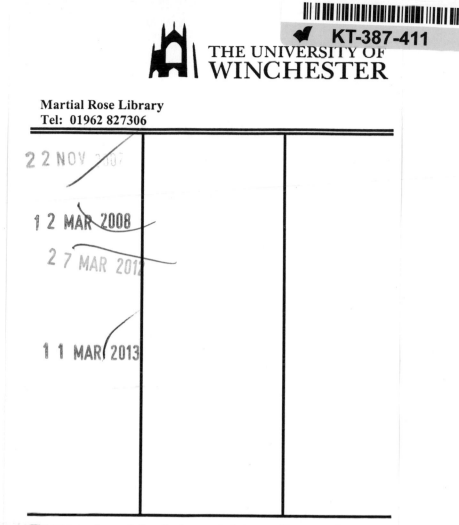

|||||||| ||| |||| |||||| ||| ||||| KT-387-411

THE UNIVERSITY OF
WINCHESTER

Sir Robert Walpole

Sir Robert Walpole

'Sole and Prime Minister'

BY

Brian W. Hill

HAMISH HAMILTON
LONDON

HAMISH HAMILTON LTD

Published by the Penguin Group
27 Wrights Lane, London W8 5TZ, England
Viking Penguin Inc, 40 West 23rd Street, New York, New York 10010, U.S.A.
Penguin Books Australia Ltd, Ringwood, Victoria, Australia
Penguin Books Canada Ltd, 2801 John Street, Markham, Ontario, Canada L3R 1B4
Penguin Books (N.Z.) Ltd, 182–190 Wairau Road, Auckland 10, New Zealand

Penguin Books Ltd, Registered Offices: Harmondsworth, Middlesex, England

First published in Great Britain 1989 by
Hamish Hamilton Ltd

Copyright © 1989 by Brian Hill

1 3 5 7 9 10 8 6 4 2

British Library Cataloguing in Publication Data

Hill, B.W. (Brian William)
Sir Robert Walpole
1. Great Britain, Walpole, Robert.
Earl of Orford
I. Title
941.07′2′0924
ISBN 0–241–12738–6

Typeset by Goodfellow & Egan, Cambridge

Printed and bound in Great Britain by
Richard Clay Ltd, Bungay, Suffolk

*For
my wife and children*

CONTENTS

CONTENTS

List of Illustrations

Preface

ANYONE WHO attempts a biography of Sir Robert Walpole must pay tribute to the work of two scholars, Archdeacon William Coxe and Sir John Plumb. Coxe wrote at the end of the eighteenth century but historians still draw upon his pioneer assessments and the hundreds of important documents he printed *in extenso*. Coxe's contribution was not confined to his three quarto volumes on Walpole, though these alone include over two thousand pages; he also produced biographies of Marlborough, Henry Pelham, and Horatio Walpole Sir Robert's brother, all having an important bearing on Walpole's career.

The second major historian of Walpole's life and times is Sir John Plumb, whose two-volumed but unfinished work represents much that is best in the twentieth century's approach to biography. Plumb found that Coxe, while using political correspondence with great effect, left unprinted and almost unused a vast collection of business, literary and personal documents, which are now deposited at Cambridge University Library by Plumb's intervention. This collection proved richly rewarding in the hands of a historian patient enough to piece minutiae together and combine political with social history. Plumb added a new dimension of social background to our knowledge of Walpole's career.

Since Plumb's second volume was published in 1960 more recent scholarship has again transformed the early eighteenth century, and this must be the chief ground for a new biography of Sir Robert Walpole. Each generation interprets a subject anew, and much of the current emphasis has swung back to traditional political, diplomatic and religious history. The present work is a fresh attempt to assess Walpole's career, especially in the parliamentary setting and as what his contemporaries sometimes called 'Prime' Minister.

I gratefully acknowledge the help of professional colleagues, archivists, librarians and students over a long period. As usual I am much indebted to the percipience and forebearance of three typists, Madge Robinson, Hazel Bye and Vera Durell. My wife has helped me more than she knows.

Brian Hill
School of English and American Studies,
University of East Anglia, Norwich.

Note

Dates are given in the Old Style, current before the introduction of the Gregorian Calendar into Britain in 1752; but *years* are assumed to begin on 1 January as now and not, as in contemporary practice, on Lady Day (25 March).

The *place of publication* of printed works cited in the notes and Bibliography is London, unless otherwise stated.

Reports of Speeches
by Sir Robert Walpole:

Have gentlemen produced one instance of this exhorbitant power, of the influence which I extend to all parts of the nation, of the tyranny with which I oppress those who oppose, and the liberality with which I reward those who support me? But, having first invested me with a kind of mock Dignity, and styled me a Prime Minister, they impute to me an unpardonable abuse of that chimerical authority, which they only have created and conferred.

– 13 February 1741

I have sat for forty years? [Whether] I leave a good or a bad name those that sat with me must be the judges. Have been twenty-one years in this office. Continue a country gentleman, one of the Commons of Great Britain . . . If wanting a shelter had been my view it was in my power by [raising?] myself into another assembly [that] I might be saved from loss. I never begged of the C[rown] of England any one grant except the lodge at Chelsea.

– another account of the same speech

A Seat in this House is equal to any Dignity deriv'd from posts or titles, and the Approbation of this House is preferable to all that power, or even Majesty itself, can bestow.

– 1 February 1739

I have lived long enough in the world to see the effects of war on this nation; I have seen how destructive the effects, even of a successful war, have been; and shall I, who have seen this, when I am admitted to the honour to bear a share in His Majesty's Councils, advise him to enter upon a war while peace may be had? No, Sir, I am proud to own it, that I always have been, and always shall be, an advocate for peace.

– 21 November 1739

I

The Minister, the Milieu
and the Man

THE CONTEMPORARY usage of such variant terms as 'First', 'Prime' or 'Sole and Prime' Minister in some ways justifies, but in others qualifies, the long tradition that Sir Robert Walpole was the first Prime Minister. The actual post he held during the long years of his ministry was that of First Lord of the Treasury, a title still held by the Prime Minister today. Though Walpole was not the first occupant of this office he was the first to hold it in a permanent capacity. Traditionally the head of the Treasury had been styled Lord High Treasurer, but monarchs who could not find a suitable appointee, or who wished to avoid having an 'over-mighty subject', had sometimes placed the Treasury temporarily in the hands of a commission of five or so Lords of the Treasury, of whom the First Lord was the senior official. Probably for the second reason King William III, who reigned during Walpole's youth, never appointed a Lord High Treasurer. Nor did William fill the powerful post of Lord High Admiral. Queen Anne, who ruled during Walpole's first years in Parliament, was of a different mettle; she filled both posts, the first by Lord Godolphin and the second by her husband Prince George of Denmark, while her long-standing favourite Marlborough became Captain-General. But Anne was the last to maintain ancient tradition. George I, when he came to the throne in 1714, firmly reverted to William III's practice by avoiding all these dignified and possibly dangerous appointments. His successors were to follow his lead, not least by always putting the Treasury into commission. The tradition that Walpole refused the office of Lord High Treasurer because it would entail his leaving the House of Commons may reflect accurately his just appreciation of that House's importance, but it ignores the reality of George I's intention; Walpole was probably never offered the more senior office.

By the accident of an historical situation in which insecure monarchs resolved to entrust the Treasury to a committee rather than an individual, the office of First Lord was able to begin its evolution into that of Prime Minister in the hands of one of the ablest politicians of the eighteenth century. In Walpole's time, however, use of the term Prime Minister was still little better than a solecism. True, the title was used frequently, but sometimes as an accusation rather than a description, and Walpole indignantly repudiated it. Borrowed into the English language from the French term *premier ministre*, applied to the powerful Cardinal-ministers Richelieu and Mazarin, the description of Prime or Premier Minister was first used in Britain mainly as abuse, to describe Anne's successive chief ministers Godolphin and Robert Harley. As such it continued to be rejected by English ministers as late as the younger Pitt.

If the term Prime Minister was sometimes ambiguous, the position which Walpole held was by no means the exact equivalent of that occupied by his present-day successors. For one thing, Walpole was not only principal minister but a department head; like most of his successors in the Commons down to Peel in 1834 he also held appointment as Chancellor of the Exchequer and conducted the everyday financial business of the nation in a manner not emulated by modern Prime Ministers. Without a general acceptance of that title Walpole was thus both less and more than his latter-day counterparts. In a famous censure debate in the Commons near the end of his ministry he warmly rejected the charge of being 'Sole' or 'Sole and Prime' Minister of which he was accused by his opponents, and correctly asserted that his offices did not amount to the right of supremacy in government.[1] Technically he had no more authority than certain other office holders such as the two Principal Secretaries of State.[2] William Pitt the Elder was later to provide an example of a premier who preferred one of these offices to that of First Lord of the Treasury. Walpole's predominance was assured by his own abilities and practices rather than by the title of his office. Those who brought the censure motion in the House of Lords did so, they explained, 'because we are persuaded that a sole or even a First

1. See below, pp.206–7.
2. Forerunners of the modern Foreign and Home Secretaries, though they shared home business and divided foreign affairs between them, one (the 'Northern') secretary dealing with Northern Europe, Germany and the United Provinces, the other ('Southern') with France and Southern Europe.

minister is an Officer unknown to the law of Britain, inconsistent with the Constitution of the country' and because 'Sir Robert Walpole has for many years acted as such, by taking upon himself the chief, if not the sole, Direction of Affairs in the different Branches of the Administration.'[1]

British government in Walpole's time, and for most of the eighteenth century, was in a process of transition from the dominant monarchy of the Stuart era to the Cabinet government of the nineteenth century. In Anne's reign there was a Cabinet which at first sight seems recognisably modern both in its composition and in the range of business undertaken. Despite appearances, however, there was not yet full collective responsibility, so that individual ministers often assumed a semi-independent role. Moreover the Cabinet itself, being new, was not yet institutionalised, and Walpole was able to rely on an 'inner' body of about five members rather than on a full Cabinet of twelve or more. Sometimes, indeed, he appeared to rely on the advice of only two or three close colleagues of his own choosing, or simply to keep his own counsels. In this Walpole resembles the authoritarian aspect of some sixteenth- and seventeenth-century royal ministers, rather than that of a modern Prime Minister in Cabinet government. In Anne's reign and early in that of George I collective resignations by several important ministers, such as those led by Harley in 1708 and Walpole himself in 1717, sometimes seem to provide precedents towards collective ministerial action. During his ministry of 1721–1742, however, no further such events took place. Aided by George I and later by George II, Walpole preferred to surround himself by men of lesser calibre, getting rid of potential trouble-makers before they could collect enough support to challenge him. Nor did his activities stop at ensuring that decision-making was essentially a reflection of his own views; at the height of his career, especially after his brother-in-law Viscount Townshend resigned as Secretary of

1. Protest against the rejection of the motion for an Address to the King to remove Walpole from his presence and counsels, 13 February 1741, *Journals of the House of Lords*, xxv, pp.596–7. The press preferred 'Prime' to 'First' minister, e.g. 'Sir R— W—, P—me M———r of *Great-Britain, Gentleman's Magazine*, xii (1742), p.82. Samuel Johnson, elsewhere in the same periodical, makes Walpole ('Walelup') say in 'the Senate of Magna Lilliputia' that his opponents have conferred upon him 'a kind of mock Dignity, and styled me a Prime minister': *see* Reports of Speeches, p.xv above.

State in 1730, Walpole often virtually took over foreign and other affairs in addition to the financial functions of his own department.

Yet Walpole's control was never monolithic, being often challenged by a parliamentary opposition and finally overthrown by the straightforward and constitutional means of defeat in the House of Commons. He had to please two masters, Parliament and the King, and loss of support from either could have destroyed him politically at any time. In practice most of the challenges to his authority came from the former, and particularly from the Commons who had proved too strong for kings in the past and could not be entirely laid under tribute by ministers. Episodes such as that of the Excise Bill which Walpole introduced and had to withdraw in the face of defeat delineated the limits of his power. But his ability to lead, if not to drive the Commons for most of the time, and in most important matters, won him the almost continuous support of George I and George II. Walpole's ministry of twenty-one years, the longest on record, seems stable only in retrospect; it was in fact fraught with parliamentary emergencies, any of which could have unseated him had he allowed them to get out of control, so that the long term of his ministry becomes a tribute to his skill and to the essential acceptability of his policies.

In his secondary function, as finance minister, Walpole appeared superior after a generation of ailing national credit and fiscal disaster.[1] Parliament welcomed him as a saviour, initially and unrealistically, on his appointment in 1721, after the fiasco of the South Sea Bubble was brought about by his rival the Earl of Sunderland. In practice, Walpole's financial achievements only stood out by comparison with others, and he was assisted in this sphere mainly by the ineptitude of his challengers. The same is true in other areas. A transparent intriguer, to the cynical eye of George I, he was nevertheless aided by the inability of his successive rivals to secure the support of the correct lady at court, the Duchess of Kendal and

1. In the wars of William and Mary, and of Anne, government delays in redeeming bills and obsolescent wooden tallies resulted in the tallies passing at a discount of over fifty per cent at times: Sir Gilbert Heathcote to Walpole, 5 February 1710/11. Cholmondeley (Houghton) MSS.647, enclosure, at Cambridge University Library (hereafter cited as C(H)MSS).

later George II's Queen Caroline. With Townshend's failure to pursue the right foreign policy in Europe, Walpole was almost forced by his own better judgement to take control and accept the Secretary's resignation. Thereafter his chief rivals were to be found only in opposition, and their failure to unite with each other for more than brief intervals simply enhanced contemporary opinion, including the all-important judgement of the first two Georges, that Walpole was the best man for the job. A more brilliant figure was Henry St John, Viscount Bolingbroke, but this politician was tainted by his frequent u-turns, both political and personal. The almost equally scintillating William Pulteney was a fallen angel, a former supporter of Walpole whose challenges to his authority led to many years of fruitless opposition which smacked more of pique and ambition than of the patriotism he laid claim to. None of Walpole's enemies even approached him in personal popularity, for their cleverness was no match for the combination of political common sense and shrewd good nature which made him acceptable as a man, even to most of those who opposed him for his policies.

Public life in the first half of the eighteenth century centred upon the royal court and on Parliament at Westminster. Before the Revolution of 1688 only the former had possessed a continuous existence: parliaments under the House of Stuart met only intermittently. By Walpole's time, however, the representatives of the nation were in session regularly for at least half the year and in many cases, including Walpole's own, their social life in the metropolis continued for the greater part of each year. When Parliament stood prorogued there was still the flourishing society revolving around the great town houses of the aristocracy and the fashionable hostesses of the day. Above all there was the presence of the court, where the monarch's regular audiences were open to a wide range of the gentry and their families, and where the closet and 'backstairs' were available to a more favoured clientele.

Despite appearances the monarchy's power was restricted. Its parliamentary grant, the post-Revolution Civil List, covered little more than household expenses and the so-called 'secret service' money, which curiously included the crown's charitable expenses. Monetary restrictions imposed by William and

Mary's Parliament, especially by voting supplies of money only on an annual basis for general governmental expenses, meant that the monarch's executive role was greatly limited in practice after 1688. William III managed to retain the initiative during the earlier part of his reign while Britain was at war, but lost it to Parliament during his last years. Queen Anne was largely content to leave political management in the hands of her favourites, first Marlborough and Godolphin and then Harley, and by this means managed to see that many of her intentions were carried out. George I, when he came to Britain, attempted to govern upon the advice of his German entourage but after 1716 their policies were largely frustrated by Walpole's opposition, and their dismissal from the court was ensured in 1719. British-born ministers thereafter gained the Royal confidence, and of these ministers Walpole became the most important after 1721.

He has sometimes been portrayed, by both contemporaries and modern historians, as having to carry out a difficult balancing act in order to retain his favour at court. In point of fact his position was not too difficult; he did not need to keep the royal pretensions in check – Parliament could be relied upon to jump on any suspected monarchical infringements of accepted practice, as when George II demanded a vote of credit for an undisclosed purpose, leaving Walpole to pose as a sympathiser to the baffled monarch while privately agreeing heartily with the parliamentary standpoint.[1] A further restraint upon the post-Revolution court's activities came from the rival influence of prospective successors, in league with the parliamentary opposition. William had to endure the passive political intransigence of the Princess Anne, while Anne herself when she came to the throne was inhibited by the existence of her nominated successor, the Princess Sophia, George I's mother, who died only three months before Anne herself. George I had to endure the setting up of an avowedly opposition court by his son at Leicester House, and George II had to face similar rivalry from his son Prince Frederick. The court retained and even enhanced its social eminence in the age of the splendour of Louis XIV and Louis XV of France, but such comparison

1. See pp.149–50 below.

with European absolutist monarchies did not fulfil its *political* aspirations in parliamentary Britain.

Walpole, like all politicians who made good after the fall of James II in 1688, was a Parliament man. The House of Commons which he entered in 1701 was elected by fewer than one tenth of the male population, but was reasonably representative of the nation and certainly far more so than it was to become by 1800 after a population explosion and industrial revolution. The two-member constituencies which remained normal well into the nineteenth century are unfamiliar to modern eyes, as are the month-long elections which often included bribery, violence and even occasional murder for political purposes. From the Triennial Act of 1694 until its replacement by the Septennial Act of 1716, the latter passed with Walpole's approval, elections took place theoretically every three years and on average every two years, bringing about an atmosphere of almost continuous electoral excitement throughout the country. The lucky few who were elected came almost entirely from the landowning class or its mercantile equals, enjoying a much enhanced status compared with their predecessors of fifty years earlier. Conscious of their power in the new permanent setting of Parliament, these men legislated for the benefit of their own class in the firm conviction that what was best for them was best for the country as a whole. Walpole was no exception, and throughout his career he saw political necessity through the eyes of the landed gentlemen. His opposition to the Peerage Bill which would have prevented deserving gentry from obtaining a title, his Excise Bill intended to alleviate the burden of the Land Tax upon the greater landowners, and several aspects of his foreign policy all illustrate his belief in the interests of the gentlemen of England.

The most notorious aspect of the parliamentary system of Walpole's time was the existence of closed boroughs, including the completely 'rotten' boroughs of later reformist literature. Though less completely under control than they were to be just prior to the 1832 Reform Act, such boroughs were the chief resource open to a gentry avid for parliamentary status, as they had been for centuries. But not all seats were controlled by one person or one gentle family. Apart from genuinely open constituencies, such as the English counties and large-franchise boroughs with thousands of voters each, there were many boroughs of under one thousand or even under five hundred voters which were by no means in someone's pocket. Traditionally rival gentry families had struggled for control of their local borough seats, and the result of such struggles varied from generation to generation. A family strong enough to control even one seat in a two-member constituency over several generations was untypical, though not unusual; the control of the two members over a similar period was quite uncommon.[1]

Rivalries which helped to keep seats from being reduced to a cipher were enhanced in the post-Revolution world by the development of Whig and Tory political parties which swept long-standing constituency 'interests' into the train of a greater national struggle. Constant changes in party ascendancy in Parliament between 1689 and 1714 helped to keep the borough seats relatively open, though the long Whig ascendancy which began with the accession of George I increasingly encouraged borough pocketability. The worst effects of this trend were not seen during Walpole's ministry, though that ministry's longevity undoubtedly contributed to the trend. In his day, more than in the four succeeding decades from the 1740s to the 1770s, popular voting could greatly affect the composition and nature of the legislative body, despite the handicaps of the 'unreformed' system. The party landslides of 1710, 1713 and 1715 may have owed something to governmental pressure, especially upon the last occasion, but they chiefly represented a genuine swing by the floating voters.[2] Walpole's losses in the 1734 and 1741 elections were not simply the result of patronage withdrawal by influential opponents but were due also to governmental defeats in open constituencies and even in supposedly controlled boroughs.[3]

Political parties were still in an early stage of their development. First used in national politics round about 1680, the names Whig and Tory had previously denoted respectively the covenanting extremists of Scotland and the Catholic extremists

1. John A. Phillips, *Electoral Behaviour in Unreformed England, Plumpers, Splitters and Straights* (Princeton, 1982)
2. W. A. Speck, *Tory and Whig, the Struggle in the Constituencies, 1701–1715* (1970).
3. H. T. Dickinson, 'Popular Politics in the Age of Walpole', in Jeremy Black (ed), *Britain in the Age of Walpole* (1984), pp.45–68.

of Ireland. The transformation of these descriptions from terms of abuse to legitimate labels of parties at Westminster was a relatively slow one, and the original connotation of extremism, verging on banditry, was slow to disappear.

From the Popish Plot, which gave currency to party names, until the accession of Queen Anne in 1702 the number of M.P.s admitting allegiance to one party or the other was only a part of the House of Commons, and a much lower proportion of the Lords. In the first heyday of party divisions, fanned by a catenation of issues both domestic and foreign during Anne's reign, the parties divided practically all members of the House of Commons between them. But by the time of Walpole's great ministry in the 1720s and 1730s there was no longer a full two-party alignment, for the overwhelming Whig domination which resulted from the 1715 election and the support of the House of Hanover led first to a weakening of internal Whig party ties and then to actual schism. Walpole himself led a substantial band of Whigs into opposition to a Whig government, and voted alongside the Tories, during three years prior to his rise to power. Nevertheless much of his skill as minister lay in the stress he put upon his own Whiggism and in his exploitation of differences between rival segments of the opposition, Tories and disaffected Whigs. Walpole's efforts to prevent more than temporary junctures between these two elements, by constantly reviving the party issues which stood between Tories and all Whigs, were an important contribution to his ministerial longevity. He was helped by the continued threat of a Jacobite restoration which divided the opposition, continually frustrating all Bolingbroke's efforts to fuse Tories and dissident Whigs into a united whole. The issues which continued to alienate Whig from Tory strengthened the loyalty to Walpole's administration of many Whigs who were bound to him by no ties of patronage or obligation. He could never have survived so long except as the leader of a Whig government devoted to maintaining the Hanoverian succession, religious toleration and Britain's independence of French absolutism.

The famed, and at the time much-publicised 'corruption' by which Walpole sought to assist his parliamentary majority was in fact no more than the use of classic methods of patronage management raised to a new standard of perfection by a master manipulator. At the height of his power about half his supporters constituted what contemporaries called the 'court and treasury party', a loose amalgam of Whig office holders held in varying degrees of allegiance according to the value and importance of their places.¹ Ranging from men whose total income was from office-holding to virtually independent individuals who enjoyed only a minor gratification from public funds or honours, the 'placemen' were Whigs to a man; but they did not constitute the whole of the body of government Whigs who came to be denoted the Old Corps of Walpole's following, as he handed it on to his nominated successors, the Pelhams. A large and respected portion of Walpole's supporters consisted of completely independent and usually socially superior Whigs, referred to as members of 'the court' only by a heterogeneous opposition anxious to demonstrate an alleged polarity between a completely corrupt court party and their own allegedly uncorrupt and patriotic 'country' party.

Nevertheless the court and treasury party, properly so-called, was an important element in Walpole's dominance, building up a hard core of compliant men who would support the government on most issues on the given signal by Walpole himself or one of his spokesmen such as Philip Yorke, Sir William Yonge, the Duke of Newcastle or Newcastle's brother Henry Pelham. In the House of Lords, with its far fewer attending members, the presence of a court and treasury element was all-important and was supplemented by the presence of a docile bench of bishops, of whom all but one or two could be relied upon by the early 1730s to vote for Walpole in return either for preferment or for the protection which he gave the established church against its rivals. Only in the House of Lords, with its subservient bishops, its elected and easily-tamed Scottish peers and its many English peers willing to be swayed by honours or advantages, was the corruption alleged in opposition taunts more than a minority element in Walpole's political management.

*

1. Walpole was, however, too wise to have believed the political axiom often attributed to him, that 'all men have their price'. As Coxe assures us, those to whom Walpole actually referred were his opponents, the opposition Whigs, self-styled Patriots under Pulteney's leadership, and what he actually said was, 'All those men have their price' – William Coxe, *Memoirs of the Life and Administration of Sir Robert Walpole, Earl of Orford* (1798), i, p.757.

If Walpole's most enduring personal reputation is that of a country squire who made good in politics, a good-natured country gentleman among his equals in Parliament, this must count as a triumph for his power of self-projection as well as a sign of his general popularity. For in his own time he was the subject of a continuous campaign of opposition vilification, especially in the press. The newspapers, pamphlets and caricatures of the day were crueller and more effective than their modern counterparts, and less inhibited by a rudimentary law of libel. Year in and year out he was saturated by vicious verbal abuse ranging from two-line squibs to tracts whose pages of vituperation ran to three figures. Nothing about Walpole's public or private life was sacred: his friendship with Queen Caroline was the subject of the same lewd speculation as his relationship with his regular mistress, later second wife, Maria Skerrett (1702–1738). His friends and relations, his houses and art treasures were pilloried, along with his political measures ranging from the never-allowed-to-be-forgotten 'screening' of politicians responsible for the South Sea crisis to his attempts to spread the burden of taxation and keep Britain out of war. He was compared with Sejanus, Nero, James I's homosexual favourites, Henry VIII and Wolsey, French Cardinal politicians, Chinese emperors, Bunyan's Mr Badman and even the Devil himself. He was caricatured as a highwayman, tartar chief, child murderer, dancing master, boot-licker, despoiler of Magna Carta, serpent, and in a host of other unsavoury roles.

The opposition image-makers certainly caught one aspect of Walpole: in almost every facet of his style he was larger than life. In person he was large, and in later years great of girth – inevitably portrayed by the cartoonists as a 'Norfolk dumpling'. As a parliamentary speaker he attracted attention immediately by reason of his command of detail and earthy accuracy of assessment. For administration he had a quick mind, an eye for the essential and an enormous capacity for hard work. His memory was more than adequate for the immense quantity of data he commanded, and his energy was quite sufficient for the wide political as well as administrative expertise he had to display. He made friends easily, even among political enemies, and this ability often helped to preserve him when he was attacked on personal grounds. The Tories, in particular, were aware that although he never lost the opportunity to attack them as a party he usually softened his political stance when dealing with them as individuals. His carefully cultivated image as a typical landed gentleman only partially concealed from contemporaries the fact that he was built to a larger scale than most of his type; few typical squires lead their country's government for over two decades.

Yet Walpole was representative of his age and his social order in most respects. In a fiercely competitive society he succeeded in elevating his family from average gentry to aristocracy, not an easy task at a time when social barriers were harder to surmount than at most times in modern British history. His father, with frugality, had raised the estate income from £750 to £2,000 per annum by the time of his death. By office-holding and the perquisites and opportunities which office brought, Robert Walpole raised this figure by a large though unknown multiple. In four years between 1714 and 1718, Sir John Plumb has estimated, he spent over £60,00 on investments, at a time when his expenses were enormous. Walpole was 'determined to make his family so rich that it would be immune to the natural disasters of the time'.[1]

The four households he ran at the height of his power were headed by the mansion rebuilt on the site of the family manor of Houghton in Norfolk during the early years of his ministry. His combination of artistic taste and desire for ostentation demanded furniture by Kent, chimney pieces by Rysbrack, and a collection of paintings which was the envy of all Europe. Not least among his overt demonstrations of affluence and power was the scale of his entertainment. As the minister to whom all seekers of office and favours had to pay court he was expected to hold frequent audiences and to entertain on lavish lines, not only in his Norfolk and London homes but at the Treasury and the royal palaces where he might be in attendance on the King. His suites at St James's Palace and Hampton Court were almost as thronged as those of his royal masters. His total outlay on food has been computed by Plumb to be 'well over £1,000 per annum', and in 1733 he is known to have returned 552 dozen empty wine bottles to one supplier.[2]

1. Plumb, 'The Walpoles: Father and Son', in *Men and Places* (1966), pp.136–63.
2. Plumb, 'Sir Robert Walpole's Food', *op. cit.*, p.174, and 'The Walpoles: Father and Son', *op.cit.*, p.168.

In his displays of opulence the flamboyant hospitality and vast expenditure should not be seen as merely the vulgarity of the *novus homo*. Ostentatious entertainment was part and parcel of the political life of the eighteenth century and Walpole's life style differed only in scale, not in kind, from that of his fellow politicians. He did, however, have some of the instincts of the new rich, rightly or wrongly feeling himself a self-made man when he looked back on the straitened circumstances, the old-fashioned surroundings of his boyhood. Like the rich industrialists of Victorian England and the self-made merchants or bankers of any age, he loved to let the world see what he had made of himself. His instinct was right. In an age when men were bursting with self-confidence in their own achievement, in a post-Renaissance world when the introspection of a mature society was yet to come, a successful man was expected to act like one. If Walpole had not displayed his own virtues and achievements he would hardly have been valued for them. If he was ostentatious and vulgar so was his age, and he was not a man to stand aside from the accepted practices of his day.

A careless and generous spender, a jovial talker, shrewd and intelligent, Walpole had the necessary qualities for distinction. He could be ruthless on impulse, but was rarely vindictive. His political motives were fairly simple. After the Europe-wide conflict which took up most of his first fifteen years in Parliament he developed a dislike of war and the expense it entailed. War went against all his instincts as an inheritor of landed stability and as a despiser of any kind of incompetence, of which war might well seem the supreme example. He did not believe in grandiose plans. 'My *politics*', he wrote to his impetuous brother-in-law Lord Townshend, '*are to keep free from all engagements, as long as we possibly can*'.[1] This aim probably served throughout his career to keep him from fixed commitments other than the need to maintain stability and keep low the national taxation which fell mainly upon his class.

Walpole was a patriotic man who saw the welfare of his own landed type as necessary for the welfare of the nation as a whole. The main political mistakes he made were bound up with this assumption. The ill-timed determination to carry the Excise scheme, which could have wrecked his career prematurely

1. Coxe, *Memoirs of Walpole*, ii, p.263.

in 1733, arose out of a conviction that this scheme would benefit landowners. By the same token he always under-estimated the force of public opinion outside Parliament, believing, in common with most of his parliamentary contemporaries, that the views of the House of Commons were those of the public at large. Nine times out of ten he was right, but on the tenth occasion he could endanger the stability he sought. The Excise scheme together with several crises in foreign policy provide the best examples of this. In particular he underrated the force of war fever which could sweep through the nation after a generation of peace, and his last years in office were to be saddened by this mistake.

The less desirable aspects of public life fathered by Walpole's administration were, like the better ones, of large dimension. As a protector of public order he was largely responsible for the strengthening and indeed over-strengthening of penal legislation including capital statutes, of which the notorious Waltham Black Act was the most prominent, and legislation against early trade unions or 'combinations'. Legislation which bore down upon wrongdoers among the lower orders was to accumulate for several decades during and after his time, producing the tangled mass of punitive law which had become almost unenforceable by the time Sir Robert Peel cut through and simplified it a century later.[1] Walpole could also be minded on occasion to ride roughshod over disturbers of the peace, as when he was tempted to penalise the Porteous riots of 1736 by punishing the City of Edinburgh as a whole.[2] But perhaps his most dramatic moves against public liberties concerned his dealings with the media. He was often infuriated not only by outright abuse but also by a general misreporting of parliamentary affairs which today would incur the censure of the Press Council. He used a Stamp Act and the law of seditious libel to muzzle publishers, invoked House of Commons standing orders to prevent reporting of debates, and solicited the Lord Chamberlain's powers to curb hostile theatrical performances.

Such measures must, however, be judged, if at all, in the context of their time. The Tories had borne down heavily on

1. E. P. Thompson, *Whigs and Hunters: the Origin of the Black Act* (1975). See also Douglas Hay, E. P. Thompson *et al.* (eds) *Albion's Fatal Tree: Crime and Society in Eighteenth Century England* (1975).
2. See below, pp.192–3.

Whig press and writers in Anne's reign. Callousness towards the poor, and a tendency to confuse them with criminals, went hand in hand with a national indifference to unseen suffering. In 1713 the Assiento, or monopoly of the Atlantic slave trade, was obtained for Britain without a murmur of humanitarian protest from Parliament. Walpole was pre-eminent in his time, but not ahead of his time.

2

Background and Early Career

THE WESTERN world into which Robert Walpole was born on 26 August 1676 was more than usually disturbed and was also in the course of remarkable intellectual changes. The effects of the Reformation and Counter-Reformation of the previous century were not yet fully worked out. Various forms of the Protestant faith were firmly established in England, Scotland, the Dutch United Provinces and north Germany; but Catholic France under its current ruler Louis XIV was ruthlessly engaged in stamping out the new religion in its own territories and those of its neighbours, so that even the Dutch were not certain of their safety. When Walpole was nine years old Louis rescinded the last privileges of his remaining Protestant subjects, threatening to carry his crusade even against England through a Catholic ruler James II. Not until Walpole was in his late thirties was the final defeat of the French King's plans for Europe certain.

At the same time there was taking place in Europe in the late seventeenth century the most fruitful stage of an intellectual revolution which had begun with the Renaissance and continued throughout the religious wars. In England the manifestations of this revolution were seen in the foundation of the Royal Society a few years before Walpole's birth, and in a mass of discoveries and improvements on existing scientific knowledge by such figures as Newton, Halley, Boyle and the naturalist John Ray. The leading figures in British intellectual life, tiring of the doctrinal differences between Catholic and Protestant which seemed to have led to an endless succession of wars, were pioneering new tenets of moderation and toleration which were to serve as the 'Latitudinarian' orthodoxy of the next generation. The latter part of Walpole's lifetime, his ministerial career, was passed in a very different mental climate from that in which he was born. Walpole had to adapt greatly to changing times, and did so successfully. Many of his contemporaries did likewise, but to few of them was given the chance to play so great a part in the changes.

The estate of Houghton lies in the north-west of Norfolk, fairly remote by primitive roads from the centre of government in south-east England. In some ways it was closer to the life and commerce of continental Europe, which could be reached very easily through the nearby busy North Sea ports of King's Lynn and Wells or the slightly more distant Norwich and Yarmouth. For centuries Dutch, German and other European immigrants had settled in East Anglia, as they continue to do until this day, bringing with them their skills and tastes to leave a permanent mark on the commerce, industry, architecture and lively intellectual interests of the region. The old manor house of Houghton, surrounded by its tenant farms, was no more insulated from the busy life of Europe than its owners wished to be.

Walpoles had lived on the estate and been buried in its churchyard for four centuries. They were gentry playing their part in the administration of the county through the magistracy and other local offices but rarely venturing upon the national scene. They once provided a bishop (of Ely), and once offered up a Jesuit martyr before they became firmly settled in the new established faith of the nation. They were not important or rich enough to control a family borough before the time of Walpole's father and so did not provide a regular flow of Members to Parliament, though they furnished occasional ones. Walpole's grandfather, Sir Edward, weathered the storms of the Civil War and supported Charles II at the Restoration in 1660 with such effect as to be knighted and establish himself as a suitable figure for election in the Cavalier Parliament. But Sir Edward died in 1667 leaving a son of seventeen to guide the family fortunes and support four siblings. At this point the family might have fallen back among the ruck of the English squirearchy and been heard of no more in English history.

Not that English squires were a class whose wealth or ability were to be despised. Sir Edward's estate income of around £750 per annum at the time of his death may be seen as a large one when it is remembered that Goldsmith's vicar of Wakefield a generation or two later was maintaining his gentle family on £40 a year. The squires of England were on the whole neither illiterate nor unread, as they have sometimes been portrayed, though they included a minority who were both, providing fuel for satirical novelists and caricaturists. They had no daily newspapers before 1701 but they bought and read the numerous pamphlets of the day, providing themselves with information on world affairs and national political life. Some also read the longer and more speculative works of Filmer, Locke and other political theorists. They absorbed the discoveries of the great scientists and other thinkers through popularising writers and were cajoled into better behaviour patterns by the prose of Bunyan or, later, Addison and Steele. Some gentry dabbled in such intellectual pursuits as philosophy, theology, poetry or drama. They bought stocks in commercial ventures, sent their younger sons into trade and the Church, and made marriage alliances with successful men of commerce for their daughters. They lorded it among their tenants and employees, domestic and agricultural, but saw to it that these dependants, whose services they could not do without, were provided for according to the standards of the day.

Walpole's father, usually known as Colonel Robert from his later rank in the militia, was in many ways set for the life of a typical squire when he came into his inheritance in 1667. Though unable to succeed to Sir Edward's seat in Parliament, the new squire otherwise held his own among his equals in his home 'country' of Norfolk. Intellectually Colonel Robert soon showed that he was well above average for his type. Still at Trinity College, Cambridge, when his father died, he had already made his mark as an exceptional student when called away prematurely to assume his new family responsibilities. Throughout the rest of his life he built up the library at Houghton with classics, ancient and modern, one of the few areas where his son and namesake Sir Robert did not exceed his contribution to the size and splendour of the house and its contents. A pioneer, like several advanced neighbours, in the 'Norfolk' rotation of crops, Sir Robert was well in advance of most of the squires of his day in methods of estate management. The avoidance of fallow, use of new root crops for winter fodder, marling and the use of clover to improve the soil greatly raised the value of his estate in his lifetime, well before the Norfolk system became widely known and used in the eighteenth century. He ran a profitable sideline in fattening Scottish cattle on their long journey from the north to the London market and proved a frugal and prudent landowner who was nevertheless willing to spend large sums of money for improvement when necessary. It was by good management and shrewd purchase of new property, when he could afford it, that he greatly increased the income of the Walpole estates in his lifetime.

In 1671 Colonel Robert Walpole married Mary Burwell, aged sixteen, whose father's Suffolk property at Rougham was near a subsidiary Walpole estate in that county. Little is known of her except that she was possibly 'something of a blue stocking',[1] rather detached and aloof from her children or at least from her most famous son, and extravagant on the limited occasions when her prudent husband allowed her a spree in Lynn or even London. Many children came of the marriage although, as in the case of all families of the day, infant ailments resulted in frequent mortality under the age of five. Those who survived into adolescence were sometimes struck down by one of many uncontrollable scourges of which smallpox was the most serious. The third son, Robert, destined for the Church, arrived after five years of marriage, to be followed in 1678 by Horatio, his lifelong companion and political associate, and in 1683 by Galfridus, also a much-loved brother.

Young Robert's eldest brother Edward, earmarked as their father's successor at a time when estates were usually strictly settled in their entirety on the first son, was to die in early manhood and thus change the entire course of Robert's life by marking him out as the future head of the family.[2] Robert's later success in Parliament enabled him and Horatio to carve out substantial fortunes for themselves and sire separate dynasties of Walpole landowners in Norfolk. Galfridus entered the Navy, but there are signs that he too would have had a share of the family incomes out of public employment had he not died in early middle age. Still looking ahead we may note that the brothers' eldest sister Mary aided the family's advancement by marrying, in 1689, Sir Charles Turner, a substantial wine-merchant and later Member of Parliament for King's Lynn, thereby making an alliance between Walpoles and Turners which was to result in their dual control of the borough for which Robert sat during most of his political career. At a much

1. Plumb, *Walpole*, i, p.83.
2. By this time Sir Robert's second son, Burwell, had already been killed, at the naval battle of La Hogue in 1692.

later date Robert's favourite younger sister, Dorothy, consolidated an already crucial co-operation between the Walpoles and a great Norfolk aristocratic family by marrying Viscount Townshend and bringing her husband and brother together in the most fruitful period of their famous political careers. Like most other gentry families of the day the Walpoles made their marriage alliances work for them.

At the early age of six Robert left home and was boarded with the Reverend Richard Ransome of Great Dunham for his initial education. Great Dunham, a full day's journey on horseback from home, must have seemed a world away from Houghton to the boy, who rarely came home more than twice a year. It was at this period, no doubt, that his unusually close relationship with his brothers, similarly exiled, was forged. It is not known how much of affairs in the outer world were communicated by the boys' clerical tutor to his pupils, but some news of the great events of the Popish Plot and Exclusion Crisis were already well-known and discussed at Houghton while Robert was yet at home, and further news of these strange affairs must have filtered through even to the remote vicarage at Great Dunham. In 1678, when Robert was only two years of age, unease at the presence of a Catholic heir to the throne – James, the King's brother – had manifested itself in hysterical and unlikely accusations of a plot against Charles II by members of James's Catholic entourage. Rigged trials and perjured witnesses like the notorious Titus Oates followed in swift succession, resulting in the judicial murder of several eminent Catholics.

But while it became clear to the few unbiased observers that there was no Catholic plot against the King, himself a Catholic sympathiser and a firm supporter of his brother's succession, there was also clearly an intention at the Duke of York's court to use his future reign as the opportunity to rescue the old religion from the penal disadvantages under which it now laboured and, if possible, restore it as the national faith. Concurrently, however, a more specific plot existed to prevent revived Catholic aspirations by excluding James from the succession in favour of some less well-qualified but Protestant rival such as Prince William of Orange or the Duke of Monmouth, Charles II's eldest illegitimate son. A strong party in the House of Commons, soon to be known as Whiggamores, or Whigs for short, made a series of attempts to obtain legislation excluding James from the succession, only to find their efforts frustrated either in the House of Lords or by the King himself, who dissolved successive Parliaments to protect his brother.

The body of support for the Whig point of view was highly formidable, especially in the boroughs and in the City of London, and it included many squires who, if forced to make a choice, put their love for the Church of England before their loyalty to the throne. In the aftermath of three Exclusion Parliaments, when the King decided that he had a large enough subsidy from Louis XIV to do without the legislature, the trial of conspirators who attempted Charles's assassination resulted in the execution of some leading Whigs and exile for many others. Over the next few years, while Robert and his brothers remained at their books, the political world remained in turmoil. The King attempted to alter the composition of the House of Commons, for any future meeting, by amending the franchise of dozens of important boroughs, those in which the small electorate was identical with membership of the chartered corporation. Writs of *quo warranto* heralded the appointment of entirely new sets of corporation members in most of the constituencies concerned. Known Whigs were driven out and replaced by those Tories who supported the Duke of York's succession. Even so, Charles II never ventured to test the effectiveness of his attempts at borough manipulation, and no further Parliament was called until the Duke of York succeeded as James II in 1685.

James's first action was to execute his most accessible rival, the Duke of Monmouth, after an abortive rebellion. A more dangerous challenger, the Prince of Orange, virtual ruler of Holland and the other United Provinces, remained aloof and unreachable. From this point Colonel Robert Walpole and his growing family had to watch public affairs ever more closely as crisis succeeded crisis. King James's first Parliament, though Tory, proved unwilling to meet his desires by making concessions to his Catholic co-religionists; instead he was forced to rely upon royal prerogative to make such amelioration of their penalised condition as he could, at the same time extending a

measure of toleration to Protestant dissenters who suffered
many of the same disabilities in worship and public life. James's
intention was to drive a wedge in the ranks of the Protestants
and provide the Roman Catholics with a potent set of allies,
those same dissenters who had demonstrated in Charles I's
time their ability to overthrow the episcopate. But the Church
of England of young Robert Walpole's childhood was a much
stronger, more united and widely-supported institution than it
had been forty years earlier, and in the long run it was more
than a match for all rivals. National revulsion followed James's
attacks on the Church, especially his dismissal of its supporters
in the ministry and persecution of the seven bishops who defied
his grants of toleration. Within three years of his accession the
division between the King and his former supporters was
almost complete.

Only a critical event was needed to tip the balance against
James II's hopes. This was provided by the birth of his son, the
future Old Pretender, otherwise James III, borne by his second
wife but becoming Catholic heir ahead of the Protestant
Princesses Mary and Anne. One by one James's supporters
slipped away. Despite his earlier efforts to re-stock the borough
corporations again, this time by replacing recalcitrant Tories
with others, or even with Whigs, the King could expect little
support from his new men in an election.[1] Like the Protestant
dissenters who benefited from his extension of toleration
without committing themselves to his cause, most new corporation members determined to support the long-term interest of
the Church of England. By October 1688 Whigs and Tories
were united in the intention of removing James II from the
throne. The final train of events was set off with an invasion by
the Princess Mary's husband, William of Orange, at the head of
a Dutch army. William met no resistance, for the British army
under the Earl of Marlborough was united with most civilians
in deserting the King in support of Prince and Princess.

When young Robert Walpole was ready to leave Great
Dunham for another school the Revolution of 1688 had taken
place, and William and Mary were upon the throne as joint
monarchs. By the time Robert was settled at Eton as a King's

1. Near the end of his active reign, James reversed this process in a belated
attempt to appease the Tories. For full details of the royal manipulation of
boroughs, see: J. R. Jones, *The Revolution of 1688 in England* (1972).

scholar in 1690 his father had become a Member of Parliament and hence a man of consequence at a national level. Robert too, from the vantage point of Windsor among the sons of the greatest in the nation, was now in a better position to observe national affairs for himself. While absorbing the classical education Eton offered, and also picking up the smattering of spoken French which was to serve him well in later life, he was able to make contacts equally valuable for his subsequent career. Among those in residence, for instance, was the young Viscount Townshend, his Norfolk neighbour at Raynham; though Townshend, as befitted his greater wealth and position in life, was an oppidan rather than a colleger and accordingly mixed with even more elevated friends.

Meanwhile Colonel Walpole was making as much use of his new parliamentary standing as the onset of chronic ill health allowed. Like his son in later life the Colonel suffered from frequent bouts of fever and ague, terms which could cover a number of ailments ranging from malaria to influenza, and from gravel and stone. The elder Walpole's health and relatively late entry into the House of Commons help to explain why he did not make a greater mark there despite his considerable abilities. He threw in his lot with the Whig party who were in the ascendant for most of William III's reign. As befitted his parliamentary status Colonel Walpole became a leader of the Whigs in Norfolk, particularly as their natural leaders, the Pastons, were Catholics excluded from office while the rising Townshends had as their present head the schoolboy who was for the moment the Colonel's ward. The elder Walpole represented the borough of Castle Rising, where the right of franchise lay in the possession of its burgages or properties. Although he owned a few of these burgages the majority were in the possession of either the Duke of Norfolk or Norfolk's relative, Thomas Howard, and it was with the agreement of one or other of the Howards that Walpole first secured his seat. Thereafter, however, he devoted his efforts to building up his own electoral 'interest' by purchasing cottages – and hence votes – whenever possible and at any expense.

Membership of the House of Commons was a growing asset, especially now that there was every sign that Parliament would no longer be the plaything of Stuart Kings, to be called or dismissed at their royal will. Colonel Robert was a careful and far-sighted man who knew the value of an investment, and it is not likely that he would let slip the opportunity of obtaining a pocket seat in Parliament. For the purpose of further securing the seat relations and friends were called upon to assist the cause, and several of them purchased and subsequently split burgages in order to multiply the number of voters under control. Close relatives such as the Colonel's brother, Colonel Horatio Walpole, together with such relations by marriage as Sir John Turner and James Hoste of Sandringham, became allies in the struggle to control the borough. By the mid-1690s Colonel Robert Walpole was acknowledged by the Howards to be in a position to demand one of the two seats for Castle Rising by right of his own patronage.

By 1696 Robert was ready to proceed by a natural progression from Eton to King Henry VI's twin foundation at King's College, Cambridge, rather than to his father's old college. He was to stay only two years, however, because of the death of his brother Edward. Had he stayed at King's Robert might, like his younger brother Horatio, have become a Fellow of that institution in due course. As it was, he had to return to Houghton to help his increasingly ailing father and to learn the arts of estate management and building a political backing, to prepare him for the position in life – and seat in Parliament – which were now virtually his inheritance. Colonel Walpole was also anxious to provide a suitable wife for his heir, an essential requisite for both dynastic and economic reasons, for recent political expenses and land purchases had left him in a situation of temporary financial embarrassment. The Colonel's choice fell upon Catherine Shorter, daughter of a London merchant family. The marriage proved to be, on Robert's part at least, a love affair; but there is little doubt that the dowry which Catherine brought to the marriage was a great help in paying off some of the debts.[1]

The young couple were married in London on 30 July 1700, but matches concluded for dynastic reasons, even if accompanied by love, are not always for the best. Catherine had an excitable temperament and soon exhibited an extravagance which exceeded her mother-in-law's both in scale and in opportunity; Catherine, unlike Mary, was assured from the

1. Plumb, *Walpole*, i, p.89.

beginning of a life in London, Europe's second largest centre of conspicuous consumption after Paris. Though many years were to pass before incompatibilities of temperament drove them apart, and though they produced the required successors, the Walpoles' marriage was under strain from the start. For Robert the death of his father within a few months of his marriage gave him heavy new family responsibilities and the immediate prospect of entry into Parliament.

Politics during Colonel Walpole's parliamentary career had been dominated by the needs and amibitions of King William III, for Queen Mary always acceded to her husband's policies and in any case died after only six years on the throne at his side. For many years, before being given the crowns of England and Scotland in 1689, William had been, as virtual ruler of Holland, the spearhead of European opposition to the ambitions of Louis XIV. William's dearest wish was not only to turn Britain from commercial hostility to his native United Provinces, which had resulted in three wars in his lifetime, but to enlist her active aid in the war against France. He was successful in persuading post-Revolution Parliament to raise the greatest army sent abroad since the Hundred Years War in furtherance of his lifetime's ambition. His principal supporters, the Whigs, at first earned his displeasure by active attempts to extract vengeance against their Tory opponents throughout the land, threatening to embroil Parliament in vendetta when he wanted only tranquility for the voting of war supplies. But the King saw this intransigence pass and a new Whiggism emerge.

With the coming into prominence of new leaders, a group of men commonly known as the Junto, the Whigs assumed an apparently more modern aspect and were willing to humour William in his desire not to persecute the Tory party, who probably represented the majority of the nation and certainly had the support of the all-powerful Church of England. From then until the end of the King's war with France, at the Treaty of Ryswick in 1697, William and the Junto ministers worked hand in hand at providing the financial supplies needed for the campaign in Flanders. A revolution in the system of government credit was brought about by the City of London's willingness to lend to the post-Revolution monarchs, as distinct from Charles II and James II whose ability to repay loans had never been trusted. Much of this fiscal revolution was the brilliant management of one of the Junto, Charles Montagu, later Earl of Halifax. Loans of unprecedented size were followed in 1694 by the foundation of the Bank of England. Numbering the city's greatest creditors among its stockholders, the Bank was able to lend enormous sums for the needs of the new army, confident of the ministry's ability to provide interest payments out of taxation, particularly a new Land Tax. Over the next generation Whig political fortunes became inextricably mixed up with the fortunes of the commercial community, as Robert Walpole was to observe at close range.

The indecisive end of the war of the League of Augsburg, really a truce while both sides gathered strength for a renewed conflict, brought about a new situation in British politics roughly at the time when the young Robert Walpole was leaving Cambridge for his new duties. National revulsion against wartime levels of taxation, together with distaste for the ostentatious way in which William III favoured his Dutch friends and his Dutch regiments over their English counter-parts, brought about a reaction as soon as hostilities were concluded. In Parliament Tory discontent was reinforced by a substantial 'Old Whig' element in calling for a reduction in the army to peacetime garrison strength and at the same time launching a major attack upon the Junto ministers. Such was the intense pressure in the Commons that the ministers lost control and were retained in office only by William's stubbornness. Such a situation could not last, and by the year of Colonel Robert's death all members of the Junto had taken refuge in the House of Lords, either with the King's agreement or by the timely chance of inheriting a title.

The situation was complicated by two successive Partition Treaties concluded by William in 1698 and 1700 with Louis XIV to settle the disputed succession to the key throne of Spain on the expected death of King Carlos II. By the second treaty the Spanish Empire, including the Americas, was to be divided between the Dauphin of France and a prince of the House of Austria. The treaties were obtained unknown to the great majority of Englishmen, even in Parliament, but with the connivance of the ministers. When news inevitably leaked out the treaties incurred great unpopularity as being deleterious to British commercial interests. William III, a European statesman over and above his British responsibilities, was indeed more concerned with overall problems of international strategy than with the narrower aspirations of his island subjects.

While Walpole was making preparations for his election at Castle Rising the Tories and Robert Harley, now leader of opposition in the Commons, were coming to terms with the King for setting up a new ministry.[1] The need for this, so far as William was concerned, arose not only from the enforced removal of his Whig ministers but from dynastic considerations. The line of succession as laid down in the Bill of Rights on his acquisition of the throne stated that he should be succeeded by Princess Anne and her heirs. In June 1700, however, the Princess's only surviving son, the Duke of Gloucester, died in childhood, leaving Anne as the only apparent successor to William. To avoid a possible Stuart restoration it was necessary to obtain parliamentary sanction for a new line of succession. William's choice fell upon the Dowager Princess Sophia of Hanover and her son George, Elector of Hanover, the nearest Protestant relatives of royal blood. The Tories had little relish for a restored James II, or even his son as James III, but they were determined to extract from William the utmost concessions for their agreement to the House of Hanover. Appointment of a Tory ministry was to be followed by a general election, and the subsequent Act for settling the succession was to include a number of provisions limiting the powers of monarchy after the Hanoverian succession. A further Tory intention, it subsequently transpired, was the punishment of William's former ministers and even a personal Dutch friend, Willem Bentinck, Earl of Portland, who had been instrumental in treaty diplomacy over several years.

Before Walpole could obtain the writ for a by-election, consequent upon his father's death, the existing House of Commons was dissolved, and in January 1701 a general election took place in accordance with the new ministers' agreement with the King. As Castle Rising returned two members of Parliament, like most constituencies, Robert Walpole was returned together with a fellow member Thomas Howard, repre-

1. B. W. Hill, *The Growth of Parliamentary Parties, 1689–1742* (1976), p.83.

senting the Howard interest.[1] Walpole was ready to take his place among the fortunate gentry of England who could boast a place in the nation's principal debating chamber.

For most members of his class, though not Walpole himself, membership of Parliament was the ultimate ambition. Through its activities the affairs of the nation were managed by landed gentry and their richer but otherwise indistinguishable counterparts, the aristocracy. Squires rubbed shoulders in the confined and often unsalubrious chamber of the House of Commons with the sons of peers, for Britain's system of primogeniture ensured that the ranks of the gentry were constantly being swollen by entrants born into a higher estate. Social mobility was two-way, and an ambitious member of the gentry could hope, once he was in Parliament, for a successful career and opportunity to make enough wealth to raise him ultimately to the peerage. Walpole's inclination always continued to be preservation of England's relatively flexible social system; he intended to use it to further his own fortunes. Born thirty years later he would have had to struggle against a socio-economic trend which widened the gap between aristocracy and the lower gentry. Social differentiation in the upper classes never, however, reached the same peaks as in much of continental Europe.

In the closed world of English landed society rank was closely allied with wealth, so that all concerned knew what title should be linked with every income; an earldom could not be supported by the wealth appropriate to a viscount, nor could a viscountcy be awarded to someone whose possessions clearly entitled him only to a baronetcy or some lesser distinction. Dukedoms were reserved for the fortunate possessors of the greatest fortunes of all, and were likely to be acquired only by the sons of monarchs or in the exceptional circumstance of outstanding service to the nation. Walpole probably never aspired to a dukedom but he intended to use his abilities and position in life to amass a sufficient fortune for his family to join the ranks of the aristocracy at a high level. In this he was successful, and his well-known preference for staying in the House of Commons during most of his career was partly a

1. In such constituencies, the candidates with the highest and second highest number of votes were both returned to the House of Commons. If only two candidates appeared, both were returned without a poll.

means to an end – he could make money and obtain power best in the Commons. But his ultimate aim, like those of most of his major contemporaries including his rivals, Harley, Henry St John and William Pulteney, was the assurance of arrival in the House of Lords. Not that Walpole despised his own class or the men of trade. His family was too bound in the intricate relationships between different varieties of wealth to overlook the importance of anyone, except perhaps the lower orders whose lack of any substantial possessions excluded them from political power. Colonel Robert Walpole's cousin was a London linen draper, Viscount Townshend's uncle a merchant of the same city, and Robert Walpole himself was now firmly married into trade. Such alliances paved the path to wealth and higher distinction.

Robert and Catherine Walpole were already settled at Houghton, where the dowager and her daughters moved out, as was customary, soon after Colonel Robert's death. With his father's debts still not fully paid off Walpole had some difficulty in making the equally customary provisions of a jointure for his mother and annuities for his sisters. His solution to this and other financial problems was to borrow heavily and widely, a habit which became a feature of his life no matter how large his income grew in later years. The young couple began an expensive programme of alterations to the old manor house, with sash windows, marble fireplaces and wood interior panelling in the modern trend.[1]

Nevertheless the young Walpoles' main residence from now on, until they obtained a permanent London home themselves, was an apartment in a house in Berkeley Street belonging to Catherine's grandmother. When they set out for the meeting of the new Parliament, Walpole's second period of permanent residence in the home of his birth was at an end, and he did not live principally there again, except during the summer and autumn recess, until the end of his career over forty years later. The glittering prospects of metropolitan life beckoned the Walpoles and their kind. From the manor houses and greater residences of the nation its gentry and the sons of its aristocracy took their coaches and mounts to move towards the capital city. There, in the Parliament which for centuries had been periodi-

1. Plumb, *Walpole*, i and ii, *passim*.

cally the political centre for landed society, Robert Walpole hoped to make his mark among those who were now his equals and might one day be numbered among his followers.

3

Young Parliamentarian

IN THE new Parliament which assembled on February 1701
Walpole already had a number of relations and friends.[1]
Foremost among the former were his relations by marriage, the
Turners, who controlled both seats at King's Lynn, the nearest
borough constituency to Castle Rising. The senior member of
this family of prosperous wine merchants was Sir John Turner,
who had received his knighthood from James II but, along with
so many others whose support had been sought by that king,
had deserted to William and Mary in 1689. In the same year Sir
John's nephew Charles marked his family's inevitable move
into the ranks of the gentry by marrying Walpole's eldest sister
Mary. Charles was himself elected to Parliament for the second
seat at King's Lynn in the general election of 1695 and shortly
afterwards received a knighthood from William III. Both
Turners welcomed the return of Colonel Robert's son to
Westminster, and Sir Charles was to become Walpole's lifelong
follower despite the early death of Mary.

An even more important potential ally, also united by close
personal ties, was the young Viscount Townshend, Walpole's
former schoolfellow. In Norfolk the Townshends of Raynham
were the challengers to the old-established ascendancy of the
Pastons as principal county family. The Pastons made the
mistake of adhering to the cause of James II after 1688, and
were to transfer their support to his son 'James III' after James
II's death, thus increasingly putting themselves at odds with the
great majority of county families, both Whig and Tory, who
accepted the Hanoverian succession. Excluded by post-
Revolution governments from enjoyment of office and prestige
at both national and regional levels, the Pastons lost power in
local politics to the Townshends and other Protestant families.[2]
In the course of 1701 the young Townshend acquired the

1. James Brydges, one of his parliamentary associates, remarked a few years
later that Walpole had 'the most friendly nature I have known' – Geoffrey
Holmes, *British Politics in the Age of Anne* (1967), p.231.
2. R. W. Ketton Cremer, 'The End of the Pastons', *Norfolk Portraits* (1944).

important county post of Lord Lieutenant of Norfolk. This gave a large measure of control in local appointments including Justices of the Peace, some of the revenue collectors and even the sheriffs, who became vital at election times when they sometimes served as returning officers. Though Townshend did not finally conclude his personal alliance with the Walpoles until some years later, by marrying Walpole's favourite sister Dorothy, he was already a political associate of some years standing.

In addition to the Turners and Townshend there were many other members of both Houses of Parliament connected to Walpole by ties of geographical proximity or family relationship. Perhaps the most influential connection was Admiral Edward Russell, Earl of Orford, a member of the powerful family headed by the Duke of Bedford. Few grandees were more impeccable Revolution Whigs than the Russells, who had provided a martyr, Lord William, executed in the cause of Exclusion. Orford himself was famed as the victor of the Battle of La Hogue in 1692 which had been the turning point of William III's sea war with Louis XIV. More importantly for Walpole, Orford was one of the four original members of the Junto, a group of leading Whigs who emerged after 1688 to replace the decimated ranks of Whig leadership and adapt the Whig party to its post-Revolution role in support of the new monarchy. Walpole was quick to attach himself to this powerful patron, who in return recognised the younger man's potential as a future leader of the party. Through Orford lay access to all the important figures of the party: Charles Montagu, Earl of Halifax, financial expert and godfather of the Bank of England; John, Lord Somers, formerly Lord Chancellor of England; Thomas, Lord Wharton, who had published in 'Lilli Burlero' the tune which became the musical signature of the 'Glorious' Revolution; and the newest member of the Junto, Charles Spencer, third Earl of Sunderland.

There were future enemies too. The same general election which sent Walpole as representative for Castle Rising also saw the first return for Wootton Bassett of Henry St John, who as Viscount Bolingbroke was to be Walpole's greatest lifelong opponent. At the outset St John's party, the Tories, were in the ascendant. With their leading financial expert Lord Godolphin at the Treasury, and the High-Churchman Rochester and other leading Tories in the newly-appointed ministry, the Tories were poised to curb the King's activities and purge leading members of the former ministry.

The principal business of the session was settlement of the line of succession to the throne, following William himself and his sister-in-law the Princess Anne, on the Protestant House of Hanover. Though Robert Harley's recent understanding with the King had arranged the new succession in principle, the Tories had every intention of using the enacting bill as a commentary on William's own often arbitrary actions since 1689. Under the observant eye of the new member of Castle Rising this was accomplished by debating what constitutional limitations were to be placed upon the crown when the House of Hanover came to the throne. Halting short of placing such limitations upon William himself or Anne, the Tories nevertheless made certain that the excesses of the present monarch could never be repeated under a future ruler. Not that most Whigs were entirely averse from such limitations upon the royal powers; many of them, especially those of the old-fashioned 'country' inclination, were at one with the Tories in wishing to see the powers of the new monarchy clipped. For though the House of Hanover might be expected to be generally in favour of Whig supporters there was no denying that monarchical actions had often damaged Whig as well as Tory aspirations.

There was thus no difficulty in the passing of articles requiring that national policy should be discussed openly in the Privy Council, and that foreign courtiers should not be allowed to take part in government as office holders or Members of Parliament under the future ruling house. To protect the judiciary from interference a clause was inserted requiring that judges should be removable only on addresses from both Houses of Parliament. Provision was also made in the settlement to prevent future foreign monarchs from involving Britain in war on behalf of their overseas possessions without consent of Parliament. This hit at William's use of British resources to aid his native Holland in its struggle against Louis XIV was to prove useful to Walpole during his ministerial struggles with George I and George II. Though Walpole could not know it in 1701, his later peace policy would often have been imperilled but for such a provision in the Act of Settlement.

Another matter in which Walpole was soon involved was the expected Tory impeachment of Orford, Somers and Halifax for their acquiescence in the King's first Partition Treaty in 1698. For good measure William's personal friend Portland was also accused and impeached by the Commons. The Junto's defenders, of whom Walpole was one, were unable to prevail in the new House but they put their faith in the King and were not disappointed; William placed strong pressure upon the peers to acquit his favourite and his former ministers, and the House of Lords in its judicial capacity acquitted two of the accused and dismissed the cases against the others.

Meanwhile Walpole made his first mark in the Lower House by piloting through a bill for building a workhouse at King's Lynn.¹ Though of no great consequence, such matters were all-important to constituencies and took up a great deal of the Commons' time. Walpole's ability to obtain the measure he wanted was no doubt noted by the Whig leaders when they could spare time from their own more important affairs. More importantly, for the moment, it was applauded in King's Lynn and remembered later when Walpole had cause to seek a seat there.

Foreign affairs took up a good deal of time during Walpole's first session, for Europe was beginning to move again towards a war stance after several years of uneasy peace. Late in 1700 the balance of power was altered by the death of the Spanish King, who ignored partition treaties made without his consent and left his vast and widespread possessions by will to Philip, Duke of Anjou, grandson of the French King. Anjou was not in direct line of the French succession and was generally acceptable in Spain, but he soon proved correct the worst fears of those who believed that he would be amenable to Louis XIV's strategic ambitions. Early in the New Year came the news that French troops had turned out Dutch garrisons occupying 'barrier' fortresses in the Spanish Netherlands, modern Belgium, in the name of the new King of Spain. The Commons voted immediately to fulfil treaty obligations to the United Provinces, for the French action not only deprived the Dutch of their first line of defence but also put a virtual end to British trade with Europe through the Low Countries.

1. Plumb, *Walpole*, i. pp.98–9.

Nevertheless the Tory ministry did not press on for war nearly quickly enough to please either the King or the Whigs, and the latter seized upon the issue as a useful diversion from the impeachment proceedings. At the instigation of the Grand Jury of Kent a petition was introduced into the Commons asking for greater protection for the Protestant religion and national interests, demanding that Parliament should listen to 'the voice of the people' on this issue. Incensed Tory ministers obtained the imprisonment of the Kentish petitioners but the incident provoked a widespread campaign, organised by the Junto in the constituencies, to protest against ministerial failure to make adequate military preparations. Walpole's first session ended on a bitter note but provided him with a spectacle of parliamentary activity unparalleled since the great events of the Revolution settlement in 1689.

While the King began arrangements to obtain an alliance against France and her new ally Spain, the young Walpoles set the pattern of their new life by dividing their time in the summer recess between building up their contacts in London and briefer visits to Norfolk. In the capital their life assumed an ostentatious and very extravagant aspect even from the start. Hospitality on a large scale was part of the accepted mode of life, and the young couple were soon greatly in debt. In Norfolk there were the changes to the house at Houghton to be supervised, constituency allies to be visited and voters conciliated. In addition it was necessary to organise the steady flow of farm produce from the estate, and wine from the Turner cellars, needed in London to maintain the Walpoles' way of life there. In the autumn too came the need for a new election at Castle Rising, for William had decided after his experience with the recent short but violent Parliament that dissolution of Parliament would be the wise course.

Though Walpole had no difficulty in securing his return, the general election was indecisive for the Whigs, giving the King at best a narrow majority and no encouragement to reinstate the recently impeached Junto as his ministers. The mainly Tory Cabinet was replaced by one containing a mixture of party politicians among whom Whigs of the second rank predominated. Preparations went ahead quietly for the war which was made inevitable by the Grand Alliance of England, Austria, the United Provinces and other nations against Louis XIV, a document signed by Marlborough on behalf of the King. With Marlborough's patron, the Princess Anne, and his friend Lord Godolphin backing William, the more moderate Tories were now coming round to the view that Louis XIV's actions had made a renewal of hostilities inevitable. This view was reinforced in September 1701 when James II died in exile and his son was immediately recognized by the French king as 'James III'.

Walpole's second session in Parliament saw little of the intransigence of the first, and financial supplies were voted quietly and steadily for the army and navy. An unexpected attempt by St John in February 1702 to revive the recent impeachments led to an impassioned debate, but the motion was rejected by the close margin of fourteen votes in a full House. Voting went the other way shortly afterwards, when the Tories obtained a retrospective endorsement by the new House of their treatment of the Kentish petitioners; but the close voting continued to swing first one way then another.

At this point Fate changed the course of politics. William III suffered a riding accident and, after a short illness, died on 8 March. Despite his often professed desire to keep the balance between parties, William's basic sympathies had almost always been with the Whigs so long as they behaved in a moderate manner. Queen Anne, though she too abhorred the extremism of both parties, was a churchwoman and upholder of moderate Toryism. From now on Walpole and the Whigs had to work in a more hostile atmosphere.

During most of the reign of William and Mary, Princess Anne and her husband, Prince George of Denmark, had remained discreetly in the background, for King William had no desire for a rival court to which discontented politicians could pay homage. The principal influences upon Anne, other than the Church, were her friend Sarah Churchill and Sarah's husband Marlborough. Though Marlborough had the chief credit for making the Revolution of 1688 bloodless, by leading King James's army over to support the invading Prince of Orange, he had been kept out of place during most of William's reign by the latter's suspicion and jealousy. Now Marlborough became Captain-General, a position which gave him supreme command of the new Queen's land forces, while Prince George became Lord High Admiral in charge of naval affairs. Marlborough's brother Admiral George Churchill became the actual ruler of the navy, and Godolphin took the office of Lord High Treasurer. Junto adherents, including Walpole's patron Orford, were removed to make way for other Tory appointments. The Queen's uncle Rochester re-entered the government as Lord Lieutenant of Ireland while the rigidly High-Church Earl of Nottingham became Southern and senior Secretary of State.

Nor were Anne's initial actions more auspicious than her appointments. Obliged to dismiss the existing Parliament within six months, she chose on her ministers' advice to do so much earlier and told outgoing members, in words written by those ministers, that 'my own principles must always keep me entirely firm to the interests and religion of the Church of England, and will incline me to countenance those who have the truest zeal to support it'.[1] Such remarks upon important occasions were eagerly scanned by the public as an indication of the monarch's intentions. In many constituencies Tory candidates would benefit from the Queen's known wishes.

In his third election within eighteen months, Walpole was now faced by a problem which was not helped by the monarch's remarks. One of the lesser owners of burgages in the borough of Castle Rising was the late Colonel Walpole's younger brother, Horatio. Colonel Horatio Walpole, however, was a Tory who had married a daughter of the powerful Tory Duke of Leeds[2] and had long nursed an aspiration to enter Parliament. Unfortunately Colonel Horatio was able to enforce his demand for one of the seats at Castle Rising, for as well as representing the interest favoured by the Queen he had a financial hold over Walpole. As trustee of his late brother's estate he was in a position to refuse consent to the sale of an estate in Suffolk, which Walpole desired urgently in view of his indebtedness. Foreseeing the problem earlier, Walpole had tried mildly to establish the Walpoles' right to a second seat in the borough a year earlier, when Thomas Howard died. He was frustrated when Howard's daughter threw her influence behind Walpole's friend William Cavendish, the Marquess of Hartington, whose courtesy title did not prevent his sitting in the House of

1. William Cobbett, *Parliamentary History of England* (1806–20), vi, p.5.
2. Known better, when leading minister of King Charles II, as Earl of Danby.

Commons. Walpole therefore reluctantly decided to give up his own seat to his uncle, even though this meant letting in a Tory for the borough. Fortunately the Turners were willing to help out at the borough of King's Lynn, where old Sir John Turner stood down from his own seat in order to accommodate Walpole as fellow member for Sir Charles.[1] King's Lynn was a more important seat than Castle Rising, and Walpole was happy to transfer there. He was to continue to represent his new constituency for the rest of his career in the Commons.

The next three years were a time of extreme difficulty for the Whigs, but Walpole was able greatly to further his own standing in the party. Even before the end of the last Parliament he had made his mark in a major political matter, by seconding a motion for adding a clause to the important Abjuration Bill, extending the application of the oath abjuring the Old Pretender to clergymen and Fellows of Oxford and Cambridge colleges. Walpole's conviction of the need for this addition to the Bill almost certainly arose, as can be seen from an early letter written by his brother Horatio at Cambridge, out of his own observation of the antics of near-Jacobite Fellows at his former university.[2] He is also recorded as teller in a division against a Tory bill which would, among other things, have prevented the translation of bishops from one see to another. Bishops were voters in the House of Lords, and Walpole, during his ministerial years, was to derive great political advantage from the system which placed the often poorly paid bishops under an obligation to the minister who translated them to a more lucrative bishopric. For the moment, however, his principal aim was simply to place obstacles in the way of any Tory measure intended to protect the interests of the Church of England.[3]

The first political gesture which gave Walpole a certain celebrity was his decision to challenge in debate, just before Christmas, 1702, a motion by no less respected a Tory parliamentarian than former Speaker Sir Edward Seymour, himself once the successful impeacher of the great Clarendon and veteran of parliamentary in-fighting almost since the restoration of Charles II. With a safe Tory majority in the new House

1. Plumb, *Walpole*, i, pp.101–2.
2. Coxe, *Walpole*, i, p.16 and ii, p.3.
3. *Ibid*, i. p.13.

of Commons, Seymour had no difficulty in carrying his call for a project dear to Tory hearts, the resumption of land grants made by the late King to his favourites and political supporters. Walpole showed some temerity, though with no hope of success, when he riposted by moving that similar grants made by King James II, mainly to Tories, should also be resumed.[1]

Walpole's bold gesture made a strong impression among the embattled Whigs. He already moved confidently in the circle of rising young Commons men who were taking the place of members of the Junto raised to the Lords in the closing years of the last reign. In addition to personal friends such as Hartington there were two men who were to hold the Treasury, Spencer Compton and James Stanhope, Walpole's future rivals but at present his close allies. Nor were his associates confined to the Lower House. He soon became a member of the fashionable Kit-Cat Club, whose members included Wharton, Halifax, Somers and Sunderland as well as other leading figures in the House of Lords and fashionable Whig society. The Whigs, women as well as men, were a socially close-knit group in face of a strong Tory majority in the nation as a whole.

Resurgent Toryism in the first years of Queen Anne's reign took many extreme forms. A primary grievance was the practice of 'occasional conformity' by Protestant dissenters in order to qualify themselves for offices from which they were disqualified by the anti-Puritan legislation of Charles II's reign. Required to take the sacrament of the Eucharist at a parish church before taking up any post, the dissenters had developed in William III's reign the habit of going to an Anglican church once, to qualify themselves, while continuing their regular attendance at their own chapel. The early years of Anne's reign saw three successive attempts by the High Tories to prevent what they saw as a blasphemous abuse of the Holy Sacrament as well as a political practice providing borough voters who almost invariably supported the Whigs. The dissenters and their Whig allies countered by pointing out that the legislation which used the Sacrament as a political test in order to exclude opponents from power was the true blasphemy.

Walpole and his friends struggled in vain to prevent the passage in the Commons of bills which would have imposed

1. *Ibid*, i. p.18.

heavy penalties upon dissenting office holders who lapsed to attendance at religious meetings other than those of the Church of England. But the principal obstacle to High Tory intransigence lay in the attitude of those moderate Tories in the ministry who adhered to the line laid down by Marlborough. Fearful that persecution of the dissenters would lead to a drying-up of the steady flow of loans from the mainly nonconformist financiers of the City of London needed to pay for Marlborough's campaigns in Flanders, the ministers led by Godolphin saw to it that occasional conformity bills were wrecked or rejected in the House of Lords where the well-organised Junto were only too willing to assist in the cause.

A related cause of Tory fury in the Lower House centred upon the prowess of the Junto, particularly Wharton, in manipulating borough elections by use of those same dissenters whose evasion of the law allowed them to be voters. The whole issue erupted in the case of the election for Wharton's borough of Aylesbury in 1701, which became one of the most celebrated constitutional causes of the period. Walpole placed himself in the centre of the fray by attempting to amend a motion by the Tory solicitor-general, Sir Simon Harcourt, maintaining that the sole right of determining who should legitimately represent the borough lay in the House of Commons. Walpole took the view, as did all Whigs, that it was inexpedient for the Commons to determine the qualification of electors: this should be decided in the Law Courts.[1] The controversy went on for several sessions. In the course of the involved and prolonged debates on both occasional conformity and the Aylesbury case, Walpole learned a sure-footed acquaintance with the rules and procedure of the House of Commons, together with considerable respect for the usefulness of the upper chamber as a means of frustrating unwelcome measures in his own House.

By the time the Walpoles had been resident in London for four years their style of life and the need for a grander scale of entertainment dictated a change of house. In 1705 they moved out from the apartment in Lady Phillips' house in Berkeley Street and took up residence in Dover Street. The change was signalled by the giving of a famous ball in the new house, at which many of the leading Whigs were present. More than ever

1. Cobbett, *Parliamentary History of England*, vi, pp.288–300

the estate in Norfolk was ransacked to provide culinary delicacies for the more lavish entertainment now possible; but the new needs exceeded the capacities of Houghton, and from now on the usual London retail markets provided most of the large quantities of food and wine essential to the furtherance of any political career.

This enhanced standard of living carried drawbacks. Greater expenses brought larger debts, and the possibility of entertaining more house guests led to personal tensions. An example of the sort of difficulty which could arise from having a bigger house arose when Walpole entertained his sister Dorothy, now twenty years old and a beauty, for a winter season. She quickly became a subject of interest to the fashionable rakes, many of whom were to be found among those Whigs who visited the Walpoles. One such was no less important a person than Lord Wharton, as famous for his sexual escapades as for his legendary successes in political management. When Dolly, who had a temper, quarrelled with Catherine and left the house, it was to the Whartons that she turned for succour; Lady Wharton was a tolerant wife. Walpole quickly retrieved the situation by collecting his sister and upbraiding Lady Wharton in direct terms. Dolly was then lodged with Townshend, with the result that she acquired Townshend's affection and afterwards, on the death of Lady Townshend, became his second wife. The Wharton affair and its prolonged aftermath was to provide material for the scandal sheets for many a year.[1]

Meanwhile a change of ministerial policy brought Walpole his first political reward. The Tories' continued campaign against the dissenters culminated in the winter of 1704–1705 in an attempt to overcome the ministry's blocking tactics by 'tacking' the occasional conformity bill to a Land Tax bill, effectively making the former a clause of the latter. If the measure reached the Upper House it would be accepted unchanged as a money bill. The response of the ministry, now controlled by Godolphin and Harley with Marlborough in the background, was to persuade moderate Tories in the Commons to vote alongside Whigs in rejecting the bill outright in that House. The High-Church Tories' fury knew no bounds, and Godolphin decided in the general election of 1705 that the

1. Plumb, *Walpole*, i, pp.123–6.

government's weight should be thrown against the 'tackers' in their constituencies. At the same time the loyalty of moderate Whigs who had supported the ministry on this issue for several sessions was to be rewarded by some promotions. Among those who benefited was Walpole, who in June 1705 became a member of the council which served to advise Prince George on naval affairs. Walpole's obvious ability recommended him for some such post, though it was probably the influence of Orford which determined that this should be his first sphere of executive activity. Walpole's duties were not very onerous, however, for naval affairs were actually conducted by Admiral Churchill, and ultimately by Marlborough, so that the role of even the Queen's husband on the council over which he nominally presided was limited.

Walpole certainly made use of his opportunity by furthering his own interests. Within a short time he became partner with Josiah Burchett, the much-respected Secretary of the Admiralty, in a craft for smuggling wines from Holland. This escapade, involving the use of an Admiralty launch and naval know-how, was not untypical of the current standards of political morality and was merely an extension of Walpole's usual business with the smugglers of East Anglia. Like many great contemporaries he differed from the squires and parsons of his day only in the scale, not the fact, of his smuggling operations. Little of the Holland linen which he acquired, or of the brandy at his board at Houghton, had passed through the hands of the Norfolk customs officers.[1]

Even more in line with current custom was the manipulation of patronage, which Walpole now became able to exercise as a member of the government under Churchill and his brother Marlborough. Galfridus received promotion in the Navy, obtaining his first independent command after only three years in the service, and Horatio was started off in his diplomatic career by being appointed as James Stanhope's secretary at Barcelona. With Robert Walpole's promotion, indeed, the whole family was advanced. The Walpoles were on the first step of the ladder.

1. Sir John Plumb pointed out that 'when Walpole was Chancellor of the Exchequer, he was still buying contraband lace from Holland' – Plumb, *Walpole*, i, pp. 120–22.

4
Junior Minister

THE GENERAL election of 1705, the fourth in Walpole's four years of Parliament, necessitated his presence in King's Lynn for a short time, between other pressing affairs in London. With the strong Turner influence behind him he had few of the worries at the new constituency which he had experienced at Castle Rising. In the country as a whole, however, the general election was indecisive, even though Marlborough's victory at Blenheim the previous year had brought immense prestige to the ministry and given Britain a new self-respect as a leading nation in the European power struggle. A governmental campaign against those Tories who had supported the 'tack' of the occasional conformity bill resulted in a setback for their party, but these losses were not sufficient to give the Whigs a majority. There were now effectively three elements to be reckoned with in Parliament: Whigs, Tories and a 'court' group consisting of Robert Harley's anti-tacking Tories together with Walpole and other Whigs who had recently accepted office.

Differences arose as to how this situation was to be handled. Godolphin tended to the view that the Whigs' superior organisation in the Commons, and their recent record of cooperation with the government, entitled them to an increasing role in office under himself. Harley, who had recently replaced the extremist Nottingham as Secretary of State in a court struggle for power, was of the opinion that the High Tories were now effectively contained, and that further Whig appointments would overset the ministerial balance. However, this view took little account of Whig ambition and determination to obtain office by any means. Many of this party were still excluded, among them the Junto on whose cooperation the ministry would continue to depend. Several new contentious issues were beginning to arise, and Whig cooperation could not be taken for granted. But for the moment the ministers remained outwardly united about their policy of management, and for a further session the court Tories were forced to accept the need to work together with the likes of Walpole and his friend John

Smith, who became Speaker of the House of Commons with court backing.

The immediate problem facing Parliament was England's relations with Scotland. Joined with the larger country since 1603 in union under the crown, the Scots still had their own legislature sitting in Edinburgh as well as their different religious, legal and educational systems. Increasingly since the latter part of William III's reign, however, feeling in the Northern Kingdom had tended towards exploring the possibility of parliamentary union between the two countries. The reasons for this trend were many and complex, but they centred on a feeling that their nation was falling behind in the new ranking of European nations. England had been rising since 1689 through its military involvement in continental affairs, especially the successes of Marlborough in the Low Countries, the Earl of Peterborough in the Iberian peninsula and the Navy in acquiring the barren rock of Gibraltar. Scotland, on the other hand, seemed further distanced from the continent by her increasingly powerful neighbour, and was also falling behind in the race for American colonies and the lucrative trans-Atlantic trade they brought. Walpole could see political advantage in acceding to the Scots' increasing willingness to unite the two Parliaments; the great majority of representatives from the mainly Calvinist kingdom in any united Parliament was likely to be Whig.

After Scotland's Parliament had brought pressure on its Southern counterpart by passing an Act of Security which threatened that Scotland might not accept the Hanoverian succession after Anne's death, and after a retaliatory Aliens Act was passed by the English Parliament to make Scottish nationals technically alien and commercially disadvantaged, the two sides were ready to talk. Walpole was one of the tellers for a motion appointing commissioners to meet with the Scots and prepare the terms of union, though he was not yet of sufficient standing to be appointed himself. No proposal which involved bringing Scottish members to Westminster could be expected to excite sympathy from the Tories, and this explains the ministry's arrangements for the English contingent of commissioners: Walpole wrote to Horatio Walpole, now settled in Barcelona, "Tis altogether constituted of Whigs, lords, and commoners; Lord Somers, Lord Wharton, Lord Townshend, etc; the

Speaker, Lord Hartington, Mr Boyle etc.; one and thirty for each nation. They meet daily, and are very busy. What propositions are on foot is a great secrett, butt they seem to think the commissioners of both nations will certainly agree in a scheme to be laid before the two Parliaments.'[1]

Another concern which occupied the attention of all Whigs was the Hanoverian succession. The matter arose with a High Tory motion in the House of Lords for an address to the Queen asking her to invite the Hanoverian heiress, Princess Sophia, to take up residence in England. This request was unwelcome, for its instigators well knew that Anne was highly averse from having a rival and possible successor on her doorstep. The Whigs were again able to show their value to the government when Somers obtained a deferment of the motion. The matter did not end there, however, for with this Whig obstruction to a proposal which was highly acceptable at the court of Herrenhausen it became necessary to reassure the Hanoverian royal family that their succession under the Act of Settlement was safe without the presence of one of their number in England. The Junto hastened to give assurances to the Princess and her son George, in a spate of correspondence which continued from this time until Queen Anne's death many years later. Somers also immediately proposed a more substantial reassurance, in the form of a bill designating a Council of the Regency which was to come into operation immediately upon Anne's death until the Hanoverian successor reached the shores of England. The Council would carry out the monarch's functions and a majority of its members was to be named by the Hanoverian royal house itself, in secret and sealed documents deposited in the care of the Lord Chancellor, the Archbishop of Canterbury, and other authorities in England. The personal presence in London of a member of the electoral house would be unnecessary.

A member of the Junto, Halifax, was despatched to the anxious German court to present the Whig case. Walpole described this event in the letter which has already been quoted: 'Lord Hallifax is gone over to Hanover to present the garter to the young prince, the act for naturalisation of the princess Sophia, and the regency-act. – My brother Galfridus

1. Coxe, *Walpole*, ii, pp.5–6.

continues still upon the Lynn station, where he finds the sweet that tempts him to continue there, contrary to my opinion: 'tis not yet known whether Sir Cloudesley Shovell goes; but an expedition seems resolved upon, with a body of land forces on board . . .'. Admiral Shovell, having already assisted Peterborough at Barcelona, was to go on to meet the French Mediterranean fleet in a successful engagement before being disastrously wrecked and perishing on the rocks of the Scilly Islands. Fortunately Galfridus continued his naval career and did not share the same fate.

While Walpole's knowledge of naval affairs was being broadened on Prince George's Council throughout 1706, leading politicians were engaged behind the scenes in a desperate struggle to control ministerial policy. Godolphin had calculated that although there was still a slight preponderance of Tories over Whigs in the new House of Commons the balance would be swung by a body of 'Queen's Servants' or office-holders.[1] After the end of the first session he was more than ever of this opinion, and carried out a minor purge of uncooperative Tory placemen. This action was far from pleasing to his colleague Harley who, as Secretary of State, was aware that overseas affairs were also taking a course which would inevitably lead to more intransigence among his moderate Tory followers. Marlborough, by winning the impressive victory of Ramillies in May 1706, effectively prevented any further danger of French incursion into the homeland of the United Provinces. The result, however, was to make the Dutch more eager for peace to relieve their already overstretched financial resources. When their naval and military quotas to the allied war effort fell even further behind than before, this could only serve to infuriate the Tories and make them more recalcitrant.

But the Whigs, mindful of the ardent desire of their new friends in Hanover to continue the war, were in no mood to relieve the military pressure on Louis XIV. And Godolphin remained determined not to lose the support of the Whigs, which he deemed essential for the continuance of Marlborough's highly successful campaigns. The Lord Treasurer accordingly acceded to the Junto's pressure for further places

1. Historical Manuscripts Commission (hereafter cited as HMC), *Portland*, iv, p.291.

in the ministerial ranks. In addition to Walpole and Smith the eminent lawyer William Cowper had already been accommodated, as Lord Keeper of the Great Seal. But the Junto determined that one of their own close circle must have an even more effective office; this time they wanted the Secretaryship of State currently occupied by the Tory Sir Charles Hedges.

The individual chosen for preferment was not one of the original Junto members but their newest adherent, the Earl of Sunderland, who as Marlborough's son-in-law could be expected to have the advantage of backing from the General himself. Early in September Sunderland was writing jubilantly of the Junto's open threat to withdraw their support, or at least to disrupt government business in Parliament during the next session, if their wishes were not granted.[1] Sunderland's strongest opponent proved to be Queen Anne, who pleaded desperately with Godolphin that to appoint Sunderland would be 'throwing myself into the hands of a party'.[2] The Queen's objection came partly from a general desire to keep any kind of extremists out of the Cabinet, for Sunderland was well known to be an ardent convert to his party, and partly from a growing feeling of estrangement from the fanatically whiggish Duchess of Marlborough who nagged her incessantly in the interests of the Whigs. Anne found an ally in Harley, but the pair's efforts were to no avail against sustained pressure from Marlborough and Godolphin. Sunderland became Secretary of State.

The prestige brought to the Whigs by this political victory came none too soon to assist in the carrying of union with Scotland. The Tories attempted by both direct and indirect means to wreck this measure, but the ministerial majority held good. During the most important period of the Scottish debate, early in 1707, Walpole took two months off in Norfolk to conclude the lengthy negotiations for a financial settlement in connection with the marriage of his sister Susan. In the end, he informed Horatio, the terms offered by the groom's father were 'too considerable I thought to be refused'. He concluded, 'I believe they will be married in a fortnight, and I hope in God we shall be able to dispose of poor Dolly very well too'.[3] Dolly, however, still had several years to wait. Walpole returned to

1. William Coxe, *Memoirs of the Duke of Marlborough*, ii, p.139.
2. HMC, *9th Report*, part 2, p.471.
3. Coxe, *Walpole*, ii, pp.7–8.

London to find the union of Parliaments an accomplished fact, though the ministers had been forced to prorogue the sitting in order to put an end to disputes at Westminster. When both Houses met again in the Autumn it was as the Parliament of Great Britain, with forty-five Scottish members sitting in the Commons and sixteen Scottish peers in the Lords.

Even before the meeting in the autumn of 1707 the Junto decided that the time was ripe for an all-out campaign to install themselves in the ministry by removing Harley, possibly with associates such as Henry St John, Secretary of War since 1704.[1] Walpole's position was now a delicate one; he owed his office to Marlborough and Godolphin, and such was the fury of the Junto's onslaught that even these ministers might not be spared if they showed any hesitation in acceding to the Junto's wishes. At first, however, the interests of the ministers and Lords of the Junto were the same. A brief initial skirmish in the Commons, in which the Whigs achieved a considerable accession of strength from their new Scottish colleagues, ensured that several sitting Tories were excluded from the House on the technicality that a clause of the Regency Act had declared their offices untenable by members in any new Parliament – even though no general election had taken place so that Parliament was only 'new' by reason of the recent union.

Thereafter, however, Walpole became increasingly disquieted at the course taken by those Whigs in the House of Commons who followed the Junto's lead. The naval and military campaigns of the summer had brought little success to British arms, and Marlborough had been unable to provide yet another spectacular victory, so that there were substantial grounds for criticism in the Commons. To a long history of naval mismanagement under the Prince's and Admiral George Churchill's direction of the Admiralty were added the failure of a planned naval and military attack upon Toulon and the defeat of the British army at Almanza during the absence of Peterborough from the Iberian peninsula. The Whigs determined upon an assault on the Admiralty as likely to put pressure on both the Queen, through her husband, and Marlborough through his brother. This was going too far, and

1. G. V. Bennett, 'Robert Harley, the Godolphin Ministry, and the bishoprics crisis of 1707', *English Historical Review* (hereafter cited as *EHR*), lxxxii (1967), p.740.

Walpole was one of a number of 'Lord Treasurer's Whigs' who rallied to the government, defending the council on which he served against those of his party who were attacking it. For the first time it became clear to all that Walpole was not only a formidable young Whig politician but one capable of acting upon his own judgement, in defiance of the terrible Junto themselves if need be. The decision to oppose his party cannot have been an easy one, but Walpole showed no more hesitation now than he was to show in 1717 when he decided to oppose Stanhope's Whig ministry. Future leaders are rarely made by a track record of subservience.

Not that Walpole was alone in his action. He was joined by a substantial band of younger Whigs including his associates Compton and Smith and his friend Hartington, who had recently inherited the title of Duke of Devonshire. After a desperate struggle the Admiralty was saved from censure by their efforts in combination, for once, with the Tories. But in the House of Lords the Junto were allowed to have their way with a famous motion on 19 December 1707 stating that no peace should be made while Spain remained in the hands of its Bourbon King, Philip V. This assertion of policy was received sceptically by most Tories, mindful of the British defeat at Almanza and the increasing cost of war in the difficult terrain of Spain, but was politically acceptable to Marlborough and Godolphin.

The 'no peace without Spain' motion just before Christmas was but a preliminary to even more important business on which Godolphin and the Junto could agree, the necessity of getting rid of Harley. Their opportunity came during January 1708, when the Secretary himself took the initiative with a plot to overthrow them. When the Commons debated the late defeat at Almanza, Harley and St John, as ministers with some responsibility for the unprepared state of the defeated army, were thrown upon the defensive. On the 29th they were rescued only by a narrow majority with Walpole acting as a teller on the ministerial side.[1] His demonstration of ministerial solidarity on this occasion, however, was not out of line with Whig party tactics, for the Junto's followers in the lower House apparently decided to ease the pressure on government at this

1. Coxe, *Walpole*, i, p.19n.

point in order to give Marlborough and Godolphin a last chance to obtain the dismissal of Harley and his Tory colleagues without incurring defeat in the Commons. But when the Queen's regard for Harley was seen to continue, the Junto unleashed the full force of their opposition and voted in the resumed debate a few days later that the battle had been lost by ministerial mismanagement in the form of the absence of thousands of British troops who should have been at Almanza.[1]

This brought the required result: the Queen reluctantly agreed to the removal of her favoured minister, who was followed out of office by St John and other associates. But for the moment nothing would persuade Anne to follow the logic of this action by bringing more Whigs into the ministry. The Junto still had several months to wait before they were at last, grudgingly and piecemeal, brought in on an equal footing with Godolphin and Marlborough. An important exception had to be made, however, to fill the important post of Secretary at War left vacant by St John's resignation. Walpole had shown himself throughout the crisis to be as loyal to his responsibilities in office as to the cause of the party. He now had his reward.

Taking up his new appointment in February 1708, Walpole had considerable grounds for satisfaction at his progress after seven years in Parliament. Henry St John, whom he replaced, had preceded him at Eton, where he had been three years ahead of Walpole, and in obtaining a major office. During their exactly equal period in the Commons, St John's brilliance had often outshone Walpole's more steady qualities. Now, however, Walpole was called upon to make good some of the defects in military management which even the older man had not been able to eradicate. Within a month of Walpole's appointment an attempted Jacobite invasion with strong French naval and military support revealed the inadequacy of the land forces in Scotland to cope with the situation had the French landed. Walpole also had to build up the denuded forces in Spain, whose short-comings had been so glaringly revealed during the

1. G. S. Holmes and W. A. Speck, 'The Fall of Harley in 1708 Reconsidered', *EHR* lxxx (1965), p.694.

recent debates on Almanza. Much of his energy was taken up with these tasks over the next two years.

It was, however, the Low Countries which absorbed most of the new Secretary at War's attention. He was Marlborough's political and administrative arm in England, with heavy responsibilities for the provision of troops and considerable power in army promotions and patronage. Though still not a member of the Cabinet he attended it frequently during its discussion of military affairs, continuing a practice which he had begun as a member of the Prince's Council in respect of naval business. In these circles he had to tread warily, especially as he had incurred the jealousy of no less a personage than Marlborough's brother, the none-too-competent ruler of the Queen's navy, at the elevation of a subordinate. One of Walpole's early tasks was to defend himself with the General against George Churchill's claim that as Secretary at War he had given a regiment to a certain Colonel Jones to please Harley.[1] The story was an unlikely one, and fortunately it did not sour Walpole's relations with his superior.

The great ones had more important problems than the quarrels of subordinates. The Junto's pressure for office for themselves increased overnight after Walpole's appointment, but the Queen remained adamant that she would not give way to these abhorred politicians. Instead she gave advancement to such moderate 'Treasurer's Whigs' of Walpole's set as Henry Boyle, who became Secretary for the Northern Department, and John Smith who replaced Boyle as Chancellor of the Exchequer. With Walpole himself in the Office at War, Marlborough and Godolphin were quite satisfied with the new arrangements; the entry of more extreme Whig politicians could only be a challenge to their own power. However, a general election was due under the Triennial Act, and it was not possible to prevent a further swing in the Whigs' favour in the aftermath of the attempted Jacobite invasion and after vigorous electoral activity by Walpole, Sunderland, and other Whig ministers.

In Norfolk, which Walpole hastened to visit for the several weeks of polling in May, the Whigs claimed almost all the returns, and this situation was repeated in many other areas so

1. Coxe, *Walpole*, ii, pp.9–11.

that, by the best modern calculations, the contest returned a theoretical majority of nearly seventy Whigs.[1] Walpole wrote exultantly to Marlborough 'the elections are now allmost over in England where the whigs have had the advantage very much. I believe by the most modest computation there are nearly thirty more whigs chosen in the room of toryes than toryes in the room of whigs, which makes them in Parliament stronger by double that number . . .'[2]

A general election was clearly no time for the continuance of quarrels within a party, and about this time Walpole became reconciled with the Junto after the strains imposed by recent differences. When the new Commons assembled the Junto would clearly have a much stronger hand.

Victory did not come easily. The Queen had quite withdrawn her favour from the Duchess of Marlborough, who was now replaced as favourite by Abigail Masham. Mrs Masham was distantly related to Harley and served to keep his views in the forefront of her mistress's mind. But royal determination, on this occasion, was not enough. The Whigs had no scruple about making Prince George their target, and the Prince was dying. In October the members of the Junto were joined by several other influential Whig peers, including Townshend, in threatening Anne with withdrawal of support in the forthcoming session unless George were replaced at the Admiralty and posts released for Somers and Wharton. The deputation even threatened to oppose the ministerial nomination for the Speakership. Godolphin thereupon added his pleas to their pressure. But while the Treasurer was attempting to reason with the Queen, Prince George died. Deprived of her husband, Queen Anne listlessly agreed to the appointment of Somers as Lord President and Wharton as Lord Lieutenant of Ireland.

With the admittance of these powerful personalities to office, soon to be joined by Orford at the Admiralty, the ministry now lost the last rags of its pretension to rise above parties. Within a few months, indeed, Godolphin himself was to appear almost as whiggish in his policies as his new Cabinet colleagues, and even Marlborough moved in the same direction. In such circumstances it was not likely that Walpole would swim against

1. W. A. Speck, *Tory and Whig, the Struggle in the Constituencies, 1701–1715* (1970), p.123.
2. Plumb, *Walpole*, i, p.138.

the tide, though later events were to show interestingly that he did not lose the reputation for relative moderation he had gained as 'Lord Treasurer's Whig'.

In 1709 the Junto's principal aim was to keep the war going, despite the many signs of strain being shown by all participating nations after seven years of continuous hostilities. To this end Townshend was despatched on a diplomatic mission to Holland to keep the Dutch steady. Their continued failure to provide their contribution to allied naval and military forces was overlooked, and instead they were given inducement to remain, nominally at least, an ally in the increasingly difficult task of conquering Spain on behalf of the Imperial candidate. The inducements offered to the Dutch were no less than a share in the expected benefits of trade with Spain and her colonies, in the event of a successful conclusion, together with administrative privileges in the Low Countries. Such concessions were hardly in the long-term interests of British trade. That Godolphin and Marlborough as well as Somers, Wharton, Orford, and Sunderland, were prepared to contemplate the potentially disadvantageous terms of the Townshend Treaty is a measure of their determination to humble Louis XIV and please the Elector of Hanover.

The ministerial desire to continue the war was increasingly abhorrent to the Queen, and to Tories who felt that they were overtaxed to pay for unnecessary military commitments. Nor were the doubters relieved of their objections when the ministry engaged in a peace negotiation called by the French King at Gertruydenberg. For though Louis's representatives gave way on almost every point, they would not agree to the use of French forces to remove their King's grandson Philip from the throne of Spain, a condition insisted upon by the British diplomats. The negotiation was broken off, and dissatisfied British observers found it difficult to resist the conclusion that the ministry's insistence upon unacceptable articles had been intended to obtain this end.

In 1709 Marlborough's great battle at Malplaquet, technically a victory, had the result of exhausting his army with heavy casualties and failing to effect his hoped-for invasion of France, so that what should have been a cause for celebration in Britain became the occasion of yet more mutterings. Walpole wrote to Adam Cardonnel, the Duke's secretary: 'The malice and ill nature of some people here makes them very industrious to lessen the advantages of the late glorious victory and to magnify the loss on our side which nobody has been able to refute for want of an authentick account of the numbers of our killed and wounded and I'm satisfied it is whispered to be double what it is really . . .'[1] Despite his genuine indignation at Marlborough's detractors, Walpole could see the writing on the wall and knew that in terms of political advantage the battle was counter-productive.

Nevertheless Walpole was himself about to take a major part in the affair which became the ministry's most costly mistake. The Whigs' ranks were unusually divided by disagreements brought about by their first opportunity for a decade or more to carry some desired projects. A bill to stiffen Scottish treason law in line with English practice aroused strong dissent among the Scottish Whigs, mindful of their national honour. Wharton's project for a total removal of the sacramental tests for dissenters aroused no enthusiasm among his Anglican colleagues. Walpole's own proposals for a measure of conscription to make good shortfalls in the land forces failed to obtain the approval of his party and hence of the Commons. Morale was lowered still further by the autumn of 1709 when it became clear that a poor harvest following an unprecedentedly severe winter, in which the Thames froze at London, was likely to bring about local famine and general unrest. It was in these unpropitious circumstances that the ministry attempted to raise their popularity by undertaking the greatest religious *cause célèbre* of the period, the impeachment of the Tory clergyman, Dr Henry Sacheverell.

For several years Sacheverell's high-flying sermons had gained notoriety by coming close to restating the doctrines of non-resistance and passive obedience to monarchy which had been popular in the reigns of Charles II and James II, though largely discredited since the Revolution of 1688. Sacheverell's flair for publicity led him several times to commit his inflammatory orations to print, so that they gained a far wider audience. The sermon which determined the ministry to take action was delivered, provocatively, at St Paul's Cathedral on 5 November 1709, the anniversary not only of Guy Fawkes' plot

1. Plumb, *Walpole*, i, p.145.

but also of the Prince of Orange's landing in Torbay in 1688. Before an assembly which included the Lord Mayor of London and many other dignitaries Sacheverell dilated upon his usual topics and added, for spice, a personal attack upon Godolphin for alleged abandonment of the Church of England.

Godolphin, stung by Sacheverell's characterisation of him as Volpone, the unsavoury character in Jonson's play of the same name (sub-titled *The Fox*), readily agreed to make an example of the Doctor. The clumsy device of a state impeachment was chosen to give maximum publicity to the religio-political issues which the ministry wished to bring to the fore. In the Commons all Whigs rallied together to condemn the presumptuous cleric and the Jacobite doctrines which he was held to represent. But the House of Lords, which early in the New Year 1710 was called upon to act in collective judgement in the Commons' prosecution, was a more difficult problem. Despite its usual Whig majority this House had a reputation for acting fairly and in defiance of party when called upon to assume its judicial role. Sensing the alarm of much of the nation at this apparent attack on the Church of England, via one of its clergy, the ministers belatedly made Walpole one of the Commons managers to appear before the Lords and strengthen the team.

Walpole's presentation of the prosecution case, when he came to make it in the Upper House, was not a hurried or unconsidered one. He concentrated upon the first article of the charges, which maintained Sacheverell had claimed that the means used to bring about 'the said Happy Revolution, were odious and unjustifiable'. But while maintaining that the 1688 Revolution was justifiable Walpole knew, unlike some of his more extreme colleagues, that he must not give grounds for the conclusion that general resistance to government was justified. He was careful to make sure that maintenance of government appeared as his first priority, and that he considered resistance to be a wholly exceptional thing. He asked their Lordships, 'Because any man or party of men, may not . . . make their own discontents, ill principles or disguised affections to another interest a pretence to resist the supreme power, will it follow from thence that the utmost necessity ought not to engage a nation in its own defence for the preservation of the whole?'

Walpole's need to make reservations illustrated the Whigs' difficulties. In general the speeches of the more far-seeing managers amounted to an assertion that the Revolution was a justified but unrepeatable episode: a weak case for condemning Sacheverell, though a statesmanlike assertion for men who hoped to retain office without further revolutionary disturbance. Sacheverell and his lawyers cleverly exploited his tormentors' dilemma by maintaining that his dogma of the rectitude of non-resistance applied only to crown-in-parliament rather than to the crown alone, a fine distinction which nevertheless found listeners among judges who were ready to sympathise for other reasons.[1]

The waters were sufficiently muddied, and public opinion against the trial running sufficiently high, that the House of Lords imposed only a nominal sentence and left the ministry to face the consequences of their own misjudgement in daring to challenge the Church which had toppled James II. But Walpole had come out of the affair as well as could be expected and was given temporarily, soon more regularly, the lucrative post of Treasurer of the Navy on the death of the last holder of this office, to be held alongside his existing post of Secretary at War. The income brought by his new employment was a welcome one, for neither his expenses nor the extravagance of Catherine had declined over the years and he was more in debt than ever. But his prospects for retaining his posts long enough to retrieve his fortune depended upon the continuance of his party in office, and a question mark hung over their future.

Queen Anne took heart from the Whigs' discomfiture and began to make active plans with Harley for their removal together with that, if necessary, of Godolphin and even Marlborough. As soon as the parliamentary session ended in April 1710 and the Lord Treasurer departed to the races at Newmarket, the Queen took her first step by forbidding the Duchess of Marlborough to come into her presence. Next she appointed the moderate Whig Duke of Shrewsbury to be her Lord Chamberlain in place of the less amenable Marquess of Kent. With the Junto demoralised and unable to respond, and with public opinion mounting steadily behind her, Anne now took the decisive step through Shrewsbury and Harley of informing Godolphin that she intended to dismiss Sunderland from his

1. T. B. Howell, *A Complete Collection of State Trials* (1809–28), xv, pp.61–2, 115 and 127; see also Geoffrey Holmes, *The Trial of Dr Sacheverell* (1973).

Secretaryship of State. This was duly done, and in June Sunderland was replaced by the Tory Earl of Dartmouth.

There was little doubt that the ministry was coming to its end. Parallel with the new appointments went intrigues. Colonel Masham, husband of the new favourite, was promoted Brigadier, with Walpole advising the reluctant Marlborough that this mark of confidence in the lady who had displaced Sarah could not with safety be withheld.[1] All the Queen's signals were watched and debated anxiously by the Whig leaders, tantalised by their hope that Anne would not dare go further and tortured by the fear that if they resigned immediately they would make little impact in the existing situation. Three days after Sunderland's dismissal in June Walpole wrote that he 'expected this desperate stroke [of resignation] in a few days';[2] but despite Wharton's pleas from Dublin for an immediate joint laying-down of offices, the other members of the Junto decided to hang on a little longer.

The uncertainty of the situation could not last for long, and several events conspired to push the Queen into the final logical step of changing her ministry. In Yorkshire several regiments mutinied, driven to this extreme by the government's inability to bring their pay up to date and by the civilian population's discontent at prices, the result of prolonged war and bad harvests. While Walpole picked up the pieces news came through of the final breakdown of renewed negotiations for peace at Gertruydenberg, adding further fuel to the peace party's demands. Finally the Bank of England, which had its own interested reasons of high interest rates for wishing for a continuance of the war until Spain could be overrun, sent a deputation of its directors to ask the Queen for an assurance that she would retain Godolphin at the Treasury and refrain from dissolving the existing House of Commons.[3] By now, however, Anne felt strong enough to take the opposite course. Early in August she replaced Godolphin by a treasury commission among whom Harley was Chancellor of the Exchequer,[4]

1. Coxe, *Walpole*, ii, pp.13–14.
2. Plumb, *Walpole*, i, p.156, note 2.
3. B. W. Hill, 'The Change of Government and the "Loss of the City", 1710–1711', *Economic History Review* xxiv (1971), pp.395–413.
4. The First Lord, Earl Poulet, was a figurehead nominated by Harley.

and soon afterwards she put an end to Parliament on the latter's advice.

Elections were called and the Junto resigned or were dismissed, though the new ministry made an attempt to retain Walpole's goodwill, or at least muzzle him, by removing him only from the Secretaryship at War while leaving him with the recently-acquired Treasurership of the Navy. Walpole's defiance of the Junto in the autumn of 1707 had not been forgotten, and Harley had the idea of obtaining the service of a powerful ally. Indeed Walpole's financial position led him to accept the gift proferred. This did not mean that he ceased to think of himself as a Whig but merely that he was prepared to accept, for the moment, the minister's assurances of moderate intention. But Walpole's uncertain future rested in the hands of the nation, or rather on the small but not unrepresentative section of it which was entitled to vote at elections and was now preparing to register its verdict on the Whigs' brief but eventful administration.

5
The Tower,
and Return to the Commons

DURING QUEEN ANNE'S last ministry Walpole's political fortunes, like those of his party, reached their lowest point. With the benefit of hindsight it would be easy to see the smooth succession of George I to the throne in 1714 and the succeeding era of Whig domination as inevitable. To Walpole and most of his friends in 1710 such an outcome seemed unlikely. The Tories, under the able and experienced leadership of Harley, were poised to rally with the support of court and country. Their party included a substantial number of Jacobites, and if this faction prevailed they might conclude peace with the Pretender's mentor Louis XIV and engineer a Stuart restoration. More likely, given Harley's well-known preference for the Hanoverian candidate, the Tories might use the threat of a rival to negotiate the German Elector's accession under terms which would establish them permanently under the new dynasty. Either way the prospect was not enticing. Walpole's own experiences under the new ministry were to be even worse than those of other Whigs, with expulsion from the Commons and a sojourn in the Tower as the nadir of his career.

Nor did Walpole's private life give much hope of comfort. During the first five years of his marriage there had been three surviving children, Robert, Catherine, and Edward. But Catherine Walpole's subsequent miscarriages, family quarrels such as that over Walpole's sister Dorothy, and the consequent promiscuity of both husband and wife all conspired to ensure that there were no more children until some years later when Catherine produced young Horace, whose suppositious fatherhood by himself Walpole accepted.[1]

In 1711 his mother died, leaving Dorothy to be taken care of again, and her settlement in the household of Colonel Horatio

1. Sir John Plumb gives some cogent, if circumstantial evidence for supposing that the youngest Horace Walpole was in fact the natural son of Carr, Lord Hervey or at least someone other than Robert Walpole. Plumb, *Walpole*, i, pp.257–9.

Walpole was, given the Colonel's aggressively Tory tendencies, only the best of a bad job. Her seemingly hopeless entanglement with Townshend and failure to find a suitable husband now became a pressing problem. Fortunately brother Horatio, now at The Hague as Townshend's secretary, remained a tower of strength. But in general Walpole's private life reflected his public one in the preponderance of problems over pleasures. The Walpoles' continued extravagant life style and the façade of a family life were little comfort in facing the loss of one lucrative office and the prospect of losing another if he put a foot wrong.

Action provided a welcome relief from worry. The calling of a general election after only two years made Walpole's presence in Norfolk essential. Such were the Whigs' fears for their prospects that they had need of their best men, and Walpole was this time nominated for the county as well as for re-election at King's Lynn. In the event their worst fears were proved to be justified. Militant Toryism swept almost every Norfolk constituency, and Walpole's desperate stand for one of the county seats failed miserably. He even had doubts about Lynn itself and took the precaution of standing for a third seat, his old place at Castle Rising; but when the electors of his more recent constituency proved loyal, the seat went to his brother Horatio, who transferred from Lostwithiel where he had been returned at a bye-election earlier in the year.

Everywhere else in the country the Tories swept the board with a majority of nearly two to one, with Whigs failing to hold long-safe boroughs and even gilt-edged nomination seats. The massive swing in public opinion, a result of recent Whig mismanagements, went ahead without the benefit of strong patronage assistance from the government, for the moderate Harley still had hopes of obtaining a government of the centre which might continue to include some of the more responsible Whigs such as Walpole. But Church sentiment was too strong for restraint, and from all parts came unanimous reports of the return of ardent Tories, many of them never having sat in Parliament before, whose intention was to overset everything for which the Whigs had worked over many years. Their desire was that peace should be made with France as soon as possible and all Whigs be rooted out from government and offices, pensionerships and magistracies. If anyone stood in the way of this cleansing process, the jubilant Tories proclaimed, so much the worse for him.[1]

A prime example of their mood was Walpole's rival Henry St John, excluded in the 1708 election after his resignation along with Harley but now returned to the House of Commons a changed man, no longer willing to follow placidly the moderate line laid down by his old leader. St John was desirous of placing himself at the head of a militant High Church party to challenge any attempt by Harley at mercy for the fallen party. With such knowledge in mind, Walpole must have returned to Westminster in the autumn of 1710, after the usual round of consultation and entertainment with friends and helpers in Norfolk, with a heavy heart.

Despite the auspices, Walpole was determined from the start to make clear his independence of the government of which he was still nominally a part. The first clash came in a committee to draw up the Commons' Address of Thanks for the Queen's opening speech. Walpole sat and took notes of the proposed Address, with the obvious purpose of devising a later amendment; he remained undeterred when the chairman, Sir Thomas Hanmer, told him that note-taking in these circumstances was 'unparliamentary'. Walpole pointed out that pen and paper had been provided for members of the committee, and asked why this should have been done if members were not allowed to write as they pleased. Winning his point after a squabble, he continued to write. But the matter was not yet closed, and when business was concluded his colleagues required him to give up his notes. Making no answer he defied them and took his paper away without further hindrance. No doubt his intransigent behaviour was reported almost immediately to Harley.

In the succeeding debate Walpole and his friends, using the information he had provided, suggested alterations which the Tories claimed made arrant nonsense of the usual eulogy upon the royal speech. There was no hope in the new House of carrying what was virtually an anti-government motion, though Walpole did succeed in inserting into the Address a mention of the Pretender, a point which was yielded by Harley himself. But Walpole's recalcitrance upon this and subsequent days left no doubt as to his position, and by the end of December the

1. B. W. Hill, *Growth of Parliamentary Parties*, p.128.

inevitable note of dismissal from his last remaining office was conveyed to him by Lord Dartmouth.[1]

From this point ministerial attempts to conciliate some of the more effective Whigs virtually ceased, though such moderate aristocrats as Shrewsbury and the Duke of Somerset, whose wife was high in Queen Anne's favour, retained their places on the Privy Council, a factor which was to become important in the Tory ministry's last days. Along with Walpole, however, went the ardently whiggish Duchess of Marlborough, now dismissed from her household offices as the Queen had long desired, though the Duke himself remained Captain-General because he was indispensable as a means of forcing Louis XIV to accede to a good peace treaty. In the Commons after Christmas the gloves were off, and Walpole joined in a persistent and general Whig assault upon all government proposals, great and small, in an effort to make clear that extremist measures would not have an easy passage despite the enormous disparity of votes. In the long sequence of readings, debates and committee meetings which attended every piece of legislation the expertise of an experienced opposition leader could gain time and even win substantive points by the process of attrition in debate.

In February 1711 the ministry's slow rate of progress in passing legislation punishing members of the last ministry resulted in the formation of the October Club, a powerful new body of Tory backbenchers devoted to furthering political extremism while consuming the heavy ale of the previous October. The activities of these members were as embarrassing to Harley as they were potentially devastating to the Whigs. To take the pressure off himself, the Chancellor devised a hurried programme of concessions to church and landed men, including fifty new Anglican churches to be built in the dissenting stronghold of the City of London and a Property Qualification Act making membership of the House of Commons dependent upon possession of land valued at three hundred pounds income annually, or six hundred for representatives of the county seats. Though Walpole opposed most of these measures he also learned from them. Later in his career he was to show,

1. J. J. Cartwright (ed)., *The Wentworth Papers* (1833), p.160.

as minister of the crown, that he knew the value of conciliating the Church and the landed interest.

In addition to the more positive measures taken to please the Tory backbenchers, the ministry gave rein to House of Commons committees to investigate the conduct of the last ministry. The examinations conducted by these committees were exhaustive and did not reach completion before the end of the session, though they were accompanied by frequent 'leaks' to other members of the House as to the alleged conduct of particular culprits including Walpole himself. In response Walpole wrote two major pamphlets, *The Debts of the Nation Considered* and *A State of the Five and Thirty Millions*. Both works were devoted to a defence of the last ministry against accusations of corruption which were made freely by the Tories. In the Commons towards the end of the session he also led the Whig attack on details of Harley's South Sea Company scheme, which the Whigs saw as likely to set up a company rivalling their own foundation of the Bank of England as an agency for raising public credit.[1] The scheme's main purpose was to fund existing government debts and in this it was successful, though Walpole's distrust seemed justified when an extension of it some years later led to the crisis of the South Sea Bubble. For the moment, however, the Company was approved, and, as this was the first time for several years that Walpole was free from ministerial responsibilities, he could retire to Norfolk at the end of the session in order to sort out family affairs which needed attention as a result of his mother's recent death. He was now established as the main Whig leader in the Commons, a position of some pride but also one which marked him out for attack by the vengeful Tories.

During the same summer the ministry were making their preparations for concluding with France a preliminary peace treaty which would at one and the same time reduce the colossal burden of the land tax and free future British commerce from the disadvantages which Townshend's Barrier Treaty with Holland had imposed upon it. The dextrous

1. At the time of the last ministry's fall, government debt to the Bank of England alone was over six million pounds, half of it in respect of exchequer bills, C(H)MSS 'Public Debts and Incumbrancies, 27 July, 1710'.

Harley, now promoted to the post of Lord Treasurer with the title of Earl of Oxford, had prepared the way by a secret negotiation with French representatives, a proceeding known only to his colleague Shrewsbury. When the negotiation was handed over to St John as Secretary he gave it a new turn both by his great vigour and by his willingness to abandon the Austrian and Dutch allies if such an action would result in a speedy conclusion. Shrewsbury, the last Whig of ability with any say in public affairs, now withdrew his services in disgust at St John's new direction, though he later consented to play a part in concluding the definitive treaty. By September the preliminary articles were signed, and the problem of obtaining Parliament's consent could not long be deferred. In the Commons the outcome was a foregone conclusion; but the Whigs' remaining majority in the House of Lords might well, with the assistance of some 'Hanoverian' Tory defectors, wreck the treaty before it had fairly begun.

Here lay the Whigs' opportunity. In October Walpole attended a party meeting, principally of the Junto and other Whig lords, held at the Cambridgeshire home of his old mentor Orford. Their plan envisaged that the main attack on the peace proposals would, of necessity, be in the House of Lords, though a substantial demonstration led by Walpole would also take place in the Lower House. An opening gambit was provided when the ministry revealed the terms of the preliminary articles to the Austrian Emperor, whose envoy in London communicated them to the Whig leaders. The peace terms were immediately published in the Whig *Daily Courant*, providing a focus of opposition for all critics of the peace policy, including Tory dissidents. The ministers, for their part, commissioned Jonathan Swift to publish one of his most effective political pamphlets, *The Conduct of the Allies*, to justify the proposed abandonment of some of the Allies' interests.

The Elector of Hanover and prospective ruler of Britain was known to be as critical of a hurried peace as was his Imperial suzerain, though for slightly different reasons; George was still of the opinion that the continuance of war would further his own chances of undisputed succession while the Pretender remained firmly in the enemy's camp. Early in December his representative Baron Bothmer handed to the British ministry a declaration that no peace could be concluded on the basis of

Philip V remaining King of Spain. At this juncture several leading Whigs including Somers, Halifax, Townshend and Walpole were sounded out by Lord Treasurer Oxford with a view to securing their immediate support for the peace preliminaries; what Oxford offered in return was probably the promise of a softer line towards Austria and Holland, possibly even a cross-party alliance of moderates in order to exclude St John.[1] The Whigs quickly rejected these proposals. They now knew that they had the support of a group of Tory peers centred upon the Earl of Nottingham, a High Churchman but ardent proponent of the Hanoverian succession whose support in the House of Lords would be of vital importance.

'Dismal', to use Nottingham's usual soubriquet, demanded a price for his support. He wanted nothing less than Whig agreement to an occasional conformity bill against Protestant dissent such as those which had convulsed Parliament in Walpole's earliest years there. The Whigs, in their anxiety to prevent the peace proposals, were willing to pay this price. Privately they assured the Dissenters that as soon as the principal object of securing the Hanoverian succession was obtained, this persecuting measure would be removed. On the day before Parliament's meeting, on 6 December, they threw down their challenge to government by publishing, again in the *Daily Courant*, the Elector's recent protest against the peace proposals, the text of which they received from Bothmer. Henceforth it was generally known that the issue was not simply peace or war but the approval of the heir to the British throne for the latter.

The events leading to Walpole's downfall now followed in swift succession. In the House of Commons the Queen's Speech to both Houses, asking for their support for the peace proposals, was opposed by 195 Whig votes and 11 Tory, but was passed by a resounding majority of 126. Walpole's oratory, though in vain, stung the ministers again. In the House of Lords an amendment to the Speech was moved by Nottingham, and by a majority of one vote that House resolved that no peace could be safe or honourable which allotted Spain or the Spanish Indies to a Bourbon monarch. The charged atmosphere

1. Oxford to [?Townshend], 26 Nov. 1711, C(H)MSS; Hill, *Growth of Parliamentary Parties*, p.134.

of this occasion was brought to a flash-point by Wharton's threat that if ministers attempted to carry any other peace they might pay with their head on the block. No doubt similar threats were made in private, if not openly, in the House of Commons too. In response the ministry persuaded the Queen to create twelve new Tory peers in order to pass the measure in the Lords, and on 31 December 1711 the *London Gazette* carried the names of twelve Tory commoners now elevated to baronies for the purpose.

The extent of Whig dismay at this unusual move would be hard to exaggerate. Worse was to follow. The ministry now decided that the recent threats should be returned, and an example made of leading opponents. The balance in the House of Lords was still too fine for an attack on the Junto to have a sure chance of success, but other scapegoats were at hand. In December the Commons' commissioners for public accounts, appointed in the previous session, laid before the House a report which accused Marlborough and Walpole of malversation in the army accounts. The Captain-General was in an unusually vulnerable position in that he was the last major opponent of government in high office; moreover his removal was now urgently necessary lest he should take it into his head to refuse to obey the ministry's planned withdrawal of the British contingent from allied forces in the field against France. But Walpole was also implicated, as the late Secretary at War. An example needed to be made of a politician, and he was marked down as the leader of Whig opposition in the House of Commons.

Before Parliament reassembled after the Christmas recess Marlborough had been dismissed and the case against Walpole prepared. He was accused of obtaining for his friend and banker Robert Mann a cut from a forage contract for the army. Walpole and his clerk James Taylor were alleged to have received illicit financial benefits out of this and other transactions. Mann admitted that he had benefited but claimed to have done so alone, completely exculpating his friend. Walpole denied receiving anything for himself and could claim that the whole transaction was not an unusual one by the standards then prevailing. Indeed in comparison with Paymaster-General Brydges, whose later dukedom of Chandos was founded on the proceeds of his term of office, Walpole's guilt was not grievous.

But his real fault being political he had to pay the penalty. He suffered more than Marlborough, to whose disgrace his own was intended as a prelude. On 17 January 1712 he was committed to the Tower by order of the Commons and expelled from the House. Despite the ministry's normal huge majority Walpole's popularity, and the strength of his case, was such that an attempt to prevent his expulsion failed by only twelve votes.[1] Marlborough's much greater culpability was established soon afterwards, for he had long been guilty of receiving 'kickbacks' for Brydges' complicated transactions; but though dismissed and disgraced the General was not otherwise punished. His military successes guaranteed his safety, and his exile to Holland was self-imposed.

Walpole remained in the Tower for six months, until Parliament rose for the summer recess. His physical well-being was ensured by a reasonably comfortable apartment, but the effect of imprisonment on his mind was bitter. He wrote to Dorothy: 'I am sure it will be a satisfaction to you to know that this barbarous injustice being only the effect of party malice does not concern me at all and I heartily despise what I shall one day revenge'. He added, 'my innocence was so evident that I am confident that they [that voted me] guilty did not believe me so . . . '.[2] He was later to have the satisfaction of seeing Oxford lodged in the same place, for a longer period, and St John deprived of the seat in the House of Lords which he received, along with the title of Viscount Bolingbroke, in the aftermath of Walpole's prosecution. He busied himself in the Tower by writing more tracts, including *A Short History of Parliament*, exonerating himself, defending his party and answering the government case against the Allies.

Released on 8 July 1712, Walpole was not allowed to take up his place in Parliament again until after a general election. For a year he was accordingly a bystander while important events in the history of Europe were taking place. Marlborough was replaced as Captain-General by the Duke of Ormonde, who in due course obeyed the ministry's command to hold back the British army from cooperation with allied forces while the main peace negotiations were taking place at Utrecht. Bolingbroke

1. Plumb, *Walpole*, i, pp.179–80, Coxe, *Walpole*, i, pp.35–40.
2. Plumb, *Walpole*, i, p.181.

pressed ahead with his intention of peace at almost any price to the Allies, but was fortunately restrained in his worst intentions by Oxford, who managed to secure a just if not over-generous settlement for the United Provinces. In the Commons the Whigs, in Walpole's absence, were dispirited and ill-organised. A key motion on 28 July 1712 by William Pulteney, his principal lieutenant, calling for a more active participation by Ormonde in the Flanders campaign, was so mismanaged by Pulteney's failure to notify the Scottish Whigs of his intention that the opposition achieved only 73 votes against 203.[1] Thereafter Parliament was tranquillised in a way which Walpole would certainly not have allowed, and kept in abeyance by a series of prorogations until the peace treaties were signed in March 1713.

In London news of the Peace of Utrecht arrived on 3 April 1713. Parliament prepared for the coming struggle over ratification of the peace terms. For despite the general popularity of the Peace, after so many years of war, parliamentary consent for executive diplomacy could no longer be taken for granted in the post-Williamite nation. There was known to be considerable unease among the Hanoverian Tories about the way in which the Allies had been treated by Bolingbroke and his negotiators, and there was thus reasonable expectation that Whig criticism would be reinforced from back benches on the government side. The Whigs' main hope for defeating the ministry centred upon the recent commercial treaty between Britain and France, a separate document from the main political treaties, carried through by the Secretary in furtherance of a long-term scheme for closer relations between the two countries. The main provision of this measure was a mutually reduced scale of tariffs on many commodities; but Bolingbroke, in his haste to conclude the treaty, overlooked some vital British interests when he allowed woollen goods to be left out of the list of tariff reductions. There was no doubt that members for wool-exporting counties would oppose ratification, and some hope that others would join them. Until the last moment the matter remained in doubt but on 18 June

1. Hill, *Growth of Parliamentary Parties*, p.137.

Tory unity broke spectacularly when Sir Thomas Hanmer, Walpole's Suffolk neighbour and old opponent in the Commons, led a substantial revolt. With good Whig organisation restored, the help of the dissident Tories enabled the government to be defeated by nine votes over the ratification.

This vote, though not all contemporaries were yet aware of the fact, was a turning point in the fortunes of the Whig party in the Commons, permitting them better hopes of safeguarding the Hanoverian succession than had been possible for the last three years. Only a minority of the Tories who followed Hanmer were principally concerned with the production of British wool; the majority voted with him because of more general concern over the tenor of Bolingbroke's policy and its obviously pro-French bias, with all that this might imply in terms of a desire to restore the Pretender.[1] The task of following up the success was entrusted to Walpole's old associate General James Stanhope, recently returned to the Commons after enforced absence; Stanhope had the misfortune to lose the battle of Brihuega in Spain, thereby making the dislodgment of the French candidate from its throne impossible, and subsequently spent two years as a prisoner of war. Stanhope had little difficulty in obtaining a motion for an Address to the Queen requesting that she should press the French king for the removal of the Pretender to some place outside France. Both victories were of significance in directing attention to the succession issue in a general election which was due in the autumn.

As a prelude to a general election there was a happy event when Walpole's sister Dorothy married Townshend, after the death of his first wife, ensuring the continuance of the Walpole-Townshend alliance for many years to come as well as providing personal happiness for the married couple. The summer months were mainly spent in electioneering. The tide which had carried the Tories into power in 1710 was still strong, and though Walpole again secured his seat at King's Lynn without difficulty he had little success in helping friends in the county seats or elsewhere in East Anglia. Throughout the country the

1. Geoffrey Holmes and Clyve Jones, 'Trade, the Scots and the Parliamentary Crisis of 1713', *Parliamentary History*, i (1982).

picture was much the same, giving the Tories a similar majority to their previous one.

But compared with 1710 the new result concealed a more auspicious situation for the Whigs because a large, if as yet unclearly defined number of the victorious Tories was of 'Hanoverian' sympathies, the result of due note taken by the constituencies after the events of the last session. From many localities there were indications that the succession was now the principal issue for the electors, with Queen Anne's health known to be ailing and the problems of war now past. A further straw in the wind was that Oxford, whose ameliorating role in the conclusion of the peace treaties was not generally known, now began to reveal himself cautiously by throwing his weight behind Hanmer for the Chair of the House of Commons, a key post in any future struggle.

Walpole's desire to bring the Hanoverian issue to a head in the new House was at first frustrated when its meeting was delayed, as in the previous year, until well after Christmas. Internal struggles in the ministry between Oxford and Bolingbroke were responsible for the delay at first, but in December 1713, Queen Anne suffered a severe illness, nearly dying on Christmas Eve, and for a further month her life was in the balance. Meanwhile ministers corresponded with James Edward the Pretender, Bolingbroke possibly sincerely but Oxford less so. Parliament remained in abeyance, but the Whig press provided a substitute for debate, and a full campaign of propaganda was directed towards obtaining the sympathy of the many Tories for whom a restoration of the House of Stuart would be anathema. The most powerful pamphlet was *The Crisis* by Richard Steele, better known to posterity as a master of *belles-lettres* but elected as a committed Whig member for the borough of Stockbridge. Steele had no scruple in declaring that at this moment of decision, for the Queen lay between life and death, the Hanoverian succession as laid down in the Act of Settlement was in serious danger. Walpole firmly believed that this assertion was true, though he lacked the evidence to prove it. When the Queen was well enough to open Parliament in March 1714 the ministry, having learned that James Edward had indignantly rejected their suggestion that he should abandon the Roman Catholic religion, decided to make an example of the member for Stockbridge. Steele's contribution to the controversy as a pamphleteer was no more than that of many other Whigs, but as a Member of Parliament he was a convenient target for the raw and bewildered levies of the Tory ranks.

Steele's chief defender in the debate, when it took place on 18 March, was Walpole. In a sweeping survey of the ministry's recent policies in war and peace, aided by the considerable thought he had given to the matter in composing his own recent pamphlet as well as studying Steele's, Walpole placed his colleague's defence of the Protestant succession in its context in order to construct a defence. He wondered openly why Steele was being singled out for punishment at all, when his views were so representative of the press and the nation. Walpole emphasized that the attack from the government benches on Steele was an attack on the Protestant succession itself.[1] The outcome of the next election was to endorse this view. But though the debate was long and acrimonious the House was not yet ready to accept Walpole's contentions; Hanoverian Tories would only go as far as absenting themselves from the vote, rather than joining the Whigs, and Steele's expulsion was carried without difficulty.

After Easter, however, the succession issue became more central. On 12 April the Hanoverian envoy handed in a request from his court that the electoral Prince George (the future George II) should be allowed to take a seat in the House of Lords by his title of Duke of Cambridge. In the Commons the Whigs immediately rallied, and in committee on the 15th, with an exceptional turnout of 467 members present, they engineered a vote as to whether the succession was in danger. Walpole was now sharing the lead of the House on important occasions with Stanhope, whose political career was prospering more than his military one. The star of the day, however, was neither of the two leading Whigs but Sir Thomas Hanmer, who being out of the Chair on a committee occasion stated in a sensational contribution to debate that 'he hoped the House would never descend so low by this vote as to screen a ministry'. Hanmer's speech was decisive, and no fewer than fifty other Tories followed him in voting alongside the Whigs against the ministry. Though the outcome was a technical government victory, with a majority of forty-eight votes, few observers

1. C(H)MSS., 90. Walpole's notes.

outside the walls of Westminster doubted that it was the long-held Whig view of the ministry's intentions which had been exonerated.

The final scenes of this extraordinary session were preceded by an apparent ministerial rally, when Bolingbroke's associate William Wyndham carried through the Lower House a Schism Bill designed to rally all Tories behind an attack on the Protestant dissenters by destroying their advanced educational system. Walpole and Stanhope in the Commons in vain led opposition to a measure which required that all schoolmasters should be licensed by a bishop and placed in jeopardy the elaborate system of academies up to university level which characterised the dissenters' system. But this revival of the Church issue proved only a temporary means of rallying the Tory backbenchers, for other events were conspiring to continue the Hanoverian Tories' unease. They soon heard of a promise by Bolingbroke to a backbenchers' meeting that 'he would not leave a Whig in employ' by the end of the session; and the succeeding hurried removal of Whigs from their military offices, often the only ones left to them, aroused the worst suspicions among Hanmer's friends of the Secretary's intentions.[1]

Tory backbench unease was exacerbated now by open ministerial schism. The long-standing quarrel between Oxford and Bolingbroke culminated in a struggle for the Queen, whose favour, by the beginning of 1714, was largely transferred to Bolingbroke through his astute alliance with the royal favourite Mrs Masham. By June the Lord Treasurer had decided that his only recourse was to join with the opposition, and on the ninth he threw his weight behind a resolution in the Commons asking for an Address to the Queen to give up a scheme by which, with Bolingbroke's collusion, a share of profits from the South Sea Company had been secretly assigned to Mrs Masham. Walpole and the other Whigs naturally made the utmost use of the amazing spectacle of the ministerial falling out. They were aided by further revelations. The last few days of this memorable session were devoted in both Houses to an extensive and startling investigation of the web of chicanery which Bol-

1. A. N. Newman, 'Proceedings . . . March–June 1714', *Bulletin of the Institute of Historical Research*, xxxiv (1961), pp.213–4.

ingbroke had woven in another matter, the commercial treaties with France and Spain, rewarding himself or his close associates at the expense of the national commercial interest.

It was to prevent further such revelations, which might damage the court irretrievably, that Queen Anne hurriedly sent Black Rod to prorogue Parliament on 9 July, and the stormiest debates of the reign came to an end. Parliament's investigations had badly damaged Bolingbroke's reputation and ended his hopes of replacing his rival. On 27 July the Secretary had a last success when he prevailed upon the Queen to dismiss Oxford; but Bolingbroke was not given the latter's post at the head of the Treasury. The Secretary had his revenge, but was now too tainted for his rival's authority to be transferred to him. In desperation Bolingbroke now offered to parley with his enemies. Walpole had left London for Norfolk soon after the end of the session and it was thus Stanhope who on 28 July delivered the ultimatum of the Whig terms, virtually a division of offices between the parties, with Marlborough and Orford to take charge of the army and navy respectively. Bolingbroke could not accept, and two days later his hopes were further shattered when the Queen rallied herself once more to place the white staff of the Lord High Treasurer's office in the more honourable hands of the Duke of Shrewsbury. Shattered by the quarrels of her leading ministers, even in her presence, Queen Anne had now done her last duty for her nation. On the morning of 1 August 1714 she died, her end hastened by worry and exhaustion, and the news was rapidly spread throughout the country. Walpole, regretting his overhasty departure, immediately set off for London again to greet King George.

6

A Taste of Power

HAVING SPENT less time in Norfolk than he expected, Walpole had to stay in London while the new regime took over. The Jacobite *coup d'état* confidently predicted by many was forestalled by the Whigs' competent action. Under the provisions of the Regency Act a Council of Regency took over smoothly until King George should arrive in Britain. Bolingbroke was suspended by the King's special order and his office sealed, while the official correspondence of Bolingbroke's fellow Secretary of State, Bromley, was required to pass through the hands of Joseph Addison, the Council's Secretary. The King showed no undignified haste to reach his new realm. Leaving Hanover at the end of August he made a slow progress across the north German plain, pausing for several days at the Hague before taking ship to England. When George arrived at Greenwich on 19 September Walpole was among the many politicians present to greet him loyally and to manoeuvre for hoped-for office or emolument.

Just thirty-eight years old, Walpole clearly was among the very ablest politicians in the House of Commons. However, there were many claimants to office, and for the moment he had to be content with the non-Cabinet office of Paymaster-General. In the current state of his finances this was far from unwelcome, for the incumbents of this office had traditionally been able to make large sums of money from their handling of the military budget. James Brydges, who had recently held the post in war-time conditions, had made a fortune. Walpole would preside over an army of diminished size but the opportunities were still considerable; in peacetime, he would, in fact, be able to lay the foundation for his own and his family's enrichment. In addition to the possibility of depositing the army's pay in his private account, where it would accrue interest entirely for his own benefit, the post carried useful perquisites and patronage. Within its jurisdiction lay control of Chelsea Hospital, and henceforth Walpole was able to use the gracious building and ten-acre garden of Orford House behind the hospital for his own residence and recreation. Indeed this house was to continue to be his chief London home, by special arrangement, long after he ceased to be Paymaster-General, while another house which he purchased in Arlington Street to replace Dover Street became simply the office where he conducted official and informal business. Walpole's friends and relations soon benefited from his new fortune, with his brother Galfridus, Robert Mann and several others being given places connected with Chelsea or other military establishments.

Horatio Walpole, however, now had sufficient standing in his own right to account for his appointment shortly afterwards as Minister in the United Netherlands. In any case this position was in the patronage not of Walpole but of Townshend, who replaced Bromley as Northern Secretary – a surprise to many observers. George I had personally observed and approved of Townshend's career, particularly during his negotiation of the treaty with Holland in 1709. The other secretaryship went to Stanhope, also something of a newcomer to high politics but known personally to the King. George was well aware of what he owed to the older Whig Junto for their stout support of his claims over the last twenty-five years but, like William III before him, had no wish for overpowerful ministers. The Junto lords were in any case near the end of their careers and in some cases failing in health. So though Orford became First Lord of the Admiralty again, Somers and Wharton were overlooked and Halifax was disappointed of becoming Lord High Treasurer, being forced to accept instead the lower office of First Lord of the Treasury. But perhaps the most deeply disgruntled of all the leading Whigs was Sunderland, now shunted off to Ireland as its Lord Lieutenant instead of receiving one of the offices of Secretary of State which he had formerly held. Cowper became Lord Chancellor, while Marlborough was restored to his old place, as Captain-General. Walpole's former post of Secretary at War went to his protégé Pulteney.

King George's appointments thus opened the way for a fresh generation of Whigs in the leadership of the party, but he had no intention of forcing the new men to share office with their Tory rivals. The only eminent Tory in the new Cabinet was Nottingham, now appointed Lord President in recognition of his unique services to the new dynasty. Two other Hanoverian Tories, Bromley and Hanmer, were offered seats on the

Treasury Board, but both men refused to desert their party friends and rejected the opportunity. The ever-hopeful Oxford, present among the throng which greeted the new King at Greenwich, was shown George's back and knew that his career was over; and if Oxford's case was such, then other Tories could have little to hope for. Throughout the length and breadth of the land began a purge of Tories in national and local office which reversed and exceeded the thinning out of Whigs when Queen Anne had come to the throne in 1702. On this the Court's Hanoverian advisers such as Baron Bothmer were at one with Whigs like Cowper, who drew up a long memorandum for the King urging him against a non-party ministry. Cowper argued that if both parties were shown favour: 'an equal degree of power, tending at the same time different ways, would render the operations of the government slow and heavy, if not altogether impracticable'.[1] But King George needed little convincing: the Whigs' day had arrived.

In the new appointments the seeds of later dissensions were sown. Townshend and Walpole had been courteously consulted on Stanhope's appointment and they convinced themselves, on Horatio Walpole's assurance, that the Southern Secretary would be reasonably compliant. But Stanhope owed his appointment more to the King's approval than to that of the Townshend-Walpole coterie, and time was to reveal that he was no cipher.[2] Other sources of dissatisfaction soon emerged, caused by the inadequate number of major posts available to match up with the multitude of applicants. These inevitable rubs were unnecessarily exacerbated by the King's failure to reward even such long-standing services as those of ex-Speaker John Smith. Some omissions were due to the inexperience of the Hanoverian advisers; but the employment of this advice merely magnified the royal offence in the minds of the sufferers. In addition to a potential rivalry between Townshend and Stanhope, with their interlocked and sometimes overlapping duties in both foreign and home affairs, the national hatred of foreign advisers behind the throne was stimulated by the part these Germans played, or were assumed to have played, in ministerial appointments.

1. Campbell, *Lives of the Chancellors*, iv, p.427.
2. Coxe, *Walpole*, ii, pp.48–9.

As a result of Queen Anne's death a new Parliament had to be called within six months. The old House met for a few weeks in August to conclude the tail-end of recent business. A blatant attempt by the Tory leaders to curry favour with the new monarch by granting him a civil list worth three hundred thousand pounds more than Anne had enjoyed was defeated by a combination of the Whigs and some Tory backbenchers. No more than at the beginning of William III's reign were the 'country' element willing to make the King more financially independent of Parliament. Nevertheless the Whigs felt it necessary to demonstrate their greater concern for George, and in addition to hinting that better terms might be given in a new House they took a more tangible step. On Horatio Walpole's initiative, no doubt concerted with his brother, they undertook to pay arrears still owed to Hanover for the payment of electoral troops in the last war. On this note Parliament was prorogued for the last time, and both parties began to prepare for the long struggle of an election campaign. In this conflict the Whigs had the clear advantage of the King's known favour and their own control of the higher offices of state, for many voters looked to the sources of patronage for their guidance. Alterations were taking place in lord lieutenancies, revenue services and commissions of the peace, and these changes made the required impression upon electors.

In December the Tories' flagging spirits were temporarily raised by persistent reports of divisions among the victors; such optimism, however, was little justified. Differences certainly existed between Halifax and his younger colleagues; so completely had the First Lord contrived to put himself at odds with the rest of the ministry that they were already bruiting the name of Walpole to succeed him. They believed that Halifax's intransigence sprang not simply from chagrin at his inferior appointment but from a reluctance to continue the persecution of lowly Tories still in place and from his unease at the prospect of the impeachment of former ministers. His colleagues and the Whig press were calling for such action to follow up the threats they had made at the time of the Peace of Utrecht. These differences of opinion, however, brought little real assistance to the Tories, and were in any case patched up in time for the general election.

The election campaign itself was preceded by a spate of Whig

Addresses, condemning the last government in terms which showed a similarity of wording suggesting careful orchestration. A royal proclamation assisted the party cause, calling for the return of Members of Parliament 'such as showed a firmness to the Protestant succession, when it was most in danger'. By comparison Tory propaganda was subdued or counter-productive and feeble. Bishop Atterbury in his *English Advice to the Freeholders of England* made a valid point, which was often to be repeated by later opponents of the Hanoverian dynasty, when he accused the King and ministers of preparing to use British military and naval resources in support of Hanoverian electoral interests in Germany. But a Declaration by James Edward, the Pretender, widely circulated in Britain and asserting that the late ministry had intended to restore him to the throne, only did damage to the Tory cause among an electorate which already suspected that this was the case.

The Whigs left little to chance in constituencies where government or private patronage could be made to play any part, as in Radnorshire where a Receiver of Land Tax later remarked that he 'had directions . . . to overturn the interests of the Harleys'.[1] Walpole found his campaign in Norfolk greatly eased by similar means and secured King's Lynn without difficulty. Government-sponsored candidates included Galfridus Walpole, who entered the House for Lostwithiel, and Horatio Walpole who transferred from Castle Rising to Bere Alston to make way for Walpole's lifelong friend Charles Churchill, Marlborough's nephew. The 1715 election was remarkable for a new star in the firmament of Whig election managers. The young Thomas Pelham-Holles, soon to be Duke of Newcastle, was able to exercise his vast patronage effectively for the first time. In Sussex, where the Pelham estates lay, he secured the election of two Whigs for the county and two others at Lewes. Newcastle's other possessions were mostly in Nottinghamshire and Yorkshire. In the former his efforts resulted in the return of two Whigs at Nottingham, one at East Retford and one at Newark. The young magnate also took a major part in securing the return of four Whig members in Yorkshire,

1. British Library, Additional manuscripts, 34, 737, f.3 (hereafter cited as Add.MSS).

including the pamphleteer Richard Steele at Boroughbridge. But such 'management' was only one factor in an eighteenth-century election. Many floating voters were convinced that the Hanoverian succession had been in danger at the end of Queen Anne's reign, and they moved strongly to support Whig candidates in the 1715 election.[1] This swing was particularly visible in the large-franchise constituencies where the operation of patronage did not play a significant part. In all some 341 Whigs and 217 Tories were returned to the House of Commons, reflecting a new preponderance which was to continue for several decades.

In the new House Walpole immediately resumed his position at the forefront of the Whigs. Success in the elections was only the first battle of a campaign, the object of which was no less than the destruction of the Tory party for ever. Bitter memories of party warfare since the Popish Plot ensured that neither party accepted any need for the survival of its rival. Walpole had vivid memories of the Junto's impeachment in his first session in the Commons, as well as of his own imprisonment by Oxford's government in 1712. He was determined to take revenge by condign punishment of the late ministers. Parliament assembled on 17 March and the House of Commons appointed Walpole's associate Spencer Compton as Speaker. At the same time the key post of Chairman of the Committee of Elections in the Commons was given to Richard Hampden, great-grandson of John Hampden, hero of parliamentary resistance to Charles I's Ship Money. Under Hampden's competent management some thirty Tories successful in the elections, were unseated in favour of their petitioning Whig rivals, while all petitions from unsuccessful Tories were defeated.[2]

With the essential preliminary business concluded, Walpole could begin his own series of interventions. In the Address to the King which he moved on 23 March he condemned the late ministry's treaties at Utrecht, its secret negotiations with the Pretender and its general mismanagement. He demanded that

1. Speck, *Tory and Whig*, pp.113–4.
2. Hill, *Growth of Parliamentary Parties*, p.155.

the guilty ministers should be brought to justice. This plain threat proved too much for Bolingbroke, who slipped out of England a few days later and received from James Edward the title of Secretary of State in the exiled court. Walpole had not heard the last of Bolingbroke, but for the next ten years, his ablest rival was effectively removed from the scene. When a committee of the House of Commons was appointed to find evidence for the impeachment of the former ministers it was Walpole who was made its chairman. On 9 June he laid the fruits of the committee's labours before the House in a document which took five hours to read out. Walpole's concluding motion for the impeachment of Bolingbroke and Oxford was immediately adopted, and a few days later the name of Ormonde was added to the list. Such was the fury of the Whigs' attack at this point that even the great Shrewsbury, despite his vigorous denials of having approved the preliminary articles of peace in 1711, was only saved from impeachment by the King's personal intervention. But George was nevertheless forced to relieve of household office the peer who had done as much as any man to preserve the Protestant succession in 1688–1689, and again in July 1714.[1]

Much of the evidence was at best circumstantial. The lack of anything which a judicial examination in the Upper House could construe as treason was running Walpole into deep waters. The case of Ormonde, who also broke and ran after his impeachment had been voted, was a good example of the expedients used, for the evidence against the Duke was exiguous and indecisive. In the end he was given the King's leave to go, in a message conveyed from Stanhope via his brother-in-law Robert Pitt.[2] This last, celebrated only as the father of the Great Commoner, proved a useful agent in averting what might have been an embarrassing acquittal, by giving the government an excuse to convert the attack on Ormonde, along with that on Bolingbroke, into a more easily obtainable attainder. Such a legislative process, bypassing the need for better evidence, amounted to a condemnation of the accused simply by a vote of the majority.

The adoption of attainder in the cases of Bolingbroke and

1. Somerville, *The King of Hearts*, pp.343–4.
2. Add. MSS. 47,034, unfoliated: Berkeley, 8 September 1715.

Ormonde solved part of Walpole's dilemma. In the case of Oxford, however, impeachment was not superseded by an attainder; the old peer, still protesting that he had done nothing which Queen Anne had not ordered him to do, bravely disdained to follow his colleagues into exile and was duly committed to the Tower of London, there to await the promised production of further evidence. In all these proceedings the cowed Tories raised little opposition other than William Wyndham's defence of his friend Bolingbroke and some speeches by Bromley on behalf of Oxford. The trial had still not been settled, however, when proceedings were thrown into disarray in September by the news that the Earl of Mar had set up the Pretender's standard at Braemar.

Before the rising of 1715 came to its climax in defeat, significant changes took place in the government. The deaths of Halifax and Wharton brought forward two younger men well able to deal with the crisis. Walpole became First Lord of the Treasury and Chancellor of the Exchequer, while Sunderland was given Wharton's place as Lord Privy Seal. Walpole's unexpectedly early rise to these high offices of state at a time of national emergency was probably due as much to Townshend's efforts as to his own unquestioned ability and service to the House of Hanover. Moreover Walpole's first tenure of the posts was to prove temporary, for unfortunately he and Townshend were by no means as strongly entrenched as the promotion suggested. Townshend had already clashed with his fellow secretary Stanhope on a number of occasions, and the latter in alliance with Sunderland was to prove a formidable rival to the brothers-in-law. For the moment, however, all Whigs acted together; many suspected Jacobites and sympathisers were arrested, including Wyndham and several other Members of Parliament. But the precaution was hardly necessary, and in the absence of an assurance from the Pretender that he was willing to adopt the Protestant religion very few Tories stirred on his behalf in England. The Duke of Argyll was despatched north to deal with the rebellion, and by the early months of 1716 it was defeated both in Scotland and in Lancashire.

Vigorous military action was followed by energetic measures of retribution. Six Scottish peers taken in the act of rebellion were impeached and sentenced to death. Walpole was strongly in favour of making an example of them to deter others who might in the future contemplate overthrowing Hanoverian government. He met little resistance, even from the Tories, in proposing a four-shilling land tax to pay for the suppression of the Rebellion, but his unrelenting pursuit of the accused men soon met stiffer resistance. In the House of Lords Nottingham took his first step out of line with his Whig colleagues by supporting an Address to the King, requesting leniency. To prevent further opposition encouraged by this example the House of Commons was prorogued and Nottingham and his relations were dismissed from their offices. But, as often in his career, Walpole was not insensitive to strongly-based opposition. His demand for prorogation was seen as the manoeuvre it was, and met objections from many of his own party who were not in favour of further punishments. In deference to a public opinion which was now veering towards the belief that enough blood had been spilt, only two of the Scottish peers went forward to execution.

In the aftermath of the Rebellion the ministers felt strong enough to proceed further against the Tories. Their intention was no less than to repeal the Triennial Act of 1694 and replace it by a new measure permitting Parliament to sit for a maximum of seven rather than three years. Extending the life of the existing House of Commons would permit the Ministry to strengthen its patronage control of the smaller boroughs. There was, however, again a considerable resistance to be faced not only from the Tories but from some Whigs who felt, in the words of Lord Perceval, that a long-lived House of Commons was 'departing from Whig principles and perpetuating a ministry though they serve their country ever so ill'.[1] Some Whig members were also influenced by the more immediate motive of anxiety that if they voted for the measure and it subsequently became bogged down in the House of Lords they might lose their seats at the next election, their constituents objecting to the proposed reduction of electoral privileges and perquisites.

The fear that the Septennial Bill might be lost in the Upper House probably arose as a result of the Lords' intransigence in the matter of the Address concerning the Jacobite peers taken

1. Add. MSS, 47,028, pp.286–7.

in arms; but Walpole and other ministers were confident, justifiably as it proved, that this was an isolated incident arising out of humanity and the well-known sensitivity of the peers in matters touching their legal decisions. To meet the objectors' point, however, the bill was first introduced in the House of Lords. Here Shrewsbury, who had been mainly responsible for the adoption of the Triennial Act, spoke strongly for its retention. Such resistance, however, was swept aside by the government majority. In the Commons opposition now came mainly from the Tories, who opposed the Bill in more than fifty speeches. The themes most often repeated, that a seven-year life for the Commons would immeasurably strengthen the executive at the expense of the legislature, were contemptuously dismissed by ministerial Whigs as libertarian and fallacious. The government's contention was that the Triennial Act had not justified itself by giving greater power to the electors but had, on the contrary, debased them by permitting excessive popular participation leading to frequent civil tumults, rebellion and – a potent argument with many members – the financial ruin of candidates by heavy and frequent electoral expenses.

Laying heavy stress upon recent events, Walpole argued in defence of the bill that the chief beneficiaries from continual electoral excitement had been the Pretender, foreign nations who took advantage of British internal politics, and an uncontrollable element of the populace which benefited from the reluctance of magistrates to punish riotous behaviour at election times. In vain the Tories sarcastically observed that the strongest support for the bill came from those 45 members who represented what were generally regarded as the venal seats of Scotland. The crucial vote on committal in the Commons on 24 April 1716 gave the government a decisive majority of 284 to 162, the lower number including a few dissident Whigs. At various stages a total of 43 Whigs voted against the bill, and 17 office-holders absented themselves.[1] Nevertheless the ministry carried, without real difficulty, a measure which even some members who voted for it privately considered to be a violation of a basic Whig ideal of electoral freedom. A new era was at hand in which the Commons were more subjected to control by

1. Sedgwick, *History of Parliament*, i, pp.25 and 81, Note IV.

government through its enhanced powers of patronage, both in constituencies and in the House, by reason of less frequent elections. Not least of the beneficiaries was to be Walpole, in his second period of office.

For the moment the passing of the Septennial Act marked the end of unity among the ministers. The crushing blows dealt to Tory aspirations by the new dynasty, the general election, and the Act itself now allowed the victors the luxury of quarrelling among themselves. Walpole had been ill with fever during most stages of the passing of the Septennial Bill, though he strongly supported it when he could, and his absences contributed to a weakening of his position which now became evident.

After the end of the session the King prepared to go to Hanover for the summer, taking with him one of the Secretaries of State, Stanhope, but leaving Townshend in Britain. In his absence George invested his son the Prince of Wales with the regency of the Kingdom. Father and son had long been on the worst of terms, and the King gave the Prince no more power than he was obliged to. Prince George could not call Parliament, nor could he control the normal channels of patronage. While the Prince showed his resentment by encouraging the aspirations of discontented Whigs such as Argyll, and by slowly moving towards an understanding with the more cautious Walpole, Townshend unwisely involved himself in a feud with a friend of the King by the mistake of obtaining for her an Irish title, Duchess of Munster, rather than the English one she coveted.[1] The harried King was further upset and turned against the Townshend-Walpole faction. Sunderland, who had left England on the excuse of taking the waters at Aix-la-Chapelle, unexpectedly arrived at Hanover instead.

The basic division between ministers in Hanover and ministers back in England having appeared, issues were not long in coming forth. George as Elector of Hanover needed French diplomatic support in the Baltic, and Stanhope was in the

1. Coxe, *Walpole*, ii, pp.58–9. The King's mistress, Ehrengard Melusine von der Schulenberg, became Duchess of Kendal in 1719.

process of obtaining a treaty with the French minister Dubois on the basis of a mutual guarantee of the House of Hanover on the throne of Britain and the infant (and therefore vulnerable) Louis XV on that of France. But the sudden prospect of alliance with France after war for a generation was something with which many Whigs could not come to terms, and Walpole was in full agreement with the reaction of backbench opinion in the Commons. He demanded at least that Protestant Holland should be included in the treaty and went on to censure the use of the British fleet in the Baltic for furthering Hanoverian aspirations against Sweden. For good measure both Walpole and Townshend censured the King's German advisers, possibly with the Duchess of Munster among others in mind, and even criticised the King personally for the sale of certain land acquired in the West Indies in the recent war.[1]

Later in his career Walpole would not have allowed himself to be so rattled by court intrigues as to forget the need to preserve a balance between the backbench opinion he understood and the wishes of a Hanoverian monarch. Stanhope and Sunderland seized the opportunity of defending the King and his policies, for if Walpole was fearful of the mood of the House of Commons when it assembled in the autumn, Stanhope was alive to the need to conciliate the peppery King, especially in matters which involved his interests most closely as a German prince. Sunderland wrote with characteristic bluntness that His Majesty had expressed surprise at the idea that a British Parliament should not involve itself in North European politics; indeed, he wrote: 'this notion is nothing but the old Tory one that England can subsist by itself, whatever becomes of the rest of Europe, which has been so justly exploded by the Whigs ever since the Revolution'.[2]

Walpole's and Townshend's opposition to the prospect of a costly British intervention in a Hanoverian war with Sweden, and to an unpopular treaty with France, sprang from their confidence in their power base in the Commons. Unfortunately, though their judgement was basically correct, their timing was at fault. It was too soon after the Rebellion for country opinion to be able to assert itself successfully against

1. Plumb, *Walpole*, i, pp.226–35; Coxe, *Walpole*, ii, pp.58–97.
2. H.M.C., *Townshend*, p.103.

the private interests of a dynasty which, after all, stood between Britain and the return of the Catholic House of Stuart. Stanhope and Sunderland showed a better grasp of current political reality, as well as of their own interests, when they bowed to the wishes of George I. When Horatio Walpole as Minister at The Hague used his position to delay the signing of the French treaty matters went too far. Horatio himself hurried to Hanover to explain his actions to the King but did not give satisfaction. In December Walpole learned in London that Townshend, considered the chief culprit, was to suffer the loss of his post, a blow hardly softened by making him Lord Lieutenant of Ireland. A final split was avoided by the retention of Walpole. The First Lord could not find in the new arrangement sufficient excuse for resignation, but he protested vigorously to Stanhope:

> I find you are all persuaded, the scheme is so adjusted, that it can meet with no objection from the Whigs. Believe me, you will find the direct contrary true, with every unprejudiced Whig of any consequence or consideration. I, perhaps, am too nearly concerned in the consequences to gain any creditt with you. However, I can't help telling you, you don't know what you are doing . . . Such sudden changes to old sworn friends, are seldom look'd upon in the world with a favourable eye.[1]

Walpole and Townshend thus submitted with ill grace. The chief ostensible consideration influencing their retreat was the need for an appearance of Whig unity at a time when the government was about to reveal the discovery of a plot, centred on Count Gyllenborg, the Swedish minister in London, to procure an invasion by the Pretender. But the true reason for Walpole's quiescence was his desire to make certain of the support he boasted in the House of Commons. From January 1717 both he and the rival ministers were engaged in canvassing opinion in that House. Both made considerable headway in enlisting a measure of Whig support and both were even reported to be making court to the Tories. In addition Walpole was putting the finishing touches to a scheme which he hoped would considerably enhance his popularity among the country gentlemen.

1. Coxe, *Walpole*, ii, p.144.

This was no less than a plan for establishing a 'sinking fund' or sum of money set aside from current taxation for the purpose of gradually paying off the National Debt. Few contemporaries could accept that the numerous debts incurred in the late wars should continue to exist as a permanent part of the financial scheme of things. The idea of a non-redeemable National Debt was still largely in the future. The greater part of the debts stood at six per cent or more and an essential part of Walpole's scheme when it emerged in a report of the Committee of the Whole House on 23 February was a reduction of these rates, including the large ones involving the Bank of England and the South Sea Company, to five per cent. If this were not accepted, the principal sums were, it was threatened, to be paid off; but there was every probability that the government's creditors, faced with this alternative, would accept the lower rate as better than nothing. The conversion of unredeemable annuities and a good deal of consolidation of miscellaneous debts was also envisaged. The project, a logical extension of Oxford's South Sea scheme though with a rate of interest appropriate to time of peace, marked the culmination of an important phase of its author's struggle for popularity and support.

By the end of March 1717 Walpole was sufficiently advanced with his financial plans, and confident enough of his support among the Whigs, to throw down the challenge of resignation and put his case before the Commons. The King, anxious to avoid the loss of an able minister, accepted his resignation with reluctance. Stanhope and Sunderland viewed his departure with more equanimity. They had long been prepared for this move but were soon to be surprised by its corollary. Walpole did not intend to sit idly on the back benches while policies of which he did not approve were carried forward by his former colleagues. That a Whig should oppose Whig government deliberately and consistently had been unthinkable in the last generation, when the party had rarely held office by more than a thread. The situation was now very different. The main cause for which all Whigs had held together, the Hanoverian succession, was a reality, and the Tories were a chastened and ineffective minority. But if Walpole and a considerable section of the Whig party were to range themselves alongside those same Tories, without agreeing with them on principle, Stanhope and

Sunderland could be harried without endangering the fundamental tenets for which all Whigs stood.

Early in April Stanhope moved in the Commons for financial supplies to form alliances with German states against Sweden, on the excuse of Gyllenborg's recent plotting. In addition to the predictable Tory opposition the minister was surprised to find a large band of Whigs against him, headed by Speaker Compton and ex-Speaker Smith. It was clear that this opposition was a Walpolite challenge, even though Walpole himself voted for the measure in order to allow the government the possibility of re-employing him in case of ministerial defeat. In the event the combined opposition failed by fifteen votes, and King and ministers decided to fight rather than succumb. The day following this debate Townshend was dismissed from his lord lieutenancy and both sides prepared for a long struggle.

The role of Walpole as the destroyer of party unity could hardly have been imagined in August 1714 when Queen Anne died. In the nearly three years which had elapsed since then many changes had taken place. Apart from the new dynasty itself the most important were the progressive destruction of the Tory party and its reduction to the size in the House of Commons which it was to retain for the next two generations. But the accession of the Whigs to apparently unchallengeable power brought about major changes in their once monolithic unity. Long-suppressed personal rivalries can beset any party which forms a government without strong opposition. The Whigs, catapulted into supremacy with unexpected force, were more than usually susceptible to schism. Further, the number of places and perquisites available was insufficient to satisfy the large Whig majority. As a result two groups now existed, one of them in opposition led by Walpole in the Commons and Townshend in the Lords.

Though Walpole held some good cards he was chafed by losing the highest office after holding it briefly. He was never to forget that his primary allegiance lay with the House of Commons, and its often stubborn and conservative backbenchers; but if he could overcome his present difficulties and return to that position of authority to which he felt his abilities entitled him, he would learn to be more adaptable. He would need to flatter and conciliate monarchs, work closely with the Church of England which had hitherto been an unswerving ally of the Tories, and even accept the new relationship with France, the national enemy, dictated by the changed circumstances of the day. When Walpole next came to office, after three years of exclusion, it would be not only as a politician but as a statesman.

7

In Opposition

WALPOLE HAD been virtually thrust from office, this time not by the Tories but by his fellow Whigs. The ministers appear to have expected that he would take a back seat and avoid opposing them, hoping to be forgiven and taken back into the fold. In fact, however, any return to office might well depend more upon the nuisance which Walpole and his friends could make of themselves than upon any credit which they might obtain by quiescence. Walpole was pushed in the direction of outright opposition by his associates, who upon his fall hurried to resign and thereby demonstrate their extreme dissatisfaction with royal and ministerial policies. Orford immediately gave up the Admiralty, Devonshire the post of Lord President, and Paul Methuen the southern secretaryship, all of them men of substance and weight in the Whig party.

These and lesser resignations were more numerous than Stanhope had expected, and he was hard put to cobble together a satisfactory ministry. His weakness was demonstrated by the fact that no one better than Joseph Addison could be found to take over from Methuen. Addison, a leading literary figure in the Whig cause for many years, had some administrative experience but was a weak parliamentary speaker and no diplomat. Stanhope himself took Walpole's places at the Treasury and Exchequer and shortly afterward transferred to the Lords as Viscount (later Earl) Stanhope, while Sunderland was at last gratified by being brought in as Secretary for the North. Orford's post at the Admiralty was taken by the Earl of Berkeley, a little-known professional sailor, and Sunderland doubled up as Lord President in place of Devonshire. In consequential changes in the royal Household the young Newcastle was brought in as Lord Chamberlain. Newcastle's adherence brought to the government side in the Commons the much-needed support of the several voters controlled by the young duke's private patronage.

By comparison with the transparently makeshift nature of some of these ministerial arrangements the quality of Walpole's followers looked respectable. Over the next three years the Walpolites followed the classic path of ejected ministers by attacking the government at every opportunity. The fact that the ministry was a Whig one made little difference. They found plenty of the usual opportunities for criticising placemen and excessive government expenditure; but in addition they were prepared to reject Stanhope's liberal desires for religious toleration and thereby to ally themselves more closely with the Church of England. Even projects such as the repeal of the Schism Act, to which they had been pledged since its passing in 1714, met their opposition. They were also prepared to abandon the continuance of Oxford's impeachment, if by so doing they could embarrass Stanhope, and they would over the next three years be found alongside Tories in denouncing the Septennial Act. For the logic of opposition demanded that Walpolites should vie with ministers in bidding for the Tories as well as for those of their own party who had not yet taken a stand. And to this end the dissident Whigs had an advantage, for they could go further than Stanhope's official Whig line in seeking the Tory party's support. On 11 April Smith showed how far the Walpolites were prepared to go when he attacked the ministry for its failure to bring in an indemnity bill to prevent further reprisals after the Rebellion. An Act of Grace was duly brought in, whereby the imprisoned peers and some scores of other rebels still under sentence of death were released – a favour which they owed as much to the Whig schism as to politic clemency.

In offering the Tories such cooperation Walpole and his friends needed to choose causes carefully; they had to tread delicately to avoid completely alienating the King, at least as long as they hoped eventually to make their way back to office. The perceptive diarist Lord Perceval predicted that the dissident Whigs were likely to be too strong for the ministry 'in any causes where they can distinguish between the King's honour and the service and interest of Stanhope and Lord Sunderland'.[1] Nevertheless the possibilities for full-blown opposition alongside the Tories were considerable and soon again to be demonstrated. The occasion for this was Wyndham's motion that Dr Andrew Snape, a well-known High

1. Add. MSS. 47,128, pp.318–2.

Church polemicist, should be allowed to preach before the House of Commons. As Headmaster of Eton, Snape had Walpole's two elder sons and the sons of many other Whigs under his care, so that the proposal provided good ground for a trial of strength when the ministers opposed it. Walpole and his friends gave Wyndham their full support and, to the ministry's surprise, carried the day by a majority of ten votes. The issue was a minor one, but useful as providing an easy transition into opposition.

Another cause for self-congratulation among the Walpolites was the attitude of the Prince of Wales. Still on bad terms with his father, the Prince had recently shown sympathy for Walpole on several occasions by encouraging his Household followers to vote with the new opposition. Heartened by such support, Walpole determined upon a more major attack.

This was no less than a parliamentary condemnation of General Cadogan, who had relieved Argyll as Commander in Scotland during the last stage of the Rebellion and whose vigorous pursuit of the Scottish rebels was greatly resented by many Tories. The eleven or so Campbell relatives of the displaced Argyll currently sitting in the House of Commons could also be expected to join in a censure of Cadogan. His ostensible offence was corruption in the cost of transporting the six thousand Dutch troops used in suppressing the Rebellion. The case against him was canvassed for several weeks before 4 June, when it was debated in a Committee of the Whole, for which occasion both sides made desperate efforts to get every last supporter into the House. The lame and the halt were summoned to a bitter test of strength.

Popular opinion expected an opposition victory, and the numbers present at the opening stages of the debate seemed to bear this expectation out. By almost unprecedented procedural devices the government side spun the business out while the precincts of Westminster were combed for yet more supporters. The opposition attack was opened by William Pulteney, who had resigned as Secretary at War with Walpole. Pulteney was answered, on behalf of the ministry, by James Craggs the younger, and by John Aislabie, who now held Walpole's old post of Treasurer of the Navy. But the Tories, whose support Walpole had confidently expected, proved to be divided, with several of their leaders apparently unwilling to bring down the government in order to raise other Whigs. Of the usual Tory debaters only William Shippen, the unrepentantly Jacobite spokesman, took part in the attack; one prominent Tory, John Hungerford, actually spoke for Cadogan while Hanmer and Nottingham's son, Lord Finch, were conspicuous by their absence from the House. In fact no fewer than 57 Tories were absent from the final vote, which the ministry consequently carried by 204 votes to 194. This outcome ensured that the struggle would be a long one. Although this was disappointing for Walpole it had its consolatory aspects. Among the minority who voted against Cadogan were 78 Whigs, including 37 who still held civil or military offices. The Prince of Wales's 'family' and the Campbells clove, as expected, to the opposition. Of the eight members returned by the Duke of Newcastle four voted with the Walpolites, including Newcastle's brother Henry Pelham and four with the government. Though a ministerialist, Newcastle kept a foot in Walpole's camp when he could.[1]

Two days later Stanhope capitalised upon his narrow victory by introducing revised proposals for the national debt. Intensive discussions had been taking place with the Bank of England and the South Sea Company, as a result of which these two bodies were willing to come into the interest reduction scheme. But Stanhope had abandoned some of Walpole's more constructive proposals, especially in making no attempt to solve the problem of the mass of annuity holders who constituted an enormous burden, at war-inflated rates of interest, on the public income. Whether Stanhope in his anxiety to seize the initiative from Walpole had no time to assimilate these proposals, or whether the scheme was one which could only have been carried through by its original deviser's energy is not certain; probably both factors were present. Walpole was greatly incensed but in the end sensibly settled for shared credit, resigning himself to the omission of one of the most important parts of his proposed financial coup.[2] When Sunderland tried a solution of his own with the annuities two years later his attempt was to bring the government enormous

1. *Annals of Stair*, ii, pp.20–2; Abel Boyer, *The Political State of Great Britain* (1711–37), xiii, pp.702–5; Sedgwick, *History of Parliament*, i, p.81.
2. Plumb, *Walpole*, i, pp.247–8; P. G. M. Dickson, *The Financial Revolution in England* (1967), pp.84–5.

popularity at first, then the utter disaster of the South Sea Bubble.

The only important matter remaining before the end of the session concerned the Earl of Oxford, whose impeachment had been deferred throughout the previous year and who was now an embarrassing problem to both government and Walpolites. At the end of May 1717 Oxford took advantage of the Whig schism by petitioning for an early trial. Walpole, on Stanhope's suggestion, reassumed the prosecution as Chairman of the Committee of Secrecy; but he refused to let this ministerial manoeuvre embroil him with the Tories. He privately assured William Bromley, 'If I bluster you must take no notice of it, for I shall mean nothing'. When the trial came on in the Upper House, Lord Harcourt on behalf of Oxford moved that the two weakest charges, amounting to high treason, should be dealt with first and carried his point with the aid of opposition Whigs led by Townshend. When the ministerial majority in the Commons demurred there was deadlock between the two Houses. Walpole saw to it that the Commons managers did not appear before the Lords to state their case, and Oxford was formally acquitted upon all charges. The government maintained consistency, but Walpole by his actions laid some claim to political humanity.[1] This helped to oil the wheels between opposition Whigs and Tories over the next three years.

In the summer of 1717, Walpole was engrossed in his plans for further opposition and was also involved in family concerns. Although he had been estranged from his wife for some years he attended her in the birth of the child whom he was to acknowledge as his son Horace, later famous for his authorship of the 'gothic' novel *The Castle of Otranto*, and for his design of his equally gothic house at Strawberry Hill. As stated earlier, however, there are reasons for supposing that contemporary gossip which assigned the true fatherhood of the child to another was, in this case, correct. So the happy event did nothing to heal old wounds, though Walpole came to love young Horace in later years. Soon afterwards another more celebrated birth took place, that of a son to the Prince and

1. HMC, *Portland*, v, p.527; Add. MSS, 47,028, p.396.

Princess of Wales. This child was immediately the innocent cause of a right royal row. George I angered the Prince of Wales by insisting that the Lord Chamberlain should be the godparent of his grandson George. Prince George's dislike of Newcastle led him to the indiscretion of personal recrimination, which the excitable Duke interpreted as a challenge to a duel. By the time the matter had been sorted out by the King himself the Prince had been placed under arrest, belatedly released, and taken himself from the royal palace of St James's to set up a new home in a house in Leicester Square. Leicester House was to become the focus of political opposition for the Prince himself and later for his son Frederick and grandson George.

The setting up of a rival court by the 'reversionary interest' of the Prince of Wales was a clear advantage to Walpole because it assured him of continued political support. Attacks on the King's government which might otherwise have been called 'faction' could now safely be sheltered behind the façade of loyalty to a junior member of the ruling House. The value of the heir's 'reversionary interest', exploited by the Whigs under Queen Anne, thus acquired new currency in the context of discord between the two prickly Hanoverians. The ministers, for their part, demanded more support from the senior court. In public the King went out of his way to show 'marks of confidence' in the ministry; he deliberately made himself more available than hitherto and embarked upon an expensive course of entertainment by a public table for Members of Parliament and others. The Prince, with his more limited financial resources, did his best to rival this display by ostentatious favour to Walpolite Whigs and even Tories.

The Tories were encouraged to respond to this princely concession by no less an adviser than Bolingbroke, who had broken with the Pretender after the failure of the Fifteen and was, through his friend Wyndham, beginning to develop the philosophy of a country alliance of Tories and dissident Whigs which was to reach its fruition twenty years later in the most famous of his pamphlets *The Idea of a Patriot King*. By the same process of transmutation Wyndham appeared no more as Jacobite sympathiser, despite his brief imprisonment at the time of the Rebellion, but as the new leader of the Hanoverian Tories replacing the waning influence of Oxford and Hanmer.

Despite political alliance with the Prince of Wales the Tories remained an object of deep suspicion to both the Prince himself and the Whigs, and it was the Walpolites who stood to gain most from the Prince's unfilial activities.

The first working of the Tory alliance was seen in the new session. Walpole was willing to vote alongside the Tories, cashing in on traditional country disquiet about the existence of a standing army in peacetime. Though the Rebellion was long since over, wrote the poet and diplomat Matthew Prior, 'Whigs and Tories begin to think there are not a sufficient number disbanded'.[1] On 2 December Craggs presented the estimates, and two days later, in a Committee of the Whole, the first brush occurred. The opposition Whigs concurred with the Tories that the land forces should be reduced to twelve thousand men, Walpole pointing out that the actual present size was not sixteen thousand, as the government claimed, but in effect eighteen thousand. Cross-party cooperation broke down, as often in practice, and the effect of Walpole's reasoned and temperate argument was lost by a fiery attack on the King by Shippen, for which the Jacobite member was committed to the Tower for the remainder of the season. Moderate Whigs were alienated, and a motion by Walpole for a reduced army failed by over fifty votes. He then turned during the following weeks to a series of patient criticisms of the government's military expenditure and regained lost ground with the waverers, succeeding in reducing the ministry's majority to fourteen votes at one point. Even more hopeful, if Bishop Atterbury's information is correct, was the threat by some of the Whigs who had supported the ministerial side in this vote that they would not be induced to continue doing so on such issues.[2] All the powers of parliamentary obstruction at the disposal of Walpolites continued to be concentrated on the ministry's newly revealed weak spot, the army.

The opposition campaign culminated on 4 January 1718 in a clause of the annual Mutiny Bill for making mutiny or desertion punishable by death. This stipulation, the opposition claimed, was inappropriate in time of peace. The point was

1. HMC, *Bath*, iii, p.450.
2. Boyer, *Political State*, xiv, pp.580, 584–5; Add. MSS. 17,677, KKK2, ff. 390, 401–2 and 47,028, p.248; J. H. Glover, *The Stuart Papers* (1847), i, pp.13–14.

calculated to arouse sympathy, on humanitarian grounds, from many Whigs otherwise well disposed to the ministry; and a high turnout of Tories could always be relied upon to vote against the general principle of a standing army. Walpole and Compton were reported to be laying heavy wagers on their own success. Several observers commented upon the number of members present in the Commons as being unprecedently high, and the political annalist Abel Boyer noted in addition 'three Whigs and six or seven Tories who happened to be shut out when the question was put'. In the upshot the government gained its point by 247 votes to 229, but a majority of only eighteen after what a later age would have called a three-line whip was more encouraging to the losers than to the winners.[1] Moreover the ministry suffered a further setback, in that plans they had for introducing legislation for the relief of dissenters had to be put off in the face of Walpole's likely continued support for the Tories and the Church of England on this point.

Before the assembling of Parliament in the autumn of 1718 several changes were made to strengthen the ministry. Craggs took over the Southern Department from the ineffective Addison, while Stanhope gave up the Treasury to Sunderland in exchange for the Northern Secretary's office which he much preferred. In an evil moment for the ministry the post of Chancellor of the Exchequer was given to Aislabic, who shortly afterwards began co-ordinating with Sunderland plans for the future of the South Sea Company. Nicholas Lechmere, perhaps the only ministerial debater apart from Craggs who had been able to stand up to Walpole in the last session, became Attorney-General. Not all the changes, however, were seen as being to the ministry's advantage. Cowper had found more ties with the Prince of Wales than with the King and left office to drift into the opposition camp, followed in the Commons by his brother Spencer Cowper. The new ministerial arrangements were thus less successful than Stanhope could have wished.

In the summer foreign affairs added further to Stanhope's difficulties. He wished to extend his new alliance with France by the inclusion of the Holy Roman Emperor. To conciliate

---

1. Add. MSS. 47,028, pp.438–9, 443–5; HMC, *Portland*, v, p.554; Boyer, *Political State*, xv, p.187.

Austria, however, it was found necessary to assist her by supporting the Utrecht arrangements in the Mediterranean, where Philip V of Spain was doing his best to upset them. Accordingly a British fleet under Admiral Byng assisted the imperial policies by defeating a Spanish fleet on its way to capture Sicily. These events were followed closely in the British press which, with opposition encouragement, laid particular stress on the difficulties brought by the hostilities with Spain for the South Sea Company and British merchants trading in Spain or Portugal. The ministry took the hostile reporting so seriously as to distribute, a few days before Parliament was due to meet in November, seven thousand free copies of a pamphlet pointing out the dangers for British commerce of an increase in Spanish power in the Mediterranean.[1] Every effort was made by both government and opposition to get supporters to London in time for the opening of Parliament.

In the event it was the ministry who drew first blood. Byng's victory at Cape Passaro was popular, and the Whig opposition's contention that British action in the Mediterranean was illegal in the absence of a declaration of war was defeated by sixty votes in the division on the Address. To Walpole's great annoyance many Tories were among the ministry's supporters on this occasion, swayed by Bromley's argument that the Ministry's Quadruple Alliance was a desirable strengthening of the principles of Utrecht.[2] Walpole was similarly disappointed on other occasions, when the Tories demonstrated that they would not be the tools of a Whig opposition. Stanhope, encouraged by this initial success, decided that the time was ripe to bring in his long-promised legislation for relieving the plight of Protestant dissenters by repealing the Occasional Conformity and Schisms Act of Anne's reign and suspending the religious tests imposed by the Test and Corporation Acts of the Restoration period. On these issues Pulteney and other Walpolites were making cautious overtures to the ministry and might be encouraged to defect. Support for the dissenters was a basic tenet of many Whigs, and Walpole's determination to continue opposition at all costs might place him at a consider-

1. G. C. Gibbs, 'Parliament and the Treaty of Quadruple Alliance', in *William III and Louis XIV, Essays 1680–1720, by and for Mark A. Thomson*, ed. Ragnhild Hatton and J. S. Bromley (Liverpool 1968), especially pp.293–301.
2. Boyer, *Political State*, xvi, pp.469–78; Add. MSS. 17,677 KKK3, ff.1–2.

able disadvantage if he put too much strain on the consciences of his followers.

But in the event Walpole proved able to sway Whig opinion towards a pragmatic point of view. The dissenters in the boroughs had been key supporters before 1714, when the Whig party could only hope at best for a small majority, but now that larger Whig majorities were available the vastly superior numerical support of Anglicans weighed more heavily in political calculations. Moreover, despite sympathy for the dissenters, the parliamentary Whigs had always been strongly Anglican in their personal allegiance. Even the dissenters themselves, argued the Walpolites, were not over-anxious that they should be favoured too highly by the present government, lest some future resurgence of Toryism should result in new and drastic penalties. Thus when Stanhope brought before the House of Lords his plan to suspend the sacramental tests for office-holders he met an unexpected degree of opposition in that usually tranquil House, with a number of Whig peers following Townshend in opposition. The clause suspending the tests was immediately dropped, and when the bill came to the Lower House Walpole led the opposition to the remainder, maintaining that half the Whigs present were against the bill. Although the subsequent vote in favour of the ministry by a majority of forty-one showed this claim to be exaggerated, ministerial weakness was revealed. In all, twenty-two placemen and forty-seven Whigs were seen to have absented themselves from the division. Among those who voted against the government were the Prince of Wales in the House of Lords and his followers in the Lower House. Walpole himself felt strong enough in the course of the debate to throw down the gauntlet of threatened retribution: 'there would come a day', he told the House, 'when the advisers and bringers of this bill would be called to account'.[1]

Impeachment, if that is what Walpole hinted, needed a majority in the House of Lords, but the ministers took his threat seriously enough to attempt to safeguard their position. Stanhope had not been idle in the creation of new peerages from among his supporters, and at present had a small but

1. Add MSS. 47,028, pp.513 seq; HMC, *Portland*, v. pp.575–6; Sedgwick, *History of Parliament*, i, p.81.

useful majority in the Upper House. He now proposed to tamper with the constitution in order to safeguard his future position in case a change of fortune should bring Walpole to power. The ministry were mindful of the Tories' simultaneous creation of a dozen peers to carry the Treaty of Utrecht. In March, therefore, Stanhope introduced in his own House a Peerage Bill with provision for limiting the number of English titles to only six more than the existing total, except for the creation of royal peers. The sixteen Scottish representative peers were to be increased to twenty-five hereditary members. After this, it was proposed, further accession to the House would occur only when old peerages became extinct.

The Bill met no check in the House of Lords, most of the peers having no objection to the proposed enhancement of their privileged position. In the Commons, however, Walpole hoped for the support of a large body of undecided Whigs, and the press put both opposition and ministerial cases before the doubters. To counter the Walpolites' modestly-titled periodical *The Plebeian*, by Steele, there came from the ministerial side *The Patrician* and Addison's last polemical work *The Old Whig*. Among the many variations on the basic themes advanced two appear to have influenced members of the Commons more often than most, both of them opposition points. One concerned the increased importance which the proposed measure would give to the House of Lords. The case was put by Walpole's own tract *Thoughts of a Member of the Lower House* that if the power of creating new peers were removed, 'the House of Lords will be a fixed independent body, not to be called to account like a Ministry, nor to be dissolved or changed like a House of Commons'. The Lords, in fact, might if they wished hamstring the Commons without fear of disciplinary new creations. The other and even more basic consideration which weighed with members of the Commons was that the Bill would, if passed, put an end to every individual's hope of elevation to the peerage for himself and his descendants. The opinion of many country gentlemen was certainly represented by the words which Walpole claimed to have heard used by one of them: 'Shall I consent to the shutting the door upon my family ever coming into the House of Lords?'[1] It was because of

1. *Thoughts of a Member of the Lower House* . . . (1719), p.17; HMC, *14th Report*, part ix, p.459.

the difficulty of overcoming such doubts for the moment that Stanhope was forced to announce on 14 April 1719 his intention of letting the Bill lie, owing to misunderstanding and misrepresentation of its purpose. Walpole had won his first major victory.

The summer was spent by both dissident and government Whigs in preparing for the showdown which they knew must occur in the Commons the following session. Stanhope and Sunderland would have either to establish their control or come to an understanding with Walpole and Townshend to form a reunited Whig ministry. As a first step towards attempting to win the support of the whole party back Stanhope was able in November to report to his colleagues that the King had at last agreed to send his German advisers back to Hanover. The move was a measure of George's desperation at recent opposition successes and his reluctance to have a ministry foisted on him by Walpole in alliance with the Prince of Wales. At the same time Stanhope and Sunderland obtained the royal consent for an all-or-nothing package of legislation calculated to establish their own ascendancy. They proposed to bring in the Peerage Bill again, to reform the universities with a view to breaking Tory control of these institutions, and to obtain a repeal of the Septennial Act further to extend the life of the House of Commons and with it their own majority. Like the Peerage Bill, which it in some ways paralleled for the Commons, this last scheme should in theory have had the support of the sitting members whose privileges it enhanced. Sunderland, the more committed of the two devisers, thought that the repeal could be pushed along with the Peerage Bill and the Universities' Bill, and 'if this won't unite the Whigs nothing will'. Stanhope's more cautious view was 'if they are against repealing the Septennial Act I shall have very little hope of succeeding in the Peerage'.[1]

A proposal to return to the situation which had existed under the Stuarts, with the possible recurrence of something like Charles II's Cavalier Parliament of nearly two decades, could be expected to raise in an extreme form Old Whig objections to infrequent elections. Among others to whom the scheme was submitted for private consideration was Newcastle, as befitted a

1. Add. MSS. 32,686, f.149; Basil Williams, *Stanhope: a Study of Eighteenth Century War and Politics*, (Oxford, 1932), pp.459–63.

peer who controlled at least eight seats in the present House of Commons and claimed to expect sixteen in the next. Newcastle had never sat in the Commons but knew more of its sentiments than did the ministers. While professing in his reply never to think the constitution settled until the Peerage Bill was passed, and to find the University Bill 'agreeable to the party', his view of the proposed repeal of the Septennial Act was unequivocally that it would lose the ministry more than it could possibly gain. He was far from thinking, he wrote, that the repeal would make the Peerage Bill go down the better; and in addition he had no fear about obtaining a better House of Commons at the next election. Newcastle's common-sense whiggism, which was to endear him to Walpole later despite his faults, would seem to have had some effect on Stanhope and Sunderland; the King's speech when Parliament opened in November cautiously refrained from setting out the whole proposed programme but simply spoke of the intention 'to complete those measures which remained imperfect the last session'. This way Commons opinion could be tested on the Peerage Bill, but if this failed the other measures could be abandoned without loss of face.[1]

The Peerage Bill was rushed through the House of Lords during the first week of the session, but Walpole was not caught unawares and succeeded in rallying his supporters and the Tories in time for the Bill's arrival in the Lower House. The decisive debate took place on 8 December with a turnout of over 450 members. In a speech long to be remembered Walpole told his hearers that Stanhope, 'having got into the House of Peers, is now desirous to shut the door after him'. The House of Lords, he meaningly added, had given its support to the Bill in the hope of increasing its influence at the expense of the Lower House. He concluded by asking his hearers to 'recollect that the overweening disposition of the great barons, to aggrandise their own dignity, occasioned them to exclude the lesser barons, and to that circumstance may be fairly attributed the sanguinary wars which so long desolated the country'. The history-conscious Commons listened to him and agreed. The Tories voted in strength, but it was defectors from the government side who turned the balance. The motion was rejected by 269 to 177, with about 144 Whigs voting

1. Williams, *loc. cit.*; Cobbett, *Parliamentary History*, vii, pp.602–4.

against. This was one of the great occasions, more often experienced in the later part of the century, when a master orator captured the minds and votes even of many of his usual opponents.[1]

By the Christmas recess in 1719 the Walpolites found themselves in a stronger position for bargaining to obtain their re-entry into the ministry. Stanhope and Sunderland, however, were not yet ready to accept the inevitable. The planned repeal of the Septennial Act had to be abandoned, together with the Universities Bill, but such action seemed to the ministers to open the possibility of buying support from some of the Tories. This scheme soon came to nothing, however, and by early in the New Year it was known that no Tories would enter into any agreement except as a party. This was clearly unacceptable, but the ministers still had the King's support and were confident that Walpole would not risk losing sympathisers among the Whig backbenchers by opposing routine business. This was true, and the session thus continued without immediate ministerial changes. Nevertheless there was one important matter which could not be brought in by the ministry. An accumulated debt on the King's Civil List now amounted to £500,000, but this urgent matter could only be carried by an extraordinary vote of supply in the House of Commons. Without Walpole's agreement the ministry did not care to hazard a request, which might well be rejected. Thus by April the two sets of Whigs had come to terms, with the ministers willing to accept their opponents' return to office.

Walpole's hand was not yet strong enough for him to demand the posts of which he had been deprived in 1717, and he contented himself for the moment with the useful and lucrative place he had held from 1714 to 1715, that of Paymaster General. At the same time Townshend became Lord President of the Council, a Cabinet appointment though one with no important executive responsibilities. Other Walpolites received lesser posts, including two on the Treasury Board, the Lord Lieutenancy of Ireland for the Duke of Grafton, and the Comptrollership of the Household for Methuen. The new arrangement was sealed by a formal reconciliation between the King and the Prince of Wales, though few who were present at

1. Cobbett, *op. cit.*, vii, pp.609–27; Sedgwick, *History of Parliament*, i, p.81.

this occasion failed to notice the bad grace with which the two royal personages saluted each other. Walpole was able to announce to his followers that further appointments would be made available as they fell vacant; and he thus had no difficulty in persuading his friends, as part of the bargain, to support an Address to pay off the debt on the Civil List.[1]

The reunification of the Whig party was not as satisfactory to Walpole and Townshend as they might have wished, but the arrangements were probably the best which could have been obtained at that time without involving the King in an unacceptable degree of loss of face by being forced to take ministers whom he was widely known to dislike. Before the end of the session there took place a new development whose results were, within a year, to bring Sunderland and Stanhope to disgrace and elevate Walpole and Townshend into their places. This was no less than Sunderland's long contemplated scheme for using the South Sea Company to solve the problem of the government annuitants. In the Commons Aislabie and Craggs carried a bill which would enable the annuitants to exchange their securities for South Sea stock on the inducement of the Company's expected trading profit. Walpole foresaw some of the difficulties which might arise out of this scheme, particularly in its failure to fix a rigid rate of exchange between the annuities and the stock purchased. Indeed he spoke unavailingly for a scheme of his own which would have got round this difficulty by using the Bank of England, with its greater stability and respectability, rather than the South Sea Company. But the ministers concerned in devising the Bill had no intention of seeing the profits which they hoped to obtain out of manipulation of the scheme prevented by so responsible a proposal. The Bill passed as planned, though in the aftermath many Members of Parliament were to remember Walpole's suggestion and wish that it had been adopted.[2]

Despite Walpole's backing for the Bank of England scheme he probably did not know for certain that the directors of the South Sea Company were bribing parliamentarians, ministers, and even members of the royal entourage with handouts of shares. He was certainly far from foreseeing the disaster of the

1. Plumb, *Walpole*, i, pp.281–92; *Diary of Mary, Countess Cowper*, pp.128–5.
2. Cobbett, *Parliamentary History*, vii, pp.628–42, 644–6.

Bubble collapse later in the summer, and his own investments at this time were highly inept, resulting in the loss of a small fortune. Just before the passing of the new South Sea Bill Walpole divested himself of the last of his South Sea stock, and at a time when shrewder investors were purchasing this stock in a rapidly rising market he held back. Only in late June, when the price had topped 1,000 does he appear to have decided that his previous judgement was at fault, and at this time he made extensive purchases. Unfortunately the market rose no higher for the next month, but even this warning sign did not prompt him to sell again.[1] When he left London for Norfolk at the end of July the market was in a highly uneasy state. A rash of 'Bubble' companies floated by promoters to cash in on the investing public's eagerness had to be stamped out by a hurriedly-passed bill in Parliament, but by this time the damage was done. Normally sensible people had caught the fever of speculation and sold their land, their pension rights, or even their jewellery in order to invest in the rocketing South Sea stock or in newer companies whose prospectuses would not have given much confidence to a careful reader.

Walpole's weeks in his home county thus proved to be critical ones for his speculations on the stock market. Although he remained in constant touch with his banker Robert Jacomb, who also happened to be his ministerial associate as deputy Paymaster-General, his absence from London made a proper assessment of the situation difficult. A further problem arose out of the distraction he experienced at the illness and death of his daughter Catherine, which occurred in the summer. Even so he found time to make some shrewd purchases of property in various parts of Norfolk, and this investment did much to improve both his financial position and his political influence in the aftermath of the South Sea crisis. But Jacomb's shrewd sales of South Sea stock could not shield Walpole from heavy losses, and when he returned to London in the middle of September it was to discover that the rapid fall of the value of his stock from about 1000 to 400 had crippled him financially and beggared hundreds of other speculators. His services were immediately called upon to try to persuade the Bank of England to shore up the sagging South Sea Company, but by the time this attempt

1. For Walpole's private investments, see Plumb, *Walpole*, i, Chapter 8, *passim*.

failed, at the end of September, Company stock had fallen to below 200 and its banker the Sword Blade Company had stopped payment. There was nothing to do but return to Norfolk, there to await the summoning of Parliament and a call for his services; for nothing was more certain than that the ministers who had been mainly responsible for the mishandling and dishonesty of the South Sea scheme would be called to account by indignant representatives of the nation.

The summer months of 1720 were not entirely taken up with the problems created by the Bubble. Despite the uncertain present, Walpole was sufficiently confident of his future to put in motion an ambitious and long-contemplated improvement to his estate. By the standards now prevailing among wealthy landowners, Houghton was a small and old-fashioned residence. New mansions were springing up around Norfolk and the whole of Britain, often purchased from the fortunes made by generals, paymasters and contractors for military materials in the wars of William III and Queen Anne. If Walpole were to rise higher, as he confidently expected, he would need visible evidence of success in the form of a house and park which could vie with the greatest. He had come to the conclusion that extensions and improvements to the existing building would not be enough, and it must be pulled down completely to make way for a residence in the fashionable Palladian style. His architect Colen Campbell set to work on the detailed plans and Walpole occupied himself in the meantime by making arrangements for the setting, which was to be a vast park landscaped by the fashionable garden designer Charles Bridgeman with grove and copse, the whole surrounded by new fencing and ditching some twelve miles long. The plantations, wrote a visitor, 'will have a very noble and fine effect; and at every angle there will be obelisks, or some other building'.[1] The village of Walpole's boyhood would have to go, for it was not in keeping with the new style and must be re-erected a mile further away. With these plans afoot the remainder of the parliamentary recess passed quickly; and Walpole was assured that house planning was in hand, new trees being set, and fencing extended when he returned to London to face one of the most portentous and difficult sessions of his life.

1. HMC, *Carlisle*, p.85, Sir Thomas Robinson.

8

High Office Again

THE AUTUMN of 1720 found London and Westminster in a state near turmoil. The general public, more convinced of Walpole's prescience than he deserved, was of the opinion that only he could clear up the mess. Unfortunately the situation was not such as could easily be set right. Time was to show that those government annuitants who had made losses by acquiring South Sea stock on a rapidly rising market could expect little in the way of compensation, while speculators in Bubble companies had not the shadow of a legal claim against the government for their penury. Yet this was a situation which could not readily be accepted by the nation, which now realised it had been misled and suspected corruption. Fortunately for the ministers, outside observers had no proof that Sunderland's scheme was basically dishonest, intended to feather the nests of some public servants and the Company's directors. These directors had been able to profit greatly from the unfixed exchange rate of stock for government securities, which Walpole had striven in vain to avoid, as the market rose. Bribery or near bribery of persons at Court and in Whitehall completed the sorry picture.

But Walpole could no more permit a witch hunt now than he could have prevented the situation from arising back in the spring. The King's government had to go on, and public confidence needed to be restored even though the scale of the disaster did not permit much in the way of compensation or even retribution. Sunderland and Stanhope still enjoyed the protection of the King, whose own dealings were by no means above suspicion. In the next few months Walpole and Townshend had to steer a dangerous course between incurring the displeasure of George, eager to protect his entourage, and further exacerbating the wrath of Parliament.

The Commons reassembled on 8 December 1720. Most members had been in town for over a fortnight, after an unexpected prorogation to allow the ministry more time for preparations. Although Walpole announced on the opening day that he was preparing a scheme to meet the disaster, he was unable to prevent an amendment to the Address calling for the punishment of offenders. The quality of the critics was significant. It was the Whig lawyer Sir Joseph Jekyll, Master of the Rolls and highly respected for his independence of mind, who voiced a general desire for a full investigation. On the 12th another usual ministerial voter, Grey Neville, carried without division a motion calling upon the South Sea Company to lay an account of its proceedings before the House. Despite the adherence of the Walpole brothers and many of their friends to the government a new Whig opposition was growing visibly. It included sometime-Speaker Smith, the Pitt family, and some of the South Sea directors' City opponents as well as others who had burned their fingers in the recent speculation and were thirsty for blood.

Walpole presented his scheme to the House on 21 December, proposing that the Company's surplus stock arising from its dishonest management of the exchange ratio for annuities should be distributed among stockholders as a partial compensation for their losses. Nearly half the Company's capital was to be cancelled by allowing it to be exchanged for Bank of England or East India stock, the capital of these institutions being increased by nine million pounds each on which interest would be paid out of public funds. Although these measures were scarcely enough to obtain the new Whig opposition's support, and indeed were mostly to prove unworkable in the long run, there seemed little alternative to letting the scheme go ahead; but when Parliament adjourned for Christmas it was with a general sense of dissatisfaction that the hoped-for panacea for public ills had not been forthcoming. This was a state of mind which gave little encouragement for the New Year.[1]

In the first months of 1721 Walpole was engaged in ferrying his scheme through Parliament and obtaining agreement with the Bank and the East India Company on suitable terms. In his anxiety to stabilise credit he became more and more involved in the attempt to protect the late administration, an effort which proved injudicious for his reputation in both the short and long

1. Coxe, *Walpole*, ii, pp.201–5; Cobbett, *Parliamentary History*, vii, pp.680–92; Add MSS, 47,029, pp.86–7.

runs. As the 'Skreenmaster-General' of every tirade and lampoon he seemed at times to exceed in unpopularity even those of his colleagues whose speculation and folly had brought about the disaster. But his reputation, unlike theirs, did not include actual guilt. And by holding the ministry together against the Tories and their new Whig allies he became its leading figure, even though he was unable entirely to turn away the wrath of the Commons from either himself or the courtiers he sought to protect.

On 4 January Jekyll introduced a bill to restrain South Sea directors from leaving the country. The bill quickly passed through all its stages in both Houses, though this did not prevent the Company's secretary from fleeing after destroying key evidence. The government were unable to prevent the setting up of a Secret Committee of the House of Commons to investigate the Company's activities, or to block the election to this committee of the opposition list of candidates. Towards the end of January, while the committee was pursing its enquiries, Aislabie attempted to divert the storm away from himself by resigning. While awaiting the result of enquiries, the House occupied itself with threats, and in this the Tories led by Shippen took a major part. Bills of attainder were freely promised not only for Aislabie but for other culpable ministers. 'I can't say it is unpleasant', wrote one Tory member to the now retired Oxford, 'to see it so quick come home upon them who so heartily joined in the unjust cry against your Lordship'.[1] Near the end of January four directors of the Company who sat in the House were expelled and two of them were placed in custody. The senior ministers' apprehensions rose that the committee's findings would blast their own reputations. Its report in February went some way towards justifying these fears.[2]

But at this point vengeance was diverted by more-or-less natural causes. On 5 February Stanhope, possibly the least culpable of the ministers, died of 'apoplexy', probably a severe stroke, after a vigorous defence of himself in the House of Lords. A few days later Secretary James Craggs died, in his case of smallpox. The principle of joint Cabinet responsibility was

1. British Library, Loan 29/136/8.
2. Cobbett, *Parliamentary History*, vii, pp.693–6, 706–48.

yet to be defined, but on this occasion all those who had been in office early in 1720 were being held responsible, and it was the fate of the least culpable to suffer alongside the guiltier ministers from the strain and emotion of the parliamentary scene. By their deaths Stanhope and Craggs perhaps allayed a little of the public wrath. Aislabie was expelled from the House and sent to the Tower, accused of having been given stock by the Company to obtain the passing of the South Sea Bill, but after this Walpole was able to shelter other lesser figures from the worst of the storm. On 15 March, however, the case of Sunderland himself came before the Commons. Of the succeeding debate an opposition Whig, Thomas Brodrick, recorded angrily that ministerialists warned Whig members 'if you come into this vote against Lord Sunderland, the ministry are blown up and must and necessarily will be succeeded by a Tory one'. The irony of being forced to defend Sunderland in order to protect his own position at court cannot have escaped Walpole. In the event Sunderland was acquitted, but 172 members of the Commons voted against him. After this vote Sunderland's days in office were strictly numbered.[1]

Early in April Walpole and Townshend received promotions which had probably been promised some time before but withheld until their compliance with the Court's wishes was assured. Townshend received the Northern Secretaryship of State and Walpole was given Sunderland's post as First Lord of Treasury, together with the Chancellorship of the Exchequer vacated by Aislabie. In practice Walpole had been carrying on the work of both offices without portfolio for two months. Sunderland's removal was expedient, despite his acquittal, but he retained his position of influence at the court with the title of Groom of the Stole and remained in the Cabinet. The Southern department was given to Sunderland's protegé, Lord Carteret, a former Hanoverian Tory who had made himself agreeable to both the King and the Stanhope-Sunderland faction over the past few years as much by his diplomatic abilities as by his courtierly qualities and useful command of the German language. Carteret was to prove a formidable rival whose influence in the Closet was difficult to eradicate despite his uncertain party pedigree.

1. Coxe, *Walpole*, ii, p.214; HMC, *Portland*, v, pp.618–9.

Sir Robert Walpole with his hounds
(by John Wootton)

Walpole and his first wife, Catherine Shorter
(*by J. G. Eckhardt*)

Family group with Walpole and his second wife, Maria Skerrett
(*by John Wootton* et al)

Charles, 2nd Viscount Townshend,
Walpole's brother in-law and ally
(*by Sir Godfrey Kneller*)

Dorothy Walpole, later Viscountess
Townshend, Sir Robert's sister
(*by Sir Godfrey Kneller*)

Horace Walpole,
Sir Robert and
Catherine Walpole's
youngest son
(*by J. G. Eckhardt*)

Houghton Hall, west front
showing exterior steps
restored as built

The Stone Hall. The picture
to the left of the fireplace is
Sir Robert Walpole with his
hounds (see plate 1)

The Saloon, with furniture by
William Kent

The Marble Parlour, Sir
Robert's dining room. To the
right of the door is the large
portrait of Walpole in Garter
robes, by Kneller

William Pulteney, 1st Earl of Bath,
early Walpole's follower but later
his most persistent opponent
(by Sir Godfrey Kneller)

Henry St John, Viscount Bolingbroke
sometime schoolfellow and lifelong
critic of Sir Robert Walpole
(by A. S. Belle)

Robert Harley,
1st Earl of Oxford
Walpole's first ma
political opponent
(by Sir Godfrey Kneller)

Sir Robert Walpole as an Excise Man, seated on a barrel, drawn by a dilapidated lion and unicorn, with the Magna Carta under the wheels; the cartoon refers to Walpole's excise scheme of 1733

Sir Robert Walpole as 'The Devil upon Two Sticks'. In preparation for the key general election in 1741, Walpole is carried by two Members of Parliament through a filthy ditch. In the background a government candidate steals money from a weeping Britannia and offers it to the electors

Sir Robert Walpole caricatured as the 'English Colossus', after the Colossus at Rhodes

When the Commons reassembled on 19 April their anger had not been assuaged by the ministerial changes, but was directed more than ever against Walpole. Certainly both the Tories and miscellaneous members of the new opposition who were beginning to appropriate to themselves the title of Old Whigs found Walpole the chief obstacle to their desire for further punitive measures. A bill to confiscate the estates of South Sea directors did not satisfy them, since the government speakers succeeded in preventing the directors from being completely ruined. Walpole's efforts to save some of Aislabie's estate from forfeiture were also regarded with anger.

But the opposition's greatest concern was reserved for the minister's efforts to assist the South Sea Company as an institution. Walpole was defeated in his first attempt to obtain remission of sums owed by the Company, including seven millions which it had undertaken in 1720 to pay the State for the privilege of taking over the National Debt. He persisted and succeeded in obtaining an Act excusing over four millions of the debt, even though his original defeat necessitated a two-day recess followed by what was technically a new session at the end of July to bring in the measure. Walpole's policy of bolstering the Company was wise. His scheme for the engraftment of part of its capital onto the Bank and the East India Company was to come to little, in view of the flagging interest of those bodies, and the future stability of the South Sea Company needed to be assured. But the annuitants who were obliged to take a newly fixed valuation of the South Sea stock to which they had subscribed at the height of the fever were vociferous in the lobby of the House during the passing of the measure. A practical settlement was necessary, but it made the new measures no more welcome.[1]

When the often tumultuous and tiring session came to an end in July, allowing Walpole to escape with relief to Norfolk, his situation was a paradoxical one. He had again reached the top of the slippery ministerial ladder, but though he was to

1. Add. MSS. 47,029, pp.107–9; Coxe, *Walpole*, ii, pp.214–9; Dickson, *Financial Revolution in England*, pp.175–6. In the longer run Walpole was able to help the former annuitants by some compensation from stock confiscated from the Company and the directors, and by putting the Company on a firmer footing, turning it into a holding company for gilts and persuading the Bank of England to buy some of its annuities.

retain office for twenty-one years this outcome was by no means certain at the time. He had never been less popular than in defending his former colleagues from the worst consequences of their own actions, and for many years his activities as a 'skreen' were revived by enemies in attempts to discredit him. That Walpole could have done little else in order to restore the stability of government, badly shaken by the Bubble crisis, was not evident, for outside the closed circle of court and Cabinet little was known of the kind of pressures which were being exerted upon him. Moreover Sunderland was still in the King's confidence and in a position of influence. With Carteret balancing Townshend in the Secretaries' office, foreign affairs were by no means fully under the control of the Walpole-Townshend element despite the ostensible disgrace of their rivals. A power base had been established, but the next three years were to see a struggle for its consolidation.

The summer of 1721 saw a series of struggles set in motion by Sunderland. He was anxious for an early general election, though one was not due until the following year under the provisions of the new Septennial Act, in order to prevent Walpole from having sufficient time to organise his newly-acquired Treasury patronage to the best advantage. This scheme was prevented by Walpole's argument of a need for continuing the existing Parliament, so as to obtain a new Civil List for the King and to carry arrangements for the South Sea Company without becoming involved in the extended debates on disputed elections which occurred in any new Commons. Equally dangerous was Sunderland's plan for obtaining the post of Treasurer of the Chamber for his follower Charles Stanhope, cousin of the late Earl Stanhope. Such a further promotion to a position close to the King would be a clear indication of the Sunderland faction's continuing influence in the Closet. Charles Stanhope had been closely involved with the seedier aspects of the South Sea Company scandal, and his very narrow acquittal in Parliament earlier in the year on a charge of taking bribes had not entirely cleared his name. Walpole was thus able to argue convincingly with the King that such a promotion might well arouse the ire of the Commons.[1] But

1. Plumb, *Walpole*, i, pp.365–6.

despite the success of his common sense arguments with the shrewd monarch, Walpole was not allowed time for rest. Allocating only a few days for essential socialising in Norfolk, he returned to London in mid-August to defend his interests at close quarters.

Perhaps as a result of rebuffs to their schemes the Sunderland faction thought it necessary to remain on overtly good terms with Walpole and Townshend. The summer months saw an apparent truce and even some fraternisation among the warring politicians. Nevertheless Carteret, now Sunderland's second-in-command, hastened to reassure one of his supporters that 'neither Lord Sunderland nor I have lost any ground with the King'. According to Carteret the main obstacle to true reconciliation was Walpole, whom he described as being restrained by the more amenable Townshend from allowing South Sea matters to dominate the next session of Parliament.[1] On this interpretation, despite Walpole's strenuous efforts over the last few months to defend the guilty ministers, he was portrayed as intending to use the Commons' continued anger as a means of defeating his rivals. No doubt the Sunderlandites took pains to ensure that their viewpoint reached the ears of the King.

In fact it was Sunderland and Carteret themselves who were about to attempt betrayal, not only of Walpole and Townshend but of Whig dominance itself. They intended to enlist the support of Carteret's old party, the Tories, against the brothers-in-law. They first approached William Bromley, doyen of the Hanoverian Tories in the Commons. Bromley reported 'promises were made to me so extravagantly large, that it was affronting me to imagine I could think them sincere, and be imposed upon by them'.[2] The promises may have been more sincerely given than the staunch old Tory supposed, but he rejected them out of hand. With Bromley on this occasion was associated William Shippen, leader of the Jacobites, who recorded their joint decision to 'enter into no concert with any of the two contending powers at court'.[3] By the time Parliament assembled, Sunderland was aware that any alliance with the

1. Add. MSS. 32,686, ff. 185 and 193.
2. HMC, *Portland*, v, p.625.
3. *Lockhart Papers*, ii, pp.70–1.

Tory party was out of the question. Much, however, would depend upon Walpole's handling of the Commons in the first full session since he had become head of the Treasury.

When Parliament assembled to hear the King's speech on 19 October the words which Walpole and Townshend had written for the monarch to read out were deliberately uncontroversial. The speech dwelled on the need to maintain peace as an aid to the export of British manufactures and import of raw materials; the balance of trade could then be preserved in Britain's favour, the carrying trade extended and numbers in employment increased.[1] Peace and revived trade were to become the watchwords of Walpole's ministry and represented some of his deepest convictions as to the needs of the country. Protection against foreign manufactured goods aided British industrial expansion.[2] Prosperity would bring contentment, political tranquillity and the likelihood of an undisturbed tenure of office for himself. Walpole deliberately pitched subsequent debates on a low key to avoid any excitement, for disruption near election time was unlikely to aid the government. Accordingly the first part of the session gave no grounds for challenge to the Walpolites' position. Attendances were low, especially on the opposition side. After business had gone on quietly for six weeks Bromley concocted with Wyndham a scheme to energise the Tories; but they were unable to arouse sufficient interest among their own followers, while the Jacobites showed little sign of further cooperation.[3]

Following the Christmas break, however, activity revived in Cabinet and Parliament. In January 1722 Sunderland, undeterred by the Tory leaders' rejection of his overtures, brought his scheme into the open in the hope of detaching some individual Tories and obtaining a ministerial reshuffle favourable to himself. According to the Jacobite source which reported the details, he gave as his reason that 'the Tory party of themselves were now formed into so great a body that nothing

1. Cobbett, *Parliamentary History*, vii, pp.912–8.
2. As Professor H.T. Dickinson points out: 'It is clear that his economic strategy was not simply a policy of letting sleeping dogs lie. He was quite ready to interfere in commercial affairs if he could promote Britain's trading interests . . .', *Walpole and the Whig Supremacy* (1973), p.112. Chapter 6 of this work is the best brief account of Walpole's economic policy.
3. HMC, *Portland*, vii, pp.309.

but dividing and breaking them could secure the Government', and believed that South Sea losses would make some stricken Tories willing to recoup by accepting office.

In answer to Walpole's enquiry, delivered with some heat in the presence of the King, as to whether Sunderland was for 'bringing in the Tories and having a Tory Parliament', the Groom is reported to have replied that 'the Tories and the Whigs were equally entitled to a share in the Administration, and that he was not for governing by brigades'. At this exchange, continued the same account, George 'stared the Earl of Sunderland in the face at the name of a Tory Parliament'. Sunderland's statement was indeed remarkable, and the King would have done more than stare had he known that his favourite was deeply engaged with the Pretender's court to obtain a Tory House of Commons, claiming that he intended this as the first step towards the restoration of the old dynasty.[1] On the question of the admission of Tories to office, as Sunderland wished, Walpole and his monarch were of one mind, and the scheme was put aside: any favour shown to the Tory party at this stage might well be taken by the electorate as a signal of royal disfavour for the Whigs. The beginnings of an understanding with the King were emerging.

In the Commons the Tories took the initiative with a bill to reduce government's manipulation of elections. By this measure election writs were to be regularised and false returns punished. At the committee stage a further clause was offered to disfranchise customs and revenue officers. Had the clause been adopted it would have brought about this reform exactly sixty years earlier than it actually took place in John Crewe's Act of 1782. However it was too much for Walpole, mindful of the need to preserve and enlarge government patronage; ministerial speakers maintained that in effect the clause was 'taking away from the said officers their birthright, as Englishmen and freeholders'. But the bill represented good opposition tactics, in view of the general election expected soon after the end of the session. Many members, even on the Whig side, were reluctant to register open opposition to the measure when they felt that their action might be publicised in voting lists placed before their constituents by the press.

1. Sedgwick, *History of Parliament*, i, p.64 and Note XXXIX, pp.108–9.

The solution reached by the Ministry was to allow the bill to pass through all its stages in the Commons but to secure its rejection in the less vulnerable House of Lords; this was a common expedient favoured by the government's superior patronage resources there. An important source of government patronage was accordingly preserved for a further two generations. In February 1722 Walpole exerted himself to save a Treasury placeman who was accused by an independent Whig member of bribery in a bye-election at Banbury. The narrow majority of four votes by which this attack was diverted was sufficient testimony to the wisdom of avoiding conflict over the Election Bill. And Walpole had begun the way he intended to continue his administration, by protecting the Treasury's power of obtaining a subservient ministerial following in Parliament.[1]

The general election took place over several weeks, as was usual, in March and April. The Sunderland faction exerted its influence against government candidates, even to the extent of supporting some Tories against ministerial Whigs. Walpole had at his disposal the formidable government patronage machine, especially the Treasury's control of various tax collection and revenue services. But Sunderland's known influence at court also carried weight, and his supporters made good use of his remaining resources as election manipulator. So busy was Walpole kept that he did not even have time on this occasion to visit his own constituency. Nevertheless he and Sir Charles Turner were easily returned, as were the sitting members for Castle Rising. Over the entire country Walpole's exertions were successful, for on the whole the Tories did not obtain the benefits they had expected from divisions among their rivals. Some 379 Whigs were returned as against 178 Tories, even before the consideration of election petitions in the new House of Commons further altered the balance in favour of the former. North of the Scottish border, where Treasury influence reigned supreme, only one Tory was returned out of the total of forty-five members, though Wales continued to return a Tory majority as did the county seats in England. The strength of the dissident Whigs proved to be relatively small. It

1. Cobbett, *Parliamentary History*, vii, pp.948–52 and 961–6; Boyer, *Political State*, xxiii, pp.200–2, 218–23 and 255–61.

was in the borough constituencies, where the influence of government or its individual supporters was most marked, that the solid ministerial majority was obtained. Cornwall, with its plethora of small boroughs under the influence of the Duchy, returned thirty-seven members of the government out of a total of forty-four. Overall the overwhelming victory of 1715 was not only equalled but exceeded.[1]

With some election results still to come in, Sunderland died unexpectedly in April of pleurisy. The sudden removal of their leader left his followers in a disarray from which they never really recovered. Though Carteret was a man of great administrative and diplomatic abilities who had made himself highly acceptable to the King by his willingness to carry out royal policies unquestioningly, he sat in the House of Lords and had never had a large personal following in the Commons. His closest associates included several members from a coterie of professional administrators and lawyers, including Trevor, Harcourt, Boyle and Brydges, all now his fellow peers. Such a group was unlikely to find much favour among the staunch Old Whigs who had always supported Walpole in the House of Commons. Carteret's best hope lay with the King. Lord Chesterfield later recalled: 'That on the death of Lord Sunderland, Lord Carteret had applied to the late King to support him, as he was then surrounded by his enemies; that the King promised it to him, but told [him] the necessity of the time forced him to temporise'.[2] George I still had little love for Walpole and Townshend, though he was increasingly appreciative of their power base in Parliament, and continued to have use for non-party or cross-party men of high ability such as Carteret and his friends. So the success of Walpole's first general election and the fortuitous death of Sunderland did not signal Walpole's and Townshend's entire control of the ministry. For a further two years they had to continue to struggle for the King's ear, and to work for Carteret's removal.

With the electoral defeat of the Tories assured, and the Sunderlandites having lost their leader, Walpole saw his task as one of ensuring that neither the opposing party nor the rival Whig faction should rise again. One way was to associate

1. Plumb, *Walpole*, i, p.377; Sedgwick, *History of Parliament*, pp.33–4 and *passim*.
2. G. H. Rose, *A Selection from the Papers of the Earls of Marchmont* (1861), i, p.3.

Carteret with Tory policies and the Tories with Jacobitism. For the remainder of Walpole's career no hint or innuendo was spared either in Parliament or in the press to make sure that this message went home. Carteret himself made the campaign easier, not only by his well-remembered Tory origins but also by attempts to continue Sunderland's dalliance with the opposition. As soon as Sunderland's death was known, Carteret was careful to point out to the Tories that they had lost 'a very good friend' in the late minister.[1] But even with Tory help, if he could obtain it, Carteret had little to hope from the House of Commons, where the expulsion of Aislabie and the death of the younger Craggs had left him without major spokesmen.

Walpole was quick to seize upon this weakness, continuing to build up his own following by turning out of Treasury-controlled offices any Whig who had shown support to the Sunderland faction in the past, and inserting nominees of his own. He could not for the moment weaken Carteret's influence in the Closet, for this process would have to be a slower and more subtle one; but at least the Secretary could be deprived of any hope of obtaining any Commons support in schemes for gratifying the King's wishes. The Tories could be dealt with more immediately by humbling them and showing that they were too dangerous for any Whig to dabble with. The method by which Walpole himself had returned to office in 1720, voting alongside the Tories, was not to be open to his Whig rivals if he could help it. Henceforth he always aimed, in the words of the acute Arthur Onslow who observed him from the Chair of the Commons for many years, 'at the uniting of Whigs against Tories as Jacobites . . . and making therefore combinations between them and any body of Whigs to be impracticable'.[2]

Almost as soon as the general election was over, material for the further disgrace of the Tory party was presented to the ministry by the activities of Bishop Francis Atterbury. This brilliant cleric was well known for his leadership of the High Church faction, and he had risen rapidly in Queen Anne's reign to become Bishop of Rochester. In this capacity, he had, as is now known, urged Bolingbroke to stage a *coup* in

1. Keith Feiling, *The Second Tory Party, 1714-1832* (1938), pp.22–3.
2. HMC, *14th Report*, part ix, p.462.

favour of the adamantly Roman Catholic Prince James Edward as soon as the Queen's demise was known. Atterbury's subsequent almost continuous plotting with the Jacobites had come to fruition by 1722 in a conspiracy to combine an Irish-officered Jacobite invasion from France with a simultaneous rising in London as soon as George I left the capital for his usual summer vacation in Hanover. The plot was revealed by Walpole's counter-espionage system and information from the French minister Dubois, who took steps to get the Irish regiments away from the vicinity of the Channel.

The news was broken to the press at the beginning of May, too late to influence elections but with great harm to the Tories in the forthcoming session. Walpole cannot be blamed for using to the full the instrument which had been placed in his hands. The King's visit was cancelled, regiments were encamped in Hyde Park and the summer was given over to a massive hunt for the conspirators. Horatio Walpole was despatched to The Hague to ask for military aid under treaty, and Atterbury, Lord Orrery and others were arrested. Government propaganda rose to new heights in stirring up national fears and indignation. For good measure Roman Catholics were ordered out of London and the Duke of Norfolk, the senior Catholic peer, was sent to sojourn in the Tower. The scene was set by skilful stage management for the meeting of the new House of Commons.

Despite his careful preparations Walpole's campaign to distress and isolate the Tories was not entirely successful in the earlier part of the session. As the Tories did not venture to divide on a provocative Address, the first test was on a ministerial bill to suspend the Habeas Corpus Act. In committee a Tory lawyer, John Hungerford, offered an amendment to reduce the period of suspension to six months, rather than the proposed year, and found himself supported by the leading Whigs still in opposition, Smith, Jekyll and Thomas Brodrick. These speakers urged that the Act had not been suspended for more than six months at any time since the Revolution. Their argument acquired the support of many independent Whigs and divided an unexpectedly high number of 193 members against the ministry's 246. But when some Tories called for the outright rejection of the bill their Whig allies forsook them, some leaving the House, others going over to the court side. As a result the Tories were reduced in the subsequent division to only 124, with the moderate Tory Hanmer and others abstaining by absence. Later, however, the Tories were again joined by some Whigs on the ministry's proposal to augment the army by four thousand men in view of the Jacobite menace. When George Treby, Secretary at War and son of the distinguished Whig of the same name, proposed this measure it was reported that 'many Whigs, to make themselves more popular, joined with the Tories in this opposition'.[1]

But the main Whig reservations about Walpole's pursuit of the plotters and alleged fellow-travellers came in the voting on his motion for placing an extra tax upon Roman Catholics, to meet the cost of government expenditure in suppressing the plot. The arguments by which the doubters were chiefly moved were, firstly, the dangerous precedent involved in mulcting the government's political opponents and, secondly, the lack of evidence that English Catholics had in fact been deeply implicated in Atterbury's machinations. If they had not, it was argued, such a tax might well drive them to extremes on some future occasion. The Tories were reinforced on this issue by Whig dissidents led by Spencer Cowper and Jekyll. With even some of the ministry's usual supporters expressing their disquiet by their absence, government majorities were much down on those of October. In committee on 23 November the proposal was carried by only forty-nine votes. Three days later, on a motion to agree to the committee's vote, the government majority sank to sixteen. The last division took place after several hours of vigorous debate, and though the ministerialists went on to obtain an order to bring in an implementing bill, the Whig observer and diarist Perceval forecast that the matter would be dropped. In this, however, Perceval was less than perceptive of Walpole's tenacity of purpose and sense of timing.[2] The implementing bill was eventually brought and passed near the end of the session, when the First Lord's plans for implicating the Tories in defence of the Atterbury plotters had fully ripened.

1. Add. MSS. 17, 677KKK5, p.383 and 47,029, pp.270–2; A.N. Newman, *The Parliamentary Diary of Sir Edward Knatchbull, 1722–1730*, Camden Society, 3rd series, xciv (1963), p.3.
2. Add. MSS. 47,029, pp.279–80; Boyer, *Political State* xxv, pp.524–5.

Before the government launched its final assault the usual consideration of election petitions assisted its cause. Predictably a number of Tories were ejected. The most useful case occurred when the election at Westminster was declared void. This contest had taken place amid unusual violence, even for this constituency, for the successful candidates had enjoyed the active support of Atterbury himself. In the bye-election which took place in November the whole electoral powers of both parties were thrown into the scale in the streets around the seat of legislature, with free use on the ministerial side of Atterbury's name. The result was that the two-to-one majority which the Tories had enjoyed in the general election was almost reversed. Patriotic opinion, as reflected by this large constituency, was now heavily influenced by the revealed plot.[1]

The lowest point of Tory fortunes came when William Pulteney, on behalf of the ministry, presented in March 1723 a report from the Secret Committee which had been set up to look into evidence on the plot. The absence of adequate witnesses, who were required by the Treason Act of 1696, made necessary a parliamentary trial by Bills of Pains and Penalties in some cases, and after hearing the evidence the House ordered bills to be brought in against Atterbury and his agents John Plunkett and the Reverend George Kelly. Such an issue detached the Whig dissidents from opposition, and Jekyll, Brodrick and Smith joined the government to take a leading part in the prosecutions. The Tories, thus deserted, made little headway in the debates. According to one exultant report 'the Tories spoke sadly, as if they were munching thistles'.[2]

The Tories could with truth say that there was little real evidence against Atterbury himself, for the Bishop had been clever and Walpole's agents were never able to ferret out enough material to make a serious charge stick in a proper trial. But a Bill of Pains and Penalties was not a trial in the normal sense, and the outcome of the proceedings was never in doubt. All three accused men were condemned, and rightly so if massive circumstantial evidence be taken into account in Atterbury's case. Regarding Plunkett the opposition were probably right in asserting that he should have been brought to trial by

1. Sedgwick, *History of Parliament*, i, pp.34 and 285–6; Add. MSS, 47,029, pp.219 and 260.
2. Add. MSS, 47,029, pp.318 and 422.

ordinary means, for in his case good evidence of guilt was available. As a result of the proceedings both Plunkett and Kelly were imprisoned for life, though the latter escaped some years later and lived to be one of the seven men who landed with the Young Pretender at Moidart in 1745. Atterbury himself was banished and retired to France, where his restless energy continued to weave a network of intrigue against the Hanoverian dynasty and a campaign of vilification against Walpole, including attempts to incriminate the First Lord of the very charge of treasonous behaviour of which Atterbury himself had been found guilty.

The parliamentary proceedings against the plotters had one of the effects which Walpole had desired. The entire Tory party rallied in support of the accused and in doing so associated itself inextricably with Jacobitism in the eyes of many of the public. Deprived of the dissident Whigs' usual aid, the Tories obtained fewer votes during the trial of Atterbury and his associates than at any other time during Walpole's career. At the same time the dissidents were obliged to declare their solidarity with the Whig cause which Walpole always insisted was as alive and flourishing as ever in face of the threat of Jacobitism. Atterbury's plot and its parliamentary aftermath therefore provided a major justification for Walpole's press campaigns for many years to come.

Perhaps most important of all, however, was the affair's effect on Walpole's relations with his monarch, for it marked a definite warming in the King's attitude after many years of little more than icy formality between the two men. Long afterwards Speaker Onslow was to sum up the importance of the episode for Walpole with the words: 'It fixed him with the King, and united for a time the whole body of the Whigs to him'.[1] The First Lord had need of his moment of triumph, for he was now about to enter the last phase of his struggle for supremacy.

Before Carteret could be dealt with, one curious concession had to be made. The well-known story that when Bishop Atterbury set foot on the French soil of exile he was greeted by the returning Bolingbroke as an 'exchange' may or may not be true; but it contains the essential truth that Walpole, in order to preserve his newly found favour with the King, had been

1. HMC, *14th Report*, part ix, p.513.

forced to give way on the readmission of his oldest and ablest enemy to Britain. The wily former Tory and sometime minister to the Old Pretender was now embarked upon a new career. For some years now Bolingbroke had been in touch with dissident Whig politicians and, more importantly, had been currying favour with the royal favourites. His reward was permission to return, in which Walpole grudgingly acquiesced. Bolingbroke's attainder was not reversed and he was not allowed to take his former place in the House of Lords; but he soon made himself the centre of a group of politicians such as his old friends Wyndham and Gower, who would in due course form the cadre of a new opposition to Walpole.

Until Bolingbroke's right of residence was confirmed he was disposed to be conciliatory. He was at pains to inform Walpole that he had received approaches from Carteret and ignored them, even offering the minister the support of his own Tory group. When Walpole rejected this poisoned gift the former deviser of the Schism Act continued to angle, while preparing at the same time to revert to the policy which he had been advocating in private correspondence for years, maintaining that the distinctions between Tories and Whigs were dead and that the new division was between court and country. Of the incident Walpole wrote to Townshend that he had told Bolingbroke 'he was doing a most imprudent thing, who was to expect his salvation from a whig parliament, to be negotiating to bring in a sett of tories; that if this should be known, his case would be desperate in parliament'. Walpole nevertheless experienced some embarrassment from Bolingbroke's overtures, for his supporters were alarmed at even the suspicion of an alliance with the old arch enemy. Townshend wrote 'I am sorry to find Lord Bolingbroke's affair continues to make ill blood among our friends'; he believed 'it will be absolutely necessary for us to rest on the whig bottom'. But because of the wind from court Walpole and Townshend could not reject Bolingbroke's overtures out of hand, and Walpole continued to plead 'the humour of the party' to Bolingbroke's importunities.[1]

Bolingbroke's hope of being to George I what the late Earl of Sunderland's father, the second Earl, had been to William III, a

1. Coxe, *op.cit.* ii, pp.260 and 264.

supra-party political 'undertaker', was foredoomed to failure even though Walpole had to handle it with kid gloves. Walpole had outlined plans to deal with the ministry's internal plotter, Carteret. And at the same time another development was moving in the minister's favour. By June 1723 at the latest the highly party-orthodox young Newcastle had drawn himself completely away from Carteret and his intrigues, even though he heard that the Secretary had now 'wrote declare off with the Tories, thinking to carry his point with the Whigs, which he knows agreeable to the King'.[1] Newcastle's support, together with that of his clients and supporters in the House of Commons, was a considerable acquisition to Walpole and Townshend.

In the way Walpole saw his ministry developing, Newcastle's adherence more than offset the potential loss of a long-standing but unreliable supporter, William Pulteney. Disappointed by Walpole of any office but Cofferer of the Household, Pulteney had recently tried to win popularity by outbidding his chief as the scourge of the Jacobites. After the last session he continued to give cause for alarm, hinting that he might bring up Bolingbroke's business in order to scotch it, and asking what would Walpole do in that case. Pulteney's impatience and ambition posed a new threat. Walpole replied meaningly that he would 'always go with the Whigs, but not call two or three the Whig party'[2] Pulteney's followers were few, but Walpole henceforth watched them with great care.

In the autumn the rivalry of the brothers-in-law with Carteret centred upon power struggles in Paris and Dublin. Horatio Walpole had been sent to France on a secret mission to undermine the inept closet diplomacy of the accredited ambassador Sir Luke Schaub, Carteret's adherent. In Ireland never-absent indignation at English rule suddenly became crystallised in the problem of a patent sold by the King's mistress, the Duchess of Kendal, to one William Wood, for minting Irish coinage. Wood's coins were demonstrated to be of good quality in an assay by Sir Isaac Newton, Master of the Mint, and the Duchess's profit from the sale of her rights was by no means an uncommon or illegal occurrence. But these matters carried

1. Add. MSS. 32,686, ff.268–70.
2. British Library, Stowe MSS.251, f.42.

little weight with a subject people who scented an opportunity to demonstrate their grievances. Aided by the Dean of St Patrick's, Jonathan Swift, in *The Drapier's Letters*, they boycotted Wood's coins and precipitated a crisis for the government in Ireland. In London Carteret attempted by assiduous attendance at the Royal Closet to deflect the new storm towards Walpole. While these conflicts went forward, Parliament's meeting was delayed until the New Year, reflecting Walpole's desire to avoid unnecessary 'cabals' during the Christmas recess.

The new session which began in January 1724 was fairly subdued. A number of Jacobite members, including Shippen, had been named in the report of the Secret Committee and had no inclination to take the limelight. Bromley, who had been feeding his indignation by reading the Whig Bishop Gilbert Burnet's newly-published *History of my own Time* (in Bromley's view, 'a strange rhapsody of chit-chat and lies, ill tacked together')[1] reported a general Tory discouragement and despondency, likely to lead to absenteeism or even defection. On 9 January the Address to the Throne was moved by Nottingham's son Lord Finch, signalling his family's return to the government side since the Atterbury plot, and went unopposed. A ministerial proposal to continue for another year the extra 4,000 troops raised at the time of the Atterbury plot was opposed by only 100 votes. Walpole took the opportunity offered by a dispirited opposition to put forward new proposals for making the customs and excise revenues more efficient and thus ease the burden on the land tax. Few backbenchers could argue with the spirit of this proposal, and the ease with which it was carried perhaps gave Walpole the germ of his later idea for an extension of the excise revenue, though this was to take place in very different circumstances and with a startlingly unsuccessful result. Even as they stood, however, his reforms since he took office forwarded his plans for restoring mercantile profits. Legitimate overseas trade, as distinct from smuggling, was improved in 1723. And by opening the way to lower taxation of landowners, Walpole hoped to reconcile the political class to his overall strategy of peaceful international cooperation and prosperity for a generation.

1. HMC, *Portland*, vii, p.367–8.

But while the House of Commons remained quiet in the aftermath of the plot and its suppression, the Closet was buzzing with activity and Walpole's machinations began to bear fruit. By the end of the session Horatio Walpole's revelation of Schaub's ineptitude in the Paris embassy had resulted in the King's agreement that Horatio should himself take over the ambassador's post. At the same time Schaub's patron, Carteret, made the mistake of alienating the Duchess of Kendal and was exposed in his Irish intrigues; his punishment was to be sent to Ireland as Lord Lieutenant, an appropriate fate which must have given Walpole and Townshend some amusement as well as removing their enemy into a sphere where he could do little further harm. For the first time they were without a serious rival in the Cabinet, the House of Commons was quiescent and the King well disposed. Twenty-three years after Walpole's entry to Parliament, ten years after the elevation of the Whigs to a position of supremacy under King George I, Walpole-Townshend influence was at last firmly in control.

9

Consolidation

AFTER THE removal of Carteret there was little further challenge from the former Sunderland element. With the exception of the small minority whom the ministry described as
'discontented', the Whigs usually formed a united court party
reflecting the wishes of their leader. The Tories, as always,
formed the permanent element of parliamentary opposition.
But until the malcontent Whigs found a new leader in William
Pulteney and made a serious attempt to work alongside the
Tory party, Parliament offered little in the way of resistance to
the ministry. With the King reconciled to the new arrangements the last three years of the reign were to be, for Walpole,
the quietest and most rewarding of his career.

To take advantage of the respite and build up his political
strength against an inevitable resurgence of opposition in the
longer term, Walpole now began systematically to extend his
following in both Houses and throughout the land by
rewarding the loyal and punishing the disaffected. Men whose
political memories went back to the sweeping changes of
personnel brought about by the Tory and Whig parties in 1702
and 1714 respectively were agreed that Walpole's activities
rivalled them. In a political system which was in some ways
more akin to the United States today than to Great Britain it
was usual for a government to make political changes not only
in ministerial posts but also in many of those lesser offices
which now make up the Civil Service and local administration.
Nor were the magistracy, armed services and Church exempt
from politically-motivated changes.

Walpole, however, was to go further than any minister
before in building up a following of office holders composed
specifically of his personal supporters within the party. He was
encouraged by three years of unchallenged power as well as by
his natural inclination to reward past services and buttress his
position with relations, friends and faithful followers. Later his
system of rewards and punishments was to bring its own
drawbacks, in the form of an increasingly embittered band of

able politicians whose claims he had slighted or overlooked, but for the moment his methods were overwhelmingly successful in securing his authority.

Walpole's greatest strength lay in the House of Commons. It is an historical truism to remark that he preferred to remain in this House, setting aside the practice of predecessors who had usually chosen at some point to commemorate success by moving to the House of Lords. Even Harley, whose pioneering methods in the post-Revolution Commons showed Walpole the way to mastery of that same body, had been misguided enough to take an earldom at the height of his career; the result was that Oxford's last years in office had been marked by a serious loss of control in the Lower House. Walpole was determined to make no such mistake. The elevation of his son Robert to a barony in 1723 had been necessary to make clear that Walpole intended to ennoble his family by other means than his own elevation to the House of Lords. He must have taken satisfaction from the fact that his own fierce resistance to Stanhope's Peerage Bill in 1719 had been the means whereby his son's new status had been obtained.

It is also true, of course, to say that Walpole's position depended on the King. No minister studied more than he to make himself the necessary, and indeed the inevitable appointment, with all that this implied in terms of power and prestige. Throughout his ministerial career Walpole's indispensability had to be constantly demonstrated to the monarch who in turn had to give the minister visible signs of his 'confidence'.

Walpole took a knighthood of the Bath in May 1725 as part of his revival of that moribund order for patronage purposes, and was a year later also rewarded by the King with a coveted knighthood of the Garter. But this is as far as Walpole went in the acquisition of honours while he remained in the Commons. His backbenchers might, in due course, receive peerages as a result of their labour in divisions; but their leader knew that since 1689 the growing importance of Parliament *vis-à-vis* the crown was partly due to the Commons' control of taxation. In the increasingly expensive modern world, the political role of the House of Lords was diminished. Financial initiatives were almost entirely in his own hands as First Lord of the Treasury and Chancellor of the Exchequer.

Walpole's ability to manage both Houses was to become a

legend in his own time. Lord Chesterfield, an able politician as well as an instructor in manners and in polished literature, was to write that he was 'the best parliament-man, and the ablest manager of Parliament, that I believe ever lived'.[1] Chesterfield lived to see, and participate in, the different style of government favoured by Walpole's successors, themselves no mean exponents of the art of 'management', so this tribute was a warm one, particularly as Chesterfield spent many years in opposition to the subject of his praise. Chesterfield knew that management was not synonymous with patronage control. It is true that under Walpole the 'court and treasury party' grew to an unprecedented size, with over one hundred and fifty members forming its solid core at the height of his career; but in a House of Commons containing 558 members, of whom another two hundred or so were either Tories or dissident Whigs, the court party would not have made much headway alone. The technically uncommitted members who held the balance and were usually the mainstay of Walpole's control of the Commons were the independent Whigs, who asked little in the way of patronage other than occasional favours which they did not consider as committing them to the Treasury upon all occasions. Such men were bound to Walpole by bonds at once more tenuous and more stable than those which kept the placemen loyal. He had to win, not buy, the independents' support, and do so by pursuing policies which they found acceptable.

First and foremost the independent Whigs demanded that the minister should pursue policies in keeping with their party tradition. If he appeared to deviate from this, in either foreign or domestic policy, he would quickly be made to realise it. In practice Walpole rarely put a foot wrong, building cunningly upon engrained party prejudices to strengthen his own support by frequently reminding the Commons of the continuing Jacobite threat, of the sympathy of some (Walpole maintained most) Tories for the Pretender, and of the dangers to be incurred by any true Whig who sullied himself by dalliance with such an opposition. In foreign affairs, as will be seen, Walpole was eventually obliged to accede to a backbench line even at the expense of quarrelling with Townshend. Such instances of the

1. Sedgwick, *History of Parliament, sub* Walpole, Sir Robert.

tail wagging the dog in politics were by no means as unusual in the eighteenth century as has sometimes been supposed; party tradition was alive and vivid to those who had lived through the stirring times of Anne's reign, and remained vivid to their sons and grandsons.

What was later to be termed the Old Corps of Whigs, the loyal body which Walpole handed over to his chosen successors at his final fall from power, consisted largely of the band of appreciative but independent Whig supporters with whom he worked in harmony for so long. The 'dunghill worms', as Perceval called the Court and Treasury party, were sometimes counted as part of the Old Corps but were less loyal and would serve any master who paid them.[1] The apparently monolithic aspect of the Old Corps at the height of Walpole's administration should not be allowed to conceal the fact that he made most of them his own by cooperation, the give and take of opinions, by keeping Britain peaceful and government expenses low, rather than by the corruption of which his opponents accused him. Patronage management was an important part of his retention of power, but it was not the only or even the most important part in the Commons.

In the House of Lords, however, patronage was all-important. Though varying in the number of its members the Upper House was far smaller than the Lower and contained a large proportion of non-attenders. As it was rare for more than a few score peers to be present, even on important occasions, the court and treasury element bulked large and there were few peers, other than Tories, who were truly independent of government. Perhaps the most solid element of the court party were the sixteen Scottish 'elected' peers and the twenty-six archbishops and bishops. The noble Scots, like their forty-five compatriots in the House of Commons, were in general poorer than their English counterparts, had higher travelling expenses, and were more susceptible to the blandishments of monetary assistance. Much of the Secret Service money allocation in the royal Civil List was in fact employed by Walpole in giving regular pensions to Scottish peers and commoners, a practice which was to continue to make the contingent from north of the border a byword for subservience to successive

1. Add. MSSS. 32,308, f.172.

ministries, for the economic difficulties under which these men laboured were usually forgotten or conveniently ignored by the opposition pamphleteers who pilloried them.

When Walpole first took office the bishops were a less well-drilled body, but within a few years he had succeeded in making them equally loyal in divisions of the Lords' chamber. The trick in this case was not to pay the bishops but to ensure that their hopes of further preferment were geared to the loyalty of their performance in their House. The opportunity which Walpole exploited more fully than any of his predecessors arose out of the very unequal incomes which were available to the incumbents of various dioceses, ranging from the few hundred pounds a year for the bishops of Bangor and Llandaff to the princely incomes amounting to thousands of pounds payable at such rich dioceses as Salisbury, Winchester and Durham. The point is well illustrated by the classic progress of Benjamin Hoadly, a Whig cleric and successful party pamphleteer who enjoyed successively the incomes of Bangor, Hereford, Salisbury and Winchester after the Whigs came to power in 1714. Hoadly held himself willing to change his loyalties from the Sunderland-Carteret clique to the Walpole-Townshend dispensation, and was rewarded accordingly. Not all bishops appointed before Walpole's ministry were as amenable, and in particular he found Archbishop William Wake of Canterbury an uncertain ally. To overcome this difficulty Walpole turned for advice on ecclesiastical promotions to Edmund Gibson, Bishop of Lincoln, whom he soon had translated to London and who thereafter managed the day-to-day business of ecclesiastical patronage.

Fortunately for the ministry five bishops died in 1723 and a sixth bishopric, that of the exiled Atterbury of Rochester, became available in the same year. This was a good beginning for the remodelling of the episcopate on thoroughly Walpolean lines. The choice of Gibson as adviser, however, was no windfall but the result of careful selection and assessment of his ambition and temperament. As Walpole wrote to Townshend after an early interview with this prelate, 'He must be Pope, and would as willingly [be] *our* Pope as anybodies'.[1] Gibson's ambition was

---

1. Plumb, *Walpole*, ii, pp.95–6. Gibson has often since been called 'Walpole's Pope'.

for power rather than further preferment, though it must be said in justice that he wanted power for the benefit of the Church itself. His insistence on selecting colleagues who were theologically orthodox as well as politically subservient was sometimes to be an embarrassment to the ministry when the next King and his blue-stocking Queen would have preferred to make bishops more in tune with the deism fashionable in their intellectual circle. That problem, however, was still in the future. For the moment Walpole and Gibson between them welded together a bench of bishops whose support of the ministry was on several occasions to save Walpole's majority in the Lords. For the rest, the peers were generally more loyal to the person of the monarch and, being richer, more easily swayed by inexpensive honours than were members of the Commons. The Upper House rarely gave much trouble or demanded the close personal attention which Walpole paid to his own chamber.

At a time when patronage was less an occasional perquisite than a way of life, when parliamentarians were unpaid and an embryo Civil Service underpaid, Walpole's tactics were sound and stood out only by reason of their unusual thoroughness.

Much of the daily life of a First Lord of the Treasury was taken up with applications, in person or by letter, from people who felt that they or their friends and relations deserved rewards or had services to offer. Walpole's lobby was even more thronged than the King's as it gradually became known that most gifts were to be filtered through the minister irrespective of whether these were technically within the competence of the Treasury or concerned ecclesiastical, naval and military, legal or other spheres.

Such considerable control of patronage was in the long run wearing, as it could not hope to feed the hunger of a nation. Morever there was a tendency for Walpole to be forced to extend his activity to the work, as well as the clientage arrange-ments, of other departments. During the summer of 1723, while both Townshend and Carteret were at Hanover in attendance on the King, Walpole took over the work of the Secretaries' office in addition to his own. This later gave him the experience necessary to steady Townshend; but it also became common for the First Lord to take over more and more control of the minutiae of business in other departments in order to meet the demands upon him. He was frequently accused of taking too much into his own hands, and there was truth in this charge.

Walpole's instinctive intolerance of able colleagues led him to dismiss Pulteney's claims and replace Carteret by Newcastle with the King's acquiescence. This preference for men of lesser abilities as colleagues further prompted him to interfere in their tasks. As often where there is a strong personality at the head of government the direction of affairs became more personalised. Much of the time the Cabinet's place was taken in practice by informal meetings of Walpole with Townshend and Newcastle, placing decision-making in the hands of three 'efficient' officers, the First Lord and two Secretaries, rather than the larger body of ministers.[1] Indeed many contemporaries suspected that even Newcastle was a cipher, and the French envoy advised his government that 'it suffices [his colleagues] that he has the docility to do and say as they dictate'.[2]

In practice, therefore, Walpole and Townshend were probably in most cases the sole ministerial arbiters of policy. A possible minor source of rivalry was eliminated in 1725 when the Duke of Roxburghe was dismissed from his post of Scottish Secretary and the post was allowed to fall into disuse. Roxburghe's faction in Scottish politics, the 'Squadrone', had adhered to Sunderland and Carteret and now paid the price. The rival Campbells, headed by the Duke of Argyll and his brother, the Earl of Islay, took over government management in the Northern Kingdom; but Walpole disliked Argyll personally and distrusted his ambition, so a continuance of the third secretaryship was not considered expedient. In such ways were born the bases of later charges that Walpole acted not only as 'prime' but as 'sole' minister.

In 1724 Walpole was at the height of his powers, and his political success was reflected in his personal life. His son Robert was recently married to an heiress of the Rolle family of broad estates and political influence in South Devonshire, though this marriage was to follow the pattern of Walpole's

1. Later in Walpole's ministry Lord Chancellor Hardwicke was added to the 'inner Cabinet', and other ministers were called upon for advice as necessary.
2. Add. MSSS. 32,308, f.172.

own, in being neither happy nor enduring. His daughter Mary was just wedded to the heir of the Earl of Cholmondeley, becoming thereby the ancestress of the family which eventually succeeded to Houghton and holds it to the present time. Walpole's second son Edward was waiting to emulate his elder brother by going on the Grand Tour of Europe, there to acquire art treasures for the new mansion. Young Horace, future man of letters and staunch defender of his family's reputation, was about to follow in his elder brothers' footsteps at Eton. The building of Houghton proceeded apace, but as yet Walpole could not take up residence on a comfortable scale. Two years later part of the new buildings were ready for occupation but his happiness was cut short by the death of his beloved sister Dorothy, soon to be followed by that of Galfridus. It was an age when death was a frequent visitor to all families, by reason of disease and especially the scourge of smallpox, but losses were no easier to bear and Walpole suffered particularly from the loss of his sister.

Meanwhile, however, a new joy had entered Walpole's personal life in the person of the mistress, more permanent than her predecessors, who was eventually to become his second wife on Catherine's death. He seems to have met Maria Skerrett in or before 1724. Her father was a wealthy Londoner, though not of the standing of Walpole's Shorter in-laws. A daughter Maria was born in 1725 and Sir Robert installed both Marias in a government residence in Richmond Park to provide a weekend home for himself. The affair appears to have been a love-match in a way that Walpole's first marriage had not been for many years, and this took the edge off the inevitable malicious gossip. As time passed and Walpole remained faithful to his new love the gossip became muted. Maria provided for him a home and tranquillity of which he often stood in need in the later, more contentious years of his administration. Not that Walpole forgot his other obligations and family ties: Catherine Walpole continued to live a life of extravagance, and not only Walpoles and Townshends but Shorters too continued to be provided with offices or other perquisites.

The Walpolean machinery of government was running smoothly. Under the alert guidance of Gibson ecclesiastical patronage was being spread down into the lower echelons at parish level, so as to modify the traditional High Church predominance among the lower clergy and counter clerical Tory influence at election times. The new style of government included low Land Tax, to keep the country gentlemen happy, and a deliberate infrequency in the bringing of new or contentious legislation. The meetings of Parliament itself were amended to political advantage, for Walpole had always disliked the unpredictability of pre-Christmas meetings, which left the House increasingly denuded when members went home in the weeks before the traditional festivities. Now Parliament did not assemble until January.

Walpole's calculatedly uneventful administration also led to a considerable measure of ritualisation in parliamentary proceedings. Members could expect that the same items of routine business would come up at approximately the same stage of the session each year, often even at approximately the same date. Stable government brought advantages. Treasury clientage, together with its Scottish, military and naval counterparts, could be deployed farsightedly for the manipulation of the borough seats even though a general election was still several years ahead. In opposition the Tories had little answer to the new dispositions. They had hardly recovered from the savage mauling they received in 1722 and the succeeding session. Never deeply implicated in active Jacobitism, in spite of their reputation, most Tories were drawing further from the court at St Germain. In the opinion of one observer, Lord Hervey, the Jacobite element 'was fallen so low . . . that in reality it consisted of only a few veterans (and those very few) who were really Jacobites by principle and some others . . .'[1] The trend was symbolised by William Wyndham who had now so emerged from his original Jacobitism as to stand forth in the Commons as the principal spokesman for the Hanoverian Tories now that the older generation of leaders was falling away.

Shortly before Christmas 1724, during the last session called in autumn for many years, Walpole took advantage of a thinning out of the Tories in the festive season to bring in a bill for further weakening them. In 1722 the City of London had returned Tory members for all its four seats. When a motion was passed in December to regulate City elections the Tories

1. John Hervey, *Some Materials towards Memoirs of the Reign of George II*, ed. Romney Sedgwick (1931), i, p.4.

brought only forty-nine votes against it. In the New Year the ministry again met little check in the Commons, though the metropolis itself offered considerable resistance, because the proposed reform included curtailment of the freeman vote in the Common Council and confirmation of the select alder-manic court's claim to veto proceedings in the more popular body. The bill received its third reading in March with a mere eighty-three votes cast against it, and passed the Lords with even less difficulty.[1] As a result the ministry was to gain two of the city's seats in the next general election.

But help was at last on the way for the Tories. William Pulteney, smouldering since Newcastle had been allowed to snatch Carteret's Secretaryship from under his nose, was ready to move into outright opposition, assisted by his friends Samuel Sandys and Sir John Rushout. Their first major effort was to join in a demand for the impeachment of Macclesfield, the Lord Chancellor whom Walpole had inherited. Macclesfield was charged with peculation and taking bribes, and Pulteney and Wyndham tried to obtain a broader parliamentary enquiry which would include other governmental practices as well as those of the accused minister. Walpole frustrated this move by agreeing to participate in the prosecution of Macclesfield, whose guilt could hardly be denied. In April Pulteney finally committed himself to opposition by attacking the King himself, protesting at a government proposal to make good debts on the Civil List. Pulteney's voting a few days later on a ministerial bill to restore Bolingbroke's estate is unfortunately not recorded.[2] Walpole supported the measure against his will and was exposed to criticism by many 'Old Whigs'. But on this matter he still had to give way to the wishes of the King and the Duchess of Kendal.

The seeds of opposition having been sown, the summer of 1725 provided new material which could be used when Parliament met again early the following year. The occasion was a treaty negotiated at Hanover by Townshend with France and

1. C.J. Henderson, *London and the National Government 1721–1742* (North Carolina, 1945), pp. 91–111. *cf* I.G. Doolittle, 'Walpole's City Elections Act (1725)', *Eng. Hist. Rev.* xcvii (1982),pp.504–529, stresses the pragmatic, rather than the political motive for this Act.
2. Newman, *Parliamentary Diary of Knatchbull*, pp.36–7, 39–40, 42–5, and 46–8; HMC, *14th Report*, part ix, p.515.

Prussia. The Secretary's reasons for reviving the French alliance of which he himself had been so critical nine years earlier centred upon his somewhat far-fetched fears of a treaty recently concluded at Vienna. This treaty between the hitherto quarrelling courts of Austria and Spain led Townshend to fear the conclusion of a royal marriage which might result in an eventual union of the Habsburg with the Bourbon dynasties of France and Spain if Louis XV died childless. This possibility was so contingent upon supposition that it was difficult for Walpole to produce it in the Commons as a defence of a policy which many Whigs still considered contrary to Britain's natural enmity with France and alliance with Austria. Walpole was thus forced to lay emphasis upon another aspect of the Austro-Spanish rapprochement, its provision for the setting up by the Emperor of a trading company at Ostend which would threaten British interests. But the Treaty of Hanover achieved no popularity and became a handle for the new parliamentary opposition. Walpole, who had to bear the brunt of criticism of the new policy, had ample time over the next five years to regret his brother-in-law's zeal.

With the Hanover Treaty fresh in the public mind Pulteney made no secret of his intention to attack the ministry. Walpole even discovered him trying to improve his case by collusion with the Emperor – for the First Lord was having his opponent's correspondence opened as it passed through the Post Office. Sir Robert was neither the first nor the last British statesman to use this convenient method of obtaining information, and throughout his ministry he derived considerable benefit from it.

The new session commenced on 20 January 1726 with the King's Speech, calling for increased naval forces in case of a war with Austria and Spain. But in the subsequent debate Walpole successfully played down the actual possibility of war over a projected Spanish attack upon Gibraltar. In amending Townshend's argument, justifying the Treaty of Hanover by reference to a threat of hostilities, Walpole accurately gauged the national revulsion at the thought of war with Austria. Although Pulteney joined the Tories in criticising the Address to the Throne he did not press his attack far, possibly because he was given some timely hope of being taken into the government. By the time this hope was shown to be false the worst danger was over, and the Address was passed without incident.

For most of this session Walpole retained the initiative. In debate on the army estimates Pulteney could not divide the House because many Tories were absent, apparently averse from putting national safety at risk, while Wyndham actually supported the enhanced forces and even Shippen toned down his criticisms. Soon after the opposition risked a division on a motion for an enquiry into the position of the National Debt, but Walpole was able to defeat this easily by 262 votes to 89. One long-standing critic of the government, Brodrick, recorded that he voted for the government in view of the international crisis and unease in the City of London, and his attitude probably reflected that of other dissident Whigs and Tories. Walpole could do little wrong. Even a ministerial motion asserting that the Commons would stand by George I if the electorate of Hanover was attacked, an undertaking which would on other occasions have been enough to alienate many of the government's usual supporters, was opposed by only 107 votes led by Pulteney with a poor turnout of Tories. In a debate on 25 March, on a vote of credit for the Navy, Walpole counter-attacked Pulteney for inciting Austrian belligerency by assuring the Emperor that the Treaty of Hanover would not be accepted in the Commons. A division of 270 to 89 again indicated a low profile by the Tories. Throughout the session they showed themselves reluctant to be lumped with Pulteney and his Whig associates as unpatriotic, by the ministry's increasingly effective assertions in Parliament and in the press.

The session which saw Pulteney's first full-time opposition also witnessed the government's bill to restore estate and income to Bolingbroke while denying him the right to regain his seat in the House of Lords. The great Tory had returned to France after his first visit but finally settled in England and remained quiet while he retained any hope of full restoration of his original status. He even went to the length of letting the ministry know that he had, and wished, for no understanding with Pulteney. But when this hope was gone, by the end of the 1725 session, Bolingbroke turned to bitter opposition, soon coming to an understanding with Pulteney. The first number of their joint and soon famous periodical, *The Craftsman*, appeared in December 1726; it aimed to set up a new and lively counter to Walpole's *London Journal* and other government periodicals. Against government propaganda which laid heavy emphasis upon party issues and the inadvisability of independent Whigs ever voting alongside the Tories, *The Craftsman* advised 'let the very name of Whig and Tory be forever buried in oblivion'. Instead the new journal proposed a 'coalition of parties' in which the upright country gentlemen of both sides would combine in opposing inept and corrupt government. In the third issue the opposition writers began the first instalment of a somewhat laboured satire about a cure-all obtainable only from one 'Dr Robert King'.[1] The image of Walpole as a King or tyrant became a favourite stock item.

Over the next few years the liveliest contributions were to come from the pen of Bolingbroke, who provided the series of essays which were later published separately as *Remarks on the History of England*. In his never-ending efforts to counter the ministry's allegations of Tory treason, Bolingbroke advocated a cross-party ministry under a Hanoverian monarch, developing the idea he later made famous in *The Idea of a Patriot King*. The excluded peer's theme of a patriot monarchy supported by all loyal politicians was one which had often been preached by the late Lord Oxford. The patriot philosophy had more effect upon the royal house, especially George I's grandson Frederick, than on the party-oriented House of Commons.

The new alliance of Bolingbroke and Pulteney had an immediate effect on the Tories and dissident Whigs, who cooperated better in the 1727 session than previously, thanks mainly to Wyndham's efforts on Bolingbroke's behalf on the Tory side. The Tories' clannishness and exclusiveness were a byword but they, or at least the non-Jacobites, mellowed temporarily. The Whig dissidents too were currently well-inclined. They now included as well as Pulteney and his personal followers such older opponents as the Irish patriot Brodrick, the unpredictable Jekyll (whose life tenure of the position of Master of the Rolls protected him from Walpole's wrath) and a number of individualists like Archibald Hutcheson. Together they displayed some sparkling talent and oratorical influence, but to be effective they needed a cause. Such a cause seemed likely to be provided by foreign affairs.

1. *The Craftsman*, 9 and 12 December 1726.

Europe was undergoing one of its periodic phases of tension. The two camps into which nations had been divided by the rival treaties of Vienna and Hanover were enlarged in the summer and autumn by new recruits. Expanding Russia, under its new Tzarina Catherine I, aligned itself with Austria and Spain, making claims to former Swedish territories flanking the Baltic. The United Provinces lined up with the Alliance of Hanover, soon to be followed by Sweden, Denmark and other lesser nations afraid of Russian or Austrian aggression. Finally Prussia, the most powerful of the German electorates, threatened to change the balance by defecting from the Hanover alliance to that of Vienna, showing the way to several smaller German principalities. The British ministry bowed to George I's insistence and sent a British squadron to the Baltic, there to show the flag in case Russian assertiveness should turn to actual aggression; for as Elector of Hanover the King would be one of the first to lose to Russia gains made from the former empire of Sweden in North Germany. But the adoption by Walpole and Townshend of Stanhope's policy, even to the extent of engaging the British Navy, was hardly likely to endear them to the Whig backbench opinion which they had mobilised against the former ministry.

At the same time another new and even more unpredictable element entered upon the scene. The youthful Louis XV's period of minority was coming to an end. The Duc de Bourbon as Regent had continued the British alliance, but in 1726 the young King began to flex his muscles and Bourbon was replaced by Louis's tutor Cardinal Fleury. Though already in his seventies at the time of his appointment Fleury was to remain the directing influence in French foreign policy for sixteen years and rank as the master statesman of his epoch. Few knew in 1726 in which direction the new minister's subtle mind would guide France, and for several years the exact nature of his policies did not become clear. But in the longer run Walpole and Townshend could expect that the presence of an effective minister in Paris and the removal of Louis's dependence on the British alliance might well gradually move France back eventually into her traditional position of hostility.

To the British ministers there appeared to be no immediate danger. Horatio Walpole in Paris soon came under the spell of the aged Cardinal's charm, and began to write in his usual enthusiastic style of the benefits likely to accrue from France's change of management. There could be no early change in direction because circumstances which had recently soured relations between France and Spain were for the moment unchanged. Bourbon had been sufficiently worried by an illness which assailed the delicate young King of France to contemplate the unwelcome possibility that Philip of Spain might soon succeed to the throne of France, his country of birth. Bourbon's reaction was to attempt to provide a healthy heir for Louis by arranging an immediate marriage. Unfortunately Louis was already betrothed to the Spanish Infanta, still a child and unable to consummate the union, so she was returned to Madrid to make possible the speedy marriage between Louis and an older princess. Spain's fury at this repudiation was not something which could be assuaged at once, and relations remained frigid between the two Bourbon courts. To this extent Horace Walpole's optimism seemed justified.

Townshend remained less worried by the possibility of a Bourbon menace than by the prospect of a future union between the thrones of Vienna and Madrid which might be brought about by a marriage between the Archduchess Maria Theresa and Don Carlos, Philip's son by his second wife. The even more horrifying if distant prospect which had haunted the Secretary until he arranged the alliance of Hanover, namely that Don Carlos might eventually succeed to all three crowns of Spain, Austria and France by the death of the young Louis XV, was now fortunately receding and Townshend was willing to accept Horatio's assurances of French goodwill. Sir Robert, propelled by both his brother and his brother-in-law, was prepared to fall in line with their views for the next parliamentary session.

Since both Townshend and Newcastle were in the Lords, the burden of justifying foreign policy fell on the First Lord. Spain was still threatening to besiege Gibraltar, and Russia had shown little sign of being deterred by the British show of force with Sir Charles Wager's squadron in the Baltic. The French alliance was still needed and would have to be defended even though its longer future was now in doubt. Walpole prepared to deploy his familiar arguments, danger to trade by the Ostend Company, the turning of the Baltic into a Russian lake, the possible losses of Minorca and Gibraltar and even a supposititious threat to the Protestant succession posed by Austria and Spain. The latter suggestion was a hard one for any level-headed British observer to swallow, but well-publicised secret clauses in the Vienna treaty could be used as evidence for this and other putative dangers to Britain.

Fortunately for the ministry the undoubted tenseness of the international situation when Parliament met in January 1727 did much to disarm the opposition. Walpole drafted a royal speech of unprecedented length to explain why the nation had been put into a posture of defence and why – a delicate point – the ministry had been forced to hire twelve thousand Hessian troops to the apparent military advantage of Hanover rather than Britain. In the subsequent debate Pulteney and other opposition speakers could only pour scorn on some of the weaker features of the government's argument; they could not deny the realities of long-term danger to British interests if Russia became too powerful in the Baltic or if Spain succeeded in taking Minorca. An opposition amendment was easily defeated. The Minority, to use a common term at this time for the combination of Tories and dissident Whigs, was able to obtain only 81 votes against the ministry's 251. Shortly afterwards Newcastle's able younger brother Henry Pelham, now Secretary at War, carried with equal ease an increase in the size of the army by about eight thousand men. Even a temporary rise in the Land Tax from two to four shillings brought no more opposition than the earlier votes, providing the best testimony that the House had accepted the ministerial case of a continuing crisis in international affairs.

Walpole was absent from the Commons for much of the later part of the session, suffering from a succession of ailments: colds, fever, then gout. Fortunately Horatio Walpole was able to delegate his diplomatic responsibilities and act as chief government spokesman in some of the foreign affairs debates. The inestimable benefit of having a younger brother of the highest ability was never more obvious. In Horatio's view the task was not a difficult one, especially as he was flanked by Pelham's financial expertise for knotty financial points. Though the opposition was becoming vociferous, especially Pulteney's following, its numbers were not dangerous. Moreover Walpole returned to the Commons before the recess and

was fortunately well-established when a major new development arose.

In June the King set out as usual for Hanover, but this time
never reached the beloved electorate. When news of his death
reached London the new monarch, George II, gave vent to
grievances by instructing Walpole to take his orders from
Spencer Compton, Speaker of the House of Commons. Compton was a Whig with good Tory family connections and a far
more assiduous flatterer of the new court than Walpole could
ever be. The next crisis of Walpole's ascendancy was at hand,
and the way he was able to deal with it was to show that just as
he had achieved mastery of the Commons so he was now more
than ever able to deal with a rival whose chief strength was, like
Carteret's, as a courtier.

10

Enter George II,
exit Townshend

IN MODERN practice demise of the monarch would make little
practical change to the personnel of a ministry. In Walpole's
time extensive changes were expected, as had been the case
when Queen Anne and George I came to the throne. That
Walpole was able to establish himself as necessary to George II
after only a few weeks of crisis in 1727 was a personal triumph
that also provided a key precedent for the future. Thirty-three
years later George III, anxious though he was to change his
despised ministers, had to scheme and manoeuvre for two
years after he became King before he dared place a favourite at
the head of public affairs, and the outcome of his action was a
decade of political strife.

The continuance of a ministry irrespective of the person of
the monarch was a logical step as the importance of Parliament
gradually increased in the eighteenth century and ministers'
power base shifted towards the House of Commons. George II
well understood that he needed the Commons' support and
thought to obtain it by securing its Speaker, Compton, as his
intermediary; but the chair of the House was not the important
governmental post it had been in the seventeenth century or
even in Anne's reign, when Harley had once held it in conjunc-
tion with a Secretaryship of State. The chair was slowly moving
towards the modern position of impartiality and independence,
which Speaker Onslow and his successors were to further over
the following decades. To direct the Commons in Walpole's
time a 'manager' needed to be not only a respected parliamentarian like Compton but a minister with the patronage
resources of the Treasury behind him. Walpole had the combination of skills needed, being an administrator of proven ability
as well as a leading Parliament man. Compton, however, lacked
talent for office.

At the time only a few people realised the real needs of the
situation. Walpole was one, and his persistence in the fight to
recover his ascendancy derived from his superior understand-

ing. George II, no fool despite his guttural accent and sometimes childish petulance, came to realise his reliance on an able
minister and the need to keep him: George on reflection did
not attempt to place Compton at the Treasury. But despite the
King's acquiescence in Walpole's overwhelming claims to continued office the first few weeks of the new reign were anxious
ones for both men. George, as Prince of Wales during his long
years of muted antagonism to his father after the 'reconciliation' of 1720, had often referred to the minister by names
which would have called for a challenge if uttered by any less
eminent personage. Walpole was ready to forgive and forget,
but the King could not immediately abandon his former stance
without loss of face. Such a situation needed careful personal
handling as well as an exhibition of Walpole's ministerial skills.

Fortunately a reasonable amount of the deference due to a
monarch was not hard to give. George, as Elector of Hanover
and lover of his country of birth, had an eminent grasp of the
minutiae of European politics and knew that Walpole's recent
policies were favourable to the Electorate. One major area of
dispute was thus quiescent for the moment. Moreover the King
was approachable by one of the means traditionally open to
courtiers. Despite the existence of a regular mistress and
perhaps others of her kind George was devoted to his wife
Caroline, a woman of ability who liked to pose as an intellectual
and enjoyed the conversation of intelligent men. Walpole was
quick to establish with Caroline a famous relationship based
upon her enjoyment of his sharp understanding of human
nature and sweeping knowledge of public affairs. He cultivated
her assiduously, and not without success. The prime need was
to convince the King, through Caroline, that only Walpole
could manage the House of Commons in such a way as would
be useful to the Crown.

If George II's preference for Compton did not put an end to
Walpole's hopes it certainly put paid to those of another.
Bolingbroke, by his own account and Walpole's, had latterly
come fairly near to persuading George I to remove Walpole.
The old King's deference to the Duchess of Kendal, who had
continued to plead the veteran schemer's case, together with
Walpole's occasional return to old objections to royal foreign
policies, may account for the expectations which the late
monarch had given Bolingbroke. The details of how the

arrangement was to be effected and presented to Parliament are not revealed, and perhaps were never drawn up. But with rumours of the scheme abroad the Prince of Wales too had thought it wise to give vague encouragement to Tory politicians. In his case the gesture was probably no more than an insurance policy, lest the Whigs' demands should at some time prove to be too great. The elevation of Compton with his close Tory connections, had the advantage of seeming to leave the door open for possible Tory appointments without actually making any concession, least of all to Bolingbroke for whom the new King felt little but contempt.

Certainly the Tories appeared at court in large numbers as soon as the Prince came to the throne and remained in its vicinity for several weeks until the situation clarified. One shrewd politician felt sufficiently certain of the King's Tory sympathies to assure Compton that 'the Tories will readily come into measures with you, and by taking in some few of the best of them (tho' this must be done with caution) and giving the rest but tolerable quarter, you may make his majesty *King of all his people*'.[1] At first George tried, via the recently appointed Lord Chancellor King, to have some magistracies allocated to Tories for the first time since 1714, but vehement Whig protests soon put an end to this gesture. On a par with this feeble attempt was the King's half-hearted move to secure the Chancery's ecclesiastical patronage for his own use, from which he desisted when the Chancellor demurred.[2] A quiet life in England and the freedom to protect his electorate were what George II really wanted; the Whigs led by Walpole were soon to show him the way to both.

If Walpole's success was materially aided by a certain wisdom in the King's outlook, it was furthered also by Compton's self-doubts and crude attempts to pick the First Lord's brains while keeping him in second place. Compton's submission to Walpole of a draft of the King's opening speech, and Walpole's improvements to it, have to be considered symbolic of the inter-relationship of the three men. George needed certain things to be done efficiently, and Walpole could do them. As

1. HMC, *Stopford-Sackville*, i, p. 375. The politician was George Bubb Dodington.
2. Peter, Lord King, *Life of John Locke*, (1830), ii, pp. 46–50 (Lord King's notes).

early as 15 June Newcastle reported that the King had 'talked a great deal to Sir Robert about the Civil List'.[1] New and better tax funds were devised and, with little resistance in the Commons except from the Jacobites, Walpole shepherded through proposals to give the new court a Civil List worth one hundred thousand pounds more than the old one had received. At the same time a useful assurance was given to George II that any future shortfall in his parliamentary income would be met and that any excess produced by the funds could be retained by the royal couple. Walpole demonstrated his command of the Commons with almost insulting ease, showing that he and his associates were the indispensable element in the ministry. Parliament ended in July with the King's personal objections to Walpole largely removed, and his preference for Compton worn down by Caroline's vehement opposition. The Tories disappeared rapidly from court after the disappointment of their hopes of a Compton administration, and Walpole's offices were confirmed under the royal seal.

Sir Robert had triumphed over his new rival but the ease of the victory called for magnanimity. Though Compton and other former members of the Leicester House set had been revealed as men of straw they were not disgraced in the eyes of their master. But it would be embarrassing for all concerned if Compton were to retain the Speakership in the Commons where his challenge to the First Lord would no doubt for long be discussed with relish. The need for a new general election, under statute, within six months of the death of the last monarch provided the opportunity for Compton's graceful withdrawal after twelve years in the Chair. Receiving the barony of Wilmington he was removed to the more dignified and less contentious scene of the House of Lords in as honourable a manner as possible. To sugar the pill he was allowed to retain the lucrative office of Paymaster-General which he had held for several years alongside that of Speaker.

Other personal friends of the monarch had to be accommodated too: the Earl of Scarborough was brought into the Cabinet as George's representative, and Walpole had to agree to the removal of his own son-in-law, Mary's husband Lord Malpas, to make way for another royal nominee as Master of

1. Add. MSS. 32, 687, f.212.

the Robes.[1] But these were minor tactical concessions masking a major strategic victory. The Walpolean political machine could function comfortably with a few hangers-on from the royal set in a way that it could never have lived in harmony with more formidable politicians. The next few years were to see some minor courtierly intrigues against Sir Robert and some discomfort from the malicious tongues of such as Lords Hervey and Chesterfield who found favour at court; but such matters were mere annoyances when compared with the reality of ever-increasing power and patronage.

The general election showed dividends for the several years during which Walpole had been making his arrangments for contesting government boroughs and other key constituencies. The Tories were able to obtain only 131 seats in all, their lowest since the accession of the House of Hanover. In Scotland they gained no foothold at all, and in Wales their former majority was at last turned into a minority, ten out of the twenty-four seats. Of the Whigs returned Pulteney could claim only about fifteen; the remaining 400, consisting of about half placemen and half independents, could be reckoned as usual supporters of the government. Walpole's friends and associates were well rewarded and new adherents were invited. Sir Edward Knatchbull, a former Tory who had left his party recently, was brought in for a government borough in Cornwall to encourage other potential deserters. Walpole may perhaps have foreseen, if he noticed Knatchbull frequently making notes in the House of Commons, that this member would be a diarist whose record of events was kind to Sir Robert himself as well as useful to future historians.

Another associate who benefited from Walpole's support was Arthur Onslow, who was elected at the start of session for the first term of his long and influential career as Speaker of the Commons in place of Compton. Onslow's first loyalty remained always to the House itself, but as he never saw any serious challenge to its traditions from the ministry his tenure of the chair was on the whole favourable to Walpole as well as beneficial to the ascendancy of Parliament. Thus began the new

1. Plumb, *Walpole*, ii, p.169.

House of Commons which saw times of stress and setback for the administration, especially towards the end of the septennial term, but on the whole marked the high point of Walpole's career.

For the sessions of 1728 and 1729 there was little serious opposition, and the most effective political criticism came not from the nation's elected representatives but from the stage and the press. *The Craftsman* continued its successful career as mouthpiece of the uneasy Bolingbroke-Pulteney combination. Not even Walpole's well-paid and highly diversified press could produce anything to equal the single-minded effectiveness of this periodical's polemic. A little earlier Swift's *Gulliver's Travels* had amusingly portrayed Walpole walking the political tight-rope in George I's court,[1] and now Gay's popular *Beggar's Opera* featured a highwayman who was clearly a caricature of the First Lord. Gay's next play, *Polly*, went too far, however, and Walpole was able to obtain its closure. Later Walpole felt obliged to take even more drastic action against the authors of political litera-ture, at some cost to his basic reputation for moderation. The stings of the gnat annoy the stallion, and the literary opponents who at various times included Pope and Swift, Fielding and Dr Johnson were no ordinary gnats. For the moment, however, with the Tories quiescent and the Pulteneyites few, Walpole could afford to be relatively lenient to the press.

During the parliamentary meeting of 1728 the nation enjoyed uneasy peace, for Spain acceded to the preliminary form of a treaty to end desultory hostilities centring on the possession of Gibraltar. The Address passed with little resistance other than formal criticism by Shippen and Wynd-ham from the Tory benches.[2] Pulteney's main attempt at criticism was on a government proposal to retain the army at war-time level. In the absence of the definitive peace treaty he made little headway.

Only towards the end of the session was there a marginal deterioration in the government position, and this concerned a measure upon which the King had insisted against the better judgement of his minister. The court's proposer, Sir George

1. As 'Flimnap', the Treasurer in Lilliput, who 'is allowed to cut a caper on the strait rope at least an inch higher than any other lord in the whole empire'.
2. Coxe, *Walpole*, ii, pp.546–7.

Oxenden, requested a vote of credit for a purpose which he thought 'of too secret a nature to be divulged'. This cloudy request proved too much for an easy passage when old Hanmer rose to denounce ringingly the practice of making credit available to government for unspecified purposes. A lively debate ranged over the precedents and the possibility that the House's control over supply, a most jealously guarded privilege, was being eroded. Walpole disclaimed 'all or any advice' in the demand but nevertheless supported it. The King was known to regard the issue as one of his receiving the same confidence as that shown by the House to his father. But there was no serious danger of rejection; since the sum involved was relatively small few members other than Tories and committed opposition Whigs cared to deny George his wish, and the matter was accordingly easily carried.[1]

The royal request was of a sort which Walpole could not, and did not, allow to happen often. That he countenanced it on this occasion is a measure of his uncertainty with regard to the new monarch's favour; but against the royal wishes had to be balanced the sensitivity of the House of Commons, born of long experience, in the case of unusual or secretive demands for money. Even the modest increase in the Minority's usual numbers marked by the 101 votes cast against on this occasion was a warning of the limitations of the Commons' tolerance. This was not a party matter, for some of the government's usual Whig supporters as well as the miscellaneous opposition members felt strongly about the danger of unconstitutional demands.

The next session saw no repetition of this incident, though some echoes from it were seen in the ministry's disquiet at the effectiveness of the opposition press in the intervening period. In the speech from the throne Walpole inserted a strong denunciation of recent literary licence. Not only had *The Craftsman's* arguments and the satire of such playwrights as Gay been painful, but there was also an ominous proliferation of newspaper reporting of debates. A resolution against this practice diminished it for a short while, but Walpole had not

1. Newman, *Knatchbull Diary*, pp. 79 and 128; Add. MSS. 47, 032, pp. 116–23.

heard the last of open and highly biased accounts of his own and his colleagues' speeches in the House.[1]

On the Address the Tories divided on a proposal by John Barnard, brought on behalf of the commercial community, that mention should be made of a need to restore trade after the hostilities with Spain; but lacking any assistance from Pulteney's Whigs on this occasion they obtained only eighty-seven votes. The opposition alliance was not functioning smoothly, and as Pulteney had openly criticised the Address itself his refusal to vote against it was ridiculed by some Tories, including the Jacobite Shippen. This was a good beginning for the ministerial side, and further offences and retaliations between the two main elements which constituted the opposition soon followed. Pulteney and his cousin Daniel spoke strongly against Pelham's usual motion for retaining the army at full strength and this time it was the turn of most of the Tories to hold back, with the exception of the half-drunk Shippen who launched a personal attack on Horatio Walpole but did nothing to further Pulteney's case. Apart from the treatment of Horatio, Sir Robert must have enjoyed the incident greatly especially as another noteworthy Tory, Thomas Winnington, chose the occasion to support the government for the first time, following Knatchbull's recent example. Pulteney did not venture to divide the House, contenting himself by ending the debate with a sneer at those who had 'enriched themselves enormously on the public and grown fat (looking at Sir Robert) by feeding on the substance of their fellow subjects'.[2]

Such weak gibes were a useful fall-back for opposition members who had nothing much of substance with which to taunt the ministerial bench. A few days after the last debate Pulteney and his cousin Daniel again found themselves but lukewarmly supported, even in a foreign affairs debate. Yet it was in this area of public life that the best hope of Walpole's opponents lay. For the remainder of the 1729 session attacks on the government centred upon foreign affairs and were more successful, especially on the subject of delays experienced by

1. Cobbett, *Parliamentary History* viii, 668–70, 672–5, 677–80; *Commons Journal* xxi, p. 238. The Commons resolution was occasioned by a report in Robert Raikes' *Gloucester Journal*.
2. Newman, *Knatchbull Diary*, pp. 80–4; HMC, *Egmont Diary*, iii, pp. 330–1, 336–45; HMC, *Carlisle*, p.57.

the ministry in finally concluding peace with Spain. The matter was fought out in late February and March, after being brought up by a petition from merchants complaining of Spanish depredations against British shipping in the West Indies. Walpole was anxious that this point should not be blown up into a first class issue but the main result of the delays was a temporary defection by many government Whigs, providing an effective demonstration of the limited nature of his control over the independent members when passions were aroused.

Fortunately most of the defectors' dissatisfaction was shown by absenteeism rather than by crossing to the opposition side, but the government's usual majority sank alarmingly. The next attack was forthcoming upon a further royal request for the remedy of an alleged deficiency in the civil list revenue. Here was another weak spot in the ministry's armour. Walpole put it round that he had not advised the request and blamed Wilmington for the King's attempt. On 23 April, in a House rapidly thinning of Tories in expectation of the end of the session, 115 members voted against the demand. Since these included sixty-nine Whigs, at least fifty who voted against the court must again have been from among the government's usual supporters.[1] Thus by May, when the King set off as usual for his visit to Hanover taking Townshend with him, Walpole was moderately alarmed about the situation and began to make preparation for changes for the next session. The time was right, with the absence of the two men who were making difficult the management of the all important Lower House, George by his financial improvidence and the Secretary by the rigidity of his policies.

Relations between Walpole and his brother-in-law had been gradually deteriorating since both men got over the first shock of Dorothy's death; the loss of Townshend's wife removed a link which had smoothed over differences on matters of policy. The basic problem was the Secretary's deep commitment to the Treaty of Hanover and to the French alliance which he had revived. For Townshend this treaty was becoming not simply a temporary expedient but a lasting prop, the linchpin of Britain's European involvement. In this view he was to some extent abetted by Horatio Walpole, who continued to be under the

1. Newman, *op. cit.*, pp. 86–7, 91–2, 96, 131–6; Hervey, *Memoirs*, i, pp. 100–1.

spell of Fleury's charm. Even after the appointment of Chauve-lin, a new and definitely anti-British foreign minister, Horatio remained convinced that signs of French reluctance to aid British diplomacy were arising in spite of, rather than because of, the senior minister's real intentions.

But Sir Robert could see that French foreign policy had little reason to value the British alliance now that the situation which had given rise to it was rapidly disappearing. Fleury did not wish to abet Britain either in war or in obtaining a favourable peace with Spain, for he saw no purpose in further antagonis-ing the court of Madrid when it was the natural potential ally for France under a cadet Bourbon monarchy. France's main continental rival was Austria, and the French ministry's princi-pal concern was accordingly to avoid entanglement in the Anglo-Spanish quarrel and concentrate on cutting the Emperor down to size. Townshend's warm adherence to the French alliance, and his often marked anti-Austrian bias, was increasingly appearing to be anachronistic and a source of future embarrassment to his brother-in-law.

Although the British ministry had believed as early as the spring of 1727 that it had good reason to expect an early peace and the cessation of the siege of Gibraltar, tension continued for a further two years. Part of the reason was a change of leadership at Madrid where Philip V had become mentally incapacitated and was replaced by a Regent, his second wife Elizabeth Farnese. When Elizabeth refused to move Spanish troops away from the vicinity of Gibraltar and Horatio Walpole turned confidently to his friend Fleury for diplomatic assis-tance nothing came of it. The old statesman was full of sympathy but gave nothing else. The two sessions of the British Parliament in which high war-time levels of taxation had to be maintained in order to keep British and mercenary troops on a wartime footing had given rise to the discontent which we have already seen. Sir Robert's growing desire for a permanent settlement with Spain was matched only by his growing disillu-sionment with the unhelpful French alliance.

With dislike of French policies came resentment at Townshend's unflagging enthusiasm for the Hanover alliance. Equally unacceptable was the Secretary's idea of satisfying Spain by giving up the *Assiento*, the profitable concession for slaving and general trade given to Britain by the Treaty of

Utrecht and regretted in Madrid ever since. If Walpole saw any merit in Townshend's proposal he soon gave it up when he reflected what would be the likely response in the Commons.[1] The retention of the Spanish trade was now not so much a commercial need as a national point of honour frequently demonstrated in the House, especially on those occasions when the British merchants sought parliamentary sympathy for atrocities perpetrated by the Spanish *Guarda Costas* against British vessels. The strong feelings which were to hurry Britain into another war with Spain nine years later, despite Walpole's forebodings, were already present in 1729.

During the absence of George II and Townshend in Hanover in the summer of 1729 Sir Robert was ripe for action which would allow him to break the *impasse* with Spain and move away from the fruitless dependence on France which he deplored. His opportunity came from Elizabeth Farnese, recently humiliated by the Emperor Charles VI's repudiation of a proposed marriage treaty between his daughter Henrietta Maria and her son Don Carlos, the second such rebuff for Spain in the course of the last few years. Burning with anger Elizabeth turned to France for sympathy and at the same time decided to remove the menace of Britain from her back by coming to terms. In Britain Walpole and Newcastle seized the opportunity with delight. Newcastle was not averse from scoring off his fellow Secretary, with whom he had been on strained terms for some time; like Walpole he had often suffered humiliation from Townshend's cast-iron assumption of his own superiority. William Stanhope was despatched to Spain as British representative and a treaty was drawn up at record speed to be signed at Seville in November. In return for British agreement to place no obstacles in the way of Elizabeth's territorial ambitions in Northern Italy at the expense of Austria, Walpole was able to obtain the restoration of the *Assiento* trade as a very material offering to Parliament.

Townshend did not raise any serious objection to the negotiation with Spain even though he had no responsibility for it. No sooner was the treaty signed, however, than the Secretary ran headlong into new disagreement with the Walpoles. Far

1. Plumb, *Walpole*, ii, pp. 189–90.

from seeing the agreement at Seville as a reason for matching France's waning enthusiasm for the Hanover treaty Townshend believed that because France was a signatory of the treaty of Seville this only served to demonstrate the continuing success of the alliance of Hanover. As Seville had forced Britain to at least concur in the anti-Austrian tenor of Spain's policy, Townshend reasoned that the logical next step would be for Britain on her own behalf to continue furthering the isolation of Austria. To this end he tried to obtain a series of subsidy treaties with minor German princes in order to detach them from their loyalty to the Emperor.

Such a policy would have been doubly unacceptable to Parliament, for not only was expense involved but, more importantly, most members of the House of Commons still believed that Austria should be cultivated as a potential ally in the inevitable next round of hostilities with France as Britain's natural enemy. At this stage the only logical course was to obtain Townshend's removal; but Walpole could not lightly contemplate removing Dorothy's widower and a neighbour and political ally of so long a standing.

By the beginning of the new session in January 1730 Sir Robert had removed some, at least, of the arguments open to the opposition. He had put an end to the dangerous period of neither peace nor war which had existed since 1727 and restored Britain's commerce with the Spanish colonies; more importantly still, he was able to announce a reduction of the four shilling wartime rate of the Land Tax to only two shillings in the pound. These were solid achievements, but Pulteney and company were not without ammunition. It was clear that the recent birth of a Dauphin to Louis XV furthered the possibility of a Franco-Spanish alliance, by providing a French heir to the throne and lessening the possibility that Philip V's family might still lay claim to the country of his birth as well as that of his adoption. Pulteney quickly seized upon the weak aspect of the treaty of Seville, its weakening of the Emperor's interest. Joined by the Tories and even by the Jacobites, who had recently been urged by the Old Pretender to work with other members of the opposition to overthrow Walpole, the dissident Whigs were able to make some headway. In particular a ministerial proposal to retain some twelve thousand Hessian soldiers on the British payroll as a precaution in the uncertain European situation could be denounced ringingly as advantageous only to the King in his electoral capacity. Anti-Hanoverian sentiments were always good for detaching a number of the government's usual supporters.[1]

In a committee on the State of the Nation, a device which was revived for the occasion after remaining unused since the early part of George I's reign, the opposition caught Walpole by surprise in February by bringing witnesses to prove that Dunkirk harbour, a notable privateering centre very harmful to British commerce in William III's and Queen Anne's days, had been rebuilt and strengthened by the French contrary to the terms of the Treaty of Utrecht. The selection of this point for attack was the work of Bolingbroke, who was responsible through his spokesman Wyndham for producing both the facts and witnesses to testify to the truth of the case. Walpole was surprised by a wave of indignation at the revelation that the French base had been restored in preparation for some future war. He knew well enough of the rebuilding of Dunkirk but had been unable to persuade the French ally to put a stop to it. With great difficulty he obtained a respite of two days to produce his reply to the House. Even this concession was a near thing.

Fortunately the Tories decided at the last moment to flout Pulteney's advice and give Walpole a chance to state his case. The minister was able to avert a quick and crushing vote at a moment when many ministerial Whigs were deeply disturbed at an apparent menace to national security. A slight cooling of tempers over the ensuing two days resulted in opposition failure to follow up the effect of the original bombshell, for on 12 February Henry Pelham requested and obtained a further fourteen days to obtain documentary evidence in the ministry's defence.

On 27 February some 450 members of the House of Commons gathered together, with half the Upper House watching from the visitors' gallery. The ministers had not been able to

1. Add. MSS. 27,981, f.11; HMC, *Egmont Diary*, i, pp.2–6, 24–31; Coxe, *Walpole*, ii, pp.671–2.

gather much of the promised evidence but they had used the interval to good purpose in urging upon their followers the need for a good turnout. The French King, Walpole claimed, had been persuaded to sign an order for the demolition of the Dunkirk harbour defences, and this palpably misleading information was enough to satisfy some members. With the connivance of the ministerialist in the chair, Richard Edgcumbe, the debate took place on a government motion for an Address of Thanks for the newly ordered demolition, rather than on Wyndham's counter-motion for a resolution that France had violated treaty obligations. Having chosen ground over which the Whigs could follow him without unduly troubling their consciences, Walpole managed to change the tenor of the debate from one of opposition censure into one of party conflict by denouncing Bolingbroke for stirring up fears by false accusations. Wyndham thereupon felt obliged to defend his old friend and was easily diverted into a defence of the last Tory ministry of Queen Anne's reign, a safe ground for ministerial counter-attack.[1]

Horatio reported gleefully 'that the Whig party were animated to the last degree, which was chiefly occasioned by Sir Robert Walpole having very artfully and vigorously fell upon the late [*sic*] Lord B'.[2] In the crowded and highly charged atmosphere of the confined chamber a large number of members were either overcome by the heat or felt themselves about to be and left with pairing arrangements. One of the casualties was the diarist Knatchbull, who fainted and had to be carried out about midnight. A few weeks later he died from a fever caught, it was thought, during the course of the debate. Knatchbull perhaps exacerbated his own fever by attending the House a few more times; another diarist, Perceval, wisely stayed at home after the debate and survived. The result of the fifteen-hour sitting was a ministerial victory by a majority of 121 votes, though the 149 who voted against included a number of the ministry's usual dependables.

Walpole was not complacent at the result of this issue, for he realised that the underlying cause of the opposition's relative

1. HMC, *Egmont Diary*, i, pp.34–44, 71–5; Newman, *Knatchbull Diary*, pp.104–5, 109–10; Hervey, *Memoirs* i, p.117.
2. Coxe, *Walpole* ii, p.669. Bolingbroke was often referred to as 'the late' after his attainder in 1715.

strength in foreign affairs debates was deterioration of the French alliance and the ministry's failure to provide any alternative. While he was still in the early stages of taking this matter in hand he did his best to provide sops. In addition to reducing the land tax ministerial speakers were able to announce the abolition of the unpopular salt tax with the prospect of disbandment for a small army of tax collectors. Even so Pulteney's henchman Sandys was able to snatch a victory by the margin of ten votes with a bill to exclude government pension holders from the Commons. Such bills had traditionally received strong support irrespective of party ties and could sometimes produce government defeat in the Lower House. Such a pension or place bill was, however, easily rejected by the ministry's solid majority in the House of Lords. The vote on the pension bill proved to be the last one of importance.

Many Tories and other country members hastened out of town in mid-March after the committee on the State of the Nation failed to produce any more surprises. Right at the end of the session the ministerial party rallied to provide proof that Wyndham and Pulteney had colluded their enquiry over Dunkirk with the unpopular Bolingbroke, and despite the two members' denials the accusation managed to throw some doubt upon their veracity.[1]

Just as Parliament rose Townshend came to a decision. He and Walpole had been on strained terms for the whole winter and spring, and the Secretary could find few to support him on his foreign policy. Devonshire, Newcastle and most of the other ministers stood by Walpole's opinion that undermining Austria was not in Britain's interest. In the end, however, it was bickering between the two Secretaries which produced the outcome desired by all but Townshend; the King took Newcastle's part in a minor quarrel, and Townshend resigned in a huff. He was never fully reconciled to Walpole for the part which the latter had played in his downfall, for it is not easy to forgive a man for being right. But at least Townshend refrained from going into opposition as he so easily could have done. Instead he chose to retire to his home in North Norfolk,

1. HMC, *Egmont Diary*, i, pp. 50, 57, 83, 85–6; Newman, *op.cit.*, p.106.

there to continue the agricultural improvements which had interested him for a number of years. His passing from the government scene was generally welcomed though this was perhaps unfair, for he had contributed substantially in earlier years to the furtherance of the Whig party cause and the advancement of Walpole personally. Later observers have seen their long relationship as an important one in which Townshend played a major part.

With the going of a Secretary of State an opportunity was taken for a ministerial reshuffle. Townshend was replaced by the Earl of Harrington, better known as William Stanhope, the diplomat chosen by Walpole to negotiate the Treaty of Seville. Carteret was dismissed from the Lord Lieutenancy of Ireland; he had not taken the hint of his transfer from the secretaryship and had displayed sympathy with the opposition. With him chose to go his friend the Earl of Winchelsea (to use the senior title which old Nottingham had now inherited), who gave up the post of Comptroller of the Household. Walpole's loyal supporter the Duke of Dorset was sent to Ireland in Carteret's place thus freeing the post of Lord Steward for satisfying, for the moment, the ambitious Earl of Chesterfield. Henry Pelham became Paymaster-General, a step in the progression of posts whereby Walpole designed that this extremely able supporter should be gradually initiated as his successor at the Treasury. Pelham's former post of Secretary at War was given to another staunch Walpolite, Sir William Strickland.

A lesser but important appointment was that of Thomas Robinson, a follower of Newcastle, as ambassador at Vienna. This diplomat's task was to obtain an Austrian alliance; his chief recommendation was his complaisance, the same virtue which a quarter of a century later briefly obtained him a secretaryship of state under Newcastle. Finally the small element of courtiers in the ministry received its due when Wilmington was given an earldom and the Privy Seal. He remained in the Cabinet but without much more influence than he had ever had. As a coda to this arrangement Wilmington was shifted a few months later to the slightly more desirable post of Lord President, and thus made way for Walpole's friend the third Duke of Devonshire as Privy Seal. The family itself was not forgotten; Horatio was retrieved from Paris and received a post in the Household as well as a privy councillorship to mark the intention that he should play an even more important role on the government benches for the future.

The new arrangements represented the greatest changes made in the ministry since 1724, and were to prove lasting. Walpole was now at the apex of his career, for the removal of Townshend was a landmark, albeit a sad and distasteful one. The next task was to bring about a major change in the direction of British foreign policy in accordance with the wishes of the nation, and thereby smother the sound of an increasingly vociferous opposition.

I I

Alliances Revised and Tax Reform Attempted

WITH THE King's support secure and Townshend's influence now removed from the ministry Walpole could at last undertake some changes, long contemplated, in Britain's alliances and the administration of taxes. That he was to be successful in the first aim but frustrated in the second was due to one and the same cause, the House of Commons. Walpole could not know it but he had already made his most successful revision of the fiscal system. It would now remain substantially unchanged until Pelham's consolidation of the National Debt and the younger Pitt's drastic revision of Treasury administration later in the century.

In the field of foreign policy, however, the Treaty of Seville was but a necessary first step in a revision of alliances which was appearing increasingly attractive to the backbenchers. Last session had shown a series of falls in government majorities, never dangerous except during the Dunkirk episode but significant enough to show that the opposition's sustained campaign over the last two or three years was beginning to have an impact on members' minds. The power of France, quiescent during the years of royal minority after the death of Louis XIV in 1715, was in the ascendant again. The obvious counterbalance, one which Walpole decided in the summer of 1730 to be ready for exploitation, was a renewal of the alliance with Austria which had served Britain well during the wars of William III and Queen Anne.

The summer of 1730 accordingly saw a shortened vacation in Norfolk, even though the new Houghton Hall was now habitable. There Walpole weighed the chances for the success of his new policy; the situation was not without danger. As the price of settlement with Spain in the Treaty of Seville, Britain had been forced to agree to the placing of Elizabeth Farnese's son in the duchies of Parma and Piacenza, currently regarded by the Emperor as well within his own sphere of influence in Northern Italy. The time limit for Austria to allow Spanish troops to occupy the duchies had already elapsed, and Charles VI still showed no sign of acceding to pressure from the Seville allies. Far from appearing a potential ally of Britain, Austria might well appear to the Commons to be on the verge of hostilities with her. This outcome Walpole was determined to avoid. But the impasse could only be broken by a determined and perhaps drastic new approach.

Fortunately there was something the Emperor wanted even more than retention of the Italian duchies, and which Walpole was in a position to offer him. For years Charles had been attempting to obtain the support of sympathetic European nations for an agreement, the Pragmatic Sanction, whereby he hoped to secure the full and bloodless succession of his daughter Maria Theresa to the hereditary Hapsburg lands even though, as a woman, she would not be eligible for election to the imperial throne. This dynastic weakness of the Emperor's lack of sons had already been exploited to the full by German electorates and principalities, who succeeded in extorting major concessions from their nominal suzerain in return for their support. It was now Britain's turn to profit by his dilemma.

Walpole returned to London determined to convince colleagues and King that an approach to Austria on the basis of Britain's support for the Pragmatic Sanction, in return for abandonment of the Emperor's claim upon the duchies and support for the Ostend company, was a viable approach. The proposed offer of alliance was undoubtedly a gamble in that when it leaked out, as it inevitably would in the lax security of the day, it would undoubtedly alienate France. Only the successful conclusion of the negotiation could justify the approach; failure might leave Britain isolated. But Walpole's belief was that a calculated risk was a justifiable one. Charles VI was well-known to be willing to sacrifice almost anything on behalf of his daughter. The problem now became one of convincing George II that the step was necessary for the preservation of his British government and at the same time not detrimental to his electoral interests in Hanover. The first theme carried more conviction than the second.

The influence of electoral interests upon George I and George II, for decades a stock subject of abuse from parliamentary opposition and press, was far from imaginary. As early as 1701, in the Act of Settlement, legislators had foreseen that the

Hanoverian dynasty might equal if not exceed William III in putting the interests of their native country before those of their adopted one. Some of the restraining provisions of that Act had already been repealed to please the Hanoverians, and others were almost a dead letter. There remained the key provision which was intended to ensure that Britain should not be involved in any war in the Hanoverian interest, and so basic was this requirement in the thinking of parliamentarians that George I and George II would flout it only at their peril.

There remained, however, a grey area in which these monarchs could and did operate as electoral princes while using the not inconsiderable threat of the Navy and other British resources as a stick with which to beat rivals in Germany and the Baltic area. Although George I had been forced within four years of his accession to give up the practice of allowing his Hanoverian advisers to take part in making British policy, a section of the electoral chancery remained in London, ostensibly to permit easy communication between the Elector and his ministers in Hanover. These advisers, though lacking their former power in British government, continued to be a major influence upon the royal thinking. Moreover on several occasions the mere threat of British intervention, without any sanction from British ministers or possibility of support from the House of Commons, had been sufficient to obtain material advantages for the electorate. British fears and suspicions, openly expressed by opposition speakers but also secretly felt by ministers, were commensurate with advantages obtained for Hanover. George II was currently occupied in a long-drawn negotiation with the Emperor over the latter's continued failure to recognise the electorate's right to the North German territories of Julich and Cleve. To the King, like his father before him, the affairs of his German possessions were apt at times to assume greater importance than those of his kingdoms of England, Scotland and Ireland. Sometimes such thinking could be tolerated, in the present situation it could not: the Austrian alliance was a political necessity.

A year later, in the aftermath of the affair, Walpole was to describe Hanover feelingly as 'a millstone round the neck of British ministers'.[1] He certainly found it necessary to make his

1. Eveline Cruickshanks, 'The Political Management of Sir Robert Walpole', in Jeremy Black (ed.), *Britain in the Age of Walpole* (1984), p.31.

position known in the strongest possible manner. Though there was no difficulty in convincing the King of Parliament's unsettled and truculent state of mind, and of the desirability of putting an end once and for all to the threat of an Ostend company to the British trade, the question of Charles VI's intransigence over the German duchies proved more difficult. But at last George gave way, though the exact arguments which Walpole used finally to convince him are not in evidence. By the beginning of September 1730 Walpole's colleagues, including Horato who was not yet withdrawn from the Paris embassy, were being informed of Britain's change of direction. Horatio's protests were swept aside, and the new policy may well have been assisted by Walpole's decision that the time had come to hand over that embassy to someone else who might be willing to receive the brunt of Chauvelin's displeasure. Protests from other ministerial colleagues were ignored. The logic of the First Lord's decision, coming from the need to placate parliamentarians in the coming session, was overwhelming. Negotiation was set on foot immediately. The Emperor was informed of current French plans to enforce the Treaty of Seville by a punitive invasion of the Austrian Netherlands, and given the inducement of British support for the Pragmatic Sanction to persuade him to revert to the traditional alliance rather than seek a rapprochement with Spain.

Although the treaty with Austria had not been signed when Parliament met in January 1731 it was nearing completion after negotiation at breakneck speed by eighteenth-century standards. The issues were clouded a few days before the session when *The Craftsman* came out with the whole story of the transaction, communicated by the opposition leaders. The source of their information was the French court, which had obtained wind of Britain's approach through its highly efficient secret service.[1] This French attempt to put a brake on the new direction in British policy proved abortive but it occasioned considerable confusion among the British opposition, which had for many years been advocating just such a policy and was now in the unenviable position of having to criticise its execution by Walpole.

Fortunately the *démarche* came too late to influence the

1. Plumb, *Walpole*, ii, pp.228–9.

negotiation itself, for the Emperor had already decided to accept Britain's proposals. If anything, the opposition's exposure did more good than harm to Walpole's position, for back-bench Whigs could not but reflect that even if his methods were necessarily secretive his aims were basically in accord with their often-stated wishes. Although news of the final conclusion of a treaty in Vienna did not reach England until near the end of the session the opposition's intended bombshell proved to be something of a damp squib. Aided by Townshend's resignation, Walpole had carried out one of the most difficult feats in politics, the complete reversal of a major policy in mid-ministry. He succeeded in eating some of his former words without choking on them, and ensured himself a new credibility in foreign affairs.

The opposition's attempt to stir up further trouble for the government, through *The Craftsman's* revelation, could have ended in the disaster of a broken negotiation. The journal's intervention was only the culmination of a series of press campaigns against the ministry, of which the most prominent had been that concerning the fortifications at Dunkirk. If attempts by Pulteney and Bolingbroke to join Tories and dissident Whigs in Parliament were often far from successful, the sustained press alliance which had been going on for five years was making an increasing impression in the country, despite the ministerial writers' vigorous replies. The new campaign's threat to Walpole's negotiation, and a further cascade of personal abuse in the press, took a toll of his nerves. The hint given by the suspension of Gay's plays having been ignored, the time was at hand for a further display of ministerial authority against Grub Street.

Walpole's treatment of the literary men is one of the least wholesome aspects of his administration. On a number of occasions he felt it necessary to make a massive demonstration against press freedom, which he saw as licence, in a manner which would not be acceptable today. Censorship laws having proved unacceptable by the end of the seventeenth century, and stamp duties having failed in and after Queen Anne's reign to achieve the purpose of muzzling criticism, there now remained the possibilities of excluding reporters from Parliament and prosecuting publishers or printers when these could be identified. Walpole was by no means the originator of such repressive governmental measures. The volume of abuse hurled at him was well in excess of the criticism which had once caused Lord Treasurer Godolphin, in a fit of pique, to unleash the full panoply of a state impeachment against the cleric and pamphleteer Dr Henry Sacheverell. Vicious attacks by such literary artists as Swift, Pope and Bolingbroke were only the respectable tip of an iceberg of shadowy and unscrupulous denigrators whose work was increasing in volume throughout the earlier part of Walpole's ministry and could not be contained either by appeals for decent restraint or by retaliation.

The reasons for this increase are not far to seek. The very success of the First Lord in controlling both Parliament and monarch, as well as in establishing undisputed ascendancy within the ministry, meant that his opponents had little recourse but to turn increasingly to the press and to public opinion for support. The images of a pure and uncorrupted country party opposed to a dictatorial and corrupt minister, appearing in sustained invective, satirical prints, literary pastiches and even house and garden design could not but impress sections of the semi-literate population by their very volume and diversity. Particularly vulnerable was Walpole's carefully cultivated stance as a representative country gentleman; for if a substantial proportion of the landed class were to be won over from government the minister had to be portrayed as a betrayer of country interests, an over-powerful minister affecting country attire and manners in order to hoodwink the decent and respectable landowners whom he claimed to represent. To Walpole all this was particularly hurtful since he genuinely felt himself to be an upholder of his type to such an extent that he was willing to subordinate all other interests to theirs.

The main outcome of Walpole's exasperation at this time proved to be no more than the arrest of *The Craftsman's* publisher Richard Francklin, on a charge of seditious libel, and a raid on the journal's office. Though such gestures might give the opposition press pause for a short while they could be of only limited value in cutting down the worst excesses of literary abuse. The problem remained and grew worse. The prints continued to portray 'Robin's Reign' as one in which public

men from bishops to courtiers queued up for bribes distributed
by the minister. Tracts continued to depict a ferocious governmental tyranny opposed by a 'Patriot' opposition. These were
the ordinary currency of opposition propaganda, and the
minister's wrath was reserved for those who overstepped the
mark either by endangering national policy or by indulging in
excessive personal abuse. Little was done about the daily output
of literary squibs and cartoons which portrayed Walpole vari-
ously as a 'skreen' (a perennial reminder of his failure to punish
the previous ministry for the South Sea fiasco), a dancing
master (directing minions through the complicated steps of the
government patronage dance) or any of a score of other stock
satirical figures.[1]

Because Members of Parliament were basically in accord with
Walpole on the matter of the Austrian treaty, the session of
1731 passed relatively smoothly even though the demolition of
Dunkirk's fortifications had not been forthcoming. The
Address was hotly debated but did not result in a division, and
when the opposition at last chanced their hand on an issue
which ought to have favoured them, the further retention of
the Hessian troops, the ministers actually obtained a slightly
larger majority than in the previous year.[2] By April Walpole
was at last able to announce the conclusion of his treaty with the
Emperor, and this was received with no more than a nominal
criticism. The minister had displayed a very considerable
sleight of hand by both retaining the better relations he had
achieved with Spain and obtaining good terms with Austria. An
attempt by Pulteney and his associates to use Dunkirk-type
tactics again, this time announcing the building of Spanish
fortifications before Gibraltar, aroused little interest as Walpole
triumphantly presented the details of his master plan for
Britain's relations with Austria for the coming years. Even the
Tories, through their leader Wyndham, foresook the Whig
dissidents and congratulated the First Lord on his achievement.[3] With his new direction in Europe, Walpole was clearly
on much firmer ground in Parliament.

1. For a further account of the political caricatures see H.M. Atherton,
Political Prints in the Age of Hogarth (Oxford, 1974), especially pp.191–208.
2. HMC, *Egmont Diary*, i, pp.125–6; Cobbett, *Parliamentary History*, viii,
pp.834–8.
3. Add. MSS. 47,033, ff. 115–25.

The summer and autumn were spent in quiet enjoyment of his domestic life without any major worries about the next session. From time to time reports came in of attempts by the dissident Whig leaders to mend their fences with the Tories, braving the hazards of a ministerial press which was quick to notice and publicise any Whig wooing of 'Jacobite' allies. Walpole may perhaps have smiled wryly when he read in one of Pulteney's intercepted letters the words, 'I will be extremely careful what I say, not to give offence and bring you into any disgrace for continuing your friendship with such a Jacobite as I am'.[1] The opposition leader well knew that his letters were opened in the post, and opposition bitterness was sauce to the ministerial repast.

The session of 1732 began quietly enough, with Walpole unable to resist a note of triumph in the King's speech concerning the strength of Britain's position as the result of new alliances in the last three years. In view of peace enjoyed throughout Europe, however, the army estimates later in the month provided more fertile ground for the opposing orators. Although the Hessian troops were no longer to be retained, the ministry proposed no further reduction in the establishment of 18,000 British troops. A motion by Lord Morpeth, the former hammer of the Hessians, for the reduction of this number to 12,000 made a wide appeal; no fewer than 77 Whigs were found in the Minority along with 94 Tories, against the government vote of 241. This promising result added Morpeth's motion to those country issues, like place and pension bills, which recurred frequently as part of the opposition's stock programme.[2]

Nevertheless in February Walpole at last saw his way clear to launching the fiscal reform which he had contemplated for many years and worked on during the previous summer. This was no less than a reorganisation of the taxation system, mainly for the benefit of the landed gentry. The most astute politician of his day did not make the mistake of revealing the least acceptable part of his plans at once, and he offered an acceptable concession. Land tax was to be reduced to one shilling in the pound, the lowest figure it ever reached. But

1. Add. MSS. 17,915, ff.6–7 and 27,732, f.49.
2. Cobbett, *op.cit.*, viii, pp.869–911; HMC, *Egmont Diary*, i, pp.214–15.

since the government's income would not bear the reduction of 500,000 pounds a year which this would entail, the deficit was to be made good by reimposing the expedient of a salt duty. Walpole also gave an outline airing to the second and greater part of his scheme, which was intended to transfer taxation on wine and tobacco from customs to excise jurisdiction, stressing that this would create more revenue by using a system capable of preventing more effectively the vast smuggling industry which evaded the customs service.

For the moment opposition speakers wasted no time on future proposals but rose to criticise the salt duty, whose abandonment as recently as 1730 had been greeted throughout the country with great relief. Its reimposition would hit the poorer sections of society. Knowing that they had a popular cause the opposition speakers took every opportunity to portray Walpole's measure as unfair and socially divisive, ignoring the fact that governments in many countries and at most times have derived their staple income from one or other form of salt tax. But although the ministerial majority fell alarmingly to twenty-nine at its lowest point the Salt Bill passed through all its stages, and Walpole remained confident that he would be able to make most independent Whigs see where their best interests lay when he brought in legislation next year for implementing the remainder of his proposals.[1]

In the same session, however, two minor matters helped to embarrass Walpole's administration and prevent a respite from opposition pressure. One was a Tory bill designed to prevent evasion of the Property Qualification Act of 1711 by obliging parliamentarians to take before the Speaker an oath testifying their possession of the necessary landed qualification. Walpole, after first supporting an unsuccessful attempt by a City member to get the qualification extended to the possession of company stock, was able to get the bill rejected, but the original proposal attracted many members and he had to resort to doing so at the unusual stage of the third reading in a thin House of Commons. The qualification bill accordingly joined Sandys' and Morpeth's in coming sessions as a hardy annual and one of particular attraction to all Tories.

1. Plumb, *Walpole*, ii, pp.239–40; Cobbett, *op.cit.*, viii, pp.943–87 and 1014–25.

The second potentially embarrassing matter was a prolonged enquiry conducted by the opposition into the financial conduct of a ministerial supporter, Sir Robert Sutton. The main hope behind the enquiry was that some of the discredit of Sutton's private misconduct would rub off on Walpole. The minister was not at his best at this time and very nearly fell into the trap. Down to 3 May he threw the government's support behind Sutton. That night, reads Perceval's diary, 'The Tories and discontented Whigs were resolved to a man to leave the House abruptly, if a division had passed this day against Mr Sandys' motion . . . It would have been represented to the nation that the majority of the House were corrupted by the Court, and that honest men could not sit any longer there'. This plan of secession came to Walpole's ears just in time for him to make an abrupt withdrawal, and Sutton's expulsion from the House was carried with only twelve or thirteen dissentient votes.[1] The opposition victory was small in itself, but was a good example of the sort of attrition which Tories and Pulteneyites could, for somewhat different reasons, sometimes agree in bringing to bear upon Walpolean whiggery.

What was left of the summer of that year was spent by Walpole at the almost completed new Houghton. He appears to have carried out to the full his usual programme of entertaining the Norfolk nobility and gentry and renewing personal contacts and friendships after the parliamentary season. But although the hospitality and, later, the hunting went on unabated in the splendidly ostentatious atmosphere of the mansion and adjacent countryside (often newly purchased), Walpole did not forget the battle which lay ahead. In announcing his intention to place wine and tobacco under the jurisdiction of the excise service he had flung down a gauntlet which the opposition was only too willing to pick up, criticising the scheme in principle and practice. Walpole for his part was immersed in the administrative detail and statistical justification for the proposed changes. Even while he remained in Norfolk a heavy correspondence with London was supplemented by the summoning of Cabinet colleagues and subordinates in the

1. HMC, *Egmont Diary*, i, pp.240–68; Cobbett, *op.cit.*, viii, pp.1077–1161.

revenue services, for consultation about future tactics in the Commons. In November, shortly before he returned to London, there was something approaching a full ministerial gathering in convivial country surroundings prior to the session.[1]

Walpole's belief in the value of extending the excise principle to more commodities was based upon a firm foundation of experience. Soon after the commencement of his ministry he had, as an experimental measure, removed the luxury items of tea and coffee from the sphere of customs duties into that of the excise. Taxing at the point of sale rather than at the ports, where only a minority of the goods were ever seen because of the activity of smugglers, had proved to be a success. Governmental income was substantially up, and the efforts of the smugglers in these beverages were largely frustrated. But the new proposal bit deeper. An insatiable national taste for alcoholic drink meant that a substantial proportion of the population would suffer as a result of advantages to be gained by the Treasury. Walpole was aware of the existence, though not perhaps the full scope, of national dissatisfaction when he prepared to present his case, but he was determined to press on.

The main argument in favour of the excise principle, apart from the clear benefit accruing to the national revenue, was that it spread the burden of taxation to a larger number of people. The current relatively low income from customs duties could have only one outcome: higher land tax, the most reliable and easiest tax to assess and collect. 'The Land Tax', penned Sir Robert in a lengthy memorandum briefing his colleagues, 'falls on 400,000 men out of 8 millions. Since 1688, they have paid £65,000,000. Great towns and moneyed men pay little or nothing'.[2] This was the nub of Walpole's complaint, as a landowner himself. Since the land tax had been invented, in the reign of King William III, to fight Britain's war with France, the burden on the landowner had been greater than that on any other section of the population; at times of the highest imposition many well-known county families had succumbed and had to sell their estates in face of this and other difficulties.

1. Plumb, *Walpole*, ii, pp.249–50.
2. Plumb, *op.cit.*, ii, p.242.

Walpole himself had suffered considerable penury during Queen Anne's reign and envied the opulence of moneyed men and merchants of the City. He had also seen for himself the scale of smuggling which was defrauding the public purse of millions; indeed as a private man he had often benefited from the purchase of smuggled goods.

The opposition too had cogent arguments, and throughout the parliamentary recess the matter was never allowed to drop in the press. *The Craftsman* poured out the message that Walpole intended to burden the poor man not only through a revived salt tax but also by the setting up of new excise duties which would certainly lead to a general excise upon all the essential commodities. Dissident Whigs and Tories were for once in agreement. A general election was due in 1734 and the electorate would have an opportunity to register its disapproval of any Member of Parliament who voted for a scheme which seemed to entail a principle of general taxation. Nor did the criticism stop with damage to the pocket; English liberties too could be damaged, it was urged, by the host of excise men who might spring up in the wake of new legislation to harass and terrorise the population at large. The activities of the excise service were already unpopular, and the nation abounded with stories of brutality exercised in the search of suspected premises and households.

Public opinion struck home when Horatio Walpole received instructions from Norwich, the constituency for which he intended to stand at the election, to oppose the excise scheme if he wished for a successful candidacy. In many other places too, including Harwich where Perceval feared for his seat, sitting members were seriously worried as electors adopted a widespread campaign of writing to their representatives to state undying opposition to the scheme. But Walpole stolidly refused to heed the straws in the wind, even so near home, and remained hopeful. Almost on the eve of the introduction of the Tobacco Excise Bill Pelham was to reflect his leader's complacency by claiming to be 'satisfied all the clamour that has been artfully worked up will end in nothing', and by maintaining that the opposition were 'half beaten before they came to the battle'.[1]

1. HMC, *Egmont Diary*, i, pp.311–12; Add. MSS. 27,732, ff. 95 and 138, and 27,733, f.35.

A certain wilful blindness visible in this attitude perhaps arose less from the ministry's faith in the strength of government voting than from necessity. The revived salt tax had proved less valuable than expected, and the Sinking Fund would need to be denuded, not for the first time, to make good the immediate deficit.

In addressing Parliament Walpole tried to make the possibility of further calls on the Sinking Fund, if his excise scheme were not passed, an additional argument for its immediate passage. Unless the proposed commodities could be excised, he further maintained, there would be a need to raise the land tax to two shillings again before the election. Thus plans went ahead which everyone knew would bring about debates of unusual excitement. The tactics of the Tories and dissident Whigs had been effective for three years, but had shown a certain ritualisation because the issues were largely manufactured. Members had tended to come to the House only for reasons of duty in an age when Cibber, Fielding, Gay and Handel had much to offer in the way of alternative entertainment. Now at last passions were stirred both in the nation and at Westminster.

Over 500 members were present on 14 March 1733 when Walpole moved that the duty on tobacco should be removed from the customs, by way of a preliminary to the proposed Excise Bill. The main ministerial argument, in a debate which lasted over eleven hours, was that the existing method of collection was inefficient and unproductive. The first opposition speakers seemed taken aback by Walpole's two-hour speech, which went into the ineffectiveness of customs collection with great detail and statistical expertise. Patriot orators did not try to meet quantification with equally reasoned argument but repeated their writers' theme asserting that British liberties would be lost or reduced by the activities of a host of new excise collectors, and the nation ruined by the proposed taxation. But ministerial optimism seemed justified when the final vote by exhausted members gave the government a majority by 61 votes against 106 Tories and 98 dissident Whigs. Such was the stifling atmosphere of the House during this debate that speakers on both sides paused to call for the building of a new and larger chamber in which to conduct their business, though their call was to go unheeded by purse-conscious ministers for over a hundred years and then be granted only after the accidental burning of the building.[1]

Measures which members were willing to approve in theory were not always acceptable in practice. In the three weeks which intervened between the foregoing vote and a substantive bill the opposition press redoubled its efforts, and waverers on the government side who had cast their votes reluctantly or absented themselves on the first occasion had time to reflect on their position, particularly in regard to the forthcoming election. As a result the full extent of Walpole's miscalculation was at last revealed. On 4 April when the Tobacco Bill was introduced it was allowed to go forward for a second reading by a majority of only thirty-six votes. The ministerial figure had dropped by twenty-nine, mainly through the absence of normal supporters, while that of the opposition was reduced by only four. Two days later the ministry's majority sank again when an opposition motion was rejected by only sixteen votes. The rot was apparently stopped a few days later, and ministerial face saved, with a majority of seventeen for refusing to receive a petition from the City of London against the bill. By this time, however, Walpole had seen enough. Having succeeded through phenomenal organisational efforts in increasing his majority by one vote in order to be able to back down relatively gracefully, he recognised that the time had come to call a halt. On 11 April he announced to a joyful House the abandonment of his schemes for tobacco and wine, thereby saving himself from almost certain defeat at a later stage.

The opponents of the Excise Bill had less cause for rejoicing than they supposed; Walpole had retreated in time, and once he gave up his scheme it became apparent that many of the Whigs who had deserted him rather than risk their constituencies were willing to return to their usual loyalty. This was first seen on 22 April when a petition brought by Barnard on behalf of dealers in tea and coffee, asking to be relieved of the burden of excise duties, was rejected by 250 votes to 150. And with the revival of the government's majority came new dissensions

1. Cobbett, *op.cit.*, viii, pp.1268–1313, and ix, pp.1–9; HMC, *Egmont Diary*, i, pp.342–61; HMC, *Carlisle*, pp.103–8; Coxe, *Walpole*, iii, pp.129–31; Sedgwick, *History of Parliament*, i, p.86; Plumb, *Walpole*, ii, pp.263–71. A modern account of the excise crisis is given by Paul Langford, *The Excise Crisis: Society and Politics in the Age of Walpole* (Oxford, 1975).

between Tories and Pulteneyites. The occasion of their quarrel was the composition of a committee which their efforts obtained, nominally to investigate frauds in the customs but actually to attack Walpole. Ministry and opposition drew up lists of their twenty-one candidates in the ballot for membership. Walpole named five independent Whigs who usually supported the ministry, together with a ballast of government placemen. He urged his followers at a meeting in the Cockpit, a usual venue for managerial rallies, to treat the matter as one of confidence and vote for his entire list. He did not scruple to tell his audience that Bolingbroke 'was at the bottom of it all' and remind them that if they did not stick together now they might let in not only Pulteney's friends but the Tories and supporters of the House of Stuart behind them. The opposition could not agree on their list of candidates, and a dispute between Pulteney and Wyndham resulted in an easy victory for the ministry, whose supporters followed Walpole's advice and stood solid. Both the number of government Whigs present on this occasion, nearly 300, and their almost unanimous vote for the minister's entire list, testified that his appeal to party instincts had succeeded irresistibly.[1]

A fortnight later the ministry scored another success, this time over a request by George II for a marriage portion for the Princess Royal. Once again the opposition fell out among themselves, with the dissident Whigs supporting the proposal for a sum of £80,000 but the Tories, reluctant as always to grant favours to the House of Hanover, insisting that this was too much.[2] The King was indignant that the matter should have been disputed at all and did not take kindly either to the information, supplied by his ministers, that the leaders of the opposition had recently been assigning themselves places in a new ministry to replace Walpole's in the event of his defeat over the excise scheme. George liked to think that he alone was responsible for the appointment of his ministries.

When Walpole, his anger unallayed by recent small victories, demanded the removal of many placemen who had voted against him in the excise crisis, the King made no objection. It is a measure of Walpole's exasperation that for once he threw

1. HMC, *Egmont Diary*, i, pp.365–7 and 371–2; Cobbett, *op.cit.*, ix, p.10.
2. Hervey, *Memoirs*, i, pp.169–71.

aside all caution and in doing so sowed a crop of dragon's teeth, dismissing former followers who were soon to spring up as opponents in both houses. Chesterfield, deprived of the Steward's staff, went into opposition followed by three Stanhope relations in the Lower House. After him went Bolton and Stair, each with a similar following, together with Marchmont, Montrose and Cobham, the last being patron of an important group of future Members of Parliament including . William Pitt, George Lyttelton and the brothers Richard and George Grenville. Some of the removals of Scottish peers from military commissions were regarded as particularly severe, but so too were the offences; at the height of the crisis even the government's majority in the House of Lords had seemed in danger, and the disaffected Scots were easy to select as scapegoats. The dismissals had the desired effect, and government control of the Upper House was restored.

Walpole had made a remarkable recovery from the dangerous situation into which his single-minded pursuit of fiscal reform had led him. His majority in both houses was intact again, and wavering supporters who had not actually been dismissed were suitably chastened. The royal couple too were secure. The King and Queen, Newcastle assured a supporter, 'talk of nothing but elections, and show all that come to court how desirous they are of a Whig Parliament'.[1] Walpole displayed a swift return of his usual political acumen when he backed down before the massive display of public opinion which opposition leaders had stirred up but not invented. Perhaps the most remarkable thing about the excise episode was not that his position had for a short while seemed seriously shaken but that he had been able to rally so quickly. Such resilience was an object lesson for would-be deserters. The recovery and its moral did not come too soon, for there now loomed a general election and new problems in Europe.

1. HMC, *Lonsdale*, p.125.

12

New Problems and New Opponents

DURING THE excise crisis the King's support for Walpole had continued unswervingly. Though George might sometimes give vent to his irritation at restrictions under which he felt that Walpole and the Whigs placed him, he always gave full support to the ministry when forced to face up to the possibility of an alternative containing Pulteney and the Tories. Queen Caroline remained enthusiastic in her admiration for Walpole, and her influence upon her husband increased rather than declined with the years. The dismissal of wavering supporters in the aftermath of the crisis was as much the royal couple's desire as the minister's, for punishments were part of the Hanoverian scheme of things. So were rewards. John Hervey, a witty if spiteful courtier who had remained loyal, was raised to the peerage as Baron Hervey. More significantly Newcastle's friend, Sir Philip Yorke, a brilliant lawyer and orator who had often carried ministerial business in the Commons, entered the House of Lords as Baron Hardwicke, at the same time joining the Cabinet to strengthen the ministry. But in some cases neither rewards nor punishments were deemed appropriate. At the height of the excise affair the Duke of Argyll had wavered, but the Campbell influence in Scotland was too vast and well entrenched for the government to risk his removal, and in any case his brother, the Earl of Islay, had remained loyal. The Campbells would bear watching, and were now added to the mounting list of problems which Walpole had to confront in addition to those posed by old and new opponents.

No sooner was the domestic crisis settled than the minister had to turn his eyes abroad. The nations of Europe were moving steadily towards a new war, which broke out in September 1733. Its nominal cause was a dispute over the elective throne of Poland, vacated by the death of Augustus II. The issue concerned the ambitions of the French and Spanish monarchs, who were now bound in a new Bourbon compact. Their interference in Eastern Europe threatened Austria directly. But when the Emperor Charles, confident in the British alliance concluded two years earlier, appealed for assistance against his two Bourbon assailants he met a polite refusal. Walpole's argument was that the alliance was a defensive one, and the Emperor was technically the aggressor in the Polish politics which had precipitated war. The First Lord's evasion of commitment reflected not only the difficulty of participating in a Central European war but also his genuine passion for peace and concern for his country's best interests. But neutrality was to bring diplomatic tension, lower Britain's reputation and provide the parliamentary opposition with frequent opportunities for belabouring his administration as timorous and lacking in appreciation of the nation's true role in Europe and the wider world.

When Parliament met for a short session on 17 January 1734, however, its debates did not at first give much attention to foreign affairs. Walpole rightly judged, and the opposition leaders feared, that a call for war on behalf of Austria would have little popular support, despite the recent clamour for alliance. The speech from the throne gave away little as to the ministry's intentions, baffling attempted opposition from the start, and Pulteneyite attempts at elucidation failed to stir up interest. In view of the tense European situation the service votes passed with less difficulty than usual. In the case of the Navy, for which Walpole proposed precautionary increases, some dissident members with mercantile interests actually supported the government, led by the vocal London representative, Sir John Barnard.

Even a customary opposition motion proposing a reduction of the army to twelve thousand men, made in frank contradiction of consistency, achieved less support than usual. Nor were attempts to revive indignation over the excise affair any more successful. In the course of the debates on the annual Mutiny Bill, opposition Whigs strove to obtain an indirect censure of the government's dismissal of serving officers for voting against the Tobacco Bill in the last session. But a motion by Morpeth for making certain officers irremovable except on professional grounds or by parliamentary address failed to warm the House, and had to be dropped without a division after Shippen and the Jacobite squadron refused point-blank to join Wyndham and Hanoverian Tories in giving countenance to a measure which appeared to be of benefit to the Whigs and the House of Hanover.[1]

The real object for all members was to make a favourable display in view of an impending general election. Despite a weak start the opposition Whigs and Tories drew together in February with an eye to the polls. Pulteney's friend Sandys was authorised to bring in a new Place Bill; such a measure would certainly please the voters. Unlike the usual Pension Bill, which would merely have reinforced existing legislation, this measure was intended to exclude officials sitting legally in the House, often because their offices had been created since the place legislation of William's and Anne's reigns. Walpole decided to risk opposing the bill in the Commons, rather than provoke a storm in the press by having it stifled in the Lords, but its rejection in a full House by only thirty-nine votes was a reminder of how easily his majority could fall on a popular issue.

This setback for the ministry encouraged some dissident Whigs to submerge their own feelings in another matter dear to the Tory party, though they did so in a confused and half-hearted manner to Walpole's ultimate advantage. In March young William Bromley, son of the old Tory of that name, introduced an attempt to restore triennial elections by repealing the Septennial Act of 1716. Walpole saw to it that the debate took on a full party flavour, thereby causing some Whigs to rally to the ministry out of party loyalty even if they saw advantages in the proposal. One independent Whig who sometimes supported the opposers, Sir William Lowther of the Yorkshire branch of that numerous family, based his support of the minister upon unashamedly partisan grounds, and other such men were similarly influenced by the government speakers' emphasis upon the dangers of resurgent Toryism inherent in the measure.

But it became clear that many members believed a restoration of the frequent elections would be popular with the voters. Bromley claimed that he was 'supported by the common voice of the people, and had it particularly recommended to me by the great majority of those I have the honour to represent in

1. Add. MSS. 27,733, f.11; Coxe, *Walpole*, iii, pp.153–6; HMC, *Carlisle*, pp.129–33.

Parliament'. Unfortunately for the opposition, however, Pulteney antagonised some likely sympathisers at the last minute by deciding to outbid the Tories and demand annual rather than triennial elections. He succeeded in pleasing no one, and Walpole won with 247 votes against the combined opposition of 184. But it was somewhat ominous that, in the pre-election situation, the minority included no fewer than seventy-seven Whigs, representing a substantial increase in the number of Pulteney's usual supporters.[1]

The preliminary skirmishes designed as a show-piece for interested spectators were now followed by the real contest in the constituencies. Here the press played a greater role than at any previous election. There had been ample time for preparation, with the opposition playing the theme of its excise campaign supplemented by the lesser tunes of foreign affairs from the Dunkirk episode to the War of the Polish Succession. As well as *The Craftsman* there were the *Grub Street Journal*, *Fog's Weekly Journal* and a host of lesser periodicals and ephemera to thunder out the message of Walpole's corruption, mismanagement and abuse of the constitution. An expanding provincial press added its contribution to the cause, and at least one such publication, *Howgrave's Stamford Journal*, was founded at this time as preparation for the election. Wide circulation was achieved by an opposition list of those ministerial members who had recently voted to retain the Septennial Act. Nor was the government press inactive. Walpole had in his service not only his long-standing organs *The Daily Courant* and *London Journal* but also *The Free Briton*, *The Weekly Register*, *Read's Weekly Journal*, *The Flying Post*, the *Hyp-Doctor* and the *Corn-cutter's Journal*.[2] Whipped up by both sides the nation enjoyed its election immensely, despite the fact that only a small proportion of the population was actually entitled to vote.

1. Cobbett, *Parliamentary History*, ix, pp.367–482; HMC, *Mar and Kellie*, i, pp.535–6; HMC, *Egmont Diary*, ii, pp.55–8.
2. D.H. Stevens, *Party Politics and English Journalism, 1702–1742*, chap. 8; Lawrence Hanson, *Government and the Press*, especially pp. 109–15; G.A. Cranfield, *Development of the Provincial Newspaper, 1700–1760*, p.21 and chap. 6 *passim*. Among local newspapers which supported Walpole at about this time were the *Northampton Mercury*, *Leeds Mercury*, *Norwich Mercury*, *York Journal*, *Gloucester Journal*, *Ipswich Journal*, *Kentish Post* and *Derby Mercury*. Against him were the *York Courant*, *Norwich Gazette*, *Chester Courant*, *Farley's Bristol Newspaper* and *Farley's Exeter Journal*.

Sometimes enthusiasm spilt over into violence or near-violence, and in some Tory villages Walpole was burned in effigy, with Guy Fawkes, the Pope and Louis of France giving up their usual place for the occasion.

Despite early signs of pressure against government candidates Walpole's patronage machinery carried those constituencies where it usually held sway, and Newcastle was able to report success in his areas of specialism despite the manifest signs of opposition activity.[1] But there were failures in some open constituencies like Yorkshire, the largest county in terms of its electorate as well as its size, and the prestigious urban shire of Middlesex where Pulteney was returned in combination with a Tory. In other counties Tories made a number of gains at the expense of ministerial and, in some cases, dissident Whigs; even in Norfolk two Tories scraped home to replace the sitting ministerial Whigs. But Horatio Walpole's fears for his candidacy at Norwich proved to be unjustified and he managed to secure his return, along with that of a Whig colleague, though the partisan behaviour of the sheriff as returning officer caused an incensed Tory newspaper editor to suggest ironically that Norwich elections might now be abolished to make way for shrieval choice.[2]

Throughout the country appeals to national distaste at the Excise Bill had a powerful influence. Nevertheless most of the English boroughs remained Whig, as they had been since 1715, while in Scotland the Campbell interest ensured that Walpole would continue to receive the support of Whigs elected in the Northern Kingdom. Overall the government's majority dropped by only about sixteen members, with the Tories gaining nineteen and opposition Whigs losing three as compared with the situation at the dissolution of the last Parliament. The fall in Walpole's following was thus insignificant in numbers, for he still had a theoretical majority of about 100.[3] But the blow to his prestige was more considerable; there was no hiding the fact that where the electorate had been allowed untrammelled

1. Add. MSS. 32,689, f. 185, 32,688, f. 190, and 27,773, ff. 63 and 102.
2. *Norwich Gazette*, 18 May and 28 August 1736. The editor was later indicted and made to apologise for his assertions.
3. B.D. Henning, A.S. Foord and Barbara L. Mathias (eds.), *Crises in English History 1066–1945* (New York 1964), pp.345–64; Plumb, *Walpole*, ii, pp.314–24; Add. MSS. 32,680, f.141.

expression of its feelings it had come down against the ministry. The result was a warning, but Walpole was at least safe for a further seven-year term.

There were indeed some observers, including able and far-sighted men, who calculated that Walpole's considerable majority could not survive the effect of recent events for a further full term. One such speculator was the fourth Duke of Bedford, who had succeeded to his peerage in the previous year. Bedford assumed that it would be better to join the government's opponents and come into office thereafter than to continue his family's adherence to the main part of the Whig party under Walpole. Such assessments were right in the long term but wrong in the time-scale which they assigned to Walpole's fall: he was to last in office for nearly eight years more and even survive the first effects of yet another general election.

Still not much past the height of his powers after the vast and time-consuming exertions of the last years' stormy passages, Walpole was indeed a formidable figure. His political status was even reflected in his appearance. He had grown enormous in weight and girth, as his portraits show. Always a large man, he now made the worst efforts of hostile caricaturists seem not unreasonable. Mentally, however, he was still alert and well in control of most situations. His decision to keep Britain out of the current continental imbroglio was carried through in face of doubts expressed by some colleagues and muted opposition from the King, whose interest as ruler of a North German province demanded support for the Emperor. The effort of convincing both George and Caroline had been particularly taxing and was likely to need repetition from time to time, for the royal couple were constantly urged towards the interventionist course by Hatorff, the Hanoverian minister resident in London. These pressures Walpole was able and more than willing to face, together with the likely attitude of the fickle public if anything went wrong. Now settled in a house at 10 Downing Street,[1] donated by the King for the use of the

1. 'The palace in Downing Street', as Walpole's youngest son called it, had undergone a complete renovation, lasting several years, since George II handed it over – *The Letters of Horace Walpole* (Cunningham ed.), i, p.324.

Treasury and its First Lord, Walpole appears to have had no doubts about either the rectitude of his policies for Britain or his ability to continue to carry them through.

Parliament was, as always, the centre of his attention. In the excise crisis the ministry's monolithic control of the House of Lords had trembled. At one point, ostensibly on a belated attempt to censure his long-term settlement of the South Sea affair, the ministerial majority in the Upper House dropped as low as one vote, and Walpole was saved only by the overwhelming majority of bishops and Scottish peers who customarily supported the ministry. The dismissals which followed this affair were severe, commensurate with the gravity of the offence. The ejected Chesterfield, Marchmont, Cobham and Bolton permanently joined Carteret and the opposition in the Lords' House. But attempts by Chesterfield in the election to wrest control of this House from Walpole by securing the election of the dissidents' nominees as the sixteen representative peers of Scotland had been frustrated by the First Lord's energetic intervention. Scotland returned sixteen government peers as usual.

In the Commons, however, the opposition peers were more successful in obtaining new supporters. The new House contained not only Marchmont's twin sons, Lord Polworth and Alexander Hume Campbell, but also several able relations and protegés of Lord Cobham, led by William Pitt, Richard Grenville and George Lyttelton. Contemptuously dubbed 'boy' Patriots by Walpole, to distinguish them from those older Whig dissidents who liked to be known as the Patriot party, these young men were nevertheless soon to be a thorn in his side. When later joined by Grenville's younger brother George the coterie included two future first ministers as well as several other forceful speakers. Together with Bedford's several followers in the Lower House and other recently disobliged members, these new opponents would constitute a formidable addition to Walpole's normal problems of control. The careful calculation and daily exertions of Commons management were from now on more important than ever.

Other potential problems could be identified. The bishops, after their spectacular rally to the government during the recent crisis, might well demand a *quid pro quo*. But the Church could not presume too much from its support; Walpole had to keep a careful balance between rival interests, and any attempt further to penalise the Protestant dissenters would have to be quashed. The royal couple too were causing some anxiety. George took the opportunity to blame his ministers petulantly for the election setbacks and at the same time remind them that Whig hegemony could not be taken for granted. According to Hervey the King 'publicly accused the Whigs of negligence; saying at the same time, that if the Tories had had a quarter of the support from the government that the Whigs had received from it for twenty years together, they would never have suffered the Crown to be pushed and the Court to be distressed in the manner it now was'. Even Caroline harped on the same theme: 'This is always the way of your nasty Whigs: though they themselves are supported by the Crown, they are always lukewarm in returning that support to the Crown'.[1] Such sentiments no doubt reflected royal frustration in the matter of Walpole's refusal to support the Emperor. But the House of Hanover, like the Church, could not be allowed to upset the well-balanced system which Walpole had so painstakingly set up over many years; the alliance with France might be dead in spirit but it was still technically in operation, despite the newer alignment with Austria, and Britain could not afford war with France for the sake of Hanoverian interests.

Finally, the Scottish contingent in the Commons, some of whom had followed Argyll's recent example of increasing restiveness, would have to be kept in line. Argyll's discontent arose from the fact that he had never been given the same degree of participation in government patronage as some of his predecessors in the management of Scottish affairs. Argyll's influence in his own country was nevertheless considerably enhanced by his alliance with government, and he might need to be sharply reminded of that fact. As for the Scottish members, the privileges they enjoyed came from Treasury patronage, whatever they might owe to Argyll at election time, and they too would need to be recalled from time to time, to a sense of their commitments.

Not all the auspices spoke of the need for wariness. The opposition's failure to more than slightly reduce Walpole's majority in the general election broke the spirit of one of its

1. Hervey, *Memoirs*, i, p.292

principal leaders. Bolingbroke was perhaps the most brilliant politician of his generation, but he had no track record of persistence in the face of adversity. Despairing after nearly a decade of attempts to bring together the disparate and often idiosyncratic elements of the opposition Whigs and Tories, he gave up the struggle and retired in 1735 to France, from whence his frequent plaints about the state of British politics had little effect upon his former followers. Bolingbroke's often-repeated assertion that party principles had disappeared was at most a half-truth whose reciprocal falsity was enough to weaken fatally his attempts to return politics to a seventeenth-century style of court versus country alignment.

The absence of Bolingbroke's energetic personality from active politics could not but harm his ambition of overthrowing Walpolean whiggery. Apart from the standard party issues which arose every session, fierce Tory reaction to attempts to repeal the Test Act was shortly to show that major former issues slept but lightly. At the same time the united Whig response to any suggestions of danger from Jacobitism, which Walpole so often turned to tactical advantage, was enough to testify that this primary 'Revolution principle' was undiminished in the array of party causes. There was, therefore, every expectation that he would continue to be able to divide his enemies and unite his followers on a party basis, so that the large body of independent Whigs who still supported the government alongside the better-publicised placemen would continue to do so. Walpole continued to be assisted by divisions among his opponents. The dilemma of those opposition leaders who tried to minimise the differences between their followers was symbolized in 1734 by the Rumpsteak Club, founded by Bedford and other dissident Whig Peers, a social and political body which excluded Tory peers from membership even when they possessed the necessary qualification for membership, namely the experience of having had the King's back turned upon them.[1]

The Commons assembled quietly enough, despite the Pulteneyites' previous threat of impeaching ministers for their foreign policy and manipulation of the Scottish peerage elections. Onslow was re-elected to the chair without opposition,

1. HMC, *Egmont Diary*, ii, p.14.

and early divisions provided no surprises: in the Address the ministry obtained a majority of eighty votes. Walpole strongly defended those portions of the speech from the throne which he had written for the King on the subject of Britain's neutrality in the War of the Polish Succession. Britain, he maintained, was close to the centre of international commerce; her expanding trade and delicate system of credit could be disrupted, or even destroyed in some areas, by the exigencies of war. The opposition claimed, in this and succeeding debates, that failure to intervene in the European conflict might lead to Austria's losing control of Naples and Sicily to Spain, to the detriment of the British trade in the Mediterranean. But this view was countered by ministerial argument that war might bring losses not just in the Mediterranean but in all oceans where British ships would encounter the formidable combination of Bourbon fleets and privateers. Pulteney contended that Britain had 'peace without rest, and war without hostilities'. Walpole retorted: 'Not one drop of English blood split, or one shilling of English money spent'. It was Walpole's stand which the Commons upheld.

In the longer run the Emperor held his own without direct British assistance, and British intervention in the interest of European stability would have proved to be difficult of execution in areas distant from Britain's usual sphere of military activity. Many of Walpole's hearers were also mindful that by refusing hostilities with France at this stage, Britain was staving off the chance of a French-sponsored Jacobite invasion which was an increasing threat since the decline of the Anglo-French alliance after 1731. Walpole's policy was not heroic, but it made good sense in that nothing in his conduct of office had prepared the nation for war.

Further debates showed a slight fall in government majorities after the success of the Address, usually when finance was involved. The votes made clear that the House was not prepared for new defence expenditure. Although opposition to the needs of the Navy was unusual, the ministry's call for a precautionary increase of 10,000 seamen, an expansion of 50%, raised passionate criticism from mercantile interests which would suffer from pressed conscriptions. On this vote the ministerial majority fell to seventy-three, and on a demand for an augmented land force of 25,000 it descended further to fifty-three. But occasional falls in support where extra expense might be involved were to be expected, and they served to demonstrate Walpole's prudence in keeping Britain generally free of higher monetary commitment to military expenditure.[1]

Much of the rest of the session was taken up with election petitions, which were contested bitterly at the bar of the House in debates sometimes extending over a number of days. Such was the persistence of the Tories and their allies that a number of divisions on the technicalities of rights of electors went against the ministry. In response Walpole roused his supporters to put on a show of force over the Wells petition on 25 March, riding rough-shod over earlier division results to vote two Whig petitioners duly elected. But such demonstrations could not be attempted too often, and when he tried to repeat this success three days later by backing some petitioners' challenge against the Tories elected for Marlborough, he was frustrated by the arguments of Jekyll, the proudly independent Master of the Rolls, in favour of the sitting members. The Tory diarist Edward Harley, nephew of Walpole's old opponent, the Earl of Oxford, recorded gleefully 'Sir Robert finding he could not spirit up his tools, he gave up the question'. With some hesitation by Walpole's independent supporters to repeat the blatant means used over the Wells election, the ministry ended the session barely a net gainer on the voting over petitions.[2]

While these hearings were continuing the Place Bill was brought in again. The debate in which this bill was rejected was generally considered remarkable less for the voting, which gave the ministry a majority of thirteen fewer than in the previous year, than for the fact that the occasion was chosen for the maiden speeches of the young hopefuls of the opposition, Grenville, Pitt and Lyttelton.[3] These orations, especially William Pitt's, heralded several years of vitriolic attacks which portrayed Walpole as corrupting British public life and the King as betraying British interests for the sake of Hanover. For the moment the efforts of the Boy Patriots could be laughed

1. For the foregoing debates, Cobbett, *Parliamentary History*, ix, pp.671–720 and 800–24; HMC, *Carlisle*, pp.147–52.
2. Harley Diary, Cambridge University Library. Add. MSS. 6,851, i, ff.15 and 18–20; HMC, *Egmont Diary*, ii, p.167; Hervey, *Memoirs*, ii, p.418.
3. Harley Diary, i, p.25.

off, albeit wryly, but no one could mistake the quality of the new youthful fervour which they brought to debate.

Having survived the first session of the new House relatively easily, Walpole found the tensions of public life considerably lightened for the moment. While Bolingbroke, from his refuge in France, demanded of his friends in England that 'a zealous High Priest may arise, and these priests of Baal may be hewed to pieces', the First Lord retired to Norfolk for an unusual period of ease.[1] In Europe no new issue arose during the summer of 1735 which seemed likely to help the opposition, for hostilities between France and Austria had by now largely ceased. As a result Parliament was poorly attended in the first two months of the next session. The ministry took credit for the cessation of European hostilities, which they attributed to Britain's non-intervention. With even Pulteney absent, and Wyndham untypically quiet, Walpole might have been forgiven for thinking that the whole meeting would pass in tranquillity. In the event it did not. The opposition leaders were communing desperately and lying low to avoid conflict among their own followers over a new issue which was about to erupt: alleged danger for the Church of England.

This matter arose with a proposal sponsored by the three leading denominations of Protestant dissenters, Presbyterians, Congregationalists and Baptists, for the repeal of the religious tests of Charles II's reign. Their endeavour promised to revive religious issues in politics on a scale not yet seen in Walpole's ministry. An earlier attempt, designed before the general election to appeal to Whig members with dissenting constituents, had been withdrawn at Walpole's instance to avoid antagonising the still more formidable interest of the Church of England. When on 12 March 1736 an opposition Whig moved for the repeal of the Test Act the First Lord again threw his weight against the attempt for fear of arousing Anglican passions. Edward Harley noted in his diary that 'most of his creatures, though in their hearts for it, voted against the repeal'. The proposal saw ministerial Whigs unwontedly supported by the Tories in a majority of 251 votes to 123. Hard on the heels of this matter came another bill, to take the recovery of tithes out of the hands of the ecclesiastical courts and

1. Add. MSS. 34,196, p.95.

prevent the undue harassment of Quakers and others who took a stand against paying Church dues. Against this measure Gibson, Bishop of London, mobilised church opposition. But Gibson found himself at odds with Walpole, who saw no harm in offering some compensation to mollify the more moderate dissenters. The bill passed in the Commons with both ministerial and opposition Whigs supporting it, but the Anglicans were safely reassured when it was rejected in the Lords, mainly by the arguments of Lord Chancellor Talbot and Hardwicke together with most of the bishops.[1]

Nor did the religious issues end here. The irrepressible Jekyll chose this moment to bring forward a Mortmain Bill with the ostensible purpose of preventing cases, of which some had occurred recently, where persons left their estates to charity, thereby depriving their legitimate heirs of inheritance. The real purpose of the bill's supporters, in the opinion of the indignant Tories, was to strike at Church institutions and other charities which were likely to receive estates by testament in mortmain. In an attempted compromise Walpole agreed to except universities from the bill, but otherwise it went forward with the support of both government and dissenting Whigs, much to the dissatisfaction of churchmen and Tories.[2] Taken together, the religious disputes of the session had the result of driving a wedge between Walpole and Gibson. The Bishop had long been taking too independent a line, in Walpole's opinion, not least by frustrating Queen Caroline's desire to promote theologically advanced prelates. Gibson was now replaced by Newcastle as the ministry's chief manager of ecclesiastical patronage. Altogether Walpole succeeded in freeing himself of an increasingly embarrassing ally, while at the same time widening divisions among the opposition by temporarily reuniting all Whigs in defence of the dissenters, short of repeal of the political tests.

Before the end of the session Walpole received overtures of reconciliation from Pulteney which were not rejected out of hand, though they came to nothing.[3] It would be possible to

1. Harley Diary, i, ff.60–1 and 62–6; Cobbett, *op.cit.*, ix, pp.1046–59; Hervey, *Memoirs*, ii, pp.530–8; HMC, *Carlisle*, p. 165; T.F.J. Kendrick, 'Sir Robert Walpole . . . and the Bishops 1733–1736', *HJ*, xi (1968), pp.430–33.
2. Harley Diary, i, pp.57–60.
3. Coxe, *Walpole*, iii, p.321.

argue that Walpole might have done better at this point to take seriously the possibility of attaching to his own side the opposition's most able leader. But such possibilities were more apparent than real; Walpole could no more have borne this ambitious politician in his ministry than he had been able to twelve years earlier, when he had preferred Newcastle to Pulteney for the secretaryship of state.

By common consent after the recent revival of contentious religious issues, both Walpole and his Whig opponents allowed them to die down again as too unpredictable and inflammatory. Walpole had quarrelled irrevocably with Gibson and was unwilling to give further offence to the Church. Pulteney and Carteret, as it transpired, had a new plan which might result in the defection of Frederick, Prince of Wales, to the opposition, and they were anxious not to further alienate the Tories. Because the King prolonged his usual stay in Hanover and then became ill on his arrival in England, the opening of Parliament took place late, on 1 February 1737. The first contentious debate was on 18 February over Walpole's intention of keeping land forces at 18,000 men. Ministerial speakers urged the dangers of Jacobitism and of internal disturbances such as those at Edinburgh the previous year. On that occasion the unpopular John Porteous, captain of the city guard, gave orders for shooting at a mob during the hanging of a smuggler sentenced to death for murder, was reprieved by the Queen acting as Regent in the King's absence, and was finally hanged by an act of mob vengeance.

The Prince of Wales was present in the gallery of the Commons during this debate. He had been resident in Britain for several years but preferred to remain out of the limelight to conciliate his father, for relations between the two men were no better than those between George I and George II in the previous generation. Opposition speakers ranged widely over old scores, seeing riots as no reason for keeping the forces at a high level. The younger Whigs were particularly prominent, concentrating their oratory on the dismissal of officers for political purposes; another instance had recently occurred, for Pitt had been dismissed from his cornetcy of horse at Walpole's instance. Despite such efforts, however, the ministry obtained a respectable majority of sixty-nine votes for the proposed size of the army.[1]

But the army debate was merely a preliminary skirmish for the Prince's business, which had been mentioned in the course of discussion but not pursued. Since Frederick came to England he had received an *ex gratia* allowance of £50,000 out of the Civil List, half the sum which his father had enjoyed under George I. Though the Whig opposition had more than once shown willingness to support the Prince's case for a much-needed increase, he had exercised caution until after his marriage, in 1735, with Augusta of Saxe-Gotha. This event placed new strains upon his finances; and to add to the bad feelings, the King made difficulty about settling a jointure upon the Princess. In allowing Pulteney to ask the Commons for an independent allowance of £100,000 the Prince was reported by Egmont to be confident of being 'assisted by the Tory party and all the malcontent Whigs' and hopeful too of sympathy from some independent supporters of the court. Inspired by a similar belief, Walpole persuaded the King on 21 February, on the eve of the intended debate, to offer to secure the £50,000 to the Prince for life and to settle the jointure immediately. The difficult errand of offering this none-too-generous arrangement to the Prince was given to Hardwicke, who on the same day had received the seals of Lord Chancellor consequent upon the death of Talbot. To the same unhappy envoy fell the duty of conveying the Prince's reply, which was an indignant refusal to stop the matter being brought before the House. The King and Queen reacted to their son's stand with the greatest wrath, vented in part on Walpole and other ministers for failing to settle the haggle out of the public eye.

The storm which followed in the Commons was largely of the King's own making. Members had not forgotten that the generous settlement of the Civil List obtained by Walpole at George's accession had been envisaged, though this was not directly specified, as including a sum for the Prince equal to that which his father had received in the same situation. Walpole took active steps to secure the support of wavering members against a motion for an increased allowance to Prince

1. Harley Diary, i, f.71; Boyer, *Political State*, liv, pp.318–24 and 409–27; HMC, *Egmont Diary*, ii, pp.350–3.

Frederick, and an interesting glimpse is obtained of the methods used by the Treasury. The diarist Harley noted that the minister or his representative approached the Jacobite member Watkin Williams Wynn and offered 'that if he or Mr Shippen would vote against it and bring over some of the Tories to do the same' the government would obtain £20,000 to be paid to the widow of one of the insurgents executed after the Rebellion of 1715, the Earl of Derwentwater. Wynn rejected this deal, but some forty-five Tories nevertheless absented themselves from the division. According to another source these included their leader Wyndham even though he spoke, almost alone among his fellows, on the Prince's behalf. Walpole was assisted by Tory reluctance to help any member of the Hanoverian house. The virtual abstention of so many opposition voters proved crucial, for Pulteney's motion was lost by 234 votes to 204. At the height of the debate Walpole affected to weep at the thought of a rupture between royal father and son. Tears came easily to eighteenth-century politicians in the emotion of rhetoric.[1]

The remainder of the session was taken up with the Porteous affair. In the House of Lords, Carteret devised a bill to make an example of the Edinburgh civic authorities for permitting the riots to get out of hand. Newcastle and Hardwicke stated their approval of the measure and thus gave it the seal of government approval, much to Walpole's embarrassment. The two ministers' motive appears to have been a private one, pursuit of a vendetta with the Duke of Argyll; but by taking this course they succeeded, as the wily Carteret fully intended, in driving a wedge between government and its principal supporter in Scotland. When the bill came before the Commons the Tories objected strongly to it on their usual principle of opposing bills smacking of 'pain and penalties'. To their delight they found allies in the Scottish members, who deserted the government side to defend the honour of their capital city.

So good an opportunity for embarrassing the ministry was not often presented, and at one point in the committee stage the bill was saved only by the chairman's casting vote. Despite this reprieve, the bill emerged from the Lower House amended almost beyond recognition. Only two penalties were left: a fine

1. Harley Diary, i, ff. 72–81; HMC, *Carlisle*, p.178; Dodington's 'Narrative' in *Dodington Diary* (ed. H.P. Wyndham, 1784), pp.443–4 and 469.

on the city of Edinburgh, to be paid as compensation to Porteous' widow, and the disablement of its Provost from holding office for the future. Having supervised this emasculation to please his Scottish supporters, Walpole saw to it that no attempt was made by ministerial speakers in the Lords to reinstate the stringent provisions originally inserted.[1] But his belated action to restrain his colleagues met only limited success. Thereafter Argyll drifted rapidly away from the ministerial camp, with results which were to be seriously detrimental to Walpole's majority in the long run.

Perhaps the most damaging effect of this session, in retrospect, was Pulteney's success in attaching the Prince of Wales to his cause. In the matter of increasing the Prince's allowance Walpole had been frustrated in his more generous intentions by the King's personal wishes, arising from the irrevocable hostility which so often characterised relations between fathers and sons of the Hanoverian royal house. Pulteney's hope of permanently attaching to his own cause the prestige of the heir's 'reversionary interest' in the throne was now to become a reality, making the opposition far more respectable by negating the ministerial argument that opposition to the crown was in some sense unconstitutional. From now on both sides had a member of the royal family among their supporters, and the heir would attract an increasing number of time-servers who calculated that their interest would be better served by joining the cause of the future.

In deference to the Prince's wishes Pulteney did not personally oppose the government on the Edinburgh Bill, and this apparent playing down of hostility led some to suppose correctly that Pulteney and his principal colleague in the Upper House, Carteret, wished to leave the way open for a reunion with Walpole, under the aegis of a reconciliation between King and Prince. A step similar to the celebrated occasion in 1720, when Walpole and Townshend had rejoined Stanhope's ministry to the accompaniment of a formal reconciliation of royal father and son, would have been difficult. Apart from private antagonism, Walpole objected to any union for want of a sufficient number of offices. But from this time a suspicion

1. Harley Diary, i, ff. 89–96; Hervey, *Memoirs*, iii, pp.734–5; Cobbett, *op.cit.*, x, pp.247–319.

remained among some elements of the Whig opposition that Pulteney was willing to come to terms with the ministry at their expense. This belief remained and deepened, even after further events in the royal family demonstrated that a reconciliation between George and Frederick was further off than ever, fuelling opposition jealousies to Walpole's advantage.

In September 1737 the Prince and Princess, with a new-born daughter, left the royal palace of St James's and set up a new establishment at Leicester House, where their son the future George III was born the following year. For Walpole the move was an ominous one. Despite dissension which the Prince's inclusion in the opposition camp might bring about there was no doubt the general effect of his presence would be to give new stimulus to the ministry's critics. The number and effectiveness of these had been increased in the last four years, partly by Walpole's dismissals, partly by the quarrel in the royal family, but above all by the calculations of an increasing number of politicians looking to the minister's eventual fall. Moreover he was weakened in November 1737 by the death of his ally at court, Queen Caroline. He had already been in high office for sixteen years, a term unprecedented in living memory and hardly paralleled in earlier periods.

In the summer of the same year a major change occurred in Walpole's personal life. For many years he had been estranged from Catherine, but her death in August at the age of 55 gave him, perhaps after some initial regrets over the failure of their early hopes, the opportunity to regularise his relationship with Maria. This he duly did, after a decent interval, and they were married early in the following year. Walpole's children by his first marriage remained loyal, especially young Horace, and for a short time Walpole was to enjoy a full family life. A group portrait attributed to Charles Gervas and John Wootton in 1738 shows Sir Robert and Maria at the centre of a group composed of their daughter Maria, Catherine's children including her two daughters who had died many years earlier, and his late sister Dorothy's husband Townshend.[1] The stilted poses conceal the family feeling which motivated the portrait's commissioning.

1. The younger Catherine died in 1722, Mary in 1731 and Townshend in 1738. The portrait is now at Houghton Hall after a long absence.

13
The End of an Era

THE MISCELLANEOUS opposition which Walpole now faced had
grown formidable with the years. Its oldest element was the
Tories. Containing a large number of Hanoverian supporters
as well as a probably smaller group of committed Jacobite
members, this party also harboured many who defy easy
classification. A substantial section had no real wish to see the
Pretender established on the throne of Britain but nevertheless
corresponded with him and even occasionally sent a small
donation as an insurance in case he should ever succeed in
returning to the country of his birth. Such men were not
Jacobites in any real sense, though the court at St Germain was
only too willing to believe that they were. The endemic muddle,
backbiting and euphoric optimism which characterised this
court gave little confidence to those in Britain who preferred to
hedge their bets.[1]

The experience of the next decade was to show that most
Tories, given the opportunity, were willing to give their allegiance to a prince of the Hanoverian line rather than to a
dimly-perceived monarch 'over the water'. The principal obstacle to a transfer of the instinctive Tory loyalism to the new royal
house lay not in the Tories themselves but in the incumbent
Hanoverian King and his son. Prince Frederick was not yet,
and his father never became, convinced that the Tory party
could be a potent ally in supporting the House of Hanover
against its cocooning Whig protectors. The Prince was to realise
this very soon after the Jacobite rising in 1745 revealed that
very few English Tories were willing to risk their lives and
estates in the old cause. But during Walpole's last years of office
the Tories remained a highly distinct and disgruntled element
of the opposition liable to show their displeasure by voting

1. Some modern historians have maintained that the Tory party was Jacobite, or mainly so, but this view has not won general acceptance. See E.
Cruickshanks, *Political Untouchables: the Tories and the '45* (1979). For the above
view see L. Colley, *In Defiance of Oligarchy: The Tory Party 1714–60* (Cambridge, 1982).

from time to time against the Prince's wishes. Tory distrust of Pulteney's set of Whigs was equally marked. Experience showed that any attempt by these Whigs to censure Walpole was by no means acceptable to the Tories if this meant that the First Lord would be succeeded by Pulteney himself.

The Whig opposition to Walpole's administration was similarly diverse and irresolute. Pulteney himself, together with his close friends Samuel Sandys, Phillips Gybbon, and Sir John Rushout, constituted the original and most formidable part of the 'Patriot' Whig opposition. But the most prestigious element was now the Prince of Wales' dozen or so followers who were members of the House of Commons. The Prince's continuing distaste for the Tories was far from causing him to refuse their assistance when offered but made him an asset to the Whig opposition, and in particular a valuable reinforcement for the Pulteneyites. The known predeliction of Carteret, their principal figure in the House of Lords, for working with the House of Hanover was a strong recommendation to the Prince, who shared his father's reservations about the 'republicanism' of many Whigs.

In the years which followed Frederick's move into opposition the Pulteney-Carteret group held themselves aloof not only from Tories but also from those Whigs who were beginning to develop the philosophy of a 'Broad Bottom', or active coalition of Whig dissidents and Tories. Such Whigs wished to overthrow Walpole and his associates to form a shared or cross-party ministry including the leading Tories.

A principal exponent of 'Broad Bottom' philosophy was the Earl of Chesterfield, who was aided by a miscellaneous group of Whigs including the Duke of Bedford, Lord Cobham and their associates in the Commons, such as William Pitt. Later these men were to be reinforced by new defectors from the ministry, among them the Duke of Argyll and George Bubb Dodington. Argyll influenced many Scots in the House of Commons, while Dodington controlled his three fellow members for the constituency of Weymouth and Melcombe Regis. For these men the overthrow of Walpole was more important than the traditional Whig bar to close cooperation with the Tories.

If Walpole's opponents were growing more formidable, he could still rely on their differences. In terms of policies there was as much to distinguish the various opposition groups from each other as from the ministry. Some had strongly advocated British participation in the War of the Polish Succession on behalf of the Emperor, others had been reluctant to sanction the expense involved. Over Hanover there was an even more marked division. Pulteney and Carteret were prepared to humour George II and the Prince of Wales by refusing to participate in attacks on the royal interest in Hanover, but the Tories and some of the Broad Bottom Whigs were active in its denunciation. Particularly vociferous was the powerful young orator Pitt, who never lost an opportunity to condemn the King's attachment to the electorate. Such were the disparate policies of the men who opposed Walpole's clear ideas and united government party. The allies who set up their banners under the Prince had little in common except a desire to overthrow the administration and enjoy the fruits of office for themselves.

The rift in the royal family was now complete, and in expectation that the question of the Prince's allowance would be raised again many manoeuvres were set on foot in the autumn of 1737. Most of these centred upon obtaining support from the Tories.

Walpole induced the King to give a pension to the impecunious daughter of the late Earl of Oxford, Lady Kinnoul, an investment which paid off handsomely in the form of gratitude from the Harley family and their parliamentary associates. The Prince of Wales too was brought by Pulteney to cultivate leading Hanoverian Tories, particularly Wyndham. Lord Stair, son of the persecutor of the Macdonalds of Glencoe and an ally of Bolingbroke, wrote to Marchmont, 'I am very far from being ashamed to take the assistance of Tories to preserve our constitution'. But Walpole had the easier task, for his purpose was the limited one of continuing to sow the seeds of dissension among the opposition. Horatio noted in January 1738 when Parliament assembled that the ground was ready: 'The opponents being a body composed of men of different principles and of different views are much disjointed, and have not any set scheme of opposition'. Prince Frederick soon bore out this judgement by refusing to join in his new friends' annual motion for reducing the army to twelve thousand men. No Hanoverian could contemplate cutting down the military basis of his family's claim to the throne. To Walpole's relief, the Tories consequently failed to lend any support to proposals for an increased allowance for the Prince.[1] It was an auspicious start for the ministry.

The first hint of the storm brewing between Britain and Spain took the form of a petition, presented to the Commons in March by merchants engaged in the West Indies trade, complaining of damage to property and atrocities committed upon British seamen by the Spanish navy in its frequent searches for contraband merchandise. The opposition strung out debates over several days by insisting on listening to the merchants in person. In winding up, Pulteney tabled several motions condemning Spanish infringements of trading rights and the often cruel manner in which the searches were carried out. Walpole's attempts to cool the debate focused upon his knowledge that not all the incidents were unprovoked and that many of the goods carried by British traders were in flagrant violation of treaty rights. But he sensed in the mood of the Commons a drift towards new conflict with Spain. In an effort to stem this he offered a moderate alternative to the opposition's motions, though such was the mood of the House that his proposal was passed by only forty-five votes in a crowded meeting.[2] For the moment the matter stopped here, but Walpole began to consider a serious negotiation with the Spanish court in order to come to an agreement about the disputed details of trade and avoid further conflict.

One more delicate problem had to be negotiated. For the last two years the reporting of parliamentary debates in newspapers and magazines had been particularly detailed and specific. On 13 April Speaker Onslow complained to the House of this constant violation of earlier standing orders. He emphasised the dangers of misrepresentation of members' speeches and mentioned a recent case when a newspaper had printed the King's reply to the Address before it had been reported from the chair. The debate made it clear that ministerial speakers, led by Walpole and his usual spokesmen, Sir William Yonge and Thomas Winnington, had concerted their line with

1. *The Wentworth Papers*, p.534; HMC, *14th Report*, ix, p.10; Add. MSS. 34,521, f.13.
2. Harley Diary, i, ff. 101–2 and 107–8; HMC, *14th Report*, ix, pp.13 and 239–40; Cobbett, *Parliamentary History*, x, pp.561–727.

the Speaker. They called for a resolution asserting that parliamentary reporting was a breach of privilege, and they defined such privilege as extending to the recess rather than as being confined, as was usually assumed, to the period when the House was in session. Walpole called for the 'utmost severity' towards any newswriter presuming to report debates or other parliamentary proceedings, whether during a session or not.

This move drove a new wedge between the opposition speakers. Pulteney agreed with the minister and was not only against the everyday reporting of speeches 'even though they were not misrepresented' but was also in favour of suppressing reports published during the recess. A year or two earlier Pulteney might have opposed the ministry on this issue; now, as the parliamentary upholder of the heir to the throne, he held back, for he saw hope of office in the not-too-distant future and was aware, and none more so than he, of the damage which a frank and untrammelled press could do to a ministry. Walpole was opposed outspokenly only by the Tories. Wyndham admitted that instances of misrepresentation had occurred, but disliked the idea of 'the prejudice which the public think they will sustain, by being deprived of all knowledge of what passes in this House, otherwise than by the printed votes.' He was against stretching the ban of the House to reporting in the recess. Contemptuously he dismissed Pulteney's suggestion of reserving the right of newspapers to publish debates after the final dissolution of Parliament, a practice which would have made such reports up to seven years out of date when they saw the light of day.[1]

In the outcome Walpole's resolution was passed, though experience was to show that the extension of the Commons' ban to the recess could not be made good without greater severity than he was willing to sustain. Such reporting as continued was largely confined to the monthly magazines rather than daily newspapers, and was couched in the quasi-concealed form of debates in 'The Political Club' or 'The Senate of Lilliput'. Considering the advantages the opposition had derived in recent years from a dissemination of detailed information about proceedings in Parliament, the resolution of

1. *Marchmont Papers*, ii, pp.99–100; Cobbett, *Parliamentary History*, x, pp.800–12.

13 April was a victory for Walpole's government and a set-back for those members of the opposition, especially the Tories, whose expectations of returning to power were least. The Pulteneyites' compliance with his suppression of news gained little advantage for themselves, but helped to preserve the Walpolean system for Walpole's successors.

The summer and autumn of 1738 were rendered comfortless for Walpole by the death of Maria at the age of 36, in childbirth on 4 June. She was buried in Houghton church, as was Catherine. The unexpectedness of the blow made it harder to bear. Maria had been a good-natured and vivacious companion, an intelligent, well-informed hostess who numbered among her friends the bluestocking Lady Mary Wortley Montagu. The loss of one whom he had so recently made his wife, and with such high hopes, left Walpole with a depression which remained in some ways for the rest of his life. Politics helped to divert him, but not to console.

Britain's negotiators were kept busy at Madrid hammering out an agreement which, Walpole hoped, would satisfy the more moderate and level-headed members of the Commons and avert the threatened conflict. As a result the speech from the throne in February 1739 announced a convention with Spain to settle outstanding differences. From the first the Convention of the Pardo came under attack, with Prince Frederick's friends prominent among the opposition. Since the full details of the agreement were still not known at Westminster, the Address passed by a good margin of 230 votes to 141. But in the following weeks the details became available and occasioned a fresh crop of petitions from West India merchants. Although Britain had secured some compensation for past atrocities the Spanish authorities refused to renounce their claimed right of search, thus the problem of regulating this right was left to be worked out later by the plenipotentiaries. This, the best Walpole could offer, was clearly less than satisfactory, and on 23 February the ministerial majority sank to thirteen. The opposition leaders, scenting possible victory, made considerable efforts to assemble their followers. As a result the next debate, on 8 March, saw about 500 members present. The debate was a long one: the diarist Edward Harley noted that he was present for seventeen hours. In the end 260 government Whigs voted for an Address of Thanks and 232 members were against. The latter included 100 Whigs of whom several were followers of the Duke of Argyll, an ominous development in view of that magnate's recent unreliability. And as if this marathon sitting were not enough, the opposition again opposed the Address at its report stage, an unusual tactic which did not take Walpole unawares, for he achieved a slightly improved majority of thirty votes. Though this was hardly a triumph, the situation was retrieved for the moment.

Walpole's dominance had been endangered but not broken, and the opposition showed some signs of their frustration and even despair by deciding, though by no means unanimously, to stay away from Parliament in order to demonstrate their case more forcibly. One Tory who did not agree with this secession noted his view of it as 'an idle project, contrary to all the rules and being of Parliament and not approved of without doors and in the country'. Walpole was happy enough at his opponents' unusual action, for this could only result in a much-needed relaxation of pressure on the ministry. Nor were the arguments of those who stayed away from Parliament readily acceptable in the country, where Members of Parliament were not expected to withdraw their services. The truth of this point was soon apparent to the seceders themselves, who complained that their action was not 'enough understood by the generality'. Within a few days many of them were reported uneasy at their inaction, though most kept it up to save face except when urgent personal or constituency interests called for their attendance. For the remainder of the session Walpole met little opposition. On 13 March most of the Tories even steeled themselves to stay away from a motion on behalf of the dissenters for repeal of the Tests, confident that the minister would do their work for them. Their confidence was justified, for Walpole still could not afford to rouse the Church of England: but many of the absentees must have been uncomfortable at reports of his caustic remarks on their absence.

Towards the end of the sittings he was able to carry easily, by 141 votes to 20, an emergency vote of credit for £500,000 to augment the armed forces in view of possible hostilities with Spain. Among the Tories' usual speakers only one, Harley, was present to raise his party's objection to this form of finance.

With a war now imminent Walpole was at least spared, by his opponents' absence, any serious objection to the means of financing it.[1]

No sooner was Parliament prorogued on 14 June than, according to Walpole's sources, opposition heart-searching over the secession came to a head. A meeting was held before members dispersed to their homes, but much confusion seems to have existed. All present agreed that some appeal to public opinion was needed, and that a campaign should be organised to obtain instructions from their constituencies, but the objects of this campaign were less clear. Walpole may have smiled at the report that some of the opposition thought it should justify the secession while others believed it should provide them with an excuse for returning to Parliament. Less pleasing was his opponents' final decision. The increasingly influential Harley was for returning, and on his insistence Wyndham and the Tories eventually agreed to end the secession.[2]

Walpole, however, had his own difficulties with associates. In May the British plenipotentiaries had met again with those of Spain and, with instructions dictated by the mood of Parliament, refused to concede the right of search to Spain. The First Lord nevertheless continued to hope throughout summer that hostilities might be averted. His vacation in Norfolk was made an uneasy one by the diplomatic situation. Subsequently in a series of agitated Cabinet meetings, Newcastle and his friends now urged that a declaration of war was unavoidable if the ministry's control over Parliament were to be retained. Reluctantly Walpole acceded, and war was declared in October.

Parliament would now be needed as soon as possible to provide further financial supplies. Despite the national mood in favour of war any call for increased taxation was unpopular. Even before the session a new hazard threatened, when the City of London produced instructions to its representatives, calling them to vote against supplies unless a Place Bill were passed. But this could be circumvented, for the Pulteneyites had no relish now for place legislation which, reported Chesterfield, 'they think might prove a clog upon their own Adminis-

1. Harley Diary, i, ff. 116, 120–1; HMC, *14th Report*, ix, p.26; Coxe, *Walpole*, iii, pp.608 and 518–20; *Commons Journal*, xxiii, p.361; *The Letters of Philip Dormer Stanhope, 4th Earl of Chesterfield*, ed. Bonamy Dobree (1932), ii, p.358.
2. Coxe, *Walpole*, iii, pp.523–4; *Marchmont Papers*, ii, pp.144–6.

tration'.[1] This Broad Bottom Whig's sour prediction of the Pulteneyites' attitude, and of their farsighted promotion of their own future needs in office, proved only too correct.

For the first time in fourteen years Parliament assembled before Christmas, in November. Debating the royal speech, announcing the state of the war, Pulteney declared his support for the government in strong terms which, according to Horatio Walpole, 'together with his having let fall some words about resigning mean suspicions of those that he acted with, [and] gave great offence to the Tories'. With possible opposition thus confused at the outset the naval and military votes as well as the Address went unopposed, except for some mild Tory demands for frugality. Soon after Christmas, however, more activity was heralded by Sandys' customary motion to bring in his Place Bill. With a large number of members present this was rejected on 29 January 1740 by only sixteen votes. The very narrow margin was partly accounted for by the moderate nature of the proposed measure, which differed from previous attempts by being intended to exclude only minor placemen. But another new factor influencing the voting was an opposition threat to obtain constituency reprimands for members who opposed the bill. Walpole was by now suffering significant losses from the Tories' mid-term campaign to appeal to the electors' opinion, and these tactics were rewarded by a greater than usual number of defections by independent Whigs from the government side.[2]

Within a day or two of this event both a worried ministry and elated opposition were making their preparations for the next move. The Ministry, wrote Newcastle, saw three possible points for the expected attack: 'The Prince's affair; the repeal of the Septennial Bill; the calling the ministers to an account for some steps relating to the late convention'. In the end it was the Convention of the Pardo upon which the opposition pitched as the most suitable issue for embarrassing the ministry. On 21 February Pulteney moved that official papers relating to the Convention should be produced, announcing that if this motion succeeded he would then move that the documents be

1. *Chesterfield Letters*, ii, pp.401–2.
2. HMC, *14th Report*, ix, pp.36 and 38; Sedgwick *History of Parliament*, i, p.89, Note xvii; Cobbett, *Parliamentary History*, xi, pp.328-30; Harley Diary, i, ff. 124–5.

committed to a secret committee of twenty-one members, who were to be appointed by ballot in the House. Walpole, confident of his preparations, met this attack head on, deliberately making the vote a matter of confidence in himself. This encouraged the experienced Wyndham to turn the minister's tactics to advantage, pointing out that Walpole 'could not apply this question solely to himself without assuming the supremacy of power, and owning that he did everything in the ministry'. For the moment Wyndham's remarks were not followed up, though they were to be remembered later. The ministerial ranks closed, and a majority of 247 to 196 rejected Pulteney's motion. After the vote Harley noted wryly: 'Sir Robert thanked many of the members for their attendance and accepted of their congratulations, as if he had been really tried and acquitted'.[1]

Although Walpole was successful on this occasion the appeal to confidence was, as Wyndham had foreseen, a two-edged sword; the minister had committed his personal fate to the success or failure of a government now at war with Spain. For the remainder of the session no military or diplomatic development showed him wrong. But over the future hung the question mark of the ministry's ability to wage the war successfully. Sir Robert Walpole was by inclination a peacetime administrator, with little recent experience of hostilities, and he was now in his sixty-fourth year.

As a preparation for the ministry's wartime footing, Walpole determined to rid it of some potentially dangerous followers and give promotion to others more deserving. He had been on strained terms with Newcastle since the latter saw fit to urge war with Spain with unusual vivacity. The Pelhams, however, were too useful to be dispensed with, particularly Henry Pelham who continued to be held in high regard by Walpole. But he took the opportunity to retire Lord Godolphin and give the Privy Seal to Hervey, much to Newcastle's displeasure. Hervey was an effective speaker in the House of Lords and would go some way towards making up the loss of Argyll, whose widening divergence from the ministry was now signalled by dismissal from his several offices. At this time too

1. Harley Diary, ii, ff.1–3; Add MSS. 32,693, ff. 51–2; HMC, *14th Report*, ix, p.39.

Dodington was removed from the Treasury board; the votes he controlled in the Commons would be a serious loss in close-fought divisions but his unreliability could not be tolerated. Dodington had himself long been preparing for a change. As a specialist in political survival he had long foreseen Walpole's political demise and was not unwilling to associate himself with the opposition.

Newcastle remained a potentially unreliable ministerial supporter, having been barely restrained from resignation at the promotion of Hervey; from now on Walpole knew that he could expect little loyalty from the Secretary of State. But if the First Lord was weaker, despite the attempted tautening of his defences, the opposition too had their problems. The summer of 1740 saw the death of Sir William Wyndham, who as Bolingbroke's associate had often acted as a bridge between his Tory followers and the dissident Whigs. For Walpole Wyndham's removal was to be a major advantage.

The last session before a general election opened relatively quietly on 18 November. In composing the King's Speech, Walpole outlined the steps leading up to the war but presented very little material for criticism. Pulteney's amendment to the Address simply proposed an enquiry into the application of last session's supplies. After a debate in which the minister defended himself ably, and Pitt and Lyttelton were reported very aggressive, the government prevailed by a majority of sixty-seven votes. Dodington and his little group, as expected, formalised their juncture with the opposition by their voting in the division. But the Prince of Wales and Pulteney showed little inclination to attack the governmental requests for supplies, and Christmas was reached with little further serious opposition. The lull continued into January 1741, for with elections imminent Walpole decided to allow the usual Place Bill to pass in the Commons on this occasion, relying upon the Lords to throw it out.[1]

The apparent agreement displayed in these issues was now followed by a more active phase. This was no less than a formal censure motion on the First Lord. Devised by the opposition Whigs, both Pulteneyite and Broad Bottom, the attempt took on a very personal flavour from the grievances of the many

1. HMC, *14th Report*, ix, p.62; *Chesterfield Letters*, ii, pp.433–5.

who had been passed over or dismissed by Walpole down the years. In the House of Lords it was Carteret who was given the honour of bringing the motion requesting that Walpole might be removed from office 'forever', but here the government's usual majority was maintained with 108 votes against the opposition's 59. In the Commons Pulteney, perhaps with an eye to maintaining the possibility of future coalition with Walpole, gave the task of bringing the same motion to his principal follower Sandys. The latter rose to the occasion with the speech of his career. The nation's present unhappy state, Sandys claimed, was the personal responsibility of one man. Three members present, Stephen Fox, Thomas Tower and Sir Dudley Ryder, took notes of the speech.

Their accounts largely agree that Sandys claimed that Walpole had assumed (in Fox's words) 'a place of French extraction, the place of sole minister' and not, as is sometimes stated, merely the position of 'Prime' Minister.[1]

Sandys' accusation was not simply that Walpole was *primus inter pares*, but that he managed all aspects of government in person or by immediate direction. The contention gained its force from the fact that it contained a substantial element of truth. Pulteney's speech introduced some more specific charges, but by comparison with his follower's opening it was subdued and made little impression. Walpole vigorously denied encompassing all government business, and defended himself against the other charges. His speech too was one of the best of his life, for he was justifying his whole political career and method of government. Rejecting the accusation of being a 'Prime' much less a 'Sole' minister he endeavoured to play down his pre-eminence and emphasised the responsibilities shared with his colleagues. His denials would not have saved him, however, but for the action of many of the Tories in abstaining or voting for him, even though it is clear they did so

1. The wording of the accounts differ somewhat from each other and from the Lords Protest (see p.3 above). Fox's account is printed in Coxe, *Walpole*, iii, pp.559–61, Ryder's in Sedgwick, *History of Parliament*, i, pp.91–95, Note XXI. The latter account has 'sole minister, a name and thing unknown to England or any free nations, but taken from a neighbouring nation'. Another account, in the *London Magazine*, has 'sole and prime minister' – reprinted in Cobbett, *Parliamentary History*, xi, p.1232. Tower's is the closest wording to Fox's: 'The taking a power of French extraction under the title of a sole minister', – I.G. Doolittle, 'A First-hand account . . . 13 February 1741', *B.I.H.R.* lxxx (1980), p.130.

without any belief in his protests. Harley broadened the charges to cover other responsible ministers and complained that 'the state of the nation is by their conduct deplorable, a war is destroying us abroad, and poverty and corruption are devouring us at home'. Yet he and others stated their belief that it would not be justifiable to censure Walpole and ignore other members of the ministry.

The Harleyite Tories had not been consulted by the Whigs who planned the motion, and they disapproved of an attack in which the accusers made no attempt to produce proof, documentary or otherwise, in support of their complaints. Over the last twenty years too many high-placed Tories, including Harley's uncle, the first Earl of Oxford, had been persecuted, imprisoned and in some cases executed by votes in Parliament for many of the party to think this proceeding desirable, even to bring down their political arch-enemy. Among the first to withdraw from the chamber before the vote was Harley himself. The veteran Jacobite member, William Shippen, declared with his usual bluntness that 'he would not pull down Robin upon republican principles', and likewise made his exit from the House. Thus those members who refused to vote included among their number both wings of the Tory party. Of the remaining Tories some voted for Walpole and some few against. The result was a victory for the minister by an unexpectedly enormous majority of 290 votes to 106.

Several explanations of the Tories' behaviour were put forward in addition to those which they stated themselves. It was agreed that their general dislike of the opposition Whigs was reinforced on this occasion by lack of adequate prior information about the intentions of their allies. The diarist Egmont also noted that, unlike Pulteney, Walpole had a certain popularity which transcended party boundaries and that he derived benefit from the fact that his 'personal behaviour towards the Tories has always been obliging altho' an enemy to them as a party'. There could have been no better testimonial to Walpole's personal popularity and his ability to charm even political opponents.[1]

1. In addition to the sources cited in the last note: Harley Diary, ii, ff. 24v–28; Yorke, *Life of Hardwicke*, i, pp.252–53; Coxe, *Walpole*, iii, pp.562–64, HMC, *Egmont Diary*, iii, pp.191–93; *Annals of Stair*, ii, p.269; *Marchmont Papers*, ii, pp.245–47; and *The Sentiments of a Tory, in respect of a late important Transaction* . . . (1741), pp.23–24.

In retrospect Walpole's surprisingly handsome victory on the censure motion was to seem only the afterglow of his former political fire. It was overtaken almost immediately in the public eye by the long-awaited election which, though conducted on a fairly low key, resulted in a significant and ultimately decisive set-back. In the open constituencies the previous election's shift away from the government was continued, though at a diminished rate. The popularity of a war which Walpole had undertaken, albeit reluctantly, and the absence of any major popular issues to compare with the excise crisis seven years earlier were sufficient to slow the decline in the ministry's electoral support. In other constituencies the decline was greater. Significant gains were made by opposition candidates in both Scotland and Cornwall. In the former there was still resentment at the ministry's unfortunate treatment of Edinburgh in the aftermath of the Porteous riots, and this was abetted by the influence of Argyll, whose weight was now thrown into the anti-ministerial scale. In Cornwall the small and decayed boroughs controlled by Prince Frederick, through the Duchy of Cornwall, affected the swing to opposition. The activities of these two magnates, together with a slight adverse balance elsewhere, brought down Walpole's following from 300 before the general election to an estimated 286 while opposition members increased to about 267.[1] With a theoretical governmental majority of only nineteen much would depend upon the luck of events as well as upon Walpole's skill, especially over the disputed elections still to be decided when Parliament met.

Events were coming to a head in the international scene, breeding differences within the ministry and bursting upon Parliament to weaken Walpole's tenuous hold. The war with Spain saw two costly failures for British arms in the West Indies. Worse still, events in Europe heralded a radical change in Britain's commitments. In May of 1740 Frederick William of Prussia had died and was succeeded by his son Frederick II, later known as Frederick the Great. Five months later died also the Emperor Charles VI, leaving his daughter Maria Theresa ruler of the Habsburg territories. In the following December Frederick invaded Silesia, one of Maria Theresa's most valuable

1. Sedgwick, *History of Parliament*, i, pp.46, 159 and *passim*; Coxe, *Walpole*, iii, pp.565–78.

hereditary possessions. Walpole, urged on by George II's fear for his electorate and lacking the excuse of 1733 that Austria had been the aggressor, reluctantly undertook to support Maria Theresa under the terms of the Treaty of Vienna which he had concluded nine years earlier. It seemed likely that a land war with Prussia might be confined within reasonable bounds.

But this calculation soon disappeared when campaigning began in 1741, for it reckoned without Prussia's military strength and the French government's desire to take advantage of the situation. In April Frederick demonstrated, by defeating the Austrians at Mollwitz, that the task of ejecting him was not going to be an easy one. His success gave encouragement to France, and within a few months Prussia had concluded alliances with both that country and with Bourbon Spain. By the time the new House of Commons assembled Britain found herself on the verge of hostilities with the most formidable power combination in Europe.

To add to Walpole's difficulties the King, during his summer visit to Hanover, concluded at Klein Schnellendorf an electoral treaty safeguarding his German territories by neutralising Hanover and promising to support the French candidate for the imperial throne against Maria Theresa's husband. This step was taken against the strong advice of Walpole, who now had to bear the brunt of accusations of 'Hanover influence' for the action he had tried to prevent. The badly-rattled Newcastle foresaw 'it will be impossible to prevent a parliamentary enquiry into this conduct'. Newcastle's friends calmed him down for the moment but were not uninfluenced by his justified alarm at the kind of use to which the opposition might put the ministry's diplomatic dilemma. Walpole later believed that it was in the autumn of 1741 Newcastle and Hardwicke came to an understanding with Carteret to ally themselves with Pulteney's associates in a new ministry.[1]

The behaviour of the Pulteneyites, increasingly over the past few years, certainly suggests an intention to get into office without the Tories and, if necessary, without many of the other opposition Whigs. If they joined forces with the Pelhams and Hardwicke the inevitable scapegoat would be Walpole, whose pre-eminence would hardly allow him to avoid responsibility

1. Yorke, *Life of Hardwicke*, i, pp.259, 264, 268–71; Add. MSS. 32,698, f.115.

for recent developments. At what point Walpole became reconciled to this likelihood is not certain, but he gradually became convinced that for the sake of a continued Whig ministry, excluding both Tories and Broad Bottom Whigs, the only solution might be his own withdrawal to make way for Pulteney's friends in a limited change. The time for this, however, was not yet: there was still a hope that the situation might improve if parliamentary wrath at the Treaty of Klein Schnellendorf could be averted, and if the ranks of government supporters could be steadied in the crucial first weeks of the House due to meet on 1 December.

For the first few days of Parliament neither Walpole nor his opponents were eager to force a trial of strength; both sides hoped to benefit by delay. With the House balanced on a knife edge and members still arriving from the country some patient spadework and intensive lobbying was needed before a division could be risked. Walpole, in his eagerness to postpone the issue until the House was more settled and some election disputes concluded, agreed to the setting up of a committee to report on the state of the nation, for 21 January, 1742.

But the preliminary clashes were not to be delayed so long, for Walpole's enemies felt themselves to be at last sufficiently united to risk some minor demonstrations. The Hanoverian Tories were now willing to move against Walpole's continuance. In June Edward Harley had succeeded his cousin as Earl of Oxford, thus removing from the Commons one of the chief critics of the censure motion of the previous February; but in any case neither Harley nor other Tories who had objected to that motion had concealed their willingness to bring down the ministry, provided the means used did not smack so obviously of 'pains and penalties'. The Jacobites were ready to move alongside their colleagues. The reason for this was a letter from the Pretender, obtained by Chesterfield on behalf of the Broad Bottom Whigs, urging supporters to join in bringing down the First Lord. These Whigs assured the Tories that, whatever the view of Pulteney and his friends, any new ministry which replaced Walpole's would contain a cross-party selection of ministers.[1]

The reinvigorated opposition's first opening was provided on

1. Sedgwick, *History of Parliament*, i, p.71.

14 December by an ill-considered ministerial attempt to prevent the hearing of a petition concerning the disputed election for Denbighshire, resulting in a ministerial defeat by 202 votes to 193. Voting over disputed elections was notoriously idiosyncratic, so the result was not in itself sufficient to indicate Walpole's loss of control. Nevertheless his elated opponents were able after this to get their candidate elected as chairman of the Committee of Elections and Privileges, a useful step on the way to control of subsequent decisions over petitions. The next test came three days before Christmas, when a petition by the opposition candidate for Westminster came before the Commons. The voting took place in a House somewhat diminished by the season, but for once this was of little advantage to the ministry, and the Westminster election was declared void by four votes. As in previous divisions there were several deserters and absentees from the court side.[1] For Walpole it was timely when Christmas intervened to give him a breathing space.

He used the Christmas recess to exert pressure on his supporters by every means at his disposal, in the hope of preventing any further flow of 'rats'. Something more than offers and promises was needed, however, to encourage men who saw him losing control in a steady flow of divisions. Walpole accordingly prevailed upon the King to make a supreme gesture of sacrifice. Prince Frederick was approached to reconcile himself and his followers in the Commons with the ministry. In return for this support he was at last offered the coveted extra £50,000 a year, together with a sum of £200,000, equivalent to arrears back to the time of his move into opposition in 1737. But the Prince, feeling the game now in his hands, scornfully refused. With his rejection of the offer the ministry's chances of survival diminished rapidly.[2]

Parliament reassembled on 18 January with the opposition thirsting for the promised debate upon foreign affairs. During the first three days Walpole delivered documents relating to current negotiations with Austria and France, which had been called for just before Christmas. On the 21st Pulteney proposed that the secret committee should examine and report on these

1. Coxe, *Walpole*, iii, pp.582–4; Sedgwick, *op. cit.* i, pp.97–9; J. B. Owen, *The Rise of the Pelhams* (1957), pp.22–4.
2. HMC, *Egmont Diary*, iii, pp.238–9; Coxe, *Walpole*, iii, p.585.

papers, a suggestion deliberately evoking memories of similar committees which at the turn of the century had heralded impeachments.

The debate which followed was one which was long remembered in the House of Commons, with both Walpole and Pulteney making the speeches of their lives. With over 500 members present in the House the atmosphere was at times stifling, especially for the invalids brought into the chamber by both sides. Carried or borne on their own crutches they would not willingly miss this day. Unfortunately for Walpole three sick government supporters who were kept in an adjacent House with a door to the Speaker's chamber, for last minute admission to the division, were locked out by some resourceful Patriot who had wind of the scheme. Nevertheless the First Lord managed to obtain the support of 253 members against the opposition's 250 and thus survived by a majority of three in one of the fullest Houses ever recorded.[1]

His hairline margin was far from the triumphant victory on the censure motion of a year earlier. But Walpole retained a faint hope and paused to regroup his forces. He controlled the Lords and still had a paper majority of fourteen or more in the Commons. Several election petitions and double returns were allowed to go in favour of the opposition without a division. But all was in the balance on the 28th when Walpole divided the House in support of ministerial supporters petitioning against the election at Chippenham. After a tense debate the ministry was defeated by a single vote. The end was near, and Walpole delayed resignation only while he assured himself that the result was indeed the work of deserters and not a failure arising from involuntary absenteeism. On 2 February, however, a further defeat on Chippenham showed that whatever may have been the case in the earlier vote, the government's waverers had made their decision: the ministry this time lost by sixteen votes. Walpole's plans were already made, and he resigned his offices on the same day despite the King's reluctance to see him go.[2] His long and active career was at last over and few of his contemporaries could but feel that a Titan had fallen.

1. Coxe, *Walpole*, iii, pp.587–88; *The Yale Edition of Horace Walpole's Correspondence* (ed. W.S. Lewis), xvii, pp.295–300; Harley Diary, ii, ff. 37–9.
2. Coxe, *Walpole*, iii, pp.590–1; *Horace Walpole's Correspondence* (ed. Lewis), xvii, pp.318–9; Sedgwick, *History of Parliament*, i, pp.99–101 and 102–3.

14
Elder Statesman

AFTER HIS fall from office Walpole lived for just over three years, and he never again took an active part in public life. He remained a valued confidant to those former colleagues who remained in office, forgiving their devious dealings with characteristic generosity. Newcastle, Pelham and Hardwicke quickly carried out their pre-arranged plan with Pulteney and Carteret, whereby Carteret took over from the accommodating Harrington as Newcastle's fellow Secretary while Pulteney's friends Sandys, Rushout and Gybbon joined a new Treasury board with Spencer Compton, now Earl of Wilmington, as First Lord. Pulteney himself stood aside to honour a longstanding undertaking not to succeed Walpole, hoping to come in later.

Even before the new appointments were complete, George II showed his continued respect for Walpole by raising him to the peerage as Earl of Orford, a title chosen out of regard for its previous holder Edward Russell, Walpole's first important patron. The King also offered a pension of £4,000 a year, though in the climate of retribution which hung over Orford in parliamentary debate he did not choose to apply for the sum until over two years later.[1] After a few months, he moved out of 10 Downing Street and took up residence in his favoured London locality of Arlington Street, this time at number 5. But he was still living at Downing Street in the spring and early summer of 1742 when he had to face the storm which was being blown up by his enemies. Many of these opponents saw a chance at last of justifying their own stance by demanding punishment for what they chose to regard as Orford's crimes while in office.

The punitive proceedings commenced on 25 March, with a motion in the Commons for an enquiry into the former minister's conduct of administration over the last ten years. The motion was passed by a small majority after an earlier unsuccessful attempt. The resulting secret committee was

1. *The Letters of Horace Walpole* (ed. Cunningham), i, p.307.

hampered from the start by the refusal of Orford's former subordinates to give evidence. John Scrope, Secretary to the Treasury, pleaded the King's personal instructions to withhold information on the fallen First Lord's use of the Secret Service allocation in the Civil List. An opposition bill to indemnify witnesses against the former minister was thrown out by his supporters, led by Hardwicke in the Lords. By the end of the session the enquiry was seen to be unsuccessful in face of ministerial obstruction, and Orford could retire thankfully to Norfolk reflecting that his friends were still more powerful than his enemies.[1]

After the summer recess there was one further attempt to keep up the vendetta against the fallen minister. In December the 'boy patriot' George Lyttelton, assisted by Pitt, strove to obtain another secret committee, but their move was easily defeated. Orford's opponents, some now in the ministry, were falling out among themselves, and little was heard of retribution after this. *The Craftsman* might meaningfully carry a description of why the Earl of Danby had been impeached in Charles II's reign as a 'wicked and corrupt minister', but the days of state trials for political reasons were over. Walpole himself had seen to that when he ensured the acquittal of Harley in 1717.[2]

Within a few months of the new ministry's formation tensions between Orford's protégés and the Pulteneyites were becoming apparent, but he soon foresaw that their union could not continue for long. Before 1742 was out he was urging Pelham to rally the Old Corps of Whigs, who had for so long been his own supporters, against Carteret and other recently-appointed 'court patriots'. Orford argued that 'no man can answer for or secure a zealous and cordial union of the Whig party, if anybody takes upon them the lead that they know have been instruments, and active in destroying the Whig party for twenty years together . . .'[3] Pelham and Newcastle needed little encouragement. They were dismayed at Carteret's play for the King's favour, by agreeing to generous subsidies to German

1. Sedgwick, *History of Parliament, 1715–1754*, ii, *sub* Scrope, John; Cobbett, *Parliamentary History*, xii, p.652.
2. *The Letters of Horace Walpole* (ed. Cunningham), i, p.217; *The Craftsman*, 2 March, 1742.
3. William Coxe, *Memoirs of . . . Henry Pelham* (1829), i, p.35.

allies, a policy which could only arouse antagonism in the Commons; and the Pelhams were alarmed at the Pulteneyites' occasional failure to support ministerial policy or tear themselves away from the opposition conceptions to which they were accustomed.

Orford's role as a bystander in the power struggle which now ensued left him more time to stay in Norfolk and enjoy the splendour of Houghton, but he continued to flood the Pelham brothers with suggestions by letter. In the spring of 1743 Wilmington was showing unmistakable signs of illness and decline, and the King's decision about a successor at the Treasury could not be long delayed. The only likely candidates were Pelham and Pulteney, and the former had the advantage of experience in financial administration as well as the support of the Old Corps Whigs. It is not certain that the King sought Orford's advice on this matter, but the old statesman gave it anyway,[1] and in any case his views were well known. To Newcastle, however, Orford wrote sage counsel that Pelham should be urged to seize any offer from the King, whatever limitations it might contain: '. . . if the offer comes to Mr P., however circumscribed, conditional or disagreeable, even under a probability of not being able to go on, it must be accepted; it will be more honourable and justifiable to resign upon practicalities, than to appear defeated and thereby disappointed, from whence no creditt or merit can arise, but we have often seen a back game at backgammon recovered'.[2]

This shrewd advice was taken, and on the day Henry Pelham accepted the office of First Lord of the Treasury Orford penned his congratulations in a further long letter setting out a manifesto for further progress. Pelham must bear patiently with being in a minority on his own board, as Wilmington had been. Some of the Pulteneyite members might be 'made reasonable' but should not be trusted. The new minister must continue to rely strongly on the Old Corps but at the same time encourage some of the Broad Bottom opposition to hope for office when the Pulteneyites were finally removed. Pitt in particular was 'able and formidable' and he must be won over.

1. In a letter to George II mentioned in Cambridge University Library's *Handlist to the Cholmondeley (Houghton) MSS* but currently not traceable in this collection.
2. Add. MSS. 32,701, f.23v. part printed in Coxe, *Pelham*, i. p.84.

In general Pelham must learn to 'forgive and gain' all Whigs, but he should always beware any commitment to the Tories. As always, Orford was convinced that no reshaped ministry could be safe which included a substantial Tory element.[1] Rarely can a senior minister have received such authoritative advice, and followed it.

Pelham's tactics over the next year bear, indeed, a close resemblance to the course suggested by his old mentor. The King's continued favour kept Carteret secure for the moment, but Pitt's bitter attacks on this 'Hanover troop master' had the effect of strengthening the Pelham case. So too, early in 1744, did an invasion scare which aroused the country to the belief that not enough of Britain's resources were being channelled into home defence. Orford had spoken little in the House of Lords since his elevation, but in February he rose to make what his son Horace described as 'a long and fine speech' calling for national support for the Hanoverian dynasty. 'The Prince was so pleased with it', reported Horace, 'that he has given him leave to go to his court which he never would before'.[2] The speech was, however, to be Orford's last major contribution to parliamentary oratory. After an autumn visit to Houghton he returned to London too ill with gout and 'stone' to take further part in public life.

Meanwhile the Pelhams continued their quarrel with Carteret, defeating him in the Cabinet over a convention in which he had committed Britain to subsidise Austria. The King had ample warning that he must soon choose between his quarrelling ministers. And by November Orford's advice had borne fruit. George was convinced by the Pelhams' threat of resignation that his ministry, as then constituted, could not successfully carry the royal wishes in the Commons. Carteret was forced out, together with his friends on the Treasury board. Harrington was restored to his former Secretaryship, and some Broad Bottom supporters including the Cobham group replaced the Pulteneyites. Only on the appointment of Pitt did the King hold out; the young orator had been disrespectful about the Hanover connection too often. Nevertheless the Pelhams were

1. Coxe, *Pelham*, i, pp.91–3.
2. *The Letters of Horace Walpole* (ed. Cunningham), i, p.293.

now in complete control of the ministry, and Orford could at last feel that his work was secure.

It was none too soon. For years he had been subject to particularly painful attacks of kidney stones, and in 1740 had even considered resignation on this account. By late 1744 he was suffering greatly and almost continuously. In December Horace wrote from Arlington Street that his father was taking 'Mrs Stephens's medicine', a fashionable remedy. Three weeks later Orford was 'extremely ill', and his relations feared that the preparation was too violent for him. The devoted Horace went out of doors only twice in the next month, when his father's life was in danger, but was able to report at the end of February 'his spirits are amazing, and his constitution more'. But by now Orford was taking an opiate which kept him asleep twenty hours a day. In this condition he remained until he died on 18 March 1745, without more than occasional recovery from the stupor which eased his pain.[1] He was in his sixty-eighth year and had outlived two wives and most of his happiness.

Horace Walpole mourned sincerely for his father. Not until nearly half a century later was he himself to succeed to the title. Orford's first son Robert, Lord Walpole, succeeded him but died six years later to be followed by his own son as third Earl of Orford. Horace was to see the third Earl disperse many of his grandfather's prize acquisitions. Sir Robert Walpole's magnificent collection of paintings was sold to Catherine the Great of Russia and the fine external staircases of Houghton Hall were dismantled to save the cost of repairing them.

Horace succeeded his nephew as fourth Earl in 1791, having outlived his other brother, Edward. On Horace's own death the estate went to the descendants of his sister Mary, who have recently restored Houghton's staircases lovingly, to show the house as its builder would have wished. For the paintings it is necessary to visit the Hermitage in Leningrad.

Sir Robert Walpole's real memorials are in other spheres than stone and oils. He left Britain a strong government with which to face and overcome the Young Pretender's challenge in 1745–6. He undoubtedly played a major part in developing the functions of a Prime Minister. In some ways his role had been anticipated by earlier ministers, notably Robert Harley who was

1. *Op.cit.*, i, pp.335, 339, 342–3.

likewise accused of being too dominant over his colleagues and of interfering with the work of other departments. But Walpole was in high office for over two decades, as against Harley's four years, and his long term gave the tradition of one minister's ascendancy time to consolidate its hold in British public life. By the time of Walpole's fall most of the features of the prime ministership were already present. The principal differences lie not so much in the absence of later aspects of this office as in the functions performed by Walpole which are not those of a modern Prime Minister.

Nineteenth and twentieth-century Prime Ministers have not combined the office of First Lord of the Treasury with that of Chancellor of the Exchequor, as did Walpole and most of his immediate successors. He had personal control of the nation's finances, and brought in the equivalent of today's budgets in the Commons. In addition he took upon himself, especially after Townshend's resignation in 1730, an overriding responsibility for foreign affairs through two capable but usually subservient Secretaries of State. Arguably in this too he exceeded the practice of most modern Prime Ministers. The contemporary opposition's charge that he was 'Sole' as well as 'Prime' Minister was intended to indicate not merely that he was *primus inter pares* but that he was a dominant authority, that he, and he alone, possessed sufficient power to formulate and execute policy. Walpole was 'Prime' Minister in the modern sense but he was also 'Sole' Minister, one who conducted most of the nation's business by personal supervision or intervention.

Only in his ultimate reliance on the crown was Walpole less than later Prime Ministers, and his usefulness to George I and George II made even this limitation a theoretical one. These monarchs' complaisance was, however, essential to his position, and in this respect he was as much the last overmighty subject as the first Prime Minister, as much a Wolsey as a Gladstone. But his long term of office was also helping to develop a new tradition of ministerial autonomy. This was not wholly without intention. From the beginning of his ministry Walpole, with Townshend's help, made himself the main source of advice to George I, manoeuvring British rivals out of the way and checking any attempted come-back by the German advisers whom even Stanhope and Sunderland had not tolerated.[1]

1. Ragnhild Hatton, *George I, Elector and King* (1978), pp.164–5.

Pelham was to follow the same policy with 'ministers behind the curtain', notably in 1746. Because Walpole and the Pelhams laid the foundation for a shift from a royal to a ministerial chief executive, albeit with no constitutional justification, George II and George III later found it difficult to recover lost ground.

In the longer term the executive power lost to monarchy was not to accrue entirely to the Prime Minister. This was the result of the parallel emergence of a rival authority, the Cabinet with a concept of collective responsibility.

In Walpole's time, however, there was only a recently-devised and weak cabinet tradition, and he was not much trammelled by it. He dealt mainly with his colleagues through an 'Inner Cabinet', and even this had only a semblance of real power. There was much truth in the opposition's arguments against Walpole's dominance over his colleagues, for if he had misused it as much as they maintained his ministry would indeed have been dangerous to the nation and repressive of future development of the constitution.

As a personality Walpole must rank, despite his many detractors, as one of the most sociable and popular of ministers. The Tories who voted decisively for him in the censure motion of 1741 were clear about this. In February 1742 they were ready to eject him as a minister who no longer appeared equal to the task of government, but they would not censure him personally. Dr Samuel Johnson, the epitome of Toryism, is reported to have said of Walpole 'that he was a fine fellow, and that his very enemies deemed him so before his death'. Johnson himself 'honoured his memory for having kept this country in peace many years, as also for the goodness and placability of his temper'.[1] If Tories who had suffered his denigration of their party for many years could rally to his support, and if a Tory intellectual who had written against him during his lifetime could pay such a tribute, Walpole's appeal to most Whigs can hardly have been less than to these determined political opponents.

For many years Walpole did succeed in keeping the European peace which Harley had with such difficulty obtained; but Walpole also had other claims to furthering peaceful conditions, by dampening internal strife. He kept both Church of England and dissenters reasonably quiet after the fratricidal

1. Donald J. Green, *The Politics of Samuel Johnson*, p.133.

strife of Anne's reign, and he relaxed the savage convention, pursued during his own early years in Parliament, of trying to extirpate the rival party. His campaigns against the Tories were pragmatic, not destructive, a fact which the Tories themselves instinctively grasped and honoured. He calmed the landed interest by keeping taxes low, and the manufacturers and merchants by a tariff policy which improved the balance of trade. His reward for his acceptable policies was twenty-one years of power and self-enrichment, neither basically unreasonable by the standards of the time though both sufficiently excessive to warn the country that the dangers postulated by his opponents might be more real in the hands of a less tolerable minister.

Sir Robert Walpole stands out among his fellows in ways not given to all leading ministers. His memory was 'prodigious', his energy boundless and his exuberance sometimes overwhelming. His very size was exceptional. Above all, the ability which took him to the top and kept him there so long was acknowledged by all to be above the ordinary. That most intellectual of later prime ministers Lord Shelburne was to write that 'by all that I have been able to learn, Sir Robert Walpole was, out of sight, the ablest man of his time and the most capable'.[1] Applied to an age which included such politicans as Harley, Bolingbroke and Pitt, this assessment was a considerable tribute.

1. Lord Edmond Fitzmaurice, *The Life of William, Earl of Shelburne* (1875), i, p.37.

Bibliography

(1) Sources

The most useful collection of documents is found in printed form in volumes II and III of William Coxe's *Memoirs of the Life and Administration of Sir Robert Walpole* (3 vols. 1798). Complementary to this are Coxe's other publications: *Memoirs of Horatio, Lord Walpole* (1820); *Memoirs of . . . Henry Pelham* (2 vols. 1829); *Memoirs of John, Duke of Marlborough* (3 vols. 1818–19); and *The Private Correspondence of . . . Shrewsbury* (1821). Most of the originals of Walpole's papers are among the Cholmondeley (Houghton) Manuscripts deposited by the Marquess of Cholmondeley at Cambridge University Library. This Library also contains the manuscript of Edward Harley's parliamentary diary (Additional Manuscript 6851). But by far the largest collection of manuscripts of all kinds is to be found in the British Library, especially among its Additional Manuscripts (the 'Add. MSS' referred to throughout this volume except only in the case of the Harley Diary). The B.L.'s holding includes most of the manuscripts of Newcastle, Hardwicke and Perceval as well as many other collections scarcely less significant. Other Walpole and related manuscripts of lesser importance are widely scattered in the Public Record Office, the libraries of Nottingham, Yale and Chicago Universities and of Churchill College, Cambridge (Erle MSS.), Norfolk and Norwich Record Office and Lord Walpole's papers at Wolterton Hall, Norfolk.

Among printed documents the selection made by the Historical Manuscripts Commission from private repositories is by far the largest and is quite beyond praise, despite some slipshod editing of the early publications. In these volumes are to be found, among many others, the major part of the Portland (Harley), Townshend, Stuart, Carlisle, Lonsdale, Mar and Kellie, Polwarth, Egmont and Bath papers. The miscellaneous small collections in the HMC's *14th Report* are also of considerable value for Walpole.

Diaries and journals are an important type of source. One of the best, for the 1720s, is that published as *The Parliamentary Diary of Sir Edward Knatchbull, 1722–1730* (containing also fragments of other diaries), edited for the Royal Historical Society by A.N. Newman (Camden Society Third Series, vol. xciv, 1963); while from 1730 onwards there is the *Diary of Viscount Percival, afterwards first Earl of Egmont*, published in three volumes by the Historical Manuscripts Commission (1920–1923). These volumes do not exhaust the papers of Perceval, much of whose political commentary from 1714 to 1730, in the form of letters or embryo journals, has been cited and quoted in this book from the unpublished manuscripts in the British Library (Add. MSS. 47,087 etc). The Harley Diary already mentioned covers the late 1730s, while Harley was still in the Commons, and early 1740s. Also falling within the category of comments by participant politicians is John, Lord Hervey's *Some Materials towards Memoirs of the Reign of George II*, in the three-volume edition by Romney Sedgwick (1931 and New York, 1970) covering the early part of George II's reign.

For Anne's reign the reports of official foreign representatives in London are often useful, especially those by the Dutch Resident L'Hermitage (Add. MSS. 17,677, many volumes, in French). From 1711 these reports begin to be supplemented by an even more valuable source, the parliamentary reporting of Abel Boyer in his *Political State of Great Britain*. Boyer's contribution from 1714 down to the mid-1730s, when his successors on the *Political State* relaxed and finally abandoned their coverage of parliamentary debates, can hardly be overestimated. His reports are the basis not only of most of the accounts in rival publications but also of Richard Chandler's collection in *The History and Proceedings of the House of Commons* (1742–1743) and William Cobbett's *Parliamentary History of England* (1806–1820). Chandler and Cobbett did not have a great deal to add to Boyer's accounts which was not easily obtainable elsewhere, though Chandler included a selection of division lists and Cobbett reprinted most of them. After Boyer ceased to be useful, Chandler and Cobbett relied mainly on the reports in the *London Magazine* and *Gentleman's Magazine* for the remainder of the period. In the present volume Cobbett has usually been cited in preference to earlier collections as being more generally available, but where Cobbett's account misses out vital information which was originally supplied by Boyer the *Political State* has been cited instead.

Other printed sources are in Henry L. Snyder, *The Marlborough-Godolphin Correspondence* (Oxford, 1975); J.M. Graham, *Annals . . . of the First and Second Earls of Stair* (Edinburgh, 1875); *The Works of Lord Bolingbroke* (Philadelphia, 1841); Bonamy Dobrée, *The Letters of Philip Dormer Stanhope, 4th Earl of Chesterfield* (1932); S. Cowper, *The Diary of Mary, Countess Cowper* (1865); H.P. Wyndham, *The Diary of . . . George Bubb Dodington* (1784). The more modern edition, *The Political Journal of George Bubb Dodington*, eds. John Carswell and L.A. Dralle, is not so useful for Walpole; J.H. Glover, *The Stuart Papers* (1847); J.J. Cartwright, *The Wentworth Papers* (1833); Philip C. Yorke, *Life and Correspondence of Hardwicke* (Cambridge, 1913); R. Phillimore, *Memoirs and Correspondence of George, Lord Lyttelton* (1845); G.H. Rose, *A Selection from the papers of the Earls of Marchmont* (1861); J.J. Murray, *An Honest Diplomat at The Hague . . . Horatio Walpole, 1715–1716* (Indiana, 1955); *The Private Correspondence of Sarah, Duchess of Marlborough* (1838); T.B. Howell, *A Complete Collection of State Trials* (1809–28). W.S. Lewis, *The Yale edition of Horace Walpole's Correspondence* (1937), and the earlier *Letters of Horace Walpole*, ed. Peter Cunningham (1861), are both cited in the footnotes. The multi-volumed *Journals of the House of Commons*, and *Journals of the House of Lords*, are useful for motions and division numbers, and the *Lords Journals* also sometimes register commentary in the form of signed Protests against votes.

(2) Secondary Works

The major study of Walpole, unfortunately incomplete, is by J.H. Plumb: *Sir Robert Walpole. The Making of a Statesman* (1956), and *Sir Robert Walpole. The King's Minister* (1960). These volumes take the story down to the 1734 election. In addition see Plumb's three chapters entitled 'The Walpoles: Father and Son', 'Sir Robert Walpole's Wine' and 'Sir Robert Walpole's Food', in *Men and Places* (1963). A useful introduction to Walpole and his times is provided by H.T. Dickinson's *Walpole and the Whig Supremacy* (1973).

General history is found in J.R. Jones, *Country and Court, England 1648–1714* (1978), and W.A. Speck, *Stability and Strife,*

England 1714–1760 (1977). Parties and opposition are covered by Sir Keith Feiling, *History of the Tory Party 1640–1714* (1924) and *The Second Tory Party 1714–1834* (1938); A.S. Foord, *His Majesty's Opposition, 1714–1830* (1964); B.W. Hill, *The Growth of Parliamentary Parties, 1689–1742* (1976) and *British Parliamentary Parties 1742–1832* (1985); and Linda Colley, *In Defiance of Oligarchy: The Tory Party, 1714–60 (Cambridge, 1982).*

No serious student can afford to ignore the relevant volumes of *The History of Parliament* which includes short biographies for all M.P.s.; Romney Sedgwick edited the two volumes on *The House of Commons 1715–1754* (1970), but the volumes for the period 1689–1714 are not yet published. The ideas which informed Walpole's Britain are dealt with by H.T. Dickinson in *Liberty and Property, Political Ideology in Eighteenth-Century Britain* (1977). P.D.G. Thomas, *The House of Commons in the Eighteenth Century* (Oxford, 1971), describes the mechanics of the House.

Eighteenth-century elections are covered by John A. Philips, *Electoral Behaviour in Unreformed England* (Princeton, 1982). John Cannon deals with the peerage in *Aristocratic Century: The Peerage of Eighteenth-Century England (Cambridge, 1984).* Walpole's dealings with the Church are described by Norman Sykes, *Church and State in England in the XVIIIth Century* (Cambridge, 1934). The land tax, an essential part of any minister's calculations, is described by W.R.Ward, *The English Land Tax in the Eighteenth Century* (Oxford, 1953). M.A. Thomson, *The Secretaries of State 1681–1782* (Oxford, 1932), is always useful.

Foreign policy is the subject of a large output of literature. For older works, not all of them outdated, reference should be made to the bibliographies and footnotes of the most recent, which include: D.B. Horn, *Great Britain and Europe in the Eighteenth Century* (Oxford, 1967); Paul Langford, *The Eighteenth Century, 1688–1815 (Modern British Foreign Policy* series, 1976); J. R. Jones, *Britain and the World 1649–1815*; and Jeremy Black, *British Foreign Policy in the Age of Walpole* (1985). Various contributions by G.C. Gibbs, among the collections listed in the paragraph after next, are of seminal importance, especially the two articles reprinted from the *English Historical Review* by Rosalind Mitcheson.

The following works deal with some specific periods or problems: J.R. Jones, *The First Whigs* (Oxford, 1961) and *The*

Revolution of 1688 in England (1972); Geoffrey Holmes, *British Politics in the Age of Anne* (2nd ed., 1986), *The Trial of Doctor Sacheverell* (1973), *Politics, Religion and Society in England, 1679–1742* (1986), and *Augustan England: Professions, State and Society 1680–1730* (1982); W.A. Speck, *Tory and Whig, the Struggle in the Constituencies, 1701–1715* (1970); John Beattie, *The English Court in the Reign of George I* (Cambridge, 1967); J.H. Plumb, *The Growth of Political Stability in England, 1675–1725* (1967); P.W.J. Riley, *The English Ministers and Scotland, 1707–1727* (1964); John B. Owen, *The Rise of the Pelhams* (1957); J.P. Kenyon, *Revolution Principles: the Politics of Party 1689–1720* (1977); C.R. Realey, *The Early Opposition to Sir Robert Walpole, 1720–1727* (Kansas, 1931); Paul Langford, *The Excise Crisis: Society and Politics in the Age of Walpole* (Oxford, 1975); G.V. Bennett, *The Tory Crisis in Church and State, 1688–1730* (Oxford, 1975); John F. Naylor, *The British Aristocracy and the Peerage Bill of 1719* (1968); H. Van Thal, *The Prime Ministers*, vol. i (1974); Eveline Cruickshanks, *Political Untouchables; the Tories and the 45* (1979), and Eveline Cruickshanks (ed.), *Ideology and Conspiracy: Aspects of Jacobitism, 1689–1759*, (1982); Bruce Lenman, *The Jacobite Risings in Britain 1689–1746* (1980); and P.G.M. Dickson, *The Financial Revolution in England* (1967).

Collections of articles by various scholars form a rich source of information for this period. They include Neil McKendrick (ed.), *Historical Perspectives . . . in Honour of J.H. Plumb* (1974); Ragnhild Hatton and M.S. Anderson (eds.), *Studies in Diplomatic History. Essays in Memory of David Bayne Horn* (1970); Ragnhild Hatton and J.S. Bromley (eds.), *William III and Louis XIV, Essays 1680–1720 by and for Mark A. Thomson* (Liverpool, 1968); John Cannon (ed.), *The Whig Ascendancy. Colloquies on Hanoverian England* (1981); Clyve Jones (ed.), *Party and Management in Parliament 1660–1784* (Leicester, 1984); and *Britain in the First Age of Party. Essays Presented to Geoffrey Holmes* (1987); Rosalind Mitcheson (ed.), *Essays in Eighteenth-Century History from the English Historical Review* (1966); Richard Pares and A.J.P. Taylor (eds.), *Essays presented to Sir Lewis Namier* (1956); Geoffrey Holmes (ed.), *Britain after the Glorious Revolution 1689–1714* (1969); and Jeremy Black (ed.), *Britain in the Age of Walpole* (1984). Many valuable articles have been published in *The English Historical Review, The Transactions of the Royal Historical Society, The Historicals Journal, The Economic History Review,*

History, The Bulletin of the Institute of Historical Research and other learned journals.

The literary and journalistic side of political life, including the work of such giants as Swift, Pope, Gay, Fielding, Johnson, Steele, Addison, Defoe and many hardly lesser figures, has produced a modern literature of its own. Some useful introductory books are: Jeremy Black, *The English Press in the Eighteenth Century* (1986); Bertrand A. Goldger, *Walpole and the Wits* (Lincoln, Nebraska, 1977); H.T. Dickinson, *Politics and Literature in the Eighteenth Century* (1974); D.H. Stevens, *Party Politics and English Journalism 1702–1742* (New York, 1916); Lawrence Hanson, *Government and the Press, 1695–1763* (Oxford, 1936); W.L. Laprade, *Public Opinion and Politics in Eighteenth-Century England* (New York, 1936); Maynard Mack, *The Garden and the City* (1969); J.H. Downie, *Jonathan Swift, Political Writer* (1984); and G.A. Cranfield, *The Development of the Provincial Newspaper, 1700–1760* (Oxford, 1962). The world of the cartoonists and caricaturists is described or illustrated in M.D. George, *English Political Caricature* (2 vols. 1969); H.M. Atherton, *Political Prints in the Age of Hogarth* (Oxford, 1974); *English Satirical Prints 1660–1832* (7 vols. 1986), especially: (ii) *Religion and the Popular Prints* by John Miller, (iv) *Walpole and the Robinocracy*, by Paul Langford, and (vi) *Caricatures and the Constitution*, by H.T. Dickinson.

Among the many biographies are: Betty Kemp, *Sir Robert Walpole* (1976); Sir Winston S. Churchill, *Marlborough, his Life and Times* (4 vols. 1933–8); Ragnhild Hatton, *George I, Elector and King* (1978); H.T. Dickinson, *Bolingbroke* (1970); Basil Williams, *Stanhope* (Oxford, 1932); Dorothy H. Somerville, *The King of Hearts . . .Shrewsbury* (1962); Norman Sykes, *Edmund Gibson, Bishop of London* (Oxford, 1926); W.L. Sachse, *Lord Somers, a Political Portrait* (Manchester 1975); Henry Horwitz, *Revolution Politics, The Career of . . . Nottingham* (Cambridge, 1968); Angus McInnes, *Robert Harley, Puritan Politician* (1970); and B.W. Hill, *Robert Harley, Speaker, Secretary of State and Premier Minister* (1988); Reed Browning, *Newcastle* (Yale, 1975).

Probably the best, and certainly the easiest way to keep (almost) up to date with the literature is to obtain the *Annual Bulletin of Historical Literature* published at very reasonable cost by the Historical Association, of 59a Kennington Park Road, London, SE11 4JH.

Index